The Last Time I Saw Her

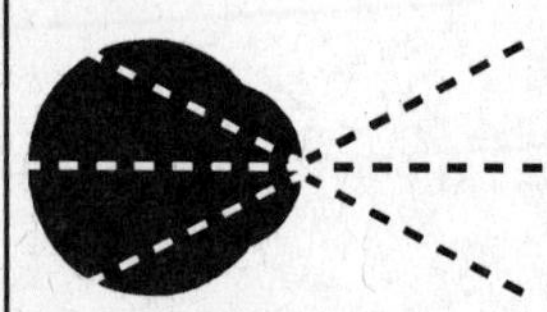

This Large Print Book carries the Seal of Approval of N.A.V.H.

THE LAST TIME I SAW HER

KAREN ROBARDS

WHEELER PUBLISHING
A part of Gale, Cengage Learning

GALE
CENGAGE Learning®

Farmington Hills, Mich • San Francisco • New York • Waterville, Maine
Meriden, Conn • Mason, Ohio • Chicago

GALE
CENGAGE Learning

Wheeler Publishing, a part of Gale, Cengage Learning.

Wheeler Publishing Large Print Hardcover.
The text of this Large Print edition is unabridged.
Other aspects of the book may vary from the original edition.
Set in 16 pt. Plantin.

LIBRARY OF CONGRESS CATALOGING-IN-PUBLICATION DATA

Robards, Karen.
The last time I saw her / Karen Robards. — Large print edition.
pages cm. — (Wheeler Publishing large print hardcover)
ISBN 978-1-4104-8048-4 (hardback) — ISBN 1-4104-8048-8 (hardcover)
1. Criminal profilers—Fiction. 2. Women psychiatrists—Fiction. 3. Serial murder investigation—Fiction. 4. Psychic ability—Fiction. 5. Large type books. 6. Paranormal romance stories. I. Title.
PS3568.O196L36 2015b
813'.54—dc23 2015025116

Published in 2015 by arrangement with Ballantine Books, an imprint of Random House, a division of Penguin Random House LLC

Printed in the United States of America
1 2 3 4 5 6 7 19 18 17 16 15

This book is dedicated
to Peter, Christopher,
and Jack, with all my love.

Chapter One

His eyes are the wrong color.

That was the panicky thought that tore screaming through Charlie's mind.

They should have been sky blue. They weren't: they were a hazelish shade of brown.

She stared up at him, unblinking, and felt the ground tilt beneath her feet.

It has to be him. Who else could it be?

His eyes were the wrong color, he had a tiny white scar beside his mouth that had never been there before, his hair was cut short and was kind of styled, and his six-foot-three-inch frame looked leaner than it should have been. Maybe that was because the black leather motorcycle jacket he was wearing with jeans and a button-up collared blue shirt (!) hid some of the truly impressive muscles that the T-shirt she was used to seeing him in had revealed.

Yeah. And maybe not.

Michael? Her heart shivered at the question, which she didn't repeat out loud.

Dr. Elisabeth Kübler-Ross had posited that there were five stages of grief: denial, anger, bargaining, depression, and acceptance. A little more than two weeks after Michael had disappeared — seventeen days, to be precise — Charlie reckoned that she'd just been torpedoed right into the third stage, because what kept running through her head was a feverish *Please God I'll do anything please.*

She stood in the small, grassy graveyard, with the crude white cross that marked Michael's grave in front of her and the viburnum hedge from which she had once gathered an armful of flowers to mark it to her left. As the steepled old First Baptist Church loomed in the background, Charlie desperately clung to a sliver of hope.

Please let it be him.

The heavy silver man's watch that hung loosely around her left wrist — Michael's watch, several sizes too large for her arm — glinted in the golden autumn sun. She didn't know if that was a good sign or a bad one.

Vacillating between joy and fear, she looked at the man frowning down at her with an intensity born of marrow-deep need. Except for those few small differences, it was all there: the square jaw, the broad cheekbones and forehead, the straight nose and beautifully cut mouth. The tawny hair, the height, the outrageous good looks. Her hand was on his arm: she could feel the solid muscles through the smooth leather of his jacket. Yet her eyes probed his and she came up empty. There was no electric *zing,* no trumpets signaling a joyous reunion going off in her head. The vibration she was picking up with every atom of sensitivity she possessed translated to *This is a stranger.* Reality hit, and the fragile little bit of hope she'd been cherishing shattered like glass.

Face it, she told herself savagely as her hand dropped away from his arm, *this gorgeous man is not Michael.* He might be turning her inside out simply by standing there, but that was because of what was going on with her rather than anything to do with him.

The multicolored pinwheels of happiness, of answered prayers, of unlikely miracles that had begun twirling through her bloodstream from the moment she had set eyes on this man faded and stilled. *It's not Michael,* she told herself again, and the world once more became the gray, colorless place that his absence from her life had made it.

"Who are you?" she asked, her voice raspy. Her throat was so tight it hurt to talk.

"Rick Hughes." The way his eyes narrowed on her face with speculation, the way the tan skin around them tightened and crinkled, made her stomach twist. The expression was all Michael, even if the brisk syllables with their total lack of a slow Southern drawl were not. "And you are?"

Okay, he apparently didn't know her. Didn't recognize her.

Pain curled through her system.

She introduced herself, still in that same strangled voice: "Charlie Stone." Still in shock from encountering the living image of the dead man she had only lately been able to admit even to herself that she loved, standing beside the grave where his body was interred. Despite everything her senses were telling her, she continued to search the man's face, his eyes, for some hint of Michael, some sign that it was him after all. She forced herself to stop, to get a grip.

Michael's gone. She knew that, but she was obviously having trouble coming to terms with it.

Rick Hughes's surprised expression was so much like Michael's that it was the equivalent of an arrow that lodged directly in her heart.

"Charlie Stone? *Dr. Charlotte* Stone?" His gaze moved over her. Watching his face, she was able to follow along: she had chestnut brown hair, a little longer than shoulder length, that today was pulled back into a low ponytail. Delicate features, fair complexion, denim blue eyes. Five-six and slender. Actually, more slender than usual, because since Michael had disappeared she'd barely been eating. Once Michael had told her men expected someone with her credentials to be butt-ugly instead of the babe he'd labeled her. Remembering this, she interpreted Hughes's expression accurately, or at least she was pretty sure it was accurately. Her spine stiffened in response to the sheer sexism of men who automatically assumed that an educated woman would be unattractive.

"Yes," she replied. And yes, okay, there was possibly a frosty overtone to her answer.

"I was just up at Wallens Ridge," he said, referring to the supermax prison where Charlie, a psychiatrist, was currently conducting research on a government grant, studying the psychology of serial killers. It was also the place where, a little more than eight weeks ago now, Michael had been murdered. "And I was told that you're the person I need to see. I was also told that you wouldn't be available for several more days, as you'd taken a temporary leave of absence."

"Yes, I did." To assist an FBI team in catching a serial killer. Less than an hour before on this late Thursday afternoon in early October, she'd arrived back at Lonesome Pine Airport with plans to take the weekend to get her head on straight before returning to work at the prison on Monday. She'd been five minutes away from her house in Big Stone Gap when, from the backseat of the taxi that was currently waiting by the curb, she had spotted his stunningly familiar figure in the graveyard. Only, of course, in the way things tended to work in her life, it turned out that he was the wrong man.

The tiny part of her brain that wasn't still reeling from shock scoffed: *You didn't really think that he was Michael standing there, alive, did you?*

But from the crushing sense of loss she was experiencing, it seemed that somewhere deep in her heart, or soul, she had.

You can't be gone. Not just like that. She sent the thought winging directly toward Michael, one of dozens that had taken that route since he'd disappeared, and immediately shut that folly down. Even if, somewhere in the misty reaches of the universe, he by some miracle did still exist (and she knew she shouldn't even begin to allow herself to hope for that), mental telepathy had never been part of their thing. And yes, sometimes bad things happened, just like that.

Bad things like Michael being destroyed.

Taking a deep breath, Charlie tried to focus. When it came to her professional life she tried to keep things, well, professional. Her hands were clenched into tight fists at her sides, she discovered. She wasn't yet able to tear her eyes away from this man's handsome face, but she made herself unclench her fingers.

"What can I do for you?" she asked, liking to think that her voice sounded less off-putting than it had before.

"I have a court order granting me access to some files that are apparently in your possession." He cocked a thumb at the grave, which, because it was still fairly new, formed a little higher mound and sported a little less grass than the ones around it. *M. A. Garland* had been hand-painted on the marker in black, slightly uneven letters, along with the dates of Michael's birth and death. Looking at it made her chest ache.

"On this guy: Michael Garland."

Once again the ground seemed to tilt beneath Charlie's feet. Hearing Michael's name spoken out loud was bad enough, but at his graveside by his doppelgänger?

Really, God? What fresh hell is this?

"Who *are* you?" she asked again, in a different intonation. If he wasn't Michael — and he wasn't, she was now *almost* convinced of that — then the fact that this man existed, that he was apparently alive and real and human and right at this moment standing close enough to touch, officially blew her mind.

Her subconscious was shouting a warning: *Hello, something's up. Big red flag here.*

All kinds of crazy possibilities started popping into her mind, running the gamut from his being some kind of shape-shifting demon to a faux-Michael from an alternate dimension to a very real-seeming hallucination brought on by grief and stress. At least, these possibilities might seem crazy to anyone who didn't live in her world. Short version was, she had the unfortunate ability to see the newly, violently dead; Michael had been one of the serial killers she was studying; had gotten himself murdered; and then, as one of those newly violently dead that only she could see, had come back as a ghost to haunt, taunt, and otherwise make her life miserable until she'd made the truly colossal mistake of falling in love with him, at which point he'd been yanked away into a purple-twilight version of purgatory, where, according to all the psychic sources she'd desperately consulted when he had disappeared, he'd almost certainly suffered a fate far worse than death or even hell: oblivion.

In other words, the possibility of a shape-shifting demon or alternate dimension or too-real hallucination wasn't as outlandish as it might sound.

To put it succinctly, in her world shit happened.

"I'm a lawyer," Hughes said, adding to her complete and utter shock. That this spitting image of Michael, whose contempt for every component of the justice system was oceans deep, was a lawyer floored her. "A criminal defense lawyer," he said. "The client I'm here on behalf of was charged with murdering his girlfriend. In the course of investigating the circumstances surrounding the crime, we discovered that it was identical in every significant detail to those committed by a serial killer known as the Southern Slasher" — he jerked a thumb at the grave again — "also known as Michael

Garland. I thought we had a winner of an alternative theory about the identity of the true killer in my client's case until I learned that Mr. Garland was in prison at the time this particular murder was committed. Still, I'm hoping that by following up on Mr. Garland I might learn something that'll shed some light on my client's case."

"Since you're here, you obviously know he's dead." She couldn't say Michael's name aloud: it just wouldn't come out. For her to *not* see Michael's grave was also impossible. It was there, in her field of vision, no matter how much she fought to not look at it. But looking at the man in front of her was even worse: it hurt. In the past two-plus weeks, she'd discovered that psychic pain could be every bit as agonizing as pain inflicted by a gun or a knife. "He's not going to be shedding light on anything. You could have just sent for the files."

"I'd also like to talk to you," Hughes said. From his voice, she was pretty sure he'd grown up somewhere north of the Mason-Dixon Line. The vibe he gave off was more big-city polished than anything Mi— no, she wasn't going there. *You have to stop thinking about him.* "I'm hoping you can help me with some questions I have."

The last thing in the world she wanted to

do was talk to him about anything, much less about Michael. Encountering him like this had shaken her badly; she had barely been keeping it together as it was. Now this — this terrible cosmic joke the universe was apparently playing on her was making her head spin, making it hard for her to catch her breath, making it impossible for her to think clearly. Looking at the man in front of her was physically painful. And it was starting to feel scary. If he wasn't Michael —

He's not. You know he's not.

At the moment she wasn't capable of much critical thinking beyond that, but she had managed to form and hold on to one crucial thought: *Until you get this figured out, you need to be careful.*

There was so much wrong with what was happening here she couldn't even begin to count the ways.

She said, "I doubt I can be of much help. Anyway, if Mr. Garland was in prison at the time the murder you're interested in was committed, I think that constitutes a fairly foolproof alibi. It's unlikely that you'll be able to deflect blame for your client's crime onto him."

Pointless as it was, Charlie realized that she was feeling defensive on Michael's behalf. Then she scolded herself: *What dif-*

ference does it make if he's accused of one more murder? It won't change anything.

"The details of the killing are so similar to the ones Mr. Garland was convicted of that I still think there's a chance he was somehow involved, possibly through an associate. I'm hoping the files you have will provide a lead, or maybe you'll remember something that might help. One of the firm's investigators would have come, but" — Hughes hesitated and gave Charlie an inscrutable look that, once again, was right out of Michael's wheelhouse — "under the circumstances I decided to check things out for myself."

"What circumstances?" Another murder that apparently fit the parameters of the brutal killings of seven women for which Michael had been sentenced to death — the possible ramifications were just starting to hit Charlie. The whole thing could be a mistake, of course; looked at by competent professionals, the evidence could prove that this murder was in no way connected to the other seven. But if the new killing did fit the parameters, if it was connected, it might be a possible avenue through which to prove that Michael was, as he had always claimed, innocent.

A spurt of excitement made Charlie's

pulse quicken. Then reality bit one more time: At this point, what did his innocence or guilt even matter?

Michael was dead. Dead and *gone.* Even if it turned out that he *was* innocent, even if that could be proved, it wouldn't change a thing. It wouldn't bring him back.

According to Tam, her daughter-of-a-voodoo-priestess, really-truly-psychic friend, it was unlikely that anything could.

Tam said that it was almost certain that Michael's soul had been terminated as soon as he'd been snatched away.

As Hughes glanced briefly to his left, toward the not-so-distant sound of a leaf blower starting up, Charlie caught an excellent view of his profile.

Oh, God. Michael to a T.

Hughes said, "I understand that you interviewed Mr. Garland, did some psychological testing, that kind of thing?"

The only answer Charlie could manage was a nod. Remembering brought back too many emotions. She didn't like recalling the hours she had spent interviewing and testing, or attempting to interview and test, Michael. At the time, he'd been a convicted serial killer on death row at Wallens Ridge, she'd been convinced of his guilt, and, even though he'd been shackled and chained to his chair and there'd been a poured concrete desk separating them and an armed guard peeping in the window at them every few minutes, she'd been secretly afraid of him. Mostly. Even then, though, there'd been moments when she'd trembled on the brink of liking him, moments when she'd been aware of his charm, moments when she'd felt attraction sizzle to life between them.

At the time, her thoughts on her reaction to him could have been summed up like this: *Girlfriend, you are one sick chick.*

"You performed the tests in person?" Hughes persisted.

Charlie nodded again, then said, "Yes." Continuing to nod because she was finding it too difficult to talk was just weak of her. At some point, she knew, the pain of Michael's loss would lessen, because even the worst heartbreak got better with time. Until then, she'd already determined her best course of action: *Fake it until you make it.* In other words, carry on as normally as possible until the raw wound that was her heart found a way to heal.

It would. She had to believe it would.

Hughes said, "Then when I tell you I'm here because I saw Michael Garland's mug shots and got curious, you'll understand what I'm talking about."

He watched her, clearly trying to gauge her reaction.

Charlie's throat felt tight as she asked, "You've — never met him? Never seen him in person?"

Hughes shook his head. "No. The mug shots were enough."

She knew what he meant. The fact that this man was physically identical to Michael in all but the tiniest of details was impossible to miss. The resemblance was still knocking her sideways, messing with her emotions, blocking her thought processes. What it meant she had no clue yet, but if he was telling the truth, if he was who and what he said he was with no kind of chicanery involved, once he'd seen Michael's picture there was no way he could have missed how much they looked alike. No one could.

If he hadn't been aware of Michael's existence until that point, the resemblance might well have been enough to bring him here. She knew that if she came across someone who looked exactly like her, she'd follow up.

"You look like him," she said. It was the understatement of the year and she was proud of how steady her voice was and how coolly objective she sounded. But as she spoke her eyes moved over his face almost compulsively, and it was all she could do not to reach up and lay her hand against the smooth-shaven plane of his way-too-familiar-looking cheek.

This is not Michael.

The refrain shivered through her body with every heartbeat even as she yearned to believe that maybe, just maybe, she was wrong. But she was getting no sense of familiarity, no feeling of connection, and the awfulness of looking at the outer shell of Michael without it being him was beyond upsetting.

"From what I could see, *exactly* like him," he said, still watching her. "Unless it was a trick of the lighting or camera angles or something when they took the mug shots."

Folding her arms over her chest to try to maintain her calm, Charlie shook her head. "No. It wasn't anything like that. It's a — very strong resemblance. Except for your eyes. Your eyes are the wrong color. His are — were — blue." She looked away from him with an effort, only to have her gaze fall fully on Michael's grave. There were a few weeds growing in tufts that were taller than the sparse grass covering it — and it looked barren. And lonely. A hard knot formed in her chest, and for a moment the pain was indescribable. She jerked her eyes back to

Hughes. "Other than that, you could be twins."

It was only then, as she said it, that the possibility shot like a missile out of the chaos churning in her brain. She didn't know why it hadn't hit her sooner: it should have first thing, as soon as she'd looked at him, as soon as she'd decided that he wasn't Michael.

If he wasn't Michael, and he was alive and human, he almost had to be Michael's relative. His brother. Maybe even his twin. Maybe even his *identical* twin.

Her eyes widened at the thought.

Could identical twins have different-colored eyes? She wasn't certain, but until she could research it she wasn't ruling it out.

Michael had been adopted at a young age. Michael wouldn't necessarily have known he had a sibling, even if that sibling was an identical twin. In fact, he certainly hadn't known it, or the fact would have surfaced during his trial.

For all intents and purposes, identical twins had identical DNA.

The DNA evidence left at the crime scenes had been the strongest evidence tying Michael to the murders.

Michael had always claimed that he was

innocent. Of course, guilty men had been proclaiming their innocence from the world's beginning, but by the time he'd disappeared she'd pretty much come to believe him. The man — ghost, whatever — she had come to know would never have brutally raped and killed seven women. It just wasn't in him.

So maybe here was the answer. Maybe this man who looked exactly like Michael was Michael's identical twin who shared his DNA and who was the *real serial killer.*

On that horrific thought, her eyes locked with his, and at what she saw in their wrong-color depths, Charlie suddenly felt cold all over.

Michael had always told her that her face was way too easy to read.

Moving closer, Hughes reached out to take hold of her upper arm. She was wearing a long-sleeved white shirt, thin and silky, with black pants. She could feel the strength of his fingers through it.

Like Michael, he was a big guy. Big enough to seem menacing even if all he did was stand there gripping her arm. Big enough that she might have some trouble getting away from him if he didn't want to let her go.

"Something wrong, Dr. Stone?" he asked.

Chapter Two

He was close enough that he loomed over her.

Looking up into that hauntingly familiar face, Charlie felt a flash of disorientation. She wanted to throw herself into his arms and pull sharply away from him at the same time. A tide of longing cut by a quick infusion of fear. It was uncanny and even kind of horrible to look up into the face of someone she knew so well — and know that it wasn't him she was seeing at all. Being afraid of Michael — that seemed impossible now, given everything that had passed between them. Only — was she? But of course if she was afraid, it wasn't of Michael: it was of this guy.

She had a sickening moment in which she found herself remembering how easily and quickly Michael had been able to kill when it suited him to do so.

A strong man could break a neck in a matter of seconds, she'd discovered.

Impossible to know whether or not Rick Hughes possessed similar skills. Stupid to assume he did not.

This is not Michael. She had to mentally formulate the words again to counteract what her eyes were telling her.

She'd come face-to-face with so much danger lately that having her heart start to pound and her pulse start to race and her breathing start to quicken felt almost normal.

Didn't mean she had to like it. But whether she liked it or not, that's what was happening to her now. She *was* afraid — of this man who *wasn't* Michael.

To hell with this.

She'd spent enough time being afraid to last a millennium. She was done with being afraid.

It was daytime. Late afternoon in a public cemetery. They were in Big Stone Gap, the kind of Mayberry-esque small town where if she screamed every neighbor within earshot would come running, and given all the houses lining the street and the occasional car driving past and the leaf blower and the sounds of hammering and sawing she could hear from the not-so-distant town square, where booths were being assembled for the fall festival scheduled for that weekend, someone was bound to be within earshot. Her taxi with the driver in it was still waiting at the curb, for God's sake.

Real serial killer or not, Hughes was not going to murder her where she stood.

"No, of course there's nothing wrong." She pulled free of his grip. He didn't try to stop her. Tearing her eyes away from his face was harder, but she did it, and glanced toward the taxi idling at the curb. The driver, a stranger who'd come with the cab she'd hailed at the airport, had his head resting against the seat back and appeared to be napping. He'd rolled the windows down, presumably to catch the woodsmoke-scented breeze.

He would definitely hear her if she screamed.

"I have to go," she said. Whether she was right or wrong in what she'd been thinking, she could no longer stand being so close to Michael's grave, or to this physical replica of him.

"Hold on a minute," he said, but she shook her head and turned away, heading for the taxi. Under the circumstances, keeping her spine straight and her gait steady required concentration, so she concentrated. She did not look back at Michael's grave.

Hughes fell into step beside her. She didn't look at him, either.

"I'd like to go over some things with you," he said. Thank God his voice didn't sound a thing like Michael's honeyed drawl. She could listen to him and not get dizzy. "Do you have some time tonight? Could I maybe take you to dinner?"

When pigs fly. Her intestines twisted at the idea of sitting across a table from him. For all kinds of reasons.

"No." Her reply was too fast and abrupt to be polite. She couldn't help it. She felt like her heart was being carved up with a butter knife. She had to get away from him, had to have a chance to clear her head.

"O-kay." There was a note in his voice that made her think that he wasn't used to having women turn him down. No surprise, with such a great-looking guy. She could feel his gaze on her face as he persisted. "What about tomorrow? I can come to your office."

She'd reached the taxi and he opened the door for her before she could grasp the handle herself. His hand was long-fingered and square-palmed and overtly masculine — and looked exactly like Michael's.

Oh, God, this was the worst pain she had suffered since the night Michael had disappeared.

"I'm not going in to work tomorrow." Sliding into the backseat, she gripped the window frame and pulled the door shut with Hughes's hand still on the handle.

He leaned down to look through the window at her. "You really can't spare an hour or so to meet with me? That means I'll have to hang around here until Monday. I do have a court order granting me access to those files, so if you're going back to work then, you're not going to be able to put me off any longer than that."

"I'm not trying to put you off," she said. The thought of having him hanging around Big Stone Gap all weekend made her shudder inwardly. His resemblance to Michael was killing her and the best explanation she could come up with for it made her skin crawl. On the other hand, if he was the killer whose crimes Michael had been convicted of, what would his purpose be in coming here? Anyway, if he was the real serial killer, the Southern Slasher's MO was to pick up hot young women in bars, not to take out unsuspecting psychiatrists in graveyards.

Although not every serial killer stayed true to his MO.

The thought brought a chill of warning with it.

"Oh? You're not?" Hughes asked dryly. She glanced at him, an automatic, unthinking response to being addressed, and felt her heart shred. He was studying her face. She liked to think that it was unreadable, but that probably wasn't the case. Michael, at least, had been able to read her expressions easily.

"No," she said.

"So set a time and place. I'll be there."

His presence in town would hang over her head like the Sword of Damocles. The way he looked was killing her. Everything else — who he was, why he was there — she could sort out later. Her first priority had to be getting him gone so she could think and breathe — and function — again.

"I can meet with you in my office tomorrow. At three," she conceded abruptly. That would give her the rest of the night and the morning to calm down. It would also give her time to get a quick background check run on Rick Hughes, attorney.

Luckily, she had friends in FBI places.

"I'll be there," he said at the same time as she tapped the back of the seat in front of her.

"Let's go," she said. The sleepy driver yawned in acknowledgment and nodded. A moment later the taxi was pulling away down the street. Charlie found herself leaning forward, watching through the side-view mirror as Michael — *No, not Michael!* — stood there in the churchyard with his arms folded over his chest, frowning after her.

She could not tear her eyes away.

It was only after the cab turned left at the intersection and she lost sight of him that it occurred to her that she'd never before seen Michael's reflection in a mirror, because ghosts — which was what he had been for the majority of their acquaintance — have no substance to reflect.

Which, by reminding her once again that the man in the churchyard was not Michael, caused a fresh wave of heartbreak to slam into her like a tidal wave.

By the time she let herself into her two-story white clapboard house, she had a lump in her throat from choking back tears she refused to shed.

Once the door closed behind her she could feel Michael's absence. A thousand images of him — walking through the front hall, stretched out on the couch watching TV, growling warnings into her ear as he followed her up the stairs — threatened to overwhelm her.

Her hands were shaking, she noticed. Taking calming breaths, she turned on the downstairs lights and the TV to combat the shadowy silence before doing what she always did as soon as she arrived home from a trip, which was lug her suitcase upstairs so that she could unpack. As a general rule, her hands never shook: since she had dealt with so much that was traumatic and horrible and terrifying over the years, keeping outwardly calm under any and all circumstances had become second nature to her. But this — this was different. This was shattering. Michael's loss was killing her, and encountering Rick Hughes in the cemetery on top of it was the psychic equivalent of ripping open stitches that barely had been holding together a near-mortal wound.

Walking inside her bedroom, she flipped on the light to brighten things up in there and then stopped dead as more memories hit her: the last time she'd been in this room, Michael had been with her, giving her crap as usual. One glance at her big brass bed with its immaculate white spread made her knees go weak.

I can't deal with this right now, she thought. Abandoning her suitcase just over the threshold, she fled back downstairs. The first time she'd had sex with Michael, it had happened in that bed; she'd slept many other nights in it with him beside her without having sex, because as an incorporeal being (i.e., a ghost) he was as insubstantial as air and ninety-nine percent of the time they couldn't physically touch. The other one percent of the time — when something like strong emotion allowed him to briefly manifest in solid form, or when she somehow managed to pull off an astral projection that landed her on his side of the life/death divide — they wound up in each other's arms as unerringly as metal flying toward a magnet. The sex was phenomenal. The friendship that had grown between them was, she was discovering now that he was no longer around, even more important to her.

She missed him so much that it was an actual ache inside her.

Without Michael, her house felt empty. It no longer felt like home.

One step at a time. That's how you're going to get through this. Focus on the here and now, on doing what comes next.

Which would be: *Check out the creepy man in the graveyard.*

Right.

Squaring her shoulders, she headed for the kitchen, fishing her phone out of her purse as she went. The number she punched into it was Tony's. Tony as in FBI Special Agent Anthony Bartoli, head of the ViCAP serial killer unit that she'd just returned from working with. Tony was tall, dark, and handsome. He was smart and capable and gainfully employed. He was also single and had a thing for her.

And she liked him, she really did. If it hadn't been for her damned (literally) ghost, they probably would have been hot and heavy by now.

As it was, she'd had to tell the closest candidate for Mr. Right that she had come across in years that she couldn't get involved in a relationship with him right now because she'd been in love with someone she'd lost (that would be Michael, although she hadn't gone into specifics about *that*) and she still hadn't gotten over it. To which Tony, great guy that he was, had replied he was willing to wait.

The trouble was, he might be waiting forever, she thought, as Tony answered the phone with a casual "Hey there" that told her he knew who was calling.

She was starting to be afraid that she was never going to get over Michael.

People did recover from broken hearts, right?

"Hi," she responded. She was still jittery

with nerves from her encounter with Hughes, and on top of that she was getting a headache. She'd been experiencing them on a regular basis since Michael had disappeared. Setting her purse down on the counter, she dug out the bottle of Advil she had started keeping with her constantly and popped the lid off. "How are you?" she asked.

Tony had been shot and severely wounded moments before she'd received her far less serious wound, both at the hands of the serial killer they'd been trying to unmask. He was off work and staying at his parents' vacation house as he recovered. He was able to walk and take care of himself, but he was still weak and had yet to regain full use of his left arm. When he'd left the hospital he'd asked her to come with him, but she'd turned him down.

Because of Michael.

"Recovering," Tony replied as she swallowed two tablets and chased them with some water from the sink. "Today I managed to lift my arm over my head."

She smiled at the humor in his voice as she walked around the breakfast bar to the kitchen table, which was piled high with mail, courtesy of the neighbor who'd watched her house while she was gone.

Through the back window she spotted Pumpkin, said neighbor's big orange tabby, stalking through the tall sunflowers that, despite being a little ratty this late in the season, still bloomed by her back fence. A short distance beyond the fence, Little Stone Mountain rose in all its fall foliage–covered glory. Once upon a time, she had run daily on the trail that wound up the mountain; she hadn't done that, or run at all, for a while.

I need to start running again. Maybe that will help.

She said, "That's great. I'm glad," into the phone as she started to riffle through her mail.

"Yeah, I might actually make it back to work in another couple of weeks. You get home all right? How are things with you?"

"Yes, and fine." That last was a lie if ever there was one, but the explanations that would be required if she responded in any other way were never going to happen. "Actually, I wondered if you could do something for me."

"Ah. And here I was hoping that you'd called just because you wanted to talk to me." The teasing note in his voice made her wish, for what must have been the millionth time, that things were different. That her life was different. That her stupid heart was different. With Tony, there really could have been something there. "What do you need?"

"Could you get a quick background check run on somebody for me?" As she spoke, she flipped past the electricity bill, the cable bill, and a sales pitch for life insurance. Just looking at them was comforting in an odd sort of way. Thinking about it, she realized that that was because they were the stuff of normal life, and normalcy was what she craved.

Once her life was back to normal again, once her routines were reestablished, maybe the pain of missing Michael would start to go away.

"Who do you want a background check run on?" Tony asked. She could hear the sudden alertness in his voice.

Charlie told him about Rick Hughes showing up out of the blue with a court order to see her files and a request to interview her. She didn't feel good about lying to Tony, so she didn't. She simply didn't tell the whole truth. What she kept back was anything about her personal ties to Michael and the whole afterlife connection to the situation. In the version she shared, Michael was simply a convicted serial killer she'd been studying who'd been killed in prison, and now a lawyer who looked identical to him had arrived with a court order allowing access to her files. Framing it as the rampant speculation it was, Charlie also floated the possibility that Hughes might have committed the crimes for which Michael had been convicted.

"Wow," Tony said when she finished. "Your life is nothing if not interesting."

"Gee, thanks." Her tone was dry. See there, she was fighting the darkness. She was fighting for normal. All was not lost in her bruised and battered psyche. "Is that supposed to be a compliment?"

"An observation, is all."

"So will you do it?"

"Anything for you, Dr. Stone."

He was flirting with her. More normal. If she faked it long enough, would she really start to feel normal again? She gave it the old college try and responded with a light "Have I mentioned lately that you're my favorite FBI agent?"

"You keep that in mind next time we're in the same zip code."

"I will." She was smiling again. God, it felt good to smile!

"So first thing you want to do is confirm this Rick Hughes's bona fides?"

"Yes," Charlie said, adding, "Anything you

can find out about him will help. And, um, if you could get me a picture of him, that would be great."

"A picture?"

"In case there actually is a Rick Hughes but this guy isn't him."

"Good thought." The silence that followed told Charlie that Tony guessed there was more to the story than she was telling him, but he didn't press her. His ability to take the off-the-wall things that happened around her in stride was one of the things she really liked about him. "You want me to come up there?"

He would, too. All she needed to do was say the word. She knew that.

"No. If it turns out that he's not who he says he is, then we'll see. But for now, you stay put and do what you're supposed to do to recuperate. Just get me that information."

"If it turns out he's not legit, I'm on my way." His tone made it a warning and a promise.

"Agreed."

"Okay, then. I'll get somebody on it now. You should have the information no later than first thing in the morning."

"Thanks." She was smiling again as they finished the conversation and disconnected. It was good to have Tony as a friend, to know that he was there if she needed him. It made her feel less alone.

Because that was exactly how she felt. Alone and bereft. No matter how much she tried to pretend otherwise.

It wasn't until Charlie put the phone down that she realized that the last envelope in the mail pile, the heavy, cream-colored vellum one that she'd been vaguely aware of all along, was from the Brain and Behavior Research Foundation. Formerly known as NARSAD, the National Alliance for Research on Schizophrenia and Affective Disorders, it was the premier brain and behavior research foundation in the world. Its panel of experts in the field included Nobel Prize winners, present and former directors of NIMH, members of the National Academy of Sciences, and the chairs of the psychiatry and neuroscience departments of a number of leading medical schools. Each year they chose recipients of the annual NARSAD Distinguished Investigator Grants and on the last Saturday in October presented the awards with much pomp and ceremony at the foundation's big annual gathering in Washington, D.C. The NARSAD awards were sort of like MacArthur Genius Grants for brain researchers, and to be selected was a really big deal.

Each award also came with a hundred thousand dollars.

Charlie was suddenly breathless as she tore open the envelope and scanned the letter it contained.

Under a gleaming gold letterhead that included an embossed illustration of the NIMH headquarters, she read:

> Dear Dr. Stone,
>
> We are pleased to inform you that you have been selected as this year's recipient of the Goldman-Rakic Prize for Outstanding Achievement in Cognitive Neuroscience.

There was more after that, much more, details including previous winners and the time and place of the ceremony, but Charlie was so floored by what she was reading that the only thing that stuck was the fact that she had won.

Oh, my God.

The NARSAD awards were the most prestigious prizes in psychiatric research. To receive one at age thirty-two was — well, she was overwhelmed.

She hadn't even known that she was under consideration. She'd never dreamed that she was under consideration.

Coming on top of everything else that had happened, it was simply too much for her to process. Pulling out a chair from the table, she sat down abruptly and stared at the letter in her hand.

It was such spectacularly good news, such an honor and a validation of her work and career, that under different conditions she would have been over the moon. Even through all the grief and turmoil and upset she was experiencing, she felt a flare of excitement.

This is huge.

Her fingers tightened on the letter. She had to tell someone. She was bursting to tell someone.

I have to tell Michael.

The thought was instant and instinctive, and it brought her crashing back to earth like nothing else could have. News like this was meant to be shared with the people you loved. The most important people in your life, the ones you could count on to be forever in your corner, the ones you automatically turned to in good times and bad.

The most important *person* in your life, the one you could count on to be forever in your corner, the one you automatically turned to in good times and bad.

When Michael had become that — well, *person* wasn't quite the word: entity, maybe? — for her she couldn't have said. But it seemed that he was.

How could I have let myself fall in love with him like this?

She'd done her best to keep it from happening. It had happened anyway.

She'd known the price all along. She'd known that it was going to be too steep to pay.

Yet here she was paying it.

Not being able to share the news with him dimmed the joy of it.

Not being able to share her life with him made the world feel like a cold, alien place.

Okay. Deep breath. Think about —

I won a NARSAD. A tiny shoot of happiness bubbled up through the pain like the first spring crocus pushing through a crust of snow. But the pain remained, grim and unrelenting and as deadening as a layer of concrete hardening around her heart.

Sitting there with the letter in her hand, Charlie glanced at her phone, which lay on the table in front of her. She should be snatching it up by this time, should be busy sharing the news. There were others she could call, others who would be glad for her: Tony, Tam, her mother. More friends, more colleagues. For God's sake, she had people. *People,* not just a heart-stealing ghost.

Then her attention was caught by what she saw through the window, the one just beyond the table that provided her with a near panoramic view of her backyard: a pair of fat white hens scratched at the dirt beneath her sunflowers, unaware that Pumpkin, tail swishing, furry body low to the ground, was closing in on them.

Knowing the mayhem that was about to ensue, and maybe even secretly a little glad that she didn't have to immediately decide who to call first with her news, Charlie jumped up, ran for the door, and flung it open.

"Shoo," she cried, flapping her hands at the hens as she sped down the back steps. "Pumpkin, stop that!"

The hens didn't shoo. They just kept calmly pecking away at the ground.

Pumpkin didn't stop what he was doing, either. Now within pouncing distance, he crouched, wriggling his rear end ominously, his eyes fixed on the hens.

Charlie scooped him up just in time.

"No, Pumpkin," she scolded him. Imprisoned in her arms, he gave her a baleful look. She could feel his tail swishing unhappily against her side.

"Oh, was he after Mrs. Norman's chickens again?" Pumpkin's twelve-year-old owner, Glory Powell, who lived next door with her parents, appeared at the fence separating their yards. She was thin and boyish-looking in jeans and a blue sweatshirt that read PROPERTY OF UNION HIGH SCHOOL. Her medium brown hair hung in one long braid down her back and her medium brown eyes were almost overshadowed by thick, dark brows. A tendency to glance shyly away from whomever she was talking to made her easy to overlook until she smiled. Usually her smile made her whole face light up. Today that smile flashed silver. "I'm sorry."

"You got braces," Charlie said in surprise, carrying Pumpkin to the fence and handing him over.

"Yesterday." From the suddenly self-conscious way Glory tried to keep her lips stretched over her teeth as she spoke, Charlie surmised that she had forgotten about the braces until Charlie had mentioned them. She was immediately sorry she had. "I hate them."

"You'll be glad you had them when you're older," Charlie told her. Glory grimaced, clearly unconvinced. Glory's mother, Melissa, who looked like a shorter-haired, late-thirties-ish version of her daughter minus the braces, stepped out of her house and onto her back porch. She waved at Charlie.

"Thanks for getting my mail," Charlie called, waving back.

Melissa nodded. "Anytime."

Glory followed Melissa inside, Pumpkin squirming unhappily in her arms. Charlie started to turn away from the fence, trying not to remember how Michael had laughed at her the last time she'd intervened in the cat-versus-chickens skirmishes that were a common occurrence in her backyard, when something — a feeling, a sixth sense, whatever — made her glance toward the street.

A car was parked across from her house.

Around here, people almost never parked on the street. They all had garages and driveways. Even guests parked in driveways. Anyway, unless something big was going on, like the Super Bowl or the Fourth of July or a funeral or a high school graduation, their street usually didn't get that many guests who needed to park.

It was a quiet residential street. The houses were older, some remodeled like hers, others not, most with large yards. Nothing fancy or expensive. The neighbors were people like Mrs. Norman, the owner of the chickens, a widow in her eighties who lived next door, and Glory's family, and Ken the deputy sheriff, who lived a little way down on the opposite side of the street with his family, and others like them. Charlie might not know them well, but she knew them all. She knew that none of them drove a car like the black Shelby GT Mustang at the curb across the street.

Looking at it, Charlie felt a frisson of unease.

A prickling at the back of her neck. A cold finger sliding down her spine.

All reactions telling her that something was wrong.

As she stared at it, the Mustang started up, pulled away from the curb, and drove off.

It was too dark to see who was driving.

What she was feeling added up to — a sense of foreboding.

If she had learned nothing else in her life, it was to pay attention to her instincts.

It was only as her view of the Mustang's progress down the street was blocked by her own house that she realized dusk had fallen.

The fading light had a purple cast. A faint line of orange on the horizon was all that remained of the sun. Trees and houses stood in black silhouette against the darkening sky. The air felt heavier.

All was quiet. Unnaturally so. No noise at all, not even the whisper of the wind or the chirping of insects or the barking of a dog.

As if everything had stilled.

Liminal: that was the word she wanted.

It meant threshold, and in that moment it felt like the world paused on the threshold between day and night.

As Charlie frowned at the place where the Mustang had been, the last bit of orange glow on the horizon began to fade away and the purple shadows that lay over everything deepened.

Then something — a quiver in the air, a kind of heat shimmer — riveted her attention to one spot.

A shadow among the many shadows creeping over the yard across the street, just beyond the place where the Mustang had been parked, seemed to take on form and substance in the shimmer's center. As she watched, the shadow resolved itself into the shape of a man.

A tall man, broad-shouldered and lean-hipped. Standing unmoving at the edge of the neatly cut yard.

It was already too dark for her to get a

good look at his face, but she thought she could make out a white tee and jeans. And his eyes staring fixedly at her house, where light blazed from the windows.

The orange glow on the horizon began to disappear. As it did, a last ray of light streamed out to touch his hair.

It was the color of burnished gold.

Chapter Three

Charlie's heart thumped. Her breath caught. Forget the threshold between day and night. What she was seeing — was it the threshold between life and death?

Then the orange glow on the horizon was swallowed up by darkness, and the ray of light disappeared.

So did the man.

Gone just like that.

"Michael!" The cry tore out of her throat, and she found herself running, flying through the gate toward the place where the man had been. "Michael! Michael!"

But of course he wasn't there.

No one was there. Nothing was there.

Cooling fall air with no hint of a shimmer. Deepening shadows with no substance to them. Chirping insects, whispering wind, ordinary outdoor sounds. Looking wildly around, Charlie saw the dark lines and angles of her own house, the lit windows with the curtains as yet undrawn that provided glimpses of the interior, and the homely, should-have-been-comforting sights of the neighborhood getting tucked in for the night.

Inside she was screaming.

It was a clear night. One by one, stars began popping into view overhead. Lights were coming on in all the houses, not just hers.

Charlie had never felt so alone in her life.

What just happened? What did I see?

If Michael had been there, he was gone.

If she had imagined him, she was in even worse psychological shape than she had thought.

If the man she had seen was Rick Hughes, where was he?

The Mustang had pulled away before the figure appeared, and there was no place where a solid, flesh-and-blood man could have gotten away to that fast.

Charlie had no answers. All she knew for sure was that the night was growing cold, and standing out there alone in the dark was starting to feel like a really bad idea.

Wrapping her arms around herself, she went inside . . .

Where her knees gave out, and she collapsed in a shivering heap on her kitchen floor.

If he was in hell, then all the preachers and all the sermons and all the holy books that had come at him over the years had gotten it only half right. Hell burned sure enough, but with a cold so intense that every second passed in it was pure agony.

But Michael was pretty sure he wasn't in hell.

He was somewhere worse.

Imprisoned by bonds he couldn't see or feel, but that surrounded him and held him fast. Trapped in darkness, suspended in a vaporous fog that smelled of sulfur and burned like dry ice, his existence an endless torment. An eternity's worth of suffering compressed into a single instant, with every torturous instant the same.

His sense of self remained. The purple twilight nightmare of Spookville was a Disney theme park compared to this icy, stinking blackness. He could see shapes, hear the screams of others who, like him, were slated for annihilation.

The monsters — he caught only glimpses, but he thought of them as hunters on steroids — that controlled this place executed souls.

He'd been brought here to be snuffed out of existence.

If he'd been in any state to find anything amusing, he would have had to at least crack a smile at the idea that he'd wound up on the afterlife's version of death row.

The more things change . . .

Too bad he was way past finding any of this funny.

He didn't know how long he'd been here. Longer than any of the others. The drill was: souls arrived, something was done to them that made them shriek like they'd been doused with gasoline and set on fire, and then they turned into what looked like a pillar of ash and vanished, blown away by the frigid, unceasing wind, to exist no more.

He watched it happening around him, again and again and again, terrible, ruthless exterminations carried out with pitiless precision, the details imperfectly concealed by gloom. Sooner or later, it was going to happen to him.

Sometimes he almost thought it would be a relief.

Just get it over with. Boom. Done.

But then he suspected that thoughts like those were part of the process of wearing him down. The monsters' whispers lodging wormlike inside his consciousness.

The searing pain that felt like it was devouring him from the inside out was excruciating. Indescribable. Never-ending. Worse than anything he had ever experienced in life, or afterward. It would have had him screaming for mercy to the heavens if he'd had a voice left with which to scream. But his outer voice was gone now, stripped away by overuse within either moments or centuries or eons (he could no longer accurately judge time) of his arrival in this place.

We can end your torment. We can make the pain stop. Your suffering is needless.

He heard the monsters talking in his head. They spoke to him constantly, in deceptively soft, gentle voices, coaxing him to give in to the inevitable, to let them wipe out his agony by ending his existence.

When he'd been alive, he would have sworn that there was nothing left in heaven or hell that could scare him. But that was before he knew that there really was a heaven and a hell, and there were things betwixt and between that could make dying seem like a day at the beach.

The thought of ceasing to exist — of having his consciousness obliterated — had disturbed him once upon a time. It still did on some level, but he rarely connected with that level of himself anymore. He recognized that the brutishness building up inside him was part of what was happening to him, was a function of this place. The knowledge didn't make him feel any less savage. If anything, it made the savagery worse, because it fed his anger exponentially. It felt like the basest, most beastly and damnable part of himself was growing like a cancer, swallowing up the last shreds of his humanity, eating away at any small pockets of decency that remained to him.

It had gradually dawned on him that the reason the monsters had not yet terminated him was because they couldn't.

The whisper that had followed him here was the constant to which he clung. It was his shield, his lifeline. The words — he had to force them into his consciousness now through the rising tide of ferocity that was slowly blocking them out — burned inside him, keeping the hellish cold from freezing him through. One day, he thought, he would no longer be able to remember the words, and that would be the day that it ended. That *he* ended.

I love you.

She'd said that to him. Charlie.

Those words were what held him to an existence. *She* was what held him to an existence. He wasn't ready to let go of them, of her, of what was between them.

What he had done while he was alive might have damned him to hell for all eternity. He might even be carrying so much darkness inside him that he deserved to cease to exist. He wouldn't argue with that. But he wasn't ready to go.

He couldn't leave her. He didn't want to leave her.

Not yet. Somewhere along the way, he'd lost the ability to pray, but that was the plea that beat fiercely inside him. *I need a little more time.*

Part of the torture he suffered was that he could feel her pain.

She cried out to him, and he knew it, and each time she called his name was like a whip lashing his soul. She ached because he was gone, and a thousand billy clubs beating him unmercifully couldn't have injured him more.

He'd never meant to hurt her.

She'd said, *I love you.*

The words were killing him and saving him at the same time. When he was snatched away, her whisper had flown after him into the dark. It had wrapped itself around what passed for his heart, and it held him fast now, like a string anchoring a kite to earth.

Sometimes his consciousness flashed along the path of the string and he could see things. Not her — but things she could see.

Lightning glimpses of a hospital room, the interior of an airplane, her house.

So tantalizingly brief. So meaningless and yet —

Each one sharper than a thousand knives.

He had little doubt that he was deliberately being shown her life in snapshots as it was happening, as she continued on without him. The glimpses were a means of softening him up.

One day he wouldn't be able to take the pain.

Holding on to her hurts.

His life had never been about love. He'd never really believed in it. He'd had bed-mates, buddies, fellow Marines who for a time had become the closest thing he'd had to family. The men in his small unit — he'd cared about them. Band of brothers and all that.

But love was something deeper, something more profound. Other men seemed to experience it, but not him. He supposed it sprang from an openness and vulnerability that he didn't possess. At its core his heart had remained a cold and distant place that allowed no one in.

He could have gone his whole life like that. But then he'd gone and died.

She's better off without you. Let her go.

More insidious voices in his head, more attempts by the monsters to fuck with him. If he did what they wanted him to, if he closed his mind to her, if he let the words she'd sent winging after him into the dark fade from his consciousness, there would be nothing left to hold the monsters off.

The thing about it was, though, he was starting to feel like the voices might be right.

She was better off without him.

He wanted her to be happy.

Alive, he thought he could make her happy, but that airship had gone the way of the Hindenburg.

Dead, he got in the way of her living her life. He was always going to get in the way of her living her life.

She was grieving for him. He could feel it. Her grief was torture to him.

But people got over grief. She would get over him.

Maybe they'd both be better off if he just gave up and let go.

Took what was coming to him.

Let the darkness win.

We can take away your pain. You can set her free.

For her sake even more than his own, he was tempted.

But then he thought, *No: I'll never stop fighting. They'll have to destroy me to win.*

Chapter Four

By the time Rick Hughes appeared in the doorway of Charlie's office at a few minutes after three p.m. the following day, nobody could have told that she had spent much of the previous night in a shivering huddle on her kitchen floor. Nobody would have guessed that she had phoned Tam, told her about what she'd seen, and begged her friend to send her psychic feelers out into the universe in search of Michael one more time, only to have Tam report back that she could find no trace of him anywhere. Nobody would have known that Charlie had managed no more than a couple of hours of sleep, only to give up and get up as soon as dawn was streaking the sky and cut a big armful of sunflowers from those that remained in her backyard. Then, when she'd taken them to the cemetery, a light rain had started to fall as she'd piled them on Michael's grave.

Can anybody say, tears from heaven?

Call her stupid: she *knew* that nothing of him that mattered was in that grave. But she'd covered his grave with sunflowers from her garden anyway, because she wanted him to have something from home.

The background check Tony had run on Rick Hughes confirmed that he was indeed a lawyer with the firm Hughes, Taybridge Associates in Baltimore. The *Hughes* in the firm's name was his father, Richard Graham Hughes Sr., who went by Graham and who at age seventy-three was still alive and practicing criminal law. Rick Hughes had had a privileged upbringing, attending private schools and a private college and the University of Maryland law school, directly after which he'd gone to work for his father. His mother, Ann Cramer Hughes, had died ten years ago, still married to Graham. Rick had no arrest record and a clean disciplinary record at the schools he had attended. No history of violence. No history of anything that wasn't squeaky clean. The picture Tony had e-mailed along with the report had, indeed, been the Rick Hughes who'd been standing in the cemetery.

In other words, he was Michael's double. And apparently he was the All-American boy who'd grown up into Mr. Upstanding

Citizen as well.

There was no indication that he'd been adopted: his birth certificate listed Richard and Ann Hughes as his parents.

His birth date was given as December 4.

Michael's was November 16 of the same year.

A little more than two weeks' difference.

The elemental markers associated with serial killers appeared to be absent in Hughes's case. Macdonald's triad, first presented as a paper after a landmark psychological study, posited that the most violent offenders tended to share three common childhood traits: obsession with fire-starting, animal cruelty, and persistent bed-wetting past the age of five. If Hughes had exhibited any of the three, there was no record of it. There was also nothing in the record about abuse or neglect suffered in childhood. No record of youthful delinquency or crimes. Not even an excessive number of speeding tickets, which also tended to be a marker for an antisocial personality. Nothing in anything she'd seen so far on Rick Hughes would have raised the smallest red flag if she'd come across it under any other circumstances.

Except that he looked exactly like Michael.

It was too big a coincidence. Hughes's appearance, the close proximity of his birth date to Michael's, the fact that he had shown up in Big Stone Gap looking for information. How could all of that not have meaning?

Her own research, conducted on a quick and superficial level that morning, had confirmed that it was possible for identical twins to have different-colored eyes.

It had also turned up at least eighty sets of identical twins in Virginia's criminal databases alone. Once an identical twin was identified, it made criminal prosecution of an individual almost impossible. Eyewitness testimony, DNA evidence, etc., became useless.

Could she prove that Hughes was Michael's identical twin?

At her request, Tony was having his people dig deeper into Hughes's background.

She was going to dig deeper.

She owed it to Michael to find the truth. He'd said a number of times that since he was dead his guilt or innocence no longer mattered, but if she could clear his name she would. If there was nothing else left she could do for him, she could at least do that.

There was something more at issue, too: if Michael was innocent, then it meant that the man who had slaughtered the seven women Michael had been convicted of killing was still at large. If she knew anything about serial killers, and that was one thing she actually knew quite a lot about, he was also still killing. Whether or not this new murder proved to be the work of the Southern Slasher, he was out there somewhere. He wouldn't have stopped. They never stopped until they *were* stopped.

At this point, Hughes was her hands-down favorite candidate to be the real Southern Slasher. Which meant that he was a vicious killer who so far had gotten away scot-free.

But speculation was just that. Without proof, there was nothing anyone could do.

If there was proof, she meant to find it.

As well as an answer to the question that was really starting to bother her: *Why is he here?*

When Hughes gave a courtesy knock on her open door and she looked up at him from where she was seated behind her desk, Charlie was as coolly composed as if her meltdown of the previous night had never happened, and she didn't suspect the man standing in her doorway of a number of heinous murders. Her hair was twisted into the no-nonsense updo she preferred for working in the prison's all-male environment, her makeup was minimal but effective in covering up any last vestiges of sleeplessness, and her only jewelry was Michael's watch and a pair of small silver hoop earrings. The long-sleeved gray silk blouse and black pants she wore under her lab coat were completely businesslike, as were her sensible shoes.

Professional to the core, that was her.

"Dr. Stone," Hughes greeted her. Sporting a briefcase, a clean-shaven face, and carefully groomed hair, he was the picture of workday elegance in a well-cut charcoal suit with a white shirt and a pale blue tie. Her lips tightened at the sight of him — the thought that he had killed at least eight women, gotten Michael imprisoned and killed, and was still walking around free as a bird gave Charlie the momentary urge to kill him herself — but she felt her expression changing and managed to control it in time, she hoped, even as she gestured at him to enter. Then as he walked toward her Charlie found herself unexpectedly blindsided by the sight of Michael all brushed and polished and *in a suit.* She'd never seen Michael in a suit, or with a good haircut, and the whole *GQ* aura he gave off was dazzling. Lips parting, she blinked at him. Finally she got it together — *Not Michael!* — stood up, and moved out from behind the desk.

"Mr. Hughes," she said, without offering to shake hands. Her aversion to him in that moment was just too strong. Their eyes met: once again, she picked up no evil vibes. But she'd figured out sometime back that picking up evil vibes wasn't exactly her strong suit, so that didn't tell her a thing. "I can give you precisely one hour."

She couldn't help it. Her voice was clipped and cold.

"I'll take what I can get. And please, call me Rick." He smiled at her. She suspected he'd killed a lot of ladies — and how was that for sick humor? — with the aid of that smile, which was wasted on her. She did not smile back. She did not invite him to call her Charlie. Instead, she grabbed her self-control with both metaphorical hands; said, "Have a seat"; and then gave herself a minute to regroup by looking beyond him at a pack of what seemed to be scruffy civilian teenagers moving past her office. Clearly they were the source of the chatter she'd been listening to since she'd opened her door to wait for Hughes to arrive.

As Hughes headed toward the chair she

had indicated, Johnson, the burly guard who was assigned to this area and who, having brought Hughes to her office, now hovered just outside the door, gestured urgently to her.

Frowning, she stepped into the hallway.

"That guy — he looks just like that bastard Garland," Johnson whispered, shooting an uneasy look past her at Hughes. "Pardon my French, Dr. Stone, but you know who I'm talking about? That research subject of yours who got shanked in the hall a couple months back? I'm not crazy, right? You see it, too?"

"I did notice a resemblance," Charlie admitted, keeping her voice low.

"Is he supposed to look like that?"

Charlie had no idea what to make of that question, so she simply raised her eyebrows at him.

Johnson wet his lips and glanced toward Hughes again. "Uh, look, uh, some of the inmates, uh, said they saw Garland. Uh, his ghost, after he was dead, I mean. Standing in front of one of the cells." Charlie remembered Michael telling her that he'd paid a visit to the prison after he'd died. Specifically, to an inmate named Nash, who'd killed him. Apparently he'd made quite an impression. Johnson continued,

"You don't think that could be possible, do you?"

"It seems unlikely," Charlie said.

His next words came out in a rush. "You don't think we could have something like a *High Plains Drifter* situation going on here with this guy, do you?"

Charlie thought she saw a flash of real fear in Johnson's eyes. It took her a second to place the reference, then from the dregs of her memory she pulled up the vague memory of a Clint Eastwood movie about a cowboy ghost. Later, when she got the chance, she would check the movie out to be sure.

"Mr. Hughes is definitely not a ghost," she replied.

"Yeah." Johnson still didn't look happy, but Charlie wasn't in the mood to talk ghosts with him any longer, especially when the ghost in question was Michael.

Instead she nodded at the teens. There were eight of them, including two girls. One girl wore a miniskirt, the rest of the kids wore jeans, and there were tattoos and piercings on both sexes. A few of them, in too-cool-for-school mode, were joking and laughing loudly. The rest, except for one pale-faced boy who was clearly frightened by his surroundings, looked sullen. Aged fifteen to seventeen was Charlie's guess. They had a civilian woman escort, plus two of the guards, and from their direction she assumed their destination was the prison library, which was farther along the hall.

She asked, "What are they doing here?"

Casting the group a disparaging look, Johnson said, "They're juvies. The court sent 'em over. You know, as part of one of those Scared Straight things."

Charlie knew what he meant: Scared Straight and its imitators were programs designed to acquaint juvenile offenders with the grim realities of adult prisons. The purpose was to scare them away from a life of crime for fear of the consequences if they continued on their ruinous path. Numerous studies had shown that such programs didn't work, and that, indeed, they had the opposite effect: a far higher percentage of offending youths who participated in them ended up in adult prisons than did offending youths who did not.

But the powers that be were not convinced, and the programs continued to run.

"We'll be bringing some Level Fours up to talk to them," Johnson told her. Level Four was prison jargon for the most violent offenders. "Another one of your guys is on the list: Gary Fleenor."

Gary Fleenor, known to the world as the Beer Can Killer because his trademark was drinking a number of Keystone Lights after committing a murder and then leaving the empty cans of the cheap beer beside the victim (which had proved to be a real boon to prosecutors when he was finally caught), had killed twenty-six women. A cold, calculating sexual sadist who was completely without remorse, he exhibited every marker of a typical serial killer. He was completely textbook. He was also one of six serial killers currently being housed at Wallens Ridge, and was part of Charlie's current study.

Charlie frowned. "Is that a good idea?"

"Not my call," Johnson replied. "Anyway, the program's called Scared Straight, and Fleenor's one scary dude."

"Yes," Charlie agreed, and looked once more at the group slouching down the hall. Whatever they might have done, they were still just kids.

"You can call down, or you can just give me a shout when your visitor's ready to leave," Johnson said as Charlie turned back to her office. At the moment she had bigger fish to fry than either the psychological well-being of a bunch of delinquent kids or Johnson's fear of ghosts. "I'll be close by," he added.

"I'll give you a shout," Charlie promised, and closed the door against the noise. Shutting herself into her small office with a man she was growing increasingly convinced was a serial killer might not seem wise, but she had moved a long way past being wise in the last few weeks. The crux of the matter was that she had to know. Not that it made any difference now, and not that it would change anything. But the idea that Michael had suffered and died because of crimes this man had committed filled her with a steely anger that left little room for fear. Plus, she seriously doubted that he was going to murder her this afternoon in her office: to begin with, Johnson was right outside, and too many people knew Hughes was there. Anyway, probing the twisted psyches of serial killers entailed a certain degree of risk. She frequently met with them alone in small rooms as part of her research. Yes, they were chained and restrained, and there were guards around, but at its most elemental level, sitting down and chatting with serial killers was what she did.

So, once more into the breach.

In the future, given everything that had happened, after winning a NARSAD with its accompanying prize money, for God's sake — she still hadn't told anybody about it; tonight, she promised herself, she would make some calls — maybe she would rethink some of that. Maybe she would wrap up her current research and start something new.

Michael had warned her that bad things were going down at the prison. Three death row inmates, including him, had been killed inside its walls within just a few months. He'd told her to stay out of Wallens Ridge. More than that, he had wanted her to find something to do that didn't involve serial killers.

Of course, *overprotective* could have been Michael's middle name. But that didn't mean he wasn't right.

Studying serial killers is my life's work, came her automatic, inward protest.

So change your life. God, that caustic rejoinder sounded so much like something Michael might have said that it sent a shiver through her. Was she really going to start hearing him in her head now?

"I appreciate you making the time to see me today." Hughes had taken a seat in one of the two white plastic chairs that faced her desk. With his arm slung over its back, he turned halfway around to watch her. He dwarfed the small chair, and she was reminded again of what a large man he was. Besides angry, *wary* was how she felt in his company, she decided, as she stopped at the coffeemaker she had just that morning added to her small, windowless, and Spartan office. Other than her desk and chair, the only furnishings were the two plastic visitors' chairs, a tall black file cabinet, an easel with a dry-erase board with data concerning her research subjects, a couple of pictures, and, as of approximately two hours ago, a folding table that held the new coffeemaker.

Because, see, she had a plan.

"I didn't have much choice, did I." Her tone made it a statement rather than a question. A borderline unfriendly statement. Whatever quirk of chemistry that had set off sparks between her and Michael from the first time he had shuffled in chains into her presence was missing here and now. No matter how much Hughes looked like Michael, she felt not the smallest degree of attraction to him.

He said, "You could have held me off until Monday."

"I'm busy on Monday. It works better for me to go ahead and get this out of the way today." Having already made the coffee, she filled two cups, saying as she did so, "I haven't had any coffee today, and I find it much easier to concentrate when I have. I hope you'll join me in a cup. I have sugar, and artificial sweetener, and nondairy creamer if you care for any of that."

"Black's fine."

He accepted the cup she handed him without further comment, and it was all she could do to suppress a triumphant smile as he took a sip.

Gotcha, she thought as she sat down behind her desk. This was the easiest, most efficient way she could think of to obtain a DNA sample from him: already, with that one sip, he would have left DNA on the cup.

If he was Michael's identical twin and the possible source of the DNA on the Southern Slasher's victims, she meant to find out. That coffee cup would be heading for the lab as soon as he left. She'd already made arrangements for a messenger to pick the cup up, and for rush testing.

She took a sip of her own coffee and put her cup down on the desk.

"Was there a reason you were parked in front of my house last night?" she asked, expression bland, tone perfectly polite. Tony's background check had also turned up the fact that Hughes drove a black Shelby GT Mustang. There couldn't be two cars like that in Big Stone Gap.

For a moment, Hughes looked startled. Then he carefully set his cup down on the part of her desk that was closest to him — the action was designed to give himself time to come up with a response, she thought — and smiled ruefully at her. She might almost have fallen for the deliberate charm in that smile if she wasn't already acquainted with Michael's original, and infinitely more charming, version: it was the smile of a guilty man caught out.

"There's not much to do in this town at night," he said, still smiling at her. At least he was too smart to deny it. As for making her think he was the man she'd glimpsed through the twilight, his confession didn't: again, the car had been pulling away before she'd seen — what she'd seen. "I ate at the inn, drove around, and ended up outside your house. I thought about knocking on your door and asking if we could go ahead and get started on some of this, but I had a feeling I might not be welcome."

Ya think? But she didn't say it out loud.

The memory of that sense of foreboding she'd experienced last night was still fresh in her mind.

CHAPTER FIVE

"You know how it is after you've been away from home for a while. Last night I had a million things to do. And I still do." Charlie gave him a brief, uncharming smile of her own, then followed up with a pointed look. "As I told you, I can only spare an hour. Shall we get started?"

"Of course." Hughes leaned forward in his chair, his hands clasped between his knees, his gaze suddenly intent on her face. "Let me start by asking you this: How well did you know Michael Garland?"

For an unguarded moment, as a thousand varied images of Michael flashed through her mind, Charlie didn't reply. That was an impossible question to answer even if she'd wanted to. Her heart said, *As well as it's possible to know anyone in any universe,* but her head warned that maybe, just maybe, she was fooling herself and she didn't know him at all.

See, the thing was, if any objective researcher (such as herself, before she'd committed the ultimate folly of falling in love with her subject) had been asked to choose between suspecting Hughes or suspecting Michael of being the Southern Slasher, Michael would have been the winner, hands down.

From an abusive childhood to a documented history of violence, Michael had so many of the markers of the serial killer he'd been convicted of being that his file would have stood out for her even if she'd been reviewing it without knowing anything else about him. There was no speculation involved about whether or not his DNA — or at least DNA that was a perfect match for his — had been found on the victims: it had been. There was so much other evidence against him — including security video of him leaving a bar with his last victim only a couple of hours before she was found murdered — that any sane investigator would consider the case a slam dunk.

Which, for the court system, was what it had been.

It was only her personal observations, her personal interactions with him, her personal feelings toward him that had persuaded her that he was innocent.

Plus the small anomaly in the evidence that was his watch. A broken and bloodied watch identical to the one she now wore on her arm had been found with the body of the Southern Slasher's last victim, Candace Hartnell. Michael had picked her up in a bar, had sex with her, and then left less than an hour before the woman had been found slaughtered. The watch Charlie wore had the Marine Corps' motto, "Semper fi," engraved on the back of its case. The watch that had been found with Candace Hartnell had no such engraving. Michael insisted that the unbroken, unbloodied, and engraved watch was his. If that was true, then Michael was innocent, and Charlie believed it was true.

I'm not wrong, she told the part of her mind that still remained coolly detached from her heart.

That detached part of her mind argued: *You feel that way because he told you he didn't do it. Because of the watch. Because you're in love with him.*

Charlie was briefly stymied. Then, slowly, she realized: it wasn't only her heart telling her that he was innocent.

I feel that way because I'm a highly skilled psychiatrist whose specialty is compiling forensic profiles of serial killers. Tops in my field, the winner of a NARSAD. Clinical observations are an important part of what I do, and my clinical observations of Michael have led me to conclude that he is not a serial killer.

Bottom line: *I'm an expert, and I believe him.*

So there.

"I met with him three times in a clinical setting. I interviewed him, tested him, observed him," she replied. "He presented no outward indicators of antisocial personality disorder" — the catchall diagnosis most commonly associated with serial killers — "his tests were inconclusive" — largely because he'd been messing with her by giving less-than-truthful answers as she'd administered them — "and he came across as intelligent and personable."

"Charismatic psychopath" was what her original diagnosis of Michael had been, but she wasn't going to tell Hughes that. Anyway, she had since concluded that her diagnosis had been influenced by her preconceived view of him as the convicted serial killer he had been presented to her as.

"Did he ever talk about his background?" Hughes asked.

"No." Not willingly, anyway, and not

under clinical conditions. Certainly she wasn't about to share with Hughes anything that he couldn't find out by reading Michael's files. "What background information I have on him is in his file."

She knew it by heart: Michael had been given over to foster care at the age of seven months; he was adopted by Stan and Susan Garland at age three; his adoptive parents divorced when he was five; his mother remarried when he was seven; the ensuing marital relationship was abusive and included frequent documented domestic violence calls, until one night when Michael was eleven he shot his stepfather to death to defend his mother and himself. His mother subsequently rejected him, giving up her parental rights. Michael was sent to a Georgia state juvenile facility until he ran away at age fourteen. Those were the facts. The damage that had been done to a sensitive child was something that she'd only once or twice glimpsed in his eyes.

Hughes sat back in his chair. "I guess what I'm trying to do is figure out how it is that he looks so much like me."

It was all Charlie could do to keep her face impassive. Was that statement intended as a kind of fishing expedition to find out how much she knew — or suspected —

about his possible genetic relationship to Michael? Hughes sounded perfectly sincere in his bewilderment, but — *Be careful. You need to think this through.*

She supposed it was possible that he'd never known about Michael before he landed the murder case he was investigating. There she paused, seized by a sudden thought: *If there even is a murder case.* Because that was an enormous coincidence, too. What were the chances that a man who looked exactly like Michael, the convicted Southern Slasher, should land another murder case possibly involving the Southern Slasher?

Her brain was not up to higher math at the moment, but she thought the chances were roughly between slim and none.

So what was Hughes's end game in coming here?

Her best professional analysis of his motivation yielded *no clue.*

Hmm.

"I can't answer that," she said.

"No, I suppose you can't. What is it they say about everybody having a double somewhere?" He flashed that ruefully charming smile again. As far as she was concerned, it missed its mark by a mile. "Looks like I found mine."

There was actually no validity to that premise, and there were no scientific studies to back it up. But Charlie didn't say so. At this point, she was doing her best to soak in any little clue that might help her determine why Hughes was here.

Hughes picked up his coffee cup, drank, and continued, "In your opinion, is it likely that Garland had a partner or some kind of associate with him when he killed?"

"No. I feel that it's highly *un*likely." If her tone was short, Charlie couldn't help it. Michael's personality was such that if he had been a killer, he would have killed alone. But he wasn't, so that point was moot.

"What do you know about his military background?"

"Very little." At least . . . God, it really would have helped if she'd gotten some sleep: her brain just wasn't up to speed today. The truthful answer was that she knew nothing she cared to share. She tried to get the conversation off on another tangent. "What was the date of the murder your client's been charged with? Knowing that could help me provide you with some insight."

He told her the date, which was approximately ten months before Michael was killed.

"Mr. Garland had been in custody for over four years at that point," she pointed out. "Even if he'd had an accomplice and the accomplice was the perpetrator, it would have been nearly impossible for the murder you're interested in to be similar enough to the others to be identified as the Southern Slasher's work if it was committed by anyone other than the Southern Slasher. Given the length of time separating the crimes and the fact that one of the principals was absent, the methodology would have changed, probably to a significant degree."

"So maybe it was a copycat," Hughes said. "Serial killers get copycats, right? Like rock stars get groupies?"

Before Charlie could answer, her cell phone rang. She would have ignored it, but a glance at the screen told her that the caller was Tony. If Tony was calling her, she assumed it was important.

"Excuse me, I need to take this," she said, and went out into the hall. Johnson and another guard whose name she didn't know lurked near the library. When they looked her way inquiringly, she waved them off: *I don't need anything.*

"I wanted you to know that we found a juvenile record on Hughes," Tony said without preamble. "It's been expunged, but it's there."

Charlie felt a flutter of excitement. "What did he do?"

"Set a neighbor's house on fire, apparently."

There it was: a marker. Fire-starting was classic. Her heart beat faster.

"Details?" she asked.

"I'm working on getting hold of the complete file. But I wanted to go ahead and let you know that there is something there, so you should probably stay away from the guy until we can get this pinned down."

"Too late. He's in my office. I gave him coffee."

"You gave him coffee?"

"To get his DNA. On the cup," Charlie explained. "It's sitting on the edge of my desk as we speak. I've already made arrangements to have it rush-tested at a lab I trust."

"Charlie —"

"Could you do something else for me? Look into this murder he's here investigating?"

She thought she heard a sigh. The sound made her smile.

Tony said, "You're determined to wade in here, aren't you?"

"Yes. Look, I have to go. I had to excuse

myself to come out into the hall and talk to you. I'll call you later, okay?"

"This isn't your —"

"Thanks, Tony." With that, she disconnected before he could say anything more.

Another piece of the puzzle had just fallen into place, and she felt a warm little glow of vindication. There were always early markers with serial killers. The trick lay in finding them.

"What files do you need?" she briskly asked Hughes as she walked back into her office. Now that she had his DNA sample and Tony was having him checked out in greater depth, she was ready to be rid of him. Looking at him bruised her heart. Being suspicious of him was nerve-racking. And this cat-and-mouse game they were playing — well, that she was playing; she hadn't yet decided what he was doing — required almost more mental energy than she was capable of mustering, especially in her sleep-deprived, grief-stricken state.

If he was what she thought he was, there would be plenty of time to deal with him as he deserved later. When the DNA results came back.

He watched her walk back behind her desk. "Whatever you have on Michael Garland. Everything."

Charlie gestured at the cardboard box full of papers that she'd had copied for him that morning. It sat on the floor beside the file cabinet. It was a large box, and it overflowed with material pertaining to Michael. By the time he'd gotten to her, Michael had been through a lot of interviews, a lot of testing, and a trial, the verdict of which he had been in the process of appealing. That meant tons of stuff.

But she wasn't handing over everything. Like, for example, Michael's watch. It was tucked up beneath the long sleeve of her lab coat. She touched it reflexively, like a talisman, her fingers searching out its heavy silver band. It was hers now, the only tangible thing of his she had.

"I want something in return," she said.

Hughes frowned at her. Again, that frown was pure Michael, and it pinched at her heart. "Like what?"

"A copy of your file on the murder that brought you here."

He pursed his lips. "I don't know if I can do that. There are confidentiality issues involved."

She wouldn't take no for an answer. "Consider me a consulting expert. Which, since you're here asking me questions and preparing to review my files on Mr. Garland, is what I technically already am."

"The court order in my briefcase doesn't say anything about me having to give you something in return for what you're legally required to turn over to me."

They looked at each other measuringly. Going through all the material she was giving him on Michael was going to take days, maybe weeks, and he had to know that. To get what she wanted, which was a chance to review his file, she was prepared to sweeten the pot.

"I'm familiar with the details of the Southern Slasher murders. I can look at the murder your client is accused of committing and tell you the similarities and differences much faster than you can wade through all that. In fact, I can give you an accurate assessment of the likelihood of the perpetrators being the same by Monday. If you give me the file."

Hughes frowned.

"I don't —" he began, but before he could get any further the sudden loud shriek of an institution-wide alarm going off made Charlie jump.

"What the hell?" Hughes said, as Charlie realized what the alarm had to be.

"Fire alarm," she informed Hughes, who was grimacing at the earsplitting whoops.

Grabbing her purse, she headed for the door, passing him on the way. She had to raise her voice to be heard. "They're anal about clearing everybody out, so we have to go. Come on."

She knew the procedure: everyone in the administrative wing procceded down the stairs to the west parking lot. As this was the least restricted part of the prison except for the visitors' area, they weren't herded into the exercise pens or the rec yard or other confined outdoor spaces. Instead, civilians such as herself simply milled around on the asphalt until the all-clear sounded. Once they were out of the building, prisoners were segregated from the others and guarded in a designated area until they could be returned to their cell blocks.

"This happen a lot?" Hughes stood up and grabbed his briefcase.

Before she could reply, there was a single loud knock and then her door was thrust open. Johnson stood there, his hand on the knob. His eyes immediately shot past her to Hughes, and he blinked nervously a couple of times. Then he looked at her.

"Got to head outside, Dr. Stone." Johnson had to yell to be heard over the commotion. In the hall beyond him, Charlie saw a river of guards, prisoners, visitors, and staff already filing toward the stairs. With the door open, the alarm was deafening. Add in clanging doors, raised voices, tramping feet, and the other noises associated with mass exodus and the racket was mind-boggling.

"We're coming," Charlie answered, moving toward him, and Johnson turned away in an obvious hurry. With Hughes following, Charlie joined the crowd in the hall. Johnson charged off ahead of them, forging through the surge of bodies, presumably to see to the evacuation of the other offices on that floor and also, she thought, to get away from Hughes. She found herself being jostled on all sides. To her consternation, as she neared the propped-open stairwell door, Charlie thought she detected a whiff of smoke. Prisons, being built largely of concrete and steel, were not particularly flammable, so an actual fire that amounted to more than a grease flare-up in the kitchen or a trash can alight would be surprising.

"This is a drill, right?" Hughes asked in her ear. He was right behind her, so close that his briefcase kept poking her in the thigh. A glance at his face told Charlie that he was worried: she guessed he smelled the same thing she did.

Behind them, a man yelled, "Fire's in the library," and someone else yelled, "Get the hell out of the way."

A jolt of alarm widened her eyes. She glanced around to see the prison fire detail in their bright yellow vests shoving their way toward the library against the tide of evacuees. As Charlie registered that apparently there really was a fire, she cast a worried look back at her office. All of her research and the material in her files existed in triplicate and were backed up online as well, but still there were some things she would hate to lose. Like, for example, the half-empty coffee cup with Hughes's DNA on it.

Nothing to do about it now.

The ramped-up rush for the exit bore Charlie along with it like flotsam on a wave. Grabbing on to the sturdy iron handrail as she started down the stairs, she found herself packed in so tightly by the larger male bodies around her that she had to hold on for dear life to keep from being knocked off her feet. Hughes was right behind her. He, too, grabbed the handrail. Out of the corner of her eye she watched his hand that looked so much like Michael's sliding along behind hers and felt her shoulder blades tighten. She suddenly felt seriously at risk. Her skin prickled.

Was it because of who was behind her?

"Keep moving," someone yelled, and they did, lurching downward in an uncoordinated mass.

The staircase was packed, nothing but shoulder-to-shoulder people, ninety-nine percent of whom were men. The noise level was unbelievable. The alarm's continuous shrieking peals echoed off the walls. The smell of stale sweat made Charlie wrinkle her nose. Right in front of her, the Scared Straight kids were descending in a tight little group with their chaperone and a pair of guards. In front of them were Dr. Creason and his staff with the infirmary patients, who were being carried on gurneys to safety. The prisoners in their orange uniforms were easy to pick out of the crowd, and as she made her way down to the next landing she spotted Gary Fleenor's tall, rangy body and narrow, sharp-featured face above her in a small group of prisoners emerging into the stairwell from the floor she had just left. His group was flanked by four guards, and Charlie concluded that they must be the prisoners who had been selected to talk to the kids.

Stepping off the last step into the short hallway that led out the door into the parking lot, Charlie saw smoke for the first time. A thin gray plume snaked over her head, probably drawn by the cool draft created by the open door in front of her. Beyond that door, rain fell in a silvery mist. The burning smell in the hallway intensified: it was now impossible to miss. Behind her, the surge toward the door increased along with the noise as those in the stairwell became aware of the smoke and pushed and shoved in an effort to get away from it. Outside, a pair of fire trucks with their strobe lights gyrating madly flashed into view. She watched them race toward the building, then split up to head in different directions, which was the first inkling she got that the administration building might not be the only one involved in the fire. Their wailing sirens added to the general confusion.

As she was propelled forward by the momentum of the crowd, someone — Charlie thought it was Hughes — grabbed her arm from behind. Then they were expelled forcefully through the door. Her toe caught on the threshold, and she stumbled out into the parking lot. The light rain that was falling spilled down on top of her.

Narrowing her eyes against the rain, Charlie tried unsuccessfully to pull her arm free — she hated having Hughes holding her arm — as she looked across the rows of parked vehicles toward where she had left her car. Since, once again, concrete and steel buildings were pretty much fireproof, she was counting on the damage in the administrative building being largely confined to the library. Her office, and the coffee cup with Hughes's DNA on it, should be safe enough until she could get back to them, which she hoped to be able to do before too long. In the meantime, she would wait in her car.

"I'm afraid our meeting is —" *Over* was what she had been going to say to Hughes, but as she turned her head to dismiss him she broke off when her gaze collided with Gary Fleenor's feral eyes.

They were approximately where she was expecting Hughes's to be. In other words, right behind her.

It took no more than a single shocked instant for her to figure out that, instead of Hughes, it was Fleenor who had been following her so closely through the press of people leaving the building that she could feel him brushing against her back, *Fleenor who had been gripping her arm.* Which was impossible. Or which would have been impossible if he was properly guarded and shackled.

Why isn't he guarded and shackled?

Fleenor leaned close to murmur in her

ear, "Keep moving, Dr. Stone." Charlie would have done no such thing, would have pulled away and screamed bloody murder and called on the combined power of every guard in the vicinity to make sure this most vicious of serial killers was secured, except that Fleenor lifted the hand that wasn't holding on to her arm long enough to let her see that he held a gun.

Then he jammed that gun hard into her side.

Chapter Six

The beginning of panic quickened Charlie's breathing and her pulse.

Okay, a ruthless murderer was holding a gun on her, but he was a known commodity: she had dealt with Fleenor before. Plus, he was still in a relatively controlled environment, which should make persuading him to let her go and give up doable. Glancing around through the veil of rain with mounting desperation, she searched for possible help. Her gaze skimmed dozens of people — guards and prisoners and staff and visitors who were streaming into the parking lot and then rushing off to do whatever it was they needed to do, get out of the rain, go wherever — and connected with no one. No one was paying attention. All were oblivious to her plight. So it looked like there wasn't going to be any immediate help.

Her breathing picked up. *You're on your own.*

More panic threatened to disrupt her nervous system. She fought to get a handle on her emotions and the situation.

Her training had taught her that eye contact was important, as was giving him respect and personalizing their interaction. Turning her head so that she could see him, she said, "Mr. Fleenor, you don't want to —"

"Shut up and keep walking or I'll shoot you right here and now." Jamming the gun harder into her side, Fleenor shoved her onward as he growled the threat. Charlie's lips clamped together even as her feet continued to move. She had no doubt that if she gave him cause he would do exactly what he said. He could kill her, kill as many people as he had bullets in the gun, and nothing would change for him.

As Michael had once told her, a man on death row has nothing to lose.

Fear dried her mouth.

Fleenor's grip on her arm felt unbreakable. His fingers dug painfully into her flesh. He ground the gun harder into her side, and that hurt, too.

How could this have happened? How did he get loose?

Another quick look around confirmed that she'd been horse-shoed in by a tight group of four orange-uniformed prisoners flanked by four blue-uniformed guards, all of whom were moving across the parking lot — moving *her* across the parking lot — at a brisk pace. The guards apparently hadn't noticed that Fleenor had grabbed her and was forcing her at gunpoint to go with them.

How can they not see this? That was the astonished thought that ran through her mind as the guards continued to hustle them along through the rain like she was supposed to be right in there with the prisoners. She tried, futilely, to signal one of them with her eyes. That's when she got a good look at the man's face and realized that the guard she was trying to signal wasn't a guard at all: she was looking at Wayne Sayers, convicted serial killer. Six feet tall, pudgy, bald, with squashed-looking features and protuberant brown eyes. Known as the Eyeball Killer because he liked to gouge his victims' eyes out before killing them, he was a death row resident and her research subject. Sayers wore a guard's uniform, complete with badge and, yes, gun.

The hair stood up on the back of her neck.

Her eyes met his. Sayers smiled at her, his tobacco-stained teeth as repulsive as the rest of him, and her stomach did a death drop toward the ground.

"Hello, blue eyes," he said, mouthing the words at her. Her insides twisted. Charlie jerked her gaze away.

Oh, my God, it's a prison break. That's what's happening here. The realization hit her with a thrill of horror even as a fast, comprehensive look around at the rest of the group identified the other uniformed "guards" escorting them: Terence Ware, Alberto Torres, and Paul Abell. They were all serial killers, death row residents, and her research subjects.

They all had guns.

She was suddenly freezing cold, the kind of cold that had nothing to do with the temperature or the rain. The kind of cold when your blood turns to ice in your veins.

The uniforms — to get them, they almost certainly had to have jumped the guards who'd been wearing them. But where did they get the guns? Prison guards don't carry guns, precisely to prevent something like this from happening.

Speculating was useless. How it was happening she had no idea, but it *was* happening. It was fact. Her heart started pounding like she'd just run a marathon as she faced it.

At that point Charlie would have

screamed, would have tried to run, would have taken her chances on breaking away from the gun and Fleenor's hand on her arm and the group hemming her in, but given all the chaos with the fire trucks and the sirens and the evacuation and the rain, there was already so much activity, so much noise, that she feared not being seen, not being heard. She would get only one chance to scream and make a run for it, she knew.

If Fleenor shot me, right here, right now, would anybody even notice?

Because of the rain, people were scattering, darting in different directions, seeking cover. The rain blunted sound, concealed telltale details, obscured faces and body language.

Somebody will surely hear a gun being fired — but by then I'll be dead.

"You don't want to do anything stupid," Fleenor warned. "We both know I won't have any problem with killing you."

She knew he was telling the absolute truth. Actually, the act of killing was more pleasurable to him than sex. And *of course* he'd been able to tell what she was thinking, she realized with chagrin. She'd been looking around everywhere. Her muscles had tightened in the first stages of fight-or-flight response. She had totally telegraphed her fears.

Stay calm.

Charlie swallowed hard as an even more horrifying thought occurred: all the convicts hurrying her away with them had guns. The carnage that might result if the situation went south was too terrible to think about. Dozens could die.

Keep it together. Wait for your chance.

Easy to say. Hard to do when her heart was racing and her thoughts were careening from possibility to possibility like they were bouncing around inside a pinball machine.

"Almost there. Keep going," Paul Abell said. The approximate size of a grizzly bear, strapped with muscle, dark hair shaved so close to his scalp that it was scarcely more than a shadow, with heavy features and waxy pale skin, Abell was known as the Midnight Rambler because he liked to break into homes in the middle of the night and kill — not all, but one or two of — the people inside. Silently. While the other residents of the house slept. He'd been convicted of twenty-two murders, and had a special preference for teenage girls. A number of his victims had been sisters. As he spoke, low-voiced, to the group, a few of the others nodded. The increasing tension among them was as tangible as the rain.

Almost where? Charlie had no clue. She only knew that wherever it was, they were taking her with them and she absolutely, positively did not want to go.

Pushing away the fear, Charlie forced herself to focus and think. The rain had worsened. It splashed down on the asphalt underfoot with a continuous low murmur, creating an obscuring curtain between her and the activity all around. The screaming fire trucks, parked now as their crews disappeared into the building she'd just left, the evacuees still spilling out into the parking lot, and the prison officials barking orders and trying to establish some kind of control were all noisy distractions that might keep onlookers from realizing what was going on with her. And like what was going on with her, all those noisy distractions were blurred and muffled by the rain.

If I fall, they might drag me with them. They won't just leave me. They can't: I'll sound the alarm, and they know that. If they don't drag me, they'll kill me.

Accepting the horrible truth of that, she tried to formulate another, better plan. The other buildings were being evacuated, too: she could see the prisoners streaming out of them. A lot of people were in the west parking lot along with her; a lot of them were heading for their cars. If she could get their attention, she could — what? Get them shot along with herself?

Excruciatingly aware of Fleenor's hand locked around her arm, of him so close behind her that she could feel the brush of his body with every step, of the gun grinding into her side, she tried to discreetly locate Hughes or anyone else who might be expected to notice that something was seriously wrong with her and the situation she was in. Two more guards strode along not too far in front of her, their uniforms striking her as blue beacons of hope until it occurred to her that they, too, might be prisoners in disguise.

From the back she couldn't tell.

Her heart pounded so hard now that she could feel it slamming against her breastbone.

The guards in front of her were escorting the Scared Straight group toward a yellow school bus that was parked in a designated visitor spot.

Even as Charlie saw the bus, the driver must have spotted his passengers approaching, because the doors opened to allow them to board.

Of course, like everyone else, the Scared

Straight kids were hurrying to get out of the rain.

"Dr. Stone!" Hughes's voice came from behind her, loud enough to cut through the din, causing her head to whip around as she sought him. Serial killer or no serial killer, at the moment he was far preferable to the group she was with. Even as her gaze locked on Hughes's, Fleenor's hand tightened so viciously on her arm that it felt as if his fingers would sink clear through to the bone. Charlie couldn't help it: she cried out. Fleenor's sharp-featured face contorted with a vicious expression that made her heart lurch.

"I'll put a bullet in you right now, bitch," Fleenor warned, and she had no doubt he would. Focusing forward, she didn't dare look back at Hughes or do anything except stride along with the group.

"Dude's coming," one of the others warned, low-voiced, behind her. "What do we do?"

"Kill him," someone else answered.

"No. Let him come," Abell said. His voice was chilling. Charlie was too jittery with nerves now to breathe properly. Should she try to warn Hughes? She couldn't — her life was on the line here, too.

She risked one more quick glance back.

Hughes was maybe twenty feet behind them and closing in fast. She could hardly see his features, much less his expression, and with the falling rain creating a rippling curtain between them, there was no way he was going to be able to read his danger in her face. There was, in fact, nothing she could do.

"Eyes front," Fleenor growled. Charlie did as he said.

"Dr. Stone! Wait up," Hughes called.

This time Charlie didn't glance around. With the mouth of Fleenor's gun digging into the space between her eleventh and twelfth ribs, she could only walk and pray. She hoped desperately that Hughes was perceptive enough to read something into that.

"Act unconcerned. Let him get to her," Abell ordered. Like his tone, his expression was terrifying. Charlie could feel menace rising in the air around her. Her breath caught. Her muscles tightened. She couldn't take this. She had to —

"Keep quiet and keep walking," Fleenor said, and ground the gun deeper into her side.

"Dr. Stone! I just need to —" Hughes called again, and from his voice she could tell that he was close behind her now. Unable to stop herself from glancing back once more, Charlie saw that he was only a few feet away, that the group had parted to let him in, and that they were closing ranks behind him.

Even with the rain hampering her vision, he looked so like Michael in that moment that she felt weirdly torn. Scared, but also — hopeful. Like she was seeing the cavalry rushing to her rescue or something.

But Hughes wasn't Michael, and the cavalry wasn't coming.

Her lips parted — *I have to warn him* — and then it was too late.

With swift brutality, Torres slammed the butt of his gun into the back of Hughes's neck. The dull *thunk* of the blow made Charlie wince.

Hughes collapsed soundlessly.

He never even hit the ground. They caught him, four of them, and carried him along with them the few yards to the school bus, which Charlie looked forward again in time to realize was their goal. Then she was being shoved onto it and forced up the narrow stairs right behind the Scared Straight kids.

Charlie was terrified. Michael experienced the sudden intensity of her fear like a lightning strike. It was an immediate, visceral sensation, so galvanizing that it jerked him out of the agony that tortured him and catapulted him along the string that still connected them.

He found himself inside a moving bus. Outside, it was raining. Too warm in the bus, the windows starting to fog up. Passengers sitting by the windows, one per seat, with men from a prison — both guards and prisoners, from their uniforms — hunkered down low on the floor beside them, shielded from the view of anyone outside the bus. A gray-haired woman in a flowered dress huddled in the seat behind the male driver, breathing noisily into a paper bag: Michael didn't know her. Wasn't interested in her or any of them.

Charlie. Where is she?

He couldn't see her, but he could feel her, feel her terror and desperation and helplessness as vividly now as if he was inside her body with her. He could feel that she was sitting, rigid with fear, fingers pressing hard into her thighs through the smooth material of her pants, her heart pounding and her pulse racing and — his brave girl! — her breathing deliberately even and slow, as if she was working hard at keeping panic at bay.

Dread: he could feel it twisting her gut, sending icy tremors snaking over her skin.

Then he felt a warm, wet, repulsive thing drag along her cheek, the sensation as physically vivid as if it was happening to him.

She recoiled, her head turning sharply toward the source of the sensation, and for a moment it was as if he could see through her eyes.

It took him a second, but then he realized that the guy in the orange peel who was leering at her, who was sitting on that bus seat hugging up to her with his arm clamped around her waist and his face so close she could smell the stink of his breath, had just licked her cheek.

Hurt her and I'll kill you was his silent promise to the guy. But he couldn't talk, couldn't move, couldn't protect her. Michael could only feel what she was feeling, see what she was seeing, and go crazy inside.

Ratlike face, small, nearly colorless eyes — he recognized the guy with a thunderclap of alarm: Dirty was his prison nickname, for Dirty 30, the thirty-can block of the cheap Keystone Light beer that was his calling card and that had led to his being called the Beer Can Killer by the media. Gary Fleenor, sick fucking bastard of a rapist, of a woman killer, from the Ridge's death row.

He had Charlie. How the hell had he gotten hold of Charlie?

If he'd been alive, Michael would have been sweating bullets at the thought of what Fleenor might do to her. But he wasn't alive: he was fucking dead. Fucking dead, and he was being shown this to torture him, and there was nothing he could do.

"You know you want some," Dirty said, waggling his tongue at her. Michael felt her horror, felt her disgust, felt the shudder of her heart, the hitch in her breathing, the tension in her muscles.

Then the bastard leaned in to lick Charlie again, this time right on her soft and vulnerable mouth. Her stomach roiled. She cringed away —

Michael exploded with rage, lunged for the guy — and just like that found himself back in hell's toilet, freezing and burning and racked with the knowledge of what was happening to her, the awareness of her fear. Everything he had seen and felt in that brief flash came together to form a single, terrible certainty: Charlie was in mortal danger. Encased in darkness, immobilized and helpless, he could only curse fate and the universe and God and every other entity that would allow someone like her to be hurt. He could only howl silently into the dark while he suffered — oh, hell, yeah, come to find out this existed, too — the torments of the damned.

How many preachers had warned him? About what would happen to him if he failed to repent, failed to heed their words, failed to turn from his evil path? Now he knew what that torment was, and that it was more real and more horrible than anything he could have imagined.

His fear for her was a hundred thousand times more acute than anything he had ever felt or ever could feel for himself.

Let me go back. He screamed it inside himself, throwing it into the stew of wordless communication that the monsters had started up again the second he'd returned to them.

Their chatter was obscene to him now. They taunted him. *She is afraid. She will be hurt. She will die.*

If he'd been able to fall on his knees, to clasp his hands like a man who actually prayed, to beseech them like that, he would have done it.

Let me go back. I'll do anything.

The voices subsided. All of a sudden there was nothing there, a void, a silence.

He begged again: *I'll do anything.* And added a word that was hard for him: *Please.*

Deeper than the rest, a single voice said, *You dare ask us to set you free . . .*

Chapter Seven

Inside the bus, the air was thick with fear. With Fleenor crowding next to her on the vinyl-covered seat, Charlie had trouble dragging in enough air.

Screaming was useless, so Charlie didn't. Crying and pleading would be worse, she knew. Fleenor fed on helplessness and fear.

Despite her instinct to recoil as far away from him as possible, Charlie just barely managed to look him in the eyes.

"Your mother would be angry at you, Mr. Fleenor," she said, and was pleased at how strong her voice sounded. From his file and her sessions with him she knew that his relationship with his mother had been the most important one in his life. It had been dysfunctional, to say the least. The woman had been controlling and abusive, but he had lived with her up until her death eight years ago. His bond with his mother was the one tool Charlie had to work with. She was horribly afraid it wouldn't be enough.

Fleenor's eyes — they were the color of dirty dishwater — flickered. That connected, Charlie could tell. Then he glared at her. His lips drew back in what looked like a snarl.

"You know jack all about my mother," he said. "She hated women like you. Social workers, they came to our house, she'd sic the dogs on 'em. Lady doctors, when she was in the hospital, she spit on 'em. She'd be proud, could she see what I'm getting ready to do to you."

His arm was around her waist; as he spoke, it tightened. Eyes vicious, he leaned toward her.

Charlie couldn't stop herself from jerking away from him, but it didn't help: she couldn't escape. Her spine came up hard against the cool metal wall of the bus. The window rattled and shook against the back of her head as it pressed futilely against the glass. Inside, she despaired. Her lungs had trouble expanding enough to allow her to inhale. She was freezing cold. Part of that was because, despite shedding her soaked lab coat, she was still damp from the rain, but shock and terror accounted for most of it. But on the outside, where he could see, she did her best to project as much calm authority as she could.

Even as his face neared hers she said, "Mimi" — Fleenor had called his mother by her first name — "would have said you were stupid to waste time bothering with a woman when —" *You should be focused on getting away* was how she was going to finish, when the muffled shriek of a siren going off behind the bus interrupted.

It was the most welcome sound Charlie had ever heard.

Fleenor's head snapped up. He glanced back, and his arm that had been locked around her waist withdrew.

"Shit," he said. "What's that?"

Charlie sagged against the side of the bus. Relief at the reprieve turned her muscles to jelly. It was all she could do not to swipe the back of her hand across her mouth, but she was afraid of drawing Fleenor's attention again. He had slurped his slimy, disgusting tongue over her lips, after previously doing the same to her cheek, and she was still shaking inside with revulsion.

And fear. Bone-deep fear.

The taste of him on her mouth made her sick.

She knew what Fleenor's MO was — first he raped, then he killed.

As an authority figure in his life, she was

the kind of victim he would particularly enjoy. He was a power killer. Power over his victims was his motivation, and wielding power over her, a woman who had exercised control over him while he was in prison, would provide him with the ultimate thrill.

Words were her only defense, along with her knowledge of him and how his mind worked. From the moment he'd slithered onto the seat beside her she'd been feverishly searching her memory for something useful to fend him off.

His mother wasn't much of a weapon, but at such short notice and under such harrowing circumstances it was the best she could come up with.

"Get back down out of sight, Dirty," Abell snapped. He was crouched between two seats, rubbing the knee of one of the girls — the thin one in the miniskirt, pretty, with short black hair, olive skin, and scarlet lips. Bree was her name: Charlie had heard her say it, haltingly, when Abell had asked her. Bree was huddled as far away from Abell as she could get, which wasn't far. Charlie tried not to think about what he had in mind for her. The girl was obviously scared to death: she'd been crying quietly off and on since the bus had been waved through the Ridge's security checkpoints and started heading unimpeded down the snaking road that led to Big Stone Gap. That's when it had become obvious that nobody in authority had any idea what was happening, that a prison break was in progress, and that the bad-news kids in the school bus (and a few others as well) were now hostages.

The fire had been the perfect diversion for a prison break. Charlie had no doubt that it had been set deliberately.

After making it through the security checkpoints, the bus had rolled through town, stopping at red lights and driving under the speed limit and in general doing nothing to attract attention while the escaping prisoners carefully stayed out of sight of the windows and kept their guns on the hostages. The teens and the women — Charlie and the gray-haired chaperone, whose name and official position Charlie didn't know — had been positioned in the seats so that their innocent-looking faces could be seen through the windows, and they'd been threatened with death if they so much as blinked wrong. The rain had helped, of course, but the people in the passing vehicles and the pedestrians hurrying along the sidewalks hadn't given the bus a second glance.

The farther away from the prison they got,

the more the atmosphere in the bus seethed with heightening emotion: fear from the hostages and tension from the escapees. The chaperone started to hyperventilate. Fortunately, the kids had brought brown-bag meals, which were stored in an open crate on a seat within Charlie's view. Unable to stand listening to the chaperone gasping for breath, Charlie had gone into doctor mode and gotten up, dumped out a bag, and given it to the woman, who she then told to breathe into it. Abell had pointed his gun at Charlie and barked, "Sit down." When Charlie did as she was told, he pointed his gun at the chaperone and said, "First to die, lady," which had caused the poor woman to wheeze so hard Charlie thought she would pass out before she could get the paper bag over her mouth and nose.

Once they were on the highway, the escapees had collected personal belongings, including Charlie's purse. They'd thrown the cell phones into a river as the bus had crossed the bridge above it and eaten the bagged food, but other than generalized threats, they'd pretty much left the hostages alone.

Except for one of the larger boys — a beanpole seventeen-year-old six-footer with stringy brown hair and thin shoulders hunched into a black hoodie — who had said something to Bree. For that, he'd been cracked in the face with a gun butt. His nose swollen and bloodied, he was now tied up and sitting on the floor between two empty seats. The real driver, who'd been left in his tighty-whities, was also tied up and sitting on the floor between two empty seats. The two guards — real, as it turned out — who'd escorted the Scared Straight group to the bus had been taken hostage as well. Unarmed themselves, faced with eight armed killers who had it in for them, they'd surrendered without a fight. They were sitting on the floor in the back row under Ware's guard, handcuffed.

Charlie didn't think the situation looked good for those four, or for Hughes, whose sheer size made him someone the escapees might perceive as a threat. The situation didn't look good for the rest of them — herself, the chaperone, the two girls, and the five remaining boys — either, but she didn't think they were on the first-to-die list.

More like the first to be raped and tortured.

At the thought, more shivers raced over her skin.

The Ridge is escape-proof. The refrain ran

at intervals through her mind. It was common knowledge: everyone who worked at the prison knew that. Warden Pugh bragged about it; it was a point of pride among the guards. Stupidly, she'd never doubted it. Even though Michael had once confessed that he'd considered trying to escape by taking her hostage, she'd never really worried about it because she'd never thought it could actually be done.

How to put this? Wrong again.

With the initial shock wearing off and hideous reality starting to set in, Charlie had her own bitter answer to that snippet of common knowledge: *The Ridge is escape-proof like the* Titanic *was unsinkable.*

From the moment she'd been forced aboard the bus and the escapees had taken over, yanking the driver from his seat, making him shed his uniform, and replacing him with one of their own while terrorizing their captives into submission, Charlie had been sure that the escape would be discovered and the bus stopped at any second. When they'd made it through Big Stone Gap, then turned at the McDonald's onto Cantrell Highway, Charlie still had been sure that they would be surrounded by an army of cops before they'd gone a mile.

Eight convicts could not just disappear

from a maximum security facility and not be missed. They could not kidnap fourteen people without anyone noticing.

Finally, with the bus on a bumpy two-lane road climbing one of the pine-ridged mountains that formed the backbone of the state, the first cop car had put in an appearance. Its siren was what had distracted Fleenor. It was back there doing its two-note whoop behind the bus.

Charlie wasn't sure whether to be glad or sorry. She doubted that the escapees would surrender without a fight: these were violent, desperate men whose lives were on the line. They wouldn't hesitate to kill every single hostage, including teenagers, including herself, if it would give them a better chance to get away.

But the thought of finding herself at Fleenor's mercy, at what might have happened just now if the siren hadn't gone off when it did, made her break out in a cold sweat.

The real nightmare begins was the thought that had flashed into Charlie's head as Fleenor had settled in beside her. Dread had knotted her stomach. Her nails had dug into her thighs as she'd fought to remain outwardly composed.

Now, with the long-delayed appearance of

law enforcement, Charlie feared a nightmare of a different sort. As in, *there's going to be a shootout and we're all going to die.*

The atmosphere inside the bus, which had stabilized into a kind of low-key fear as the minutes had ticked away with nothing too horrible happening, was suddenly turbocharged again. The teens who'd been slumping in their seats sat up, looking around, a mix of every emotion from fear to hope in their faces. The chaperone bent almost double as she huffed noisily into the paper bag. The escapees were on alert, some watching the hostages, some watching the back of the bus, wired to a man.

Having spent practically every single minute since she'd been forced into the bus trying to devise a plan of escape, Charlie had hit on nothing that had the least chance of working. She'd settled on trying to come up with a way to survive, but she wasn't having a lot of luck with that, either. Basically, she was down to using her knowledge of her research subjects to try to distract them from whatever heinous thing they attempted to do, seize any opportunity to run that presented itself, and pray for rescue.

It wasn't much, but it was the best she could do.

"*Bastardo*'s been following us for about

five miles," Torres said, as Fleenor — thank God! — slipped off the seat and into the center aisle. Crouching, Fleenor moved toward the rear, edging around Hughes, who was sprawled facedown in the aisle with his hands cuffed behind his back, presumably because his size and unconscious state made putting him anywhere else problematic and also so that Torres and Ware, who'd taken up positions in the rear, could easily keep an eye on him as well as the guards. As far as Charlie could tell, the escapees had allocated the few sets of handcuffs they apparently had managed to get hold of — guards didn't usually carry them — to the hostages they considered the most dangerous. She and the chaperone and the teens had been left unrestrained. But Hughes had made not one single threatening move since being carried aboard the bus, and Fleenor edged past him now like he was about as dangerous as a rug.

Torres squatted in front of the emergency exit door, neck craned as he peered out the exit door's window. Behind the bus, the siren continued to wail. Charlie could see the flashing blue lights reflected in the bus's big side-view mirrors. The rain had stopped, but the sky was overcast and a cloud had dropped low enough so that they were driving through gossamer fingers of mist. It wasn't yet dusk, but dusk wasn't far away. The interior of the bus was gloomy.

"You plan on telling anybody he was there?" Fleenor demanded as he reached the back of the bus.

"You got eyes just like me," Torres retorted. Like Abell, Sayers, and Ware, Torres wore a guard's uniform, one that was obviously too big for his skinny, five-foot-ten-inch frame. Charlie hated to think how he'd gotten it. His thick black hair was shaved at the sides and buzzed on top, and he had a tattoo of a cross on the right side of his neck. At thirty, he was the youngest of her research subjects, and also one of the most depraved. His specialty was young boys. Known in the media as the Carolina Cannibal, he'd killed, dismembered, and eaten the flesh of forty-three early-adolescent males that the authorities knew of. Charlie suspected there were more undiscovered victims. Since boarding the bus, he'd been looking the boys over like a dog eyeing raw meat. Charlie was terrified for them and was glad they knew nothing of his history. "You hadn't been so busy with Dr. *Puta,* you'd have noticed sooner and you wouldn't have been sitting up where the *sucio marranos* could see you."

Charlie knew enough Spanish to translate that last as "dirty pigs" and her own sobriquet as Dr. Whore.

"You blaming the pig whistle on me?" Fleenor asked, outraged, as he peeped out the exit window, too. Torres looked at him. Charlie didn't have the best angle on Torres's expression, but from her perspective it looked murderous.

Before Torres could respond, Abell said, "Can it, you two."

"Couldn't tell it was a cop until he turned on his lights," Ware told Fleenor, who was still bristling at Torres. Ware was back there, too, out of Charlie's sight between the seats.

Staying low, Abell headed down the center aisle to join them at the rear of the bus. On the way, he kicked Hughes, whose inert body made getting past him awkward, in the ribs. Charlie winced at the painful-sounding thud.

Whether Hughes was conscious or not, Charlie had no idea. He'd resurfaced once that she knew of as they were leaving Big Stone Gap, lifting his head and groaning loudly enough to attract attention. One of the orange-uniformed escapees she didn't know — she assumed he'd been with Fleenor in the library talking to the Scared Straight kids — had slammed his gun butt down on the back of Hughes's head, and he'd collapsed again, knocked unconscious for a second time. He was positioned so that he hadn't gotten in anyone's way until now, and so as far as she knew he'd been left alone.

"What do I do? You want I should gun it?" the driver — Charlie thought his name was Doyle — called back, his voice tight with anxiety. Turned sideways in her seat, which was about a third of the way down the bus, Charlie was able to see a great deal. Doyle's hands had tightened on the steering wheel. His back had stiffened. Awaiting instructions, he was looking through the rearview mirror at the men now crouched around the back door.

"No," Abell replied. He seemed to have assumed the role of leader. "Turn on your flashers and slow down, like you're getting ready to stop."

Sayers stood up abruptly. He was near the front of the bus, on her side. Charlie thought he'd been settled on the floor beside the other girl, a short, plump, platinum blonde with obvious dark roots who up until the siren had gone off had been leaning against her window with her eyes closed and her lips moving as if she were silently praying. Now she was sitting up and looking around, her heavily made-up eyes huge with fright.

Sayers said, “I’m here to tell you, stopping’s not going to happen.”

“Get down,” Abell snapped, gesturing at Sayers to get his head below the level of the windows. “And I say what happens.” To Doyle he added, “Hit the brakes. Pull over to the side of the road, then stop. But do it real gradual.”

Doyle didn’t seem to be in any doubt about who was in charge. The bus rattled and shook as it started to slow. The groan of the brakes was audible even over the following siren. Seen through the windows, the heavily forested mountain became less and less of a blur. Charlie was able to pick out individual trees among the deeply colored oaks and maples and poplars that crowded close to the road.

Her pulse quickened until she could feel it pounding in her ears. Whatever was getting ready to happen, she had a bad feeling that the escapees tamely submitting to being pulled over wasn’t it.

“I’m not going back to the Ridge.” Sayers’s tone made it a challenge. Several of the others muttered in agreement, but there was no overt show of mutiny and Sayers followed Abell’s directive and crouched in the aisle, one hand holding on to the seat nearest him for balance, the other clutching his gun.

"We're sticking with the plan, okay?" Abell said. "That barn I told you about, the one with the pickup truck, is about fifteen miles from here. Once we get there, we hide the bus in the barn and take off in the truck. Nobody's gonna be looking for a truck."

Sayers frowned. "But what about —"

Abell cut him off. "Just shut up, will you? I got it under control."

As Abell turned back to look out the exit window, tension settled heavy as a blanket over them all. Charlie had just been hit by a terrifying thought — no pickup truck she'd ever seen was big enough to hold eight escapees and fourteen hostages — when she saw that both of the girls and two of the boys — the small, scared-faced one she had noticed in the prison's hallway and a larger, heavyset boy with carroty hair — were looking at her fearfully. Bree's mouth trembled, the smaller boy was breathing hard, and from their expressions it was obvious that, with the other good-guy adults present out of commission, all four were turning to her as the authority figure in charge.

There's no one else. I'm responsible for them. I have to do whatever I can to get them out of this alive. With the realization came a fresh wave of panic. It made her chest tighten. She had to fight to keep her own breathing slow and even. The hard truth was she wasn't sure there was anything she *could* do. For them or for herself.

Feeling helpless and hating it, she mouthed *Shh* at them and shook her head slightly, a silent message warning them to be quiet and stay in their seats.

It was the best she could do.

"You think they found the guards yet?" asked one of the unknown orange-uniformed escapees. He was tall and bony, with sandy hair, pale skin, and hollowed-out cheeks. Charlie pegged him as early thirties. He wasn't a serial killer, but that left plenty of room for him to be guilty of all kinds of other horrible crimes.

"The dead ones we left in the library's supply closet?" another of the orange-uniformed unknowns responded like he was making a joke. This guy was older, shorter, and heavier, with deep lines in his face and grizzled dark hair. He grinned, revealing a missing front tooth. "Depends on if we really managed to burn that mother down."

"They found 'em," Fleenor said shortly. "They found everybody. You think this guy being on our tail is an accident? By now there's bound to be a BOLO out on this damned big yellow school bus."

"Could be something like a busted taillight," Abell said. "Not that it matters."

"I still say you shouldn't have killed Brother Frank." Ware sounded both uneasy and angry. Of medium height and weight, he was a physically attractive man with even features and thick brown hair, the kind of clean-cut, WASPy guy that nobody was afraid of on sight. Known as the Beltway Strangler, he'd murdered fourteen women, most of them prostitutes, and left their bodies beside the D.C. Beltway. "Offing a preacher — that's gonna piss God off. I *told* you."

"Makes you feel any better, the last thing Brother Frank said was a prayer," Torres said, and snickered.

"It was *prayer group.*" Ware shook his head. "Killing people there's just bad karma. And a *preacher.*"

Torres said, "Going to prayer group was the only way us *hombres muerto caminando*" — Charlie quickly translated that as dead men walking and realized he was referring to himself and his fellow residents of death row — "were going to get to the library today. Except for Fleenor. Hey, Dirty, who'd you have to suck off to get the gig with the kids?"

Fleenor snorted. "Fuck you, *amigo.* I bribed one of the guards with a month's worth of smokes to get put on that damned community outreach panel. I hadn't done that, we wouldn't even have known these little bastards were coming, much less when and where."

"So you lost some smokes," Torres retorted. "You know what kind of shit I had to put up with from that fat librarian to get those guns hid in there?"

"You killed him," Fleenor said. "You got payback."

"You could've waited till Brother Frank left," Ware said.

"You had a problem with what was going to go down, you could've stayed in your cell and taken your chances on being the next one hit," Abell said to Ware. "You didn't, so shut the fuck up. All of you, shut the fuck up. We got enough problems." He looked toward the front of the bus, his gaze skimming the hostages. "Kiddies, ladies, you just sit tight. Sayers, Creech, Ruben, make sure nobody does anything they shouldn't. Anybody gets out of line, kill 'em."

Creech and Ruben were the names of the two unknown orange uniforms who'd been talking, Charlie gathered by their reactions. They moved out into the center aisle, going down on their haunches like Sayers to keep from being spotted through the windows, casting meaningful looks at the hostages, guns at the ready. Charlie had a bad feeling about what was getting ready to happen as the bus jolted onto the gravel on the shoulder of the road. The driver had chosen to pull over to the side where the mountain rose above them; on the other side a narrow slice of young trees was all that stood between them and a drop that was obscured by floating gray mist but that Charlie estimated had to be somewhere in the region of five hundred feet.

Abell was talking to Torres, Fleenor, and Ware, all of whom were gathered around the rear exit with him now in a tight little clump, in a low tone that Charlie couldn't overhear. Their body language told her that they were edgy and primed for action. Wetting her lips, Charlie glanced at the side-view mirrors again and watched the flashing bar lights of the police car follow the bus onto the shoulder. She hoped the cops in the car knew what they were wading into.

The thought of that waiting pickup truck wouldn't leave her alone. A chill slid down her spine. Glancing at the teens, Charlie felt real desperation start to set in.

Once they get us inside that barn, it's over.

There are eight of them, they have guns, they can do whatever they want to us. Waiting for rescue isn't going to do it. Even if rescue comes, these guys will kill every one of us before they let us go. We've got to escape from the bus. With a big enough distraction — maybe these cops will create enough of a distraction — maybe we can get the front door open and run. Some of the kids might be able to make it out the windows. A few. The fast ones. The skinny ones. The skinny, fast ones.

As plans went, that was about as sucky as everything else she'd come up with so far. It had almost no chance of success — certainly no chance of everyone making it out alive — but unless something else occurred, it was going to have to do.

I have to let the kids know.

She looked around at them.

"When I tell you, lift the handle and push out," Abell ordered, loudly enough that Charlie could hear. He was talking to Ware, and something about his tone commanded her full attention. Focusing on what was happening at the rear now, she gripped the metal bar at the top of her seat back as the bus shuddered to a halt. The siren grew louder as the police car pulled up behind it. Blue flashing lights pulsed through the interior of the bus like barber pole stripes.

"Now," Abell ordered.

The emergency exit door flew open. Even as the tinny alarm attached to the door sounded, Charlie caught the merest glimpse of the police car parked a few yards away. The passenger door was open. A uniformed police officer strode toward the bus, mist swirling around his feet. Local, not state police, was all she had time to register before the staccato sound of gunfire ripped through the wailing sirens.

Pulse leaping, Charlie stayed frozen in place for long enough to watch the cop's chest explode into a pulpy mess as he got mowed down, to catch his partner emerging from the driver's side of the police car with a shout and a pointed gun, to see that same cop duck behind the open door of his cruiser as a fusillade of bullets slammed into the car. Abell, Torres, Fleenor, and Ware were all firing out the emergency door. She heard answering gunfire from the cop.

Should I try to . . . ?

Something whizzed past Charlie's head to smack into the wall behind her, then ricocheted off with a whine.

That snapped her out of it. Forget trying to go out the doors or windows. Right now the name of the game was *Don't get shot.*

"Get down!" Charlie cried to the kids as

bullets slammed into metal with a series of sharp slaps and *ping*s and the interior of the bus erupted into an explosion of gasps, screams, shouts, and curses. The clearly terrified teens obeyed instantly, throwing themselves to the floor between the seats. Charlie threw herself to the floor as well, huddling so low in the narrow space in front of her seat that she was practically kissing the dirty metal.

"Stop them! Don't let them get away!" Abell screamed. Through the resulting burst of shooting, Charlie heard what she thought was the squeal of tires on pavement, and could only hope that both officers were back in the car — after all, Abell had said "them" — and were peeling out. *Go,* she urged them silently as the gunfire from the bus intensified until it sounded like a whole Fourth of July's worth of firecrackers being detonated at once.

Torres's triumphant yell of "Yes!" was followed almost immediately by a series of metallic-sounding screeches that Charlie, horrified, had to assume was the patrol car hurtling through some kind of barrier — like, say, trees. Then the wailing siren seemed to drop away —

"He's done! He's over the side!" Ware cried, and the escapees broke into whoops and cheers.

Even as Charlie looked beneath the seats toward the rear door to try to see something, anything, of what was happening, there was the distant sound of a severe impact. The siren cut off abruptly.

Oh, no. Her head dropped to rest on her hands, which were fisted on the floor. Her shoulders slumped.

It didn't require a psychic to conclude that the cop car had gone off the side of the mountain.

That both cops were almost certainly dying or dead.

"Doyle, get this thing moving," Abell yelled. *"Now."*

There was a grinding sound: the gearshift being engaged. The bus jerked and bounced and rumbled as it took off again. The tires rattled over gravel, then swooshed onto pavement, and they picked up speed. In the distance, she thought she heard the wail of a siren. Was another cop car out there? Was it chasing them? Or was she imagining things?

"Damn *sucio marranos* must've called for backup," Torres said and groaned as Charlie caught her breath.

Her stomach tightened. Her head came up.

And her widening eyes immediately fixed on what was planted in the center aisle only a few inches in front of her face.

A man's scuffed brown cowboy boot, attached to a long, muscular leg encased in faded jeans, attached to a —

Charlie kept on looking up, and then her heart stood still.

Chapter Eight

Michael.

He stood there, in spirit form, looking as solid and real as any living, breathing human being on the bus.

If Charlie had been able to say anything, his name would have flown out of her mouth like it had wings.

"So what's your plan B?" Sayers yelled, belligerence in every syllable.

Abell or one of the others replied, but the words didn't register. All the pandemonium in the bus, the rattling and jolting and shouting and burst of feverish activity as they tried and failed to catch and close the wildly swinging rear door, even her own fear, fell away, blocked by a wave of emotion so strong that it rocked her.

Michael.

If she'd been able to move she would have flung herself at him. Not that it would have done any good, because throwing herself at ectoplasm was pretty much the same as throwing herself at thin air, but that's what she would have done anyway. Instinctively. Because she had never, ever been so glad to see anyone in her life.

Fortunately, shock paralyzed most of her muscles, including her vocal cords. In those first critical seconds she could neither move nor speak.

Having traveled up over his wide, white T-shirted chest, her eyes stayed fastened on his face.

There was no mistake. He was *there,* all six-foot-three hunky golden inches of him. Aggressively masculine despite the outrageous good looks. Seriously badass.

He wasn't looking at her. He was glancing around, frowning, and seemed maybe a little dazed, like he was having to work to get a handle on exactly where he was. She had a really good worm's-eye view of the underside of his square jaw, of the stubble that darkened it, of the flat planes of his cheeks, of his chiseled nose and high cheekbones, of the firm lines of his beautifully cut mouth. From her angle, she couldn't see his eyes. She didn't need to.

Michael. She had no doubt whatsoever about his identity, couldn't believe she had ever in a million years mistaken Hughes for him. She recognized him with something more accurate than anything her eyes could tell her. She recognized him in some deep, atavistic place in her soul.

For a moment, an agonizing moment, she wondered if he was some kind of illusion, if he would vanish as suddenly as he had appeared, if this was a repeat of the quick vision she'd had of him the previous twilight.

Her hand shot out on the thought and grabbed the nearest part of him, which happened to be the instep of his boot. At least, she tried to grab the instep of his boot. Of course her hand sank right through.

But the tingle, the electric tingle that accompanied any contact she had with him in his incorporeal state, was there.

He was real. Present. On the bus just inches away.

He must have felt the tingle, too, or sensed her eyes on him, or something, because he looked down at her.

Sayers went storming through him right then, shouting at the men in the back, waving an impatient hand at the air where Michael was standing as he passed, like he thought he'd run into a patch of cobwebs or static electricity or something.

Charlie yanked her hand out of the way of Sayers's stomping feet just in time. She heard a *thunk,* and Sayers's curse, and guessed that he'd stumbled over or kicked Hughes on his way to the back of the bus.

Michael looked after him, then looked down at her again. However dazed he might have been originally, he was clearly getting over it now. His brows rushed together in a fierce frown that was absolutely directed at her.

Her lips parted —

"Do not say a fucking word. Do not make another fucking move," he growled, and then he hunkered down, squatting in the center aisle directly in front of where she huddled on the floor beside her abandoned seat. He looked as big and bad and muscular and intimidating as he ever had. His expression was scary enough that any right-minded person on the receiving end of that look would have shrunk back as far away from him as she could get.

Charlie didn't shrink. Instead she drank in the sight of him. Her pulse hammered. She could feel the blood rushing to her head, feel it pounding against her temples. She didn't care how menacing he looked. Her heart erupted in glad hosannas.

"Oh, my God, where have you *been*?" Her voice was a barely audible croak. Not because she was deliberately keeping it low.

That wasn't a consideration; everything that wasn't him had temporarily fallen off her radar screen. She didn't wait for his answer, because she knew: his eyes were the burning, fathomless black that she'd seen before, and the savagery in his face and voice were familiar, too. The longer he stayed in Spookville, the darker he got, and this time he'd been gone longer than ever before. She didn't care. She would take him any way she could get him, darkness be damned. "I didn't think you were coming back!"

"What part of 'Do not say a fucking word' did you miss?" Those ferocious black eyes glittered at her. "Oh, I know: the same part as 'Keep away from fucking serial killers' and 'Stay out of the fucking prison' that you never seem to hear. The whole damned thing, because you refuse to listen to a word I say, because you have a fucking *death wish.*"

It was vintage Michael, all of it, and, God, she was so glad to see him, so relieved, so happy, that she could feel herself smiling at him even as he yelled at her.

"Do not," she said, forming the words with her mouth without making a sound.

"Are you fucking *smiling*?" He sounded furious. He looked furious.

"No." She shook her head. But because

she simply couldn't help it, her smile stayed in place, or maybe even grew.

Michael. To have him back —

"You are! You're smiling. Goddamn it, you're totally nuts, do you know that? Do you know what that bastard Fleenor is going to do to you if he gets the chance? Hell, yes, of course you know: you meet with him every week, so you can do your precious research that's probably going to end up getting you killed." His mouth tightened as he glanced around. He was speaking in a perfectly normal tone — actually, a louder-than-normal tone, because he was angry and yelling at her, and a tone that was deeper and more gravelly than usual, too, because that's what Spookville did to him. Listening to him, looking at him, Charlie suddenly felt better than she had in, oh, a little over two weeks. "What did you do, take your serial killer buddies on a fucking field trip? Who wouldn't have guessed *that* might go wrong?"

Giving him a mildly indignant look — as if she would! — she opened her mouth to reply and offer a quick explanation of what was happening. He shut her down with a fierce look and a warning finger pointed at her. "We're talking about this later. For now, for once in your life, just keep quiet and stay still while I try to figure out how the hell to get you out of this alive."

"We're sitting ducks! They're on our *ass*," Sayers yelled from the back of the bus, almost certainly addressing Abell. Michael cast a frowning look in their direction. Now that the first shock of his return was over, Charlie was once again becoming fully aware of the world beyond him, beyond them. She heard distant sirens — either there was an echo or there was more than one cop car chasing the bus now. She felt a shiver that combined hope and fear. Far more than before, she wanted to be rescued. She wanted to get out of there alive. They — the hostages — all wanted to be rescued and get out of there alive, of course. But for her, the stakes had just heightened dramatically. Michael was back, and he needed her to keep him grounded to the earthly plane. Michael was back, and that meant her world had regained its color and warmth and possibility. The weight that had been crushing her was gone. She felt like she could once again breathe. She felt like she could once again live.

If the escapees were cornered, though, she had no doubt at all that that could change in an instant. She knew five of them very well, and if they saw no way out for themselves they would not only have no compunction about killing everyone in the bus, they would enjoy the slaughter.

Go out with a bang and all that.

Her chest tightened again.

Abell bellowed, "You gettin' up in my face? Huh? Huh? Get back up front, Google Eyes, and let the people who know how to run things run them."

Sayers's reply was so loud it practically rattled the windows. "What did you call me?"

An unexpected sound — a soft little whimper, really — drew Charlie's attention to something closer at hand. Turning her head in the direction from which it had come, she found herself looking through the dark space beneath the seats at Bree, whose face was pressed to the floor, too. The girl had her fist shoved up against her mouth in an attempt to muffle what were obviously sobs. Her whole body shook. Tears flowed from her eyes as they met Charlie's. Her fist moved away from her mouth.

"I'm scared," she whispered.

Charlie didn't waste time by lying and telling her that everything was going to be all right. She had no way of knowing that, and feel-good platitudes were of no help to anyone.

"We have to get away," Charlie whispered back. The escalating argument between Abell and Sayers, the banging of the unsecured back door, the rattling of the bus, and various sounds from the others on board were enough to mask her barely-there whisper, she hoped. A quick glance at Michael reassured her: he was still focused on the argument at the rear. If he wasn't hearing her, she could be certain Abell and Sayers and the rest weren't, either.

Bree nodded as another head dropped into view: a boy, with buzzed brown hair and a nose ring, peering beneath the seats. Previously she'd been able to see only the lower part of his jeans-clad legs as, like the others, he knelt on the floor. He looked at Charlie, who went "Shh!" with a finger to her lips, then continued with what she'd been saying, directing it to both of them now. "When the bus stops, when there's a distraction, try to get out a window or one of the doors. These men are killers. Take any chance you get to escape."

"Are you talking to somebody?" Michael demanded. Charlie's head snapped up guiltily.

". . . think they're not going to set up roadblocks?" Sayers screamed. The bus swayed as they went around a curve, and

Charlie, on all fours now, had to brace her hands against the floor to keep her balance. "They're probably blocking every damned road off this mountain right this minute!"

"You don't know shit," Abell screamed back. There was more, but Charlie quit listening to focus on what was going on closer at hand.

"Under there," Charlie mouthed to Michael, and pointed.

Michael bent down and looked. Charlie followed suit. The kids couldn't see *him,* of course. Now the blond girl was looking beneath the seats, too. Her pale cheek rested against the floor.

"They're going to kill us, aren't they?" the girl whispered. Her voice trembled.

"Shut up, Paris," the boy responded, sending a glare her way as Bree drew in a harsh breath that was just short of a sob and then pressed her fist to her mouth again.

"We have to try to escape," Charlie repeated as quietly as before. "First chance you get: go out a door, a window, whatever, and run. Tell the others if you can."

"She won't fit out a window," the boy said, jerking a thumb at Paris.

"Suck off, dirtwad," Paris fired back.

"Shh!" Charlie cautioned fiercely, glaring, and they both clamped their mouths shut while Bree stifled another sob.

"Holy shit," Michael said, resurfacing. Charlie straightened to look at him and found her gaze colliding with those angry, burning black eyes. "Those are fucking *kids.*"

She knew he had a thing about getting involved with endangered kids. "Yes, they are."

"How the hell —"

"They were visiting the prison. A Scared Straight group. This is a prison break, and they got caught up in it."

His face tightened. His eyes looked even scarier than they had before. "Same as you did, huh? Just one of those unfortunate things that could happen to anybody."

There was no missing the sarcasm.

"Could you drop the attitude, please?"

"Drop the *attitude*? Like that's the problem here? My *attitude*?" He eyed her like there was a whole lot more he wanted to say, then made a disgusted sound and shook his head. "You know what your whole life reminds me of? That Hole album, *Live Through This.*"

Funny. Charlie didn't say it out loud, but she made a face at him. Then she caught herself smiling at him again, because it felt so good to have him there and being pissy at her and because, with him there, she was no longer quite so deathly afraid.

That last thought didn't even surprise her. Her faith in Michael as her own personal superhero was infinite, she was discovering.

"I knew it. You're insane," Michael growled in the face of her smile, only to have his attention diverted as Sayers, who'd been in the act of storming toward the front of the bus, stopped when he reached Hughes and snapped, "This asshole's in the way. Help me get him out of the aisle."

From her position on the floor, Charlie couldn't see a lot, such as who Sayers was talking to. But by looking beneath the seats again, she was able to see Hughes's body come up off the floor. She presumed Sayers and one of the others at the back were lifting him. Then Hughes was dumped in a semi-sitting position between two seats. As he slumped sideways Charlie saw his hands, which were cuffed behind him, clench into fists.

Not so unconscious, then.

She was just watching Hughes's fingers straighten and clench again, a clearly deliberate movement, when something, a sound or a vibe, she didn't know for sure, snapped her attention back to Michael.

He was looking toward where Hughes had

been. His expression was absolutely shell-shocked.

Of course, if he'd seen Hughes's face — and from the look of him he had — he would be. There was no way he could have missed the resemblance.

"Hey," she whispered. It was the merest breath of sound, but Michael heard, because he looked at her then. His face was a study in stupefaction.

"Who —" he began, while at the same time Sayers said, "He remind you of —"

Both were interrupted by Torres shouting, "*Mierda!* Here they come!"

Chapter Nine

Charlie's heart pounded in terrible anticipation. "They" could mean only the cops. Would the escapees try stopping the bus again, and would they — ?

"Punch it, Doyle," Abell yelled, giving her the answer. Already bouncing over the pavement, the bus picked up speed. The jolting of the floor beneath Charlie telegraphed the location of every pothole. Her shins hurt from the unforgiving metal slamming into them. An outbreak of curses from the escapees, coupled with the increasing loudness of the sirens, told Charlie that the cops who were behind them must be closing in fast.

Michael said, "Stay put," stood up, and walked out of her line of vision. Catching her breath — having him out of her sight rattled her, she instantly discovered — she was relieved to find that she could follow the progress of his boots down the aisle. He stopped in front of the place where Hughes now sprawled. From the position of his feet, she knew that Michael must be studying him.

She didn't think it would take Michael long to grasp the significance of what he was seeing.

"There's two of 'em this time," Ware warned, clearly referring to the cop cars.

Charlie couldn't see them, of course, but the revolving bar lights were reflected in the mirrors and the sirens were impossible to miss. The blur of trees flying past outside the windows gave silent testimony to how fast they were traveling. Charlie had a momentary mental image of the cliff edge beside the road, which made her shiver. Flying off a sheer drop in a hijacked school bus was relatively low on the list of horrible ways she could die in the next few hours, though, so she thrust it out of her mind. Shifting positions so that she could sneak a look around the seat, Charlie was just in time to watch Abell grab one of the handcuffed guards, jerk him off the seat where he'd been slumped, and force him — he didn't struggle — toward the rear door, barking, "Wedge it open," to Ware as he came.

Ware forced the door all the way open and locked it in place. Charlie caught a glimpse of roiling mist colored blue by the flashing lights before Abell, with the prisoner in tow, filled the opening.

"Back off!" Abell screamed at the cops in pursuit. Bracing his feet against the rocking of the bus, he held the unresisting guard in front of the open door, one hand twisted in his collar. He placed his gun against the back of the guard's head.

Bang.

A cloud of dark particulates mushroomed from the guard's forehead and out into the deepening fog. Inside the bus, there was a collection of gasps. Somebody let loose with a truncated scream.

Charlie's mouth fell open as she watched the guard topple limply out of the bus. She heard the thud as he landed in the road. There was not the slightest doubt in her mind that he was dead, and that she'd just watched murder being committed.

Oh, my God . . .

From behind the bus came the sudden screech of tires. She could only assume that the cops, witnessing the shooting, seeing the body hit the pavement, had slammed on their brakes.

"Jesus Christ." Michael was back, hunkering down in front of her. Charlie didn't know what she looked like, but from his expression she guessed it wasn't good. "Get back down on the floor, put your head on your knees, and cover it with your arms. And *stay there.*"

Michael was right, she knew: she was way too exposed and she needed to get down. At that moment she was kneeling, her forearms resting on the seat as she craned her neck to look toward the rear door. There was nothing left to see, nothing she could do. The guard was dead.

Numbly, she dropped to the floor, pillowed her head on her knees, clasping her hands behind her neck, and concentrated on taking deep breaths.

"I'll be right back," Michael said. Although she had her eyes closed to combat the dizziness that was assailing her and thus couldn't be sure, she got the impression that he was moving away toward the front of the bus. Her heart was pounding, and she focused on trying to slow it down. Since no bullets were flying — the cops apparently had been stopped in their tracks by the murder — there didn't seem to be a lot of point in shielding her head. Unclasping her hands, she wrapped her arms around her knees instead. She was shivering — from shock, she knew.

"We offing hostages now?" somebody —

Charlie thought it was Fleenor — asked gleefully.

"Just slowing the bastards down," Abell answered. "Scraping corpses off the pavement takes time."

"Maybe we ought to get *los marranos* some bumper stickers: we brake for dead people," Torres said, and snickered.

"Good one," Ware answered, while Abell said, "Hey, get over here and help me."

Michael hunkered down in front of her again. Charlie's eyes were still closed, but she knew he was there, and that knowledge was as stabilizing as an anchor in a storm. She expected him to tell her to cover her head, but he didn't. The sounds of quiet weeping reached her ears — Bree, or possibly Paris or even one of the boys. Of course they were terrified. *She* was terrified, and she had Michael, who she knew would do everything in his power to protect her.

"What? Wait!" It was a man's voice, one that Charlie didn't recognize, and it sounded panicky. It was accompanied by the sounds of a scuffle.

Her eyes popped open. Looking beneath the seats, she could see enough of what was happening to realize that Abell was dragging the other guard into the aisle. She sucked in a horrified breath. This guy was short and stocky, with buzzed blond hair. He struggled plenty, screaming and fighting, although given his and Abell's relative sizes — Abell dwarfed him — and the fact that his hands were cuffed behind him there wasn't a lot he could do to save himself. With Torres's help Abell had little difficulty wrestling him toward the door.

They're going to kill him, too. Charlie knew it with an icy certainty.

"I got a wife! Kids!" the guard screamed.

"There's eight of them. They're all armed," Michael said, talking to her over the commotion. Despite the lingering harshness that was a result of his sojourn in Spookville, his voice was almost back to its normal honeyed drawl. "We're in a confined space. That makes things tricky. But I'm working on it." He was trying to distract her from what was happening, Charlie realized. He was actually succeeding, a little. She was listening to him rather than —

Her eyes widened and her insides seized up as Abell pushed the guard to his knees in the open doorway. She could see the guard now, or most of him, kneeling, cowering, clearly petrified. Behind him, she could see Abell almost to the waist, see his hand holding the gun.

"Close your eyes," Michael ordered sharply.

Of course she didn't. She couldn't.

There's nothing I can do. Oh, God, I can't just —

"Don't kill me! Please, don't kill me," the guard begged. Abell's gun hand rose, disappearing from Charlie's view.

"Stop," she cried, leaping to her feet. She knew it was foolish, knew it was probably useless, but she had to try. She could not simply hide and do nothing as another man was murdered in cold blood in front of her eyes.

"What the hell are you *doing*?" Michael roared. "Get down!"

He was instantly on his feet, his big body blocking her view. Even though she knew she could walk right through it if she wanted to, having him standing there like that was enough to keep her from confronting Abell. Stopping short, refusing to look at Michael because she didn't want to see in his expression the fury and fear for her she could feel coming off him in waves, she summoned the one weapon she had to wield: her knowledge of the serial killers she was studying.

She was pretty sure it was the only weapon that she and her fellow hostages had.

Abell was looking at her now. At what she saw in his eyes, Charlie felt the blood drain from her face. His usual mask of ordinary humanity was gone, and the killer he was at his core glared at her, silently promising retribution. As the guard pleaded for his life at Abell's feet, Charlie shook that threatening look off. Squaring her shoulders, she ignored Michael's furious "Don't you dare say another fucking word."

"Mr. Abell, you still have Heidi" — Abell's twelve-year-old only child, part of his seemingly normal life as a married building contractor before his secret existence as the Midnight Rambler was revealed — "to live for. You don't want to provoke the police into —" *Killing you today* was what she was going to say, but Abell didn't let her finish.

Mouth curling, he pulled his eyes from hers to look back at the cringing guard. His hand jerked up.

Bang.

That shut her up. Abell had pulled the trigger, and the guard had been killed, all in a split second. The atmosphere in the bus was suddenly electrified as, shaken, Charlie watched Abell kick the body off the bus. Her throat closed. Her knees went weak. She had to hang on to the seat back to keep from crumpling.

Michael was livid. "Get down! Get down *now*! Jesus, are you *trying* to get yourself killed?"

Charlie felt the tingle as he grabbed her, which was a waste of time because his hands passed right through. In that single telescopic moment in the aftermath of the shooting, the bus suddenly seemed full of sounds: the rattling of the vehicle, the chaperone's rustling paper bag, the moans and sobs and heavy breathing from the other hostages, an argument between Fleenor and Ware about how to split up the dead guards' cash.

His expression ugly, Abell turned to look at her again even as the knowledge that it was too late, that the second guard had just been murdered, shot through the head right in front of them all like the first, truly hit her. The shock of it took her breath.

Abell said, "Anything else you want to say, Dr. Stone?"

Her eyes met his, held.

"No," Michael growled. "Hell, no, you don't have anything else to say."

Knowing that calling attention to herself as she had done had been incredibly stupid as well as *useless,* knowing that Michael was right and had been right all along, Charlie stayed silent.

"Thing about the death penalty is, it's like getting a kill-all-the-people-you-want-free card," Fleenor said, cackling. "I mean, what're they going to do?"

Abell broke eye contact with Charlie to give Fleenor a thumbs-up.

"So how's about we throw out another roadblock?" Abell said.

"Get down," Michael told her in the kind of voice that could have stopped a charging bull in its tracks.

Shuddering, Charlie dropped to her knees. As the seat blocked her from the view of Abell and the rest of the escapees, Michael loomed protectively over her, cursing a blue streak, his fear for her obvious in every profane word he uttered. Sinking back on her haunches, Charlie looked up at him with mute horror as the bus, slowing, started chugging up a steep incline.

She couldn't get the image of that exploding head out of her mind.

"When this is over, assuming you're still alive, you need to see a shrink," Michael said grimly.

I am a shrink, Charlie didn't reply, because her throat was still so tight that she wasn't sure she could talk, and anyway, flippancy was inappropriate at the moment, and also guaranteed to piss him off. But he must have read something in her face he didn't like, because his jaw hardened and his still-scarily-black eyes flared at her.

"I'm serious," he said.

"Speed it up, Doyle," one of the men yelled, while Charlie smiled at Michael, just a little smile because it felt so good to have him there and to have him worrying about her, and, because, really, to have a man who had been hit with diagnoses ranging from charismatic psychopath to borderline personality disorder to homicidal maniac tell her that she needed to see a shrink was kind of rich, not to mention funny.

Michael's eyes were still on her face, but his expression had changed. He was looking at her like she was worrying him.

"Everything's going to be okay, babe," Michael said, and from the gentler tone of his words, Charlie knew she'd been right. He was worried about her, and not just about her physical safety.

Probably the shock of watching those men get killed was still there in her eyes. Maybe her reactions to things were a little bit off because of it. Maybe that's what had him looking at her with such concern.

"Can't," Doyle called back. "This is as good as it gets until we reach the top of this grade."

"Floor it." Abell barked the order.

"I am," Doyle replied, adding, "I got to turn the lights on soon. You know it's getting on toward six, and with the fog and all, it's getting dark as shit."

Sayers burst out with an angry "Why not just fire off flares telling them where we are while you're at it?" and strode right through Michael again, heading toward the front this time, grabbing on to random seat backs as he went because of the steepness of the grade.

"No!" It was a girl's voice: Charlie wasn't sure if it was Bree or Paris. The fear-filled cry sent prickles of alarm racing over her skin. Even as her head whipped around in the direction from which it had come, Sayers went charging back through Michael — dragging Paris behind him. Practically sitting on the floor in an effort to resist as Sayers hauled her by one arm, the girl screamed, "Help! Help me!"

Looking wild-eyed at Charlie as she was dragged past, Paris thrust her free hand at her.

"Help! Please!"

"Paris!" With her heart in her throat, Charlie grabbed for that flailing hand, missed, and lunged for it again, diving right through Michael, who roared "No!" as he tried to stop her.

Ignoring him, Charlie scrambled down the aisle after Paris, who was looking back at her with her hand outstretched, screaming and crying and doing her best to jerk her arm free of Sayers's hold. Visions of her teenage best friend Holly Palmer, of Bayley Evans, of all the young girls in all the cases she had worked who had been horribly murdered, flashed through Charlie's mind, turning her mouth sour with fear. Whatever the risk to herself, she had to do what she could to prevent Paris, prevent any of these kids, from joining their ranks.

"Don't let him kill me," Paris cried, sobbing.

"Stop!" Charlie and Michael shouted almost simultaneously. Charlie was screaming at Sayers; Michael was yelling at her and at the same time trying to pull her back to safety with hands that were no more substantial than air. The beauty of ectoplasm was that as big and bad as Michael was, he couldn't actually physically stop her from doing anything. She managed to latch on to Paris's hand as Sayers tore past Abell and Torres, who were crowded into Hughes's seat row, attempting to pull a now wide awake, shouting and struggling Hughes from the spot he'd been occupying between the seats. Charlie had no doubt at all that Abell's intent was to shoot Hughes like he'd shot the guards, and from the way he was fighting, Hughes knew it, too.

"Damn it, Charlie!" Michael tried to grab her around the waist, with predictable results. Paris's cold and clammy hand clutched hers desperately. Charlie hung on to it with every bit of strength she had, doing her best to jerk the girl free as Sayers continued to haul her down the aisle. She knew what Sayers was capable of. The thought of him with Paris — it was enough to make Charlie's blood run cold.

"What the hell's up with you?" Abell bellowed, head turning to track Sayers. At the same time, he solved the problem of Hughes's struggles by slugging him over the head with his gun. The sharp *crack* of the blow told Charlie just how hard it had been. Hughes grunted and went limp. Abell and Torres pulled his sagging body into the aisle.

"I'm outa here," Sayers threw over his shoulder. "How hard do you think it's going to be for the millions of cops heading our way to find a *school bus*?"

"Mr. Sayers! Let her go!" Charlie cried, giving Paris's hand another frantic jerk as the girl tried digging in her heels one more time. Tightening his grip on her arm so brutally that Paris cried out, Sayers snapped, "Get the bitch." Charlie found her hair being grabbed from behind by Fleenor as Sayers dragged Paris and, by extension, her past him and Ware. Gasping at the sudden pain of it, Charlie lost her grip on Paris's hand.

"No!" Paris screamed, head twisting to look back as she strained toward Charlie. Her hand stretched out beseechingly. "Don't let go! Please!"

"Hey, sweet thing, you and me got —" Fleenor began, as Charlie, snarling, whipped around toward him. Without even thinking about it, she doubled up her fist and punched him as hard as she could in the nose. It was like slamming her fist into a rock. Her hand went numb. She felt the impact of the blow all the way up her arm.

"Bitch!" Fleenor howled.

Letting go of her hair, he staggered back, clapping a hand to his nose. Ware whooped with amusement.

There'll be hell to pay for that, Charlie thought with a fresh stab of fear as she whirled to go to Paris's assistance. The girl was doing her best to fight free of Sayers, kicking and screaming and trying to grab on to the seats without success. Elsewhere on the bus, pandemonium broke out. Bree screamed. Hughes revived with a roar, causing Abell and Torres to attack him in tandem. Ruben and Creech rushed down the aisle toward the fight —

"Help!" Paris screamed, looking back at Charlie with panic in her face as she and Sayers reached the open door. The specter of what had happened to the guards in that doorway made Charlie's heart clutch. The bus was slowing more as it rocked into a curve. A harried glance past Sayers out the door told Charlie that dusk was falling, mist lay everywhere, and the road was empty as far as she could see.

Not a cop car in sight.

"You can stay on this death ride if you want to. I'm taking my chances on the mountain," Sayers yelled, and he jumped, taking Paris with him.

Charlie watched in shock as the girl and Sayers plummeted to the road, hitting with a thud and rolling over and over.

Oh, no, no, no —

Then Fleenor charged up behind her, locked his hand around her wrist, and jumped, too, pulling her out with him.

Charlie didn't even have time to scream before she smashed hard onto the unforgiving asphalt.

Chapter Ten

Pain shot through Charlie's knees and palms. Landing on all fours, then tumbling uncontrollably, she felt the shock of the impact over every inch of her body. The surface of the road was hard and rough enough to tear clothes and skin, bruise muscles, jar bones.

Sharper even than the pain was the fear.

Fleenor's got me. Vivid images of the file pictures on Fleenor's victims flashed through her head. He liked to hurt them, make them cry and plead. And he would have particular reason to want to hurt her.

Only he didn't have her. At least the fall had made him release her wrist. The realization galvanized her. A petrified glance around found him skidding on his side along the shoulder of the road, his orange uniform making him impossible to miss even in the gathering darkness, even through the gray fingers of mist.

He was perhaps two yards to her left, bouncing along the edge of the pavement. On that side, the road was lined by a ribbon of gravel backed by a forbidding stockade of towering trees. The mountain rose steeply behind him, heavily wooded and dark. There was no sign of Paris, or Sayers, but given the choices, Charlie thought they must be somewhere up in those woods. The last she'd seen of Paris, the girl had been rolling down the middle of the road — but the good news was that Sayers had lost his grip on her just like Fleenor had lost his grip when they hit. Maybe Paris had gotten away. Maybe she was even now fleeing through the woods. Searching for the girl was not an option; Charlie had to get away from Fleenor while she could. He was looking in her direction now, cursing loudly even as his body slowed. At any second his forward momentum would stop, and then he would come after her or go for his gun.

At the thought of his gun, adrenaline shot through Charlie's veins like a giant infusion of speed.

Run. Her brain screamed the command. Despite the injuries she knew she must have suffered in the fall, her body responded. She had to get off the road; it was too open. Getting her feet beneath her, she scrambled toward the edge of the pavement, desperate to get away from Fleenor — and out of the reach of his gun. A splash of yellow amidst all the gray, the bus was already being swallowed up by mist as it rounded another turn, about to be lost from sight. The fading shouts coming from inside it almost covered the labored sound of the engine as it fought to reach the top of the steep incline. The smell of exhaust lingered in its wake, mixing with the damp scent of the mist. Charlie thought of the teens still inside, and felt her heart turn over. But there was nothing she could do for them now.

Michael. Glancing desperately around, Charlie called to him out loud. But there was no sign of him, no answer, and she couldn't wait.

Because Fleenor was on the side of the road with the rising mountain behind him, she darted for the opposite side, the side with the guardrail protecting the dizzying drop-off that, before, she'd thought was a sheer cliff.

It was a drop-off, but it wasn't sheer, she discovered. Clambering over the guardrail, plunging into the narrow strip of trees that grew on the other side of it, she glanced desperately down the rock wall that fell away into nothingness a few feet in front of her and discovered that, at least at this point, the angle of the cliff wasn't so steep that she couldn't descend it on foot, and that there was, in fact, a path.

"I'm coming for you, bitch," Fleenor yelled.

A frightened glance over her shoulder found him kneeling in the gravel on the opposite side of the road. As she watched, he rose laboriously to his feet, gun already in hand.

Charlie didn't wait to see any more. Heart pounding, she flung herself down that path, ignoring the pain in her knees, praying that her low-heeled shoes wouldn't slide on the wet leaves and moss that covered parts of the stone and send her plummeting — she dared take a look — hundreds of feet into the ravine below. Islands of gray mist floating below her like clouds made it seem like she was higher up even than she knew she was. All around her, the jagged silhouettes of mountains rose like blackened shark's teeth against a purpling sky.

Michael. She no longer dared to call his name out loud. Where he was she didn't know, but she did know that he would never leave her of his own accord. The fifty-foot rule — did that still apply? Was he gone again, sucked back into Spookville?

Even as she ran for her life, as she ducked beneath small prickly bushes growing out of the cliff face and prayed that she wouldn't catch her foot on an uneven place in the rock and go flying off the path, the thought terrified her.

Fear made her chest tight. Her lungs heaved as she fought to draw in enough air.

Bang. The bullet smacked into the stone face of the cliff beside her, so close that she felt its passing, so close that a tiny chip of rock flew in front of her eyes.

A scream tore into her throat. She swallowed it, afraid of pinpointing her location for Sayers, who was out there somewhere and might join with Fleenor to double-team her. And although attracting the cops who had to be out there on the mountain somewhere, too, would be good, she couldn't be sure that they were close enough even to hear her — so she ducked her head and ran like death was on her heels. Which, in fact, it was.

The path widened into a narrow, tree-covered ledge.

"Stop or I'll put a bullet in your back," Fleenor shouted after her, his voice echoing eerily.

Charlie's shoulders tightened. Her skin

crawled as she imagined a bullet slamming into her spine. Blessing the swirling mist and the deepening darkness equally for the cover they provided, she raced into the doubtful protection of a stand of spindly pines. Their pungent scent filled the air as she shoved through the damp branches only to discover that the ledge ended abruptly just beyond them. Coming up short as her sanctuary fell away in front of her feet in yet another sheer drop, she looked down in horror — and heard a rustle of branches warning her that Fleenor was coming after her through the trees.

Heart racing, practically teetering on the edge of the precipice as she whirled to face the copse of pines, she looked wildly around. Where she was, there was no concealment. The trees had run out, and she was standing in the open, with not even any mist in that particular spot, thanks to a cold updraft spiraling from below. It was dark, but not dark enough to hide her: the deepening charcoal of advancing dusk rather than the full-out blackness of night. The pale stone of the cliff rose starkly on one side. She was some ninety feet below the road now, and the climb up was impossible. Her only way out was back through the trees and along the path — and Fleenor, armed and murderous, was in her way.

Oh, my God, I'm trapped.

Panic had her heart pumping, reduced her breathing to ragged pants. Her palms were damp, she discovered, as her hands fisted at her sides. Turning, she looked down again. There was another ledge much like the one she was standing on some thirty feet below, down a wall of smooth, perpendicular rock. This one was maybe ten feet wide and held little in the way of cover: only a couple of large, scruffy bushes growing close to the face of the rock. Her stomach knotted as she evaluated her chances of reaching it. It wasn't a straight shot, but was maybe eight feet over, with the prospect of a fatal drop hundreds of feet into a misty, wooded chasm if she lost her grip. No way could she climb —

"Dr. Sto-o-one." Fleenor's mocking call made the hair stand up on the back of her neck. "Here I am. Good to see you decided to wait for me."

He could see her. His words, his tone, left Charlie in no doubt about that. A terrified glance back found him, a tall, dark form shoving his way through the trees. In the open as she was, she would be completely visible to him. From the deliberate way he was moving — no rushing for him now —

he must realize that she was cornered.

The knowledge was utterly terrifying.

Go.

Crouching, lowering herself over the side, she went down that cold, treacherous cliff like a lizard, pressing herself flat against the smooth rock, digging her fingers and toes into any tiny crack she could find, sliding on her stomach when there weren't any cracks, and finally semi-falling the last few yards and pitching up in a heap on the ledge.

Then she looked up to find that Fleenor stood on the ledge she had just abandoned, peering down at her.

From her position he wasn't much more than a dark shape against the paler stone, but there was just enough light left to allow her to pick out the gun in his hand. There was no mistake: he was aiming, pointing it at her, targeting her.

Throwing herself sideways, Charlie screamed.

A second figure, taller and broader of shoulder, merged with the first. A glint of silver whipped through the air and was yanked tight against Fleenor's throat. A chain, Charlie realized, even as a choked cry was followed by a brief, violent reaction on Fleenor's part. Then his knees seemed to give out, and he sank down out of her sight.

Charlie practically dissolved with relief.

A moment later, the taller figure was looking over the edge at her. She could see little more than his silhouette against the darkening sky. Sprawled on her back on the unforgiving rock, her elbows propping her up, Charlie stared at him.

The outline of an elegant suit, the faint gleam of a white shirt, a suggestion of short, fair hair.

Her pulse leaped. There was no mistaking Hughes. But —

"Michael?" Her voice had a distinct quaver.

"You hurt?" he called down to her. That laconic question was all she needed to tell her that she'd been right, it was him. The voice was dark and gravelly but unmistakably his. Oh, my God, she'd known it, although exactly how she couldn't have said. Probably from the way he'd shown up to save her — typical Michael — or the way he'd dealt with Fleenor with such ruthless efficiency — also typical Michael — or maybe because she just did. Because she had developed a sixth sense where he was concerned. She could recognize him now at any distance, anytime, anywhere, under any conditions. She was a little fuzzy on the mechanics of how it all worked, but he'd managed to take over Hughes's body.

Thank you, God.

"No," she replied. And smiled, at him and at the universe, too, for sending him back to her and making such a thing as body takeovers possible.

He didn't say anything more, just lowered himself over the edge of the cliff and climbed down, far more efficiently than she had done. The fact that his wrists were cuffed together made the feat even more impressive, she decided. She watched without moving, and in just a few minutes he was stepping onto the ledge. By then her previously pounding heart had slowed to a near normal beat and her ragged breathing had more or less stopped being ragged. But her muscles were still jelly, and various aches and pains were starting to make themselves felt, and she was so mentally and physically drained that lying there on the cold stone was just about all she could imagine doing ever again.

He came to stand over her.

"Fleenor?" she asked, although she was 99.9 percent sure she knew the answer. She'd seen Michael in action before. He'd been Marine Force Recon once upon a time, and the finer points of breaking a man's neck seemed to have stuck with him.

"Dead."

She acknowledged that with a nod.

"How'd you get the handcuffs in front?" she asked next. Because the last time she'd seen Hughes, his hands had been cuffed behind his back.

"Stepped through them."

She was sure that was far more difficult than he made it sound, but she didn't really care.

"Ah," she said.

"You scared the hell out of me back there," Michael said. His tone was flat, and she was unable to read anything in his face, partly because he was looking down at her, which placed his face deep in shadow. Menace radiated from him like rays from the sun. His powerful body was visibly tense. He looked impossibly tall and broad-shouldered, and formidable as hell looming over her like that. Charlie came to the conclusion, arrived at with all the objectivity of the research scientist she was, that she would never get enough of looking at him.

"Yeah, well, payback's a bitch," she retorted with no heat at all.

He hunkered down beside her. His eyes, she saw, were still that glittering, soulless black. Aggression came off him in waves, the result, she knew, of his recent sojourn in Spookville. "What's that mean?"

His face remained in shadow and was thus impossible to read, but he was looking her over carefully. Checking for injuries, she guessed, because for her to remain flat on her back on cold, uneven rock probably struck him as a sign that she wasn't quite herself. She was taking it as a sign of that, too.

"It means that for the last seventeen days I thought you were gone. Forever. Tam told me you'd probably been terminated. I didn't think I'd ever see you again." She said it conversationally, no drama there, while her eyes moved over what she could see of his face and her insides slowly loosened up so that her heart and her lungs and her stomach felt more or less the way they ought to feel, and her blood warmed to the point where it flowed easily through her veins. Which was when she realized just how frozen her body had been with grief since he'd disappeared.

"Miss me?" he asked. His tone was as drama-free and casual as hers had been.

To Charlie's consternation, her throat tightened and her lips quivered.

"Yes," she said. Then, aches and pains and

jellied muscles be damned, she sat up and rolled onto her knees and threw herself against him and wrapped her arms around his neck and burst into tears.

The thing about it was she never cried. Or, at least, she only ever cried over him.

"Hey, hey, hey," he murmured, pressing his lips to her ear and her cheek and the line of her jaw because she had her face buried in the crook of his neck and that was all he could reach. The feel of his mouth, warm and *real,* against her skin, destroyed the last of her defenses. She cried as though every ounce of the anguish she'd experienced over him had been building up and had finally exploded in this, a volcanic loss of control, which was, in fact, precisely what had happened. Despite the handcuffs linking his wrists, he somehow managed to maneuver them both so that he was kneeling with his arms wrapped tight around her. She was kneeling, too, and hanging on to him like she never meant to let go. As she sobbed and clung and gasped incomprehensible things into his neck while they knelt on that narrow lip of rock with the sheer cliff towering above them and the misty chill of the twilight enfolding them, he held her and rocked her and wisely didn't try to reply, until finally the storm subsided enough so that she lay more or less quietly against him. Then he kissed her cheek for what must have been the hundredth time and said in her ear, "It's all right. Everything's all right. There's nothing to be afraid of anymore. I've got you safe."

"I'm not crying because I'm afraid," she growled into his neck, with the slight interruption of a maddening little hiccupping sob that she would have stifled if she could have. "I'm crying because you vanishing like you did scared *me* to death, you jackass, which you should *know,* and now here you are and — and —"

She couldn't go on. Her voice deserted her as her throat closed up again despite her absolute determination to stop with the waterworks already. *You're stronger than this,* she told herself, but she wasn't, not where he was concerned, which was what the period without him had taught her. Where he was concerned, she was weak and vulnerable and in so much trouble, because there wasn't any possibility of a happy ending for them, and —

"Charlie. Babe." There was the briefest of pauses as he pressed his mouth to the sensitive place below her ear, to which her only response was a shuddering indrawn breath as she fought to get herself back on an even keel. Her skin tingled where his lips touched it and her heart beat faster. He kissed her neck and she shivered and tightened her grip on him. Then he lifted his head and said, "Now you're making me cry."

What? That got her attention. Blinking away the hot tears that just would not stop welling up, rearing back so that she could see his face, she frowned suspiciously.

She knew the hard, handsome face technically belonged to Hughes, but the man who was looking back at her was *Michael.* She'd thought Hughes looked identical to him, but now she saw that Hughes was only a pale copy. Michael was the vivid original, the oil painting to Hughes's print. Temperament, character, life force — whatever it was that made one individual different from any other — sculpted a face as much as bone and muscle, she discovered. The crooked half-smile with which he was regarding her was *his.* The tightening of the skin over his cheekbones, the slight lift of one eyebrow — it was as if the soul inside the body had modified the exterior just enough so that, for her at least, there was no longer any possibility of mistake.

"You are not," she said accusingly. He was *smiling.* And those glinting black eyes held not the slightest hint of tears.

"I was just trying to get you to look up," he said, and kissed her.

Fierce and possessive, his mouth slanted over hers in a way that made her heart lurch. Tilting her face up to his, she parted her lips in instant, instinctive response as everything else in the world receded. Hot and wet and intensely real, his tongue slid into her mouth. She shivered and closed her eyes, and kissed him back with an urgency fueled by those days in which she'd thought he was gone forever. The electric thrill that was always there between them had her arching up against him, sliding her fingers through his hair, responding to the controlled savagery of his mouth with a feverish hunger of her own. Heat blew through her, making her blood sizzle, causing her pulse to go haywire. Passion blazed up hotter than any wildfire, and she went all light-headed and marshmallowy as her body quickened and her mind lost focus and everything that wasn't *them* got burned away.

Michael. She must have said his name out loud, whispered it against his lips, breathed it into his mouth, something, because he lifted his head just long enough to make her blink questioningly up at him, just long enough for her to meet those scarily black eyes and have him whisper back, "I'm right here."

Then he kissed her again with a carnality that had her melting inside, that turned her blood to steam and liquefied her bones. His mouth was hard with wanting her and his body was hard with wanting her, and she was left with no doubt whatsoever about the strength of his desire. But there was tenderness for her there in his kisses, too, as well as a kind of angry desperation that echoed her own sense that the situation was getting away from them, that there was more at stake here than either of them had ever thought there would be, or had ever intended. Being in love with him absolutely blew, for a variety of reasons, but she *was* in love with him, no doing anything about that. He knew it, too, or at least she thought he did, although she had never officially told him so — yelling it after him when he'd disappeared didn't really count, and she didn't think he'd even heard — and she wasn't sure if she would or should say it *again.* But now he was there with her and corporeal, which was kind of a miracle in and of itself for however long it lasted, and she was just going to go with what they both knew they had, which was this blazing sexual attraction. She kissed him as if he was everything she had ever wanted in this existence, which, come to find out and who'd a thunk it, he was.

And he kissed her the same way.

His mouth left hers to trail down her throat. The hot, wet glide of his lips on her bare skin made her dizzy, made her cling to him as if he was the only solid thing left in the world. Tilting her so that her head rested on the hard muscle of his upper arm, he kissed her collarbone, the soft upper swell of her breast, and then his mouth slid over the silky stuff of her blouse to open over her nipple.

Charlie felt the moist heat of his mouth burning through the thin layers of her shirt and bra. Her nipple hardened instantly against what she realized was his tongue caressing it. She caught her breath at the exquisite sensation, at the scalding dampness that penetrated her clothes clear through to her skin. Her heart pounded and her blood raced and her body made a good case for the reality of spontaneous combustion. His mouth tightened, sucking at the aroused peak, pressing hard against her, until she was so totally turned on that if they'd been any place else she would have been ripping off his clothes and her own. She made an involuntary little sound of pleasure, surging up against his mouth while deep inside her body clenched and quaked.

His arms tightened in response. His mouth pulled hungrily at her breast. She was on fire for him, blazing hot, wanting him —

Then right in the midst of that blistering embrace a terrible thought hit her. Charlie pushed away from him like he'd suddenly erupted in a layer of thorns and looked at him in horror.

Chapter Eleven

"What?" Michael growled. His voice was thick and low. His eyes smoldered at her. If ever a man had looked dangerous, he looked dangerous then. His face was set in brutal lines. His eyes were black and burning. She could feel the tension in his wide shoulders and muscular arms, feel aggression coming off him in waves, feel the intense sexual energy surging through the big body she was plastered against. He was rock-hard and radiating heat. Electrically charged sparks practically crackled in the air around him. The remnants of Spookville were still with him, making him all savage and primitive, as she knew from experience it did. Lust seemed to be intensifying the effect, but the immediacy of this simply could not wait.

"Oh, my God, are you going to get snatched away again? The last time you took over someone else's body —" Charlie broke off, because she didn't need to elaborate.

He'd been there the same as she had and knew exactly what she was talking about. The last time he'd taken over someone else's — actually, Tony's — body, he'd been snatched right out of it by a hunter, and that's what had led to the worst two and a half weeks of her life. As in the last two and a half weeks.

Remembering, she cast a harried glance around the dark, mist-shrouded mountainside.

"Relax. That's not going to happen." He sounded so certain that, having gone rigid in his arms, she allowed herself to slump against him the tiniest little bit. They were kneeling chest to chest still, and she had her hands braced against his shoulders and he had his arms wrapped around her waist. His grip was slightly awkward, she noticed now, because of the handcuffs. She could feel the chain linking them bunched against her back. She loved the physicality of it, the steely strength of his arms around her, the hard muscularity of his thighs, the unmistakable evidence of his arousal pressing urgently against her. She loved the heat of him, and the slightly ragged way he was breathing and the rise and fall of his chest against her breasts. She loved having him there with her in real, live, human form.

She loved having him there with her, period.

None of that stopped her from being scared to death about what might be getting ready to happen to him at any second.

The cold breeze that she'd felt earlier blowing up the side of the mountain swirled around her, making her shiver despite the fact that she was wrapped in his arms. Easy to imagine a hunter swooping down and —

She looked at him anxiously. "How do you know?"

"I know, okay?" Meeting her gaze, he dropped another fierce, deep kiss on her mouth. She slid her arms around his neck and kissed him back because she simply couldn't do anything else, but then resolutely broke it off.

Their faces were inches apart. He was looking down at her, breathing unevenly. His face was dark with passion. His mouth was hard with it.

"But we should —" Do what? She didn't quite know. Something. Her anxiety for him was there in her voice.

He didn't let her finish.

"I'm good. We're good," he said. "Unbutton your blouse for me." That last was accompanied by a sweep of his eyes down her body, and the burning intensity in that look coupled with the roughness of his voice made her breathing quicken.

"What?" She stared up at him while her heart hammered and her pulse raced.

His eyes blazed down into hers. "Unbutton your blouse and take it off. Then take off your bra."

Suddenly her bra felt two sizes too small and she realized that she could still feel the dampness of the cloth covering her nipple, both of which were pebble-hard. She was burning hot inside despite the rising chill that was enveloping her, and that would be because she was fiercely aroused. She *wanted* to do what he told her to do, to unbutton her blouse and —

"No," she said. "Michael, this is important. I need you to *listen.*"

"I don't want to listen. I want you to take off your clothes." He lowered his head, nuzzling his face into the open vee of her collar, pressing his mouth against the place where her cleavage began, licking the sensitive skin in the hollow between her breasts.

She barely managed to swallow a moan as she was hit by a blast of sheer, unadulterated sexual desire.

Oh, my God, take me now.

"Stop," she practically yelped, and shoved at his shoulders.

He lifted his head to look at her. A dark

flush had risen to stain his cheekbones. His nostrils flared at her.

"You don't want me to stop," he said, and kissed her, a hungry, insistent kiss that had her kissing him back and molding her body against his and letting him bend her back over his arms and . . .

No. Wait. Something important to . . .

Tearing her mouth from his, she shoved at his shoulders again. "Damn it, Michael."

He looked down at her, his eyes blacker than the blackest pit in hell and so hot she could practically feel the flames. *"You're* saying 'damn it' to *me?"*

Fighting to steady her breathing, she looked at him more closely. There was a latent savagery in his face that she'd never seen there before, a barely controlled violence in the way he was holding her that she would have found alarming in anyone else. Every muscle in his body was rigid, and that would be, she decided, because he was fighting to hold himself in check. His arms around her were corded bands of steel. His chest was a rock wall. He was huge with wanting her. She could feel his erection pressing insistently against her stomach. A deep pulse of pleasure between her legs flared in yearning answer.

Part of her — no, get real, most of her —

wanted her to shut up and lie back and let him do what he wanted.

It was that other part of her that might just keep both of them from getting a really nasty surprise. The levelheaded part, which, right now, was very, very small.

Her brows knit as she frowned at him. "What happened to you in Spookville, anyway? You seem —"

He interrupted with a terse "Forget Spookville. Same old same old. Take off your blouse."

"Hunters," she reminded him with some desperation, because nothing she said really seemed to be getting through. "Big scary monsters who swoop down and carry you away. *Hello-o.*"

He made an impatient sound. "Like I said, not gonna happen."

Ignoring the taut intensity in his face and body as well as how tightly he was holding her, to say nothing of her own thrumming pulse and rising urge to just give in and go ahead and have sex with him already, she said with some astringency, "That's nice, Hellboy, but I'm going to need a little more."

"Hellboy?" His voice grated, but then something flickered in the depths of those burning eyes and some of the ferocity in his expression eased. Slowly his mouth relaxed into the slightest of wry smiles. It did unfair things to her heart. *"Hellboy?"*

"You're sprouting horns and a tail here, baby." She tapped her nails meaningfully against the nape of his neck. Message: *pay attention.* "Hunter?"

"Would you quit worrying? A hunter is not going to show up." His eyes slid over her face. "Anyway, if one does, I'm counting on you to go all Van Helsing on it and save me."

"You're hilarious." To go along with the tartness of her response, the look she gave him was severe. "I'm serious. How do you know a hunter's not going to show up?"

He sighed. "It's technical, okay? A ghost thing. I'd explain it, but you still wouldn't get it, and we'd be talking about it all night, and I'm not much in the mood to talk, in case you can't tell. How about you just trust me on this? I'm not going to get snatched away. So why don't you do me a solid and start getting naked?"

"I'm not getting naked," she told him firmly. "Would you get over this whole return-of-the-damned thing you've got going on already? It's important that you *focus.*"

"I am focused," he said, and kissed her

again, a torrid taking of her mouth that left her in no doubt about exactly what he was focused on. Because he was Michael, and because he'd already gotten her so turned on that she just couldn't help herself, she responded to the searing intensity of that kiss with a deep-seated hunger of her own. Still, there was a part of her mind that even the heat they generated couldn't quite shut down: the situation was too fraught. The single-mindedness with which he kissed her left her in no doubt as to what would be next up on the agenda if he was calling the shots. It also said that he really wasn't worried about being interrupted by a hunter, and she *was* willing to trust him on that because she had to assume that he was even less of a fan of the prospect of getting snatched away by a hunter than she was. Well, maybe not: if he was terminated, once he was terminated, he'd presumably know nothing about anything, while she would suffer for — she didn't want to think about how long. In fact, she didn't want to think about hunters at all, because if one was out there looking to carry him off there was nothing she could do about it, really. With that in mind, there was enough going on that was terrifying right there on the earth plane to worry about, so she switched over to being terrified by a problem that possibly she could actually do something about.

By the time she pulled her mouth from his, steam clouded her thought processes and warm liquid honey ran through her veins and the flare of pleasure between her legs had intensified until it was all she could do not to squirm against him. She was breathing unevenly and her bones had turned to mush and her heart was beating like a piston. Resting her forehead against his wide shoulder — the subsequent hot slide of his mouth down the side of her neck was so *not* conducive to clearing her head — she took a moment to regroup. Her eyes still felt swollen from her crying jag, but otherwise she had herself under control again. She couldn't even blame herself for losing it. The absolute, soul-wrenching agony of the last two and a half weeks coupled with barely any sleep, a lack of proper nutrition, the day's horrific events, and his miraculous return had added up to the perfect storm of stress: emotionally, she'd been a time bomb waiting to explode. Fortunately, she was now over it. Well, over the waterworks. Over him? She was afraid that wasn't going to happen in the next million or so years. But until she figured out what to do about that, there were more urgent issues to deal with.

First order of business: talking Michael the rest of the way down from his Spookville-induced primordialness and getting him to concentrate on the problems at hand. There would be time for the two of them — *God, please let there be time for the two of us!* — later.

Lifting her head, she looked at him consideringly. As he leaned in to kiss her again she could see how heavy-lidded with sexual intent his eyes were, see the passionate curve of his mouth. His hands slid down to her butt, shaping it, cupping her cheeks. Her muscles instantly went all warm and pliant and her body curved into him in totally instinctive response. His eyes never left hers as he pulled her harder against him. Holding her in place, he rocked into her suggestively, and the pleasurable clenching between her legs intensified until she practically dissolved into a little puddle right there and then. He was still in the primitive, barely civilized state that journeying through the wrong side of the afterlife reduced him to, and the thought of having sex with him when he was like this made her toes curl.

Unfortunately, one of them had to keep a cool head, and from the way this was going it was obvious she was the one.

"Please stop," she said in her best plaintive voice. "You're scaring me."

That got through to him. He froze in place, his mouth scant inches from hers, his eyes boring into hers. His hands stilled. So did his body.

"I am not scaring you." His voice was thick with desire and even more gravelly than before.

"How do you know?"

"I know."

Looking up into the way-too-handsome-for-his-own-good face just inches from her own, she had to take a breath before she could continue. "You know you're not quite yourself, right?"

His lip curled. "So?"

"You're not thinking clearly."

"I'm thinking clearly enough."

Another breath. "Michael. Take your hands off my butt."

"Why?"

"Because I'm asking you to. Because we're not having sex on this ledge."

His eyes narrowed at her. "Why not?"

She made a gesture encompassing their surroundings. "Because this is a *ledge.* Nothing but rock. On the side of a mountain. In the open. And the cold. With armed murderers probably doing terrible things to innocent people nearby as we speak, and giant winged creatures from hell possibly swooping around up there in the sky."

His lips compressed. "I told you we don't have to worry about hunters."

"Fine. Scratch the hunters. Like there aren't enough reasons to keep our clothes on without that?"

His face hardened. So did his hands on her butt. But after a moment in which the issue hung in the balance, his hands moved back up to her waist in a slow, sensuous slide. She wasn't sure that was a whole lot better. It was easier to feel the strength and heat of his hands through her thin blouse.

"Happy now?" It was a growl.

"Happier. We need to talk about something."

"For fuck's sake, what?" But for all the frustration in his voice, some of the untamed savagery had left his face. She'd been right: the idea that he was scaring her had brought him down another notch or two. Near enough to reason that he wasn't being totally ruled by the most primeval part of himself.

"Is Hughes dead?" Her tone was purposefully brisk. He frowned at her.

His arms were still locked around her —

literally, by the handcuffs, which were also, she knew, why he hadn't made any attempt to take off her clothes himself — so she was still pressed tightly up against him. Her hair had fallen to hang in what felt like an unruly mass around her shoulders. She'd tucked the bulk of it behind her ears, but loose strands of it fluttered toward him in the breeze. As one caressed his cheek he turned his head toward it and took a deep breath. She thought that she could actually see the worst of the darkness that held him in thrall recede. To keep a little space between them, to buy a little more time to get him to actually lose the beast, she placed her hands flat against his chest. The fine wool of his suit coat beneath her fingers felt different enough that she glanced down and abstractedly absorbed how slender and pale her hands looked splayed on the broad expanse of dark cloth. The white dress shirt was unbuttoned at the neck. The silk tie was crooked.

A man in a suit. Her mother had always told her that she should try to find herself a man in a suit, and now that's just what she'd done. The thought brought a bubble of near-hysterical amusement with it, and as she quelled it Charlie recognized that maybe she, too, was still not quite hitting on all cylinders.

"You're smiling again." He kissed the corner of her mouth. The touch of his lips, the brush of his cheek against hers, sent a whisper of heat over her skin. "What's up?"

"I'm just" — she paused, deciding that the conversation the man-in-the-suit story was likely to lead to was best saved for later — "smiling."

"You've got a beautiful smile," he said. "First thing I noticed about you."

"I don't remember smiling at you. Not for weeks. You were a scary convict in chains. With an attitude."

"You didn't smile at me. You smiled at the damned guards, and the Skunk" — by that he meant the Ridge's warden, Pugh — "and everybody else you saw *but* me. Me you gave this fish-eye stare. But your smile was still the first thing I noticed about you. Well, right after the great rack and killer ass."

She narrowed her eyes at him. "You're not funny."

"I'm not kidding," he said, and kissed her again.

Michael. Oh, God, she was such a sucker for him. One touch of his mouth, of his hands, and her heart throbbed and she got all woozy and fluttery inside. She kissed him back, her mouth as hot and hungry as his, but then she remembered the importance of the conversation she'd been trying to have with him before he'd succeeded in distracting her *again* and got her hands on his shoulders again and pushed.

His head came up. His eyes glittered at her through the darkness.

"What now?" There was a distinct edge to his voice.

She said in a severe tone, "I asked you if Hughes was dead."

"Hughes?" he repeated, without any apparent interest. His head dropped, his mouth slid over her cheek, and her breathing developed a hitch.

She'd forgotten he didn't know who Hughes was. As he pressed a lingering kiss to her cheekbone and she felt her lids droop in swoony response, she took a firm grip on her priorities and tugged on his lapels in a pointed "this is important" message.

"Rick Hughes is the name of the man whose body you're in. Is he dead?" The sharpness of her voice was deliberate.

Drawing an audible breath, he lifted his head to look at her. "Nope."

"So where is he?"

"How the hell should I know? Wherever spirits go when their bodies get shanghaied. Bottom line: not here," he said. His voice, his expression, even the way he was holding her told her that he was continuing to emerge from the brutishness that had gripped him since his return. She could almost see him fighting to shake off the last of Spookville's lingering effects. He took another audible breath and frowned down at her. "You're getting ready to explain to me how you came across a guy who could be my double, right? What is he, my evil twin?"

That was so exactly in line with what she suspected that Charlie could only look at him speechlessly by way of a reply.

Michael always could read her face like a neon sign. His eyes widened. *"What?"*

"It's a long story. I'll fill you in in a minute."

His lips tightened. "Charlie —"

She patted his only-very-slightly bristly jaw — Hughes apparently took shaving much more seriously than Michael did — as a way of pacifying him, and also because it was tantalizingly close and she wanted to. She breathed in —

"Patience, grasshopper. I'm loving the cologne, by the way," she said as she finally identified what seemed different about that hard, masculine jaw. Lightening the charged atmosphere that still surged between them seemed like a prudent thing to do if she could.

"Cologne?" He cocked an eyebrow at her.

"Mmm." Leaning in to him, she sniffed ostentatiously. "Smells expensive. Woodsy. Nice."

"I'm glad you like it." His voice was dry. He was looking, and sounding, more like himself with every passing moment. Less demon, more Michael. "In the interest of full disclosure, I should probably tell you that I think I'm wearing silk boxers."

"Oooh, sexy."

He shook his head. "Why am I not surprised that you think so?"

Charlie leaned close again, whispering, "Just to give you a heads-up, you also have product in your hair. Man-mousse. Or maybe spray."

"Geez."

At the aggrieved tone of that she smiled and congratulated herself on bringing him down a little bit more. But she couldn't wait any longer: there was something she absolutely needed to clarify before much more time had passed. Not that she was paranoid or anything, but the thought of a surprise return of the body's rightful owner gave her the willies.

"How sure are you that Hughes isn't going to pop back into his body at any second?" she asked. "I mean, how random is it? For example, could I start out kissing you and finish up kissing him?"

"I'll give you a heads-up if I think there's a problem."

"You sure you'll know there's a problem? In advance?"

"Yeah. I'm sure. Another one of those technical things you're going to have to trust me on."

Cautiously, she asked, "How much of a heads-up?"

"Babe, I don't want you fucking him even more than you don't want to fuck him, believe me. So count on it, plenty of time."

Charlie narrowed her eyes at him and tightened her grip on his lapels. "Pretty sure of yourself, aren't you?"

He smiled at her. Then he kissed her, a spine-tinglingly lush kiss that owed nothing to Spookville and got her all dizzy and clingy and turned on again in a heartbeat anyway. As her arms slid up around his neck and she kissed him back she gave up on even pretending that she wasn't going to be having sex with him pretty much whenever, wherever, and however he wanted. Which he knew.

Only just not now. Just not here.

Priorities, Charlie reminded herself. Like teenagers at the mercy of serial killers. To very roughly paraphrase *Casablanca,* the problems of the two of them didn't amount to much in the face of *that.* But as she dragged her lips from his she couldn't help remembering once more just exactly what had happened the last time he had possessed a body, and all the misery that had resulted. In hopes of counteracting the bad case of I-want-you he had reinfected her with, she wedged a few inches of space between them and gave him a stern look.

"Before we get completely off topic here, let me ask you something," she said. "Considering what happened the last time, did you hesitate at all? Did you even consider the possibility that stealing a body might be a bad idea?"

"Compared to what? Watching you get shot? Or raped? If I hadn't grabbed a body, that psycho would have killed you back there. Nothing I could have done. This Hughes guy was unconscious, which made it easy. I jumped in. To save your ass, just so we're clear." His face hardened as he spoke, and his eyes glinted unpleasantly at her. His tone had grown more and more grim. But it was Michael grim, not Spookville grim, and she was (mostly) relieved to know that the demon was finally in abeyance. "What would you have done if I hadn't shown up inside that school bus when I did? Hmm? You might want to think about that."

Charlie could tell that a rant on the dangers of the prison and her line of work in general was on the tip of his tongue, and she had more important things to talk to him about at the moment. To forestall the lecture — and also because having him solid like this in her arms was too good an opportunity to miss and the temptation was overwhelming — *she* kissed *him,* a quick but, she hoped, distractingly hot kiss on the mouth that felt like such a luxury because she'd almost never had the opportunity to kiss him at will before.

When she broke it off, his breathing had quickened and his eyes immediately sought her mouth. "Babe —"

Disregarding the huskiness of that, as well as the whole shivery-melty thing that was going on inside her, she interrupted him to get right back to the point. "How long do you have the body for?"

The change in his expression told her that he'd figured out that her kiss had been designed to sidetrack him.

He said, "It's not like I rented a car. I don't know precisely. Long enough. At a guess, a day or two."

A day or two. A day or two out of all eternity. A day or two in which they could touch, and kiss, and make love, and — the promise of it dazzled her, the briefness of it broke her heart. But at least he was back, and even when his time in that body was up he would still be *there,* in the earthly plane with her (that is, if a hunter didn't swoop in and get him) and that was much more than she'd ever thought she'd have again. But right now their situation, with all its potential upsides and downsides, had to be put on the back burner in favor of more pressing concerns.

He bent his head with the obvious intention of kissing her again.

"Wait." Pressing her fingers against his mouth to forestall him — he promptly kissed them, a warm and suggestive kiss that caused her heart to skip a beat — she shook her head at him and, in self-defense, curled her fingers and pulled them away. He frowned at her and she looked at him earnestly.

"Michael. Since you do have this body and are physically capable, we need to go after Paris. Sayers is — you know what he is. We have to try to rescue her. And Bree. And the boys, too. Oh, and the chaperone.

And the driver. All the hostages, but the kids first. Probably Paris first."

Chapter Twelve

Michael returned her look with a level one of his own. The black-eyed devil who'd come back to her from Spookville had been replaced by the tough and pragmatic man he was at his core. Charlie suddenly wasn't sure how much of an improvement that was.

"You have wings?" he asked.

She blinked at him. "What?"

"Because without them, you're not getting off this ledge. I could probably climb back up to where I came down from even if I am wearing handcuffs and some kind of fancy leather-soled shoes that are slick as shit, but you can't. And I'm not leaving you."

"I'll be fine here. I —"

"Also it's dark, and I'm not Superman, which means I don't have X-ray vision, and I'm not a damned bloodhound. Even if I left you here, which I'm not going to do, what do you think the chances are that I could find that girl or Sayers or anybody else, for that matter? By now they could be anywhere."

"But we have to do something."

"Not only do we not have to do something, we're not going to do something." His tone was brutal in its finality. "We're going to wait right here until a rescue crew with a damned rope shows up to get us off this ledge."

"We can't just wait here! Who knows how long it might be?"

"Daylight, at the very latest. Believe me, by now this mountain is crawling with cops. FBI, National Guard, you name it, they're all out here. You think a mass escape of death row inmates from the Ridge didn't get the big guns called out? You notice how you're not hearing any sirens, or seeing blue lights, and the road up above us isn't bumper-to-bumper cops? That tells the story right there. They've got the mountain blocked off. They're here, in the dark, searching. They're just keeping a low profile because they don't want to spook anybody into killing more hostages."

"So why don't we yell, 'Help! Help!' and go ahead and see if we can't get rescued?" Charlie asked. "Then we can tell the rescuers about the barn and the pickup truck, and any other details that might help them find those kids."

He shook his head. "The problem with that is there are seven armed killers somewhere on this mountain who probably know we overheard them talking about the barn and the pickup truck and everything else. It might even be that they're a hell of a lot closer to us than any rescuers. If we start yelling, they're going to know where we are. There's no cover on this ledge. If one of them decided to take a shot at us — from, say, the road up there or the ledge we came down from — we're sitting ducks. I don't like playing dodgeball with bullets, and we're not going to put ourselves in a position where we have to do it. What we are going to do is sit tight and stay out of the way and let the cops do their jobs."

Charlie looked at him like she couldn't believe what she was hearing. "Do you know what Sayers does? He gouges out his victims' eyes. After he rapes them. *Before* he kills them. And Abell — Abell's an animal. And Torres —"

"I know what they do," he interrupted. "I was on death row with all of them, remember? And by the way, I think it's a piece of damned idiocy that *you* know what they do and you still come within a hundred miles of them."

"It's called my job," she said.

"Uh-huh."

"You know what? If we really have to talk about this *again,* we can do it later. Right now, there are children out there at the mercy of serial killers."

"Maybe they escaped. Some of 'em were squeezing out of the bus windows when I jumped out the back after you."

"And maybe they didn't!"

"There's nothing we can do."

Charlie stiffened in his arms. "That's not your decision to make."

"Oh, so it's yours?"

They eyed each other measuringly.

"Charlie, look," Michael said. "Even if we could get off this ledge, we'd only get in the way, and might even catch a bullet for our trouble. The folks that are hunting them right now will have thermal imaging equipment, and night-vision goggles, and lots of other sophisticated equipment that we don't have. Plus they're not stuck on a damned ledge with a five-hundred-foot drop if somebody puts a foot wrong, one of 'em's not a woman with absolutely no law enforcement or weapons training, and I'm assuming that they have more than one gun with about half a clip left in it. Which would be good, considering that, as I said before, the escapees are all *armed.*"

"Michael —" It was a protest.

"You can 'Michael' me all you want. It *is* my decision, because *you* can't get off this ledge, and I'm telling you it ain't happening. We're staying put. Your savior complex is showing, babe."

Charlie's brows snapped together. Come to think of it, she absolutely preferred demon Michael.

"I do not," she said, "have a savior complex."

"You have a savior complex *and* a death wish," he retorted. "You stood up in that bus and yelled at a man with a gun who'd just murdered someone right in front of your eyes. Then you punched another armed man in the face, which, by the way, was either the bravest or the stupidest thing I ever saw. You're lucky to be alive. I wasn't kidding about you needing to see a shrink, Shrink."

"Oh, yeah?" She glared at him, but before she could verbally annihilate him as she absolutely meant to do, he said, "Look, this is hell on the knees. You want to fight, how about we get comfortable first?"

Her lips compressed. But then, because the unforgiving stone really was hurting her already bruised knees, and anyway, much as she hated to face it, he had a point about the swarming cops and high-tech equipment and the rest of it even if he was also being totally high-handed and infuriating as usual, she said, "I don't have a death wish *or* a savior complex. And I don't want to fight. But fine, let's move."

He lifted his arms over her head. She let go of his neck and sank back. Then they moved the few feet necessary so that they were sitting with their backs against the cliff. In front of them, the ledge ended in a drop into utter blackness. The two scruffy bushes growing out of the crack where the face of the cliff met the ledge were maybe three feet to Charlie's left. From their faintly spicy scent, Charlie thought they might be witch hazel. The ledge itself was about ten feet wide by twenty feet long, a tiny scar on the mountain's craggy face.

Much as it went against the grain to just give up, Charlie reluctantly accepted that she was stuck. For her at least, going up or down was problematic. She was lucky she hadn't fallen to her death the first time.

"You have a gun?" she asked as they got settled, referring to what he'd said about having a gun with only one clip.

"Yep. Took it off Dirty."

"Dirty?"

"Fleenor."

"Oh." She paused for a moment, reflecting that being with a living, breathing man who knew his way around a gun was a definite plus under the circumstances, especially since what she knew about guns could be summed up with "point and shoot," and she had an aversion to them besides. To that she added a quick mental review of the seven armed murdercrs who were presumably still on the mountain. "That's good."

"I think so."

Legs bent, Michael rested his forearms on his knees. He seemed to be doing something twisty with the handcuffs. Charlie sat beside him with her knees drawn up to her chest and her arms wrapped around them, close enough to him that their bodies brushed because, well, despite her slight level of annoyance with him she really needed to be touching him. His reappearance was still too new, and the pain she had suffered over his absence was still too raw. Between the rising wind and the temperature of the stone at her back, she was starting to get really cold. Her thin shirt and pants had not been designed to keep anyone warm during an autumn night spent outside in the mountains. She was also starting to be acutely aware of various aches and pains. If there was a part of her that wasn't bruised or sore she decided that she must be somehow overlooking it. The knuckles of her right hand felt stiff. Her pants were ripped at both the knees and various other places, and she could see through the gaps in the cloth that her legs were scraped up. Her shirt had popped its top two buttons, so that the modest vee of her neckline was now an immodest vee, revealing more than a hint of cleavage and a glimpse of her lacy white bra. She refused to think about the hint of moisture against her nipple that remained from Michael's mouth.

"How about you —" Michael began, only to break off as a shout split the air, faint but not so distant that Charlie couldn't make out the words: "Stop, or I'll put a bullet in your back."

Stiffening, she shivered. God, she hated this part of her "gift." Fleenor was dead, yet she could hear him, and would've been able to see him, too, if she'd been close enough, as his spirit reenacted the last moments of his life. A moment later, the follow-up she'd been expecting reached her ears: "Dr. Sto-o-one. Here I am. Good to see you decided to wait for me."

That was followed by a choked cry and the sounds of a struggle.

"What the hell?" Michael had gone rigid beside her. He was looking up toward the sounds, but there was nothing to see above them but a whole lot of dark.

"Fleenor," Charlie said with resignation. Then she had a thought, and cast Michael a sideways glance. "You can hear him, too, huh?"

"Hell, yes, I —" Michael broke off as he started to get to his feet, no doubt contemplating some violent action designed to defend them. She put a calming hand on his arm and added, "Don't worry, he's still dead. His spirit's on a loop, repeating the last moments of his life. It's a fairly common side effect of a violent, unexpected death. He isn't aware of us, or anything in the earth plane. Spirits go through that sometimes, you know, before they move on."

The thing about Michael was, he did know. Besides being a spirit himself, which took care of the whole I-don't-believe-in-ghosts problem she'd been running into all her life, he'd witnessed enough of what she'd gone through to know exactly what she was talking about. The supernatural world was as real as anything on the earth plane, and because of some dirty cosmic trick she was one of the few who absolutely, without a doubt, knew it. That knowledge was something she'd had to keep to herself for most of her life, and especially since she'd become a physician, as the medical community tended to frown on doctors who saw ghosts. Certainly it didn't take them seriously. Since he'd died, Michael, previously a total skeptic when it came to the paranormal, had become a reluctant convert. Which meant, among many other not-so-wonderful benefits, he got to listen to Fleenor's randomly repeating death reenactment, which Charlie was one hundred percent sure no one else on that mountain besides the two of them was able to hear. As she had previously concluded, one of the good things about having Michael in her life was that she no longer had to experience those things alone.

As he absorbed the fact that Fleenor couldn't hurt them, Michael's taut muscles slowly relaxed.

"I wasn't sure, since you're in a body now, that you'd still be able to hear things like that," she told him.

"I can." His voice was grim.

"I see." Hers wasn't.

"Your life's a damned freak show," he told her as Fleenor started up again. "You know that, right?"

Giving him a pointed look, she said, "Yes, Casper, I do."

He met her gaze, his mouth quirked as he caught her meaning, and then he leaned over to kiss her. The touch of his mouth on hers, the hard possessiveness of his kiss, the casual way he made it instantly hot and deep, got her heart thundering and made her body clench and burn just as quick as that, as if her physical response was an automatic, conditioned reaction to a familiar stimulus now. This was pure Michael, no demon at all, and it was still scorching enough to blow her mind. But besides being sexy as hell, it made her feel like they were a couple, like they were in a relationship and they both knew it and accepted it. Which she supposed was all true, and was such a disaster on so many levels that she refused to even let herself dwell on it. She slid a hand behind his head and kissed him back because she loved him, and the hard truth was that she was helpless in the face of it even if she knew that she was looking at heartbreak on the horizon.

When he straightened to return to the handcuffs, she tilted her head back against the rock wall and contemplated the sky. Fretting about her fellow hostages was as upsetting as it was apparently useless, so she pushed that out of her mind by focusing intently on the here and now. Night had fallen, and the mountain peaks around them were no more than dense black shapes against a black background. A thick cloud cover allowed only fleeting glimpses of one or two tiny, distant-looking stars, and the moon was nowhere in sight. The ledge was so dark by this time that she couldn't see where it ended, or anything much beyond Michael, who was deep in shadow. Smokelike tendrils of mist floated everywhere, the rising wind moaned through the trees and mountain passes, and it was growing colder by the minute. If she'd been by herself, she would have been miserable and afraid.

As horrible as it might be of her, she was suddenly glad Michael hadn't left her alone. Although she had a knot in her stomach that twisted tighter every time she thought of Paris, or Bree, or any of the others.

Please God watch over them and keep them safe.

"So how about you go ahead and fill me in on the evil twin?" Michael said.

Looking at him — he was frowning down at whatever he was doing with the handcuffs — Charlie took a deep breath, dragged her wandering wits back together, and said, "I think that's literally what he is. Your evil twin. As in your identical twin brother and the real Southern Slasher. I think he's the one who really murdered Candace Hartnell and those other women they said you killed."

Stopping what he was doing with the handcuffs, Michael held her gaze for a pregnant moment and then drawled, "And yet you're calmly sitting here with him."

"I'm sitting here with *you.* That's why I asked you if he was likely to pop back into his body without warning." She frowned at him. "You're sure about what you said, right? You'll know in plenty of time to warn me?"

"I'll know." His voice was grim. "But you had no way of knowing that when I climbed down here. You could have been stuck on this ledge with the animal who slaughtered all those women. Who you *think* might have slaughtered all those women."

"Well, you're the one who climbed down here."

"Because you were down here, and you're down here because you had to risk your life scrambling down a sheer cliff with a death drop to get away from another fucking serial killer."

"We've had this conversation," Charlie

said. "The interesting thing we were talking about is I think the body you're in belongs to your identical twin brother who actually committed the murders you were convicted of."

"You think that's the interesting thing."

"Yes, I do. Yes, it is."

He took a moment before replying. "You know, if I'd known that all it took to convince you that I didn't kill those women was having an evil twin turn up, I would have rounded one up a hell of a lot sooner."

She frowned at him. "You're not funny. This isn't funny."

"It's kind of funny. Come on, babe, an evil twin?"

"Does he look just like you?" she countered, then added, "Well, his eyes are a different color, but besides that."

"What color are his eyes?"

"Hazel. Yours are blue."

"I know what color my eyes are."

"Identical twins can have different-colored eyes. I researched it. Other than that, you look exactly the same. You saw it for yourself on the bus. I know you did, because I saw your face when you spotted him."

"Charlie —"

"Would you just listen?" As concisely as she could, Charlie told Michael everything she knew about Rick Hughes, starting with the moment she'd first seen him at the grave and including the background information Tony had given her. She'd just gotten to the part where she was going to have the identical-twin thing officially confirmed via the DNA from Hughes's coffee cup when Michael stopped her.

"Wait. You think this guy slaughtered all those women and your reaction is to invite him up to your office to have coffee?"

Charlie instantly knew where he was going with that. "I did not invite him up to my office to have coffee. He had a court order allowing him access to your files, which were in my office. I allowed him to come up to get the files, and in the process gave him coffee."

"So you could get his DNA."

"Seemed like the easiest way to do it to me."

"And that doesn't strike you as being a little self-destructive?"

"Would you stop with that already? Your trying to play armchair psychiatrist is getting old."

"Babe, if it walks like it needs a shrink and talks like it needs a shrink, then, take it from me, it needs a shrink."

Exasperated, she asked, "Don't you want

to know who really committed the murders that sent you to death row?"

"You know what? At this point, I don't give a shit. I'm dead now, remember? Whether the courts change their minds about if I did it or not doesn't change a thing for me." A smile just curved his mouth. "Wait a minute. Is this you finally saying you believe I'm innocent?"

"Yes."

"Well, what do you know. Glory be, it's a miracle. The beautiful but slightly pigheaded Dr. Stone admits she got something wrong."

He called me beautiful. How stupid was it that the compliment made her feel warm all over? *And pigheaded.* Well, *that* didn't make her feel warm.

"You shouldn't have messed with my inkblots," she retorted. "If you hadn't made up all those bloodcurdling descriptions of what you saw in them, and screwed around on all the other tests that were administered to you, too, I would have known right away that your psychological profile almost certainly precluded you from being a serial killer."

"Covering your ass, Doc?"

She lifted her chin at him. "Altering my professional opinion on the basis of new information."

"Ah."

He was still smiling that slight smile at her, and he looked so dear, so familiar, so damned aggravating, but still so much her person, that one person who mattered for her, her friend and family and lover all rolled into one, that her heart turned over. It didn't matter that he was gorgeous, although he was. It didn't matter that he was sexy, although he was that, too. It didn't even matter that he was dead, a spirit at that moment residing in a stolen human body. What mattered was that he was *Michael.*

She said, "You know, it would have helped if every time you came near me you'd been a little less insolent. And a little less aggressive and threatening."

"I never threatened you. And, anyway, where would the fun have been in that?"

With only limited use of his hands because of the cuffs, he caught the front of her shirt and tugged her closer, then kissed her so hotly that she could practically feel flames licking at her skin. Her hand slid around to the back of his head, and she kissed him back and burned for him.

When he lifted his head her eyes opened. Heart thudding, she blinked at him, momentarily punchy. Unfair how easy it was for him to turn her on. From his expression, she got the feeling that she might be looking a little bit dazzled.

She knew she felt dazzled.

"You sure you don't want to change your mind and just go ahead and fuck me now?" There was a wickedness to the slight smile he gave her that did unbelievable things to her body. "You know it's going to happen, and this way we could get it over with. I mean, since we're stuck here and —"

"No," Charlie said firmly, picturing herself beating off lust with a stick, and straightened away from him.

He continued to smile at her. Wickedly.

"Forget it," she said. "Not happening. No way, José."

He still said nothing, just sat there, looking at her with that maddening smile. Any reaction — a frown, further protestations — would simply add to his enjoyment. Charlie mentally gritted her teeth, girded her loins, and cast her mind back to the conversation they'd been having. Before he'd managed to make her forget everything except him.

"I'm sorry I didn't believe you about being innocent sooner," she said after a moment, and was proud of how normal her voice sounded.

"That's okay. I kinda got that you were

getting a thrill from thinking you were fucking a serial killer."

Charlie's eyes flew to his face. She practically choked with indignation. "I was not getting a thrill from —" Seeing his sudden grin, she broke off and punched his arm. "You suck," she said. "Just so you know."

He laughed. It was the first normal laugh she'd heard out of him since he'd returned, and it turned her heart inside out.

Then he said, "I appreciate the fact that you've finally seen the light, but I want you to leave this Southern Slasher thing alone."

His tone left her in no doubt that he meant what he said.

She said, "*What?* There's no way I'm going to leave it alone. Aside from the fact that you deserve to have your name cleared, Rick Hughes is a murderer. Besides the women that got blamed on you, I'm certain that there are more victims. Serial killers don't stop. The case he's supposedly working on? If that murder is identical to the Southern Slasher murders, then he must have done it, too. And there will be others, I guarantee you."

It made her feel a little better to see that Michael was at least starting to look thoughtful.

He said, "For the sake of argument, let's

say this guy *is* my identical twin. He looks like me, I was adopted, it's not completely outside the realm of possibility. But why'd he come to you? If he's the real Southern Slasher, and the Southern Slasher murders he committed were blamed on me, and I was dead, what was his purpose in coming to you and stirring the whole damned thing up again?"

"I don't know," she admitted. "I haven't figured that part out yet."

"Okay. Let that go for the moment. So here's something else: If he killed Candace Hartnell in the fifty-minute window between the time I left her and the time she was found dead, he had to have known of my existence even though I didn't know anything about him, and he had to have been stalking me, right, and waiting for his opportunity to kill a girl I'd just left my DNA all over so the blame for all seven murders would fall on me?"

"Y-yes, I guess," Charlie said. "That seems logical, although I haven't had time to work out the whole process he went through yet. I will, though, believe me."

"One more thing: Where'd he get the watch?" He shot a meaningful look at the heavy silver watch that right at that moment was pushed halfway up Charlie's forearm.

"You know, the one that was left with the Hartnell chick's body that was identical to my watch that you're wearing now. Where'd he get it?"

"Where'd *you* get it?" she asked.

For a moment she thought he wasn't going to answer. Then he said, "Afghanistan. When I first got there, I was part of a force that was sent out to rescue some warlord from insurgents. We had to synchronize the rescue perfectly, so the CO handed out identical watches. Twenty-four of us went out, four of us came back. That was me, Sean, Hoop, and Cap. After that was when we got them engraved."

Michael wasn't much on talking about his past, as she knew from experience. For him to tell her that was a measure of how far their relationship had come. She wanted to pat his arm, rub his leg, something, in sympathetic acknowledgment, but she was afraid that if she made too big a deal of his revelations he would immediately clam up. So instead she tucked the information away and said matter-of-factly, "So there were twenty watches given out at the same time as yours that weren't engraved. I take it Hughes wasn't one of the guys who got one?"

"I think somebody would have noticed if

I'd had a double over there. Hell, I probably would have noticed myself." His tone was dry.

"So no," Charlie said, adding, "It's possible that the same watch was available for purchase by anyone," and she made a mental note to check, and also to try to ascertain the whereabouts of the other, not engraved watches that had been issued that day.

"Maybe," he said. "But you realize that having that damned watch turn up at the crime scene makes it almost certain that I was deliberately framed for those murders instead of blamed by mistake. If I'm following you, you think that this Hughes guy got hold of a watch like mine to frame me — but he wouldn't have known to have it engraved — and then followed me around, waited for his chance, and killed a woman I'd been with. Why?"

"To deflect suspicion from himself," Charlie answered. *That* she'd already thought through. "He must have known about you and realized that you were the perfect fall guy for the murders he had already committed."

"Then why did he come to you and drag the whole thing up again?"

Okay, they'd just come full circle. Charlie

frowned at him. "I don't know."

"Me neither," Michael said. "And what's more, I don't care. What I do care about is that you're going to get yourself killed if you don't find a new gig that doesn't have anything to do with serial killers."

She made a face at him. "Can anybody say 'broken record'?"

"Can anybody say 'death wish'?"

"Would you stop with the —" Charlie began indignantly, but he cut her off with a kiss. His brief but thorough invasion of her mouth had her gripping his shoulders hard and kissing him back with helpless abandon. It made her shiver. It made her heart pound. It made her yearn for more. With every kiss, he was weakening her defenses, making her burn hotter, upping the chances that she would do something like climb onto his lap and get the deed done already. What's more, he knew it.

Get thee behind me, Satan.

When he straightened away from her, he said, "Babe, I think you're suffering survivor's guilt from your friend being killed all those years ago and you not being able to help her. If you don't recognize what you're doing and stop, you're going to keep pushing until you wind up like her. Dead."

That his voice was all sexy and husky in

the aftermath of their kiss did not make what he'd said any less annoying.

"Oh, my God," Charlie exclaimed, recovering from the tingly melties left behind by their kiss and glaring at him. "That's it. That's enough. One more amateur diagnosis out of you and I'll . . . I'll . . ." She couldn't think of anything bad enough to threaten him with.

He knew it, too. "You'll what?"

"I'll start laying a few diagnoses on *you.*"

"You've been doing your shrink thing with me since we met." His mouth quirked at her. "Just so you know, most of the time it gets me hot. Turns out chicks with through-the-roof IQs and my-way-or-the-highway attitudes really do it for me. Who knew?"

Charlie narrowed her eyes at him. "You are so full of —"

"What, you don't think I spent a lot of time when I was locked in my cell fantasizing about Dr. Ballbreaker with the sexy bod and the big blue eyes? 'Cause I did. Just like probably ninety-nine-point-nine percent of the men who come in contact with you in that damned prison do."

"I can't help what —"

He interrupted ruthlessly. "The thing is, I wouldn't hurt you. Those bastards in that bus? They'd love hurting you. They'd have fun doing it. You got kidnapped right out of your workplace by a bunch of psychos who were absolutely going to rape and torture and kill you. If I hadn't been there, they'd be doing it right now. Is that a normal thing that might happen to anybody in the course of their workday? No, it's fucking not. The point I'm making is, *you can't count on me always being around to save your ass.* I'm asking you, please: find a new line of work."

His tone and expression were both so completely serious that Charlie was surprised into paying attention. She frowned. This was a rehash of the argument they kept having over and over, but to have Michael looking at her this way, asking her this way, was new. It was enough to make her stop and think, at least.

"Is there a reason you're so stuck on this right now?" she asked, frowning at him. He glanced away: he was doing the twisty thing with the handcuffs again, and he looked down at them. She could read absolutely nothing in his face. But there was something — *something . . .*

He said, "You ever think maybe I want to keep you alive?"

"Michael. Talk to me."

He looked at her again then. "What we've got here — you and me, this thing that's going on with us — is temporary. We both know that. One of these days I'm going to disappear from your life for good. Nothing either of us can do to change it. I'd like to see you safe before it happens."

The thought of him disappearing forever was like a shard of fear stabbing into her heart. She didn't think she could live through a repeat of the last seventeen days, much less a lifetime of it. As she stared at him, she felt herself going cold all over.

"What is up with you?" she demanded. "Is there something you're not telling me?"

"I'm just facing facts," he replied, and made a sudden savage movement with his wrists. A metallic snapping sound followed.

Charlie's eyes widened.

"You broke the handcuffs," she said on a note of mild disbelief as he stretched his arms wide. The bracelets still adorned both wrists, but the chain dangled from his left. "I didn't think people could do that."

"Like riding a bike."

"I'm officially impressed."

"I'd rather you be officially unemployed."

"Michael —"

She broke off as what sounded like running footsteps and violently rustling foliage from somewhere above was punctuated by a short, shrill, abruptly terminated scream.

Chapter Thirteen

Charlie and Michael looked up at the same time, their reaction automatic. There was nothing to see except a craggy, near perpendicular mountainside, a shadowy fringe of trees swaying along the edge of the cliff above them, and a flotilla of nearly black clouds blowing across a higher ceiling of ink black sky. Except for the low moan of the wind and the usual night sounds, there was also now nothing to hear. But the scream — Charlie hadn't been mistaken about the scream. She thought it had come from the road, or rather the wooded verge beside the road, some hundred and twenty feet above their heads. She was about to glance at Michael when a handful of pebbles and dirt rained down on them.

Instantly, she looked up again. Her pulse quickened.

"Could be anything," Michael said in response to her wordless clutching of his arm. "An animal up there hunting. Another damned ghost reenactment. Anything."

"It sounded like a woman screamed. A girl." Charlie's mouth was dry. "You know it did."

"Could be anything," Michael repeated. Taking off his jacket, he draped it around her shoulders. "Here. Your teeth are starting to chatter."

The jacket was still warm from his body, and she accepted it gratefully, sliding her arms into the sleeves, hugging it close.

"Thank you," she said.

"You're welcome."

It was far too large, big enough to fit maybe three of her in it, the arms dangling past the tips of her fingers. She got busy rolling up the sleeves, launching straight back into the conversation they'd been having. "You have to go check it out. You said you could climb up. And now you don't even have to worry about the handcuffs."

"No."

"What do you mean 'no'? What if it's Paris? Or Bree? Or . . . or . . ."

"No."

"Why not?"

"We've been over this."

"You are not coldhearted and callous enough to just ignore that scream we heard."

"Want to bet?"

"You jumped out of the bus after me."

"Like I think I may have told you before, you're mine, Doc. I protect what's mine."

That was equal parts infuriating and heartstopping, so chauvinistic on the one hand, so backhandedly romantic on the other, that for a moment Charlie was at a loss for a reply.

Another truncated cry and a shower of debris made them both glance up again.

"You know that's not an animal." Charlie was so agitated she stood up, wrapped her arms around herself, and started to pace back and forth.

Michael looked up at her. "I do not know that's not an animal. Anyway, I'm here to save *your* damned life, not go running around this whole damned mountain on some probably fruitless bleeding-heart search-and-rescue mission."

"You wouldn't be running around the whole damned mountain. You'd be climbing right up there."

"Leaving you alone on this damned ledge."

"What on earth do you think is going to happen to me on this ledge? Nothing can get to me here. You have to —"

"Help!" The cry was thin and faint and

terrified. It was also clearly human, and almost certainly female.

"See," Charlie hissed.

"Fuck." Michael stood up. He grabbed her by the upper arms. It was at times like this that she was reminded just how very much bigger and stronger than her he was. "I don't care what happens. I don't care if it sounds like the shoot-out at the OK Corral up there or you see a hundred people falling to their deaths or ten thousand girls start screaming, you keep quiet and stay put, you understand? Do not try to climb the cliff. Do not call out. Do not —"

"Yes," Charlie interrupted. "Yes, yes, I understand. Would you just *go*?"

"Damn it to hell anyway," Michael muttered, and kissed her, a brief, hard brush of his mouth against hers. Then he let her go and shoved something — Charlie saw it was the gun as he turned to face the rock wall — more firmly into his waistband at the small of his back, where his untucked shirt hid it from view. Grabbing on to what looked like sheer rock, he proceeded to scale the cliff with the agility of an experienced mountain climber. His white shirt made it easier than it should have been to follow his progress through the darkness and the mist, and it occurred to her that she might not be the only one who could see him. She tensed at the thought, but there was no gunshot, no outcry.

Another abbreviated shower of rocks and dirt brought her heart leaping into her throat. All she could do was look up and hope that there was something Michael could do, that he wouldn't be too late, that whoever was up there would be okay.

Michael hoisted himself onto the ledge where Fleenor had died — she hadn't heard Fleenor's loop for a while, which didn't mean much because it was a random thing, but she was really hoping he'd been swept away to whatever the afterlife had in store for him — and then he was out of sight.

After that, nothing.

Nada. Zip.

Not a rustle of leaves, not a sprinkle of dirt, not a glimpse of anything where something should be happening.

Charlie's heart pounded.

Had Michael disappeared? Had whoever or whatever he'd gone up there after disappeared?

What if a hunter had been lying in wait? Or some other hideous creature had emerged from the depths of the netherworld to drag him back?

What if the whole thing had been a trap

and she'd sent him right into the jaws of it?

Charlie strained her eyes trying to see through the darkness. She strained her ears trying to hear anything that wasn't wind or natural forest sounds. Her neck ached from being craned so far back. Despite Hughes's coat, she was shivering, and not only from the cold. Her throat was so tight she could barely swallow.

What if he never came back?

The thought terrified her.

It occurred to her that the downside to having Michael in Hughes's body was that the body could be injured or killed. Presumably Michael would still be able to stay with her in spirit form if that happened. But never having had her own personal spirit before, she knew so little about the parameters of his existence that she couldn't be sure.

She couldn't be sure about anything.

Except that she was growing increasingly afraid that something had gone badly wrong. She was so nervous that she resumed pacing, back and forth, on that tiny ledge.

Finally she sat with her legs tucked up beside her and one shoulder resting against the cold stone wall as she alternated between watching the ledge and scanning the woody fringe at the edge of the cliff high above.

Nothing, nothing . . . more nothing.

When at last she saw Michael swinging his big body down from the ledge overhead and then descending toward her, she was so relieved she felt light-headed and at the same time so wired with nerves that she leaped to her feet. Or at least she tried. By then she was stiff and cold and achy and her leap was more like an awkward clamber.

She was waiting as he stepped down onto the rock shelf. When he turned to face her she hugged him, the greeting as natural as breathing, wrapping her arms around his neck and giving him a quick I'm-so-glad-to-see-you kiss. Low-voiced and anxious, she said, "Oh, my God, I was worried! What happened? Are you all right?"

Having hugged her back and returned her kiss with a brief, hard kiss of his own, he stepped back, jerked a thumb upward, and said quietly, "I'm fine. Careful, we've got an audience."

Looking up, Charlie discovered a quartet of dark-uniformed men standing on the ledge and peering down at them.

"Who are they?" she asked.

"A local search-and-rescue team." He was untying a rope from around his waist as he spoke. That was the first time Charlie realized that a rope had been snaking down the cliff with him, a rope that had been tied around his waist and which extended all the way back up to the ledge. Michael continued, "I'm Rick Hughes, remember, and you don't know me very well. You probably don't want to be seen kissing on me."

Oh. Right.

"So what happened?" she demanded impatiently.

"The scream — it was the blond girl. Google Eyes — Sayers — had knocked her out and was on top of her by the time I got there. I was able to get the drop on him, but then I had a nearly naked, unconscious girl on my hands. No way to let you know what was going down without yelling and maybe drawing attention we didn't need. So I got the girl bundled up in what was left of her clothes and carried her down the mountain until I found some help. I handed her over, and then I came back with those guys to get you off this damned ledge." Rope in hand, he reached beneath the jacket she was wearing to pass it around her waist. "Hold still. I'm going to fasten this around you and then they're going to pull you up."

"Paris. Is she going to be all right? How badly is she hurt?" Charlie asked, standing obediently still as Michael looped the rope around her to form a kind of makeshift harness. She attributed his familiarity with ropes and rock climbing and handcuff breaking and all the rest of that type of thing to his time in the military, trusted that he knew what he was doing, and dismissed it from her mind.

Michael said, “Her head was bleeding. I think Google Eyes used a rock to knock her out. It wasn’t anything life-threatening, and she was awake last I saw of her. They were taking her the rest of the way down to an ambulance.” Having passed the rope over both Charlie’s shoulders as well as between her legs and wrapped it around her waist one more time, he tied some kind of intricate knot at her waist. “She was telling a deputy that she’d been hiding in the woods until he found her and she ran. What we heard must have been him catching her. Like I said, Google Eyes had knocked her out by the time I got up there.”

Charlie shuddered. “Her eyes —”

“Didn’t touch ’em. He didn’t get that far.”

“Poor girl, did he —” She broke off, unable to put the thought into words.

A glance at her face apparently told Michael what she meant. “Rape her?” He shook his head. “No. I got there before he could." He was double-checking the ropes he'd tied around her. "You saved her life, babe."

Charlie said, "Are you kidding? *You* saved her life. Did you — is Sayers —"

"Dead." He didn't elaborate, but then, he didn't have to. Since she hadn't heard a shot, Charlie assumed he'd killed Sayers with his bare hands. If she'd been a better person, she supposed that ability of his would have bothered her, but instead it just made her feel safer. Having finished with his knot, Michael took a step back and looked her over critically. It occurred to her then that he was free of the broken handcuffs.

"What happened to the handcuffs?" she asked.

"Guy had a key," he said without elaborating. Then he took both of her hands and curled them, one hand above the other, around the rope that was rising in front of her. "Hang on to the rope and they'll pull you up. When you get close to the ledge, watch out that you don't crack your head on the underside of it. Push off from the cliff with your feet if you have to."

Charlie nodded and tightened her grip on the rope. "What about you?"

"I'll be right behind you." He looked her

over one more time and said, "Ready?" When she answered "Yes," he made a whirling gesture over his head that was clearly aimed at the men on the ledge above.

The ropes tightened around her without any more warning than that, and she caught her breath as she was lifted off her feet. An unexpected rush of nervousness was countered by having Michael's hands on her, steadying her for that first little bit as she started to rise.

Then she was on her own, dangling in mid-air as she looked out over a vast expanse of night. The rope circling her thighs cut into them as she was hoisted steadily upward. She shifted uncomfortably, which made her sway back and forth like a pendulum, which was alarming, so she quit shifting and tried to stay as still as she could. The harness Michael had devised suddenly did not feel substantial enough to be all that stood between her and what, she determined with an unwary glance down, was an unchecked plummet to certain death, but she trusted him enough to assume that it was. Still, her pulse pounded and her chest felt tight. Heights, she was rapidly discovering, were not her favorite thing. The drop beneath her was terrifying, so after that one quick glance she looked skyward instead. A few more stars were out, but if there was a moon it was hidden by the cloud cover, which was threateningly low. Jagged black peaks towered everywhere around her like waves about to crash. The wind was biting now, and strong enough to rock her into the cliff face even though she was taking care to remain perfectly still. She had to push off with her foot more than once. Mist drifted beside her, eerie and pale, smelling of damp and making the rope feel slippery in her hands. By the time she was close enough to the ledge so that she could reach up and touch it if she'd wanted to — she didn't — her heart was thumping.

"Dr. Stone, I'm Deputy George Trent. If you'll hold up your hands we can get you the rest of the way up, no problem." The voice belonged to a heavyset, fortyish man who was peering over the edge at her. Charlie held up her hands, one at a time because she was wary of releasing her grip on the rope, and felt warm, thick-fingered hands lock around her wrists. The next thing she knew she was being lifted up onto the ledge and surrounded by four deputies. At least she assumed that's what they were, because Trent had introduced himself as a deputy and because the words SHERIFF'S DEPARTMENT were emblazoned in white on their black caps.

"How do you know my name?" she asked, as two of them helped her out of her rope harness.

"We have a list of the hostages," Trent answered. "And Mr. Hughes identified himself and you."

It took her a second to associate Mr. Hughes with Michael, and that's when she knew for sure how really, really tired she was. She was going to have to take care not to forget.

The rope had been thrown over the side again, and she saw that this end of it was wrapped around one of the sturdier tree trunks for ballast and that the two men who hadn't been helping her out of her harness were anchoring it. As she pulled Hughes's jacket tight around herself again, a sideways glance found Fleenor's body sprawled near the cliff face. At some point it would be transported down the mountain, but probably not until the medical examiner could look at it, she assumed. The night was so dark she couldn't see anything much beyond the shape of it, but the angle at which the head was attached to the neck precluded the body being alive, and she hastily averted her gaze. Fleenor's spirit was nowhere in evidence, and for that she could only be thankful. If he was still experiencing the loop, she was glad to have missed an up-close-and-personal viewing of it.

"There's an ambulance standing by for you at the foot of the mountain and a truck waiting to take you there," Trent told her. "Can you walk to the road? It isn't far, just up that path. If you can't, we can get you there."

Chapter Fourteen

The truth was, her legs felt about as sturdy as cooked spaghetti, and what she really wanted to do was sit down. She was cold with the wind still swirling around her, and she thrust her hands deep into the pockets of Hughes's jacket for warmth. The men around her were scarcely more than shadows. The pines crowding the ledge were black as ink, and every sound — rustling trees, moaning wind, the crunch of the rescue team's footsteps — made her tense. She realized that she was listening for any sign of the other hostages, but there was nothing.

"I can walk, and I don't need an ambulance," Charlie responded, watching as Michael, climbing up under his own steam, hoisted himself onto the ledge. He stood up and started to untie the rope around his waist while two of the deputies, inches shorter and far less physically impressive than he was, tried to steady him. Remembering that he'd climbed down to her tethered to a rope, she assumed he had tied himself to it for both descent and ascent as a sensible safety precaution, because, as she had learned, under the right circumstances he could be a surprisingly careful man. Summoning her inner fortitude, she squared her shoulders, looked away from Michael, and got right down to what was important, saying to Trent, who seemed to be in charge, "The escapees were heading for a barn large enough to hide a school bus in. It should be within fifteen miles of here. They have a pickup truck waiting inside. You have to find that barn. I think they're planning to kill at least some of the remaining hostages once they get there." Taking a breath, she tried to calculate the amount of time that had already passed and felt her chest tighten. "There may not be much time."

"I told them all that. It's taken care of, you don't have to worry." Michael joined her. She wanted to rest against him, to have him wrap his arms around her and take her weight for a little while, but she didn't. She was exhausted and sore and emotionally wrung out and practically jumping out of her skin with anxiety, and none of that mattered. What mattered was getting the rest of the hostages back safely. But staying on her feet and keeping her concentration where it needed to be if she was going to be of any help to anyone was getting harder. Always able to read her expression too easily, Michael frowned down at her.

"You okay?" he asked quietly.

She said "Yes" and looked at Trent, who hovered nearby. She asked him, "Have any of the other hostages been rescued?"

"I don't know, ma'am," he replied. "We got a big operation going on here. Hard to know what the other hand's doing, if you know what I mean."

"The Sheriff's Department thinks they know what barn it is," one of the other deputies told her. "Only one up here that size. They've got people on the way there now."

"That's good," Charlie said, although she was horribly afraid that it might already be too late.

"If you're ready, ma'am . . ." Trent said and gestured. Charlie nodded and started walking back up the path Fleenor had chased her down what felt like a lifetime ago.

While three of the men stayed behind, Trent escorted her and Michael up to the top of the trail, where a small truck with a closed bed waited. Its lights were off, and when Trent opened the door for her to slide in along the one bench seat no interior light came on.

As the driver got out and went around to talk to Trent, Charlie clambered in out of the wind with relief and scooched over to make room for Michael. He got in beside her. The warmth he radiated was welcome, and the feel of his big body against hers was instantly comforting.

"Hughes have military training?" Michael asked under his breath.

"No, why?" Charlie replied, looking at him with a frown. He was almost impossible to see in the dark, so she guessed her frown was lost on him.

"Couple of broken necks to account for," Michael said, as the driver, a strapping man who looked to be in his early twenties, got in behind the wheel, introducing himself as Lieutenant Tim Brown, National Guard.

They started off, pulling away without turning on the headlights.

"Um, lights?" Charlie said, alarmed. She couldn't even see Michael, who was squeezed in beside her, let alone the road in front of them.

"Trying to keep a clandestine presence,

ma'am," Brown replied, which did nothing to calm Charlie's misgivings about navigating the steep, twisty road in the pitch dark. The sheer drop-off she'd just ascended, along with similar ones she'd seen on the drive up, was vivid in her memory.

"He's wearing night-vision goggles," Michael said in her ear, clearly having once again read her thoughts, or more likely her body language, because she'd gone rigid and had grabbed hold of his leg.

Charlie darted a glance at the driver. Now that Michael had alerted her to their presence, she could just see their shiny blackness against the paler skin of his face.

The ride down the mountain proved uneventful, although Charlie continued to experience spasms of unease over negotiating hairpin turns in the dark. She kept scanning the dense woods lining the road, hoping against hope that she would see one or more of the hostages who might have escaped the bus emerging from the woods. The blackness beneath the trees was impenetrable, however, and all she saw was an occasional gleaming pair of animal's eyes tracking the truck as it passed. She tried not to picture anything horrible that might have happened or might be happening in that dark forest. Upsetting herself did no one any good. Despite Hughes's jacket, which she kept wrapped tightly around her, and the fact that she was sandwiched between Michael and the driver, she was still freezing. The temperature outside had dropped to what felt like the upper forties and she'd gotten thoroughly chilled on the ledge, but it was warm enough in the truck that she knew the reason she was still so cold had little to do with the weather. A digital clock on the dashboard read 10:43. In the course of the seven-plus hours since she and Hughes had evacuated her office, so much had changed that she could barely wrap her mind around it. On the one hand, Michael was back, which filled her heart with so much lightness and joy it could have floated away like a helium balloon. On the other hand, in that same span of time at least five and possibly six people had died either in front of her or in her near proximity, all but two of them good men who hadn't deserved what had been done to them, and the lives of nine more, seven of them teenagers, were currently at risk. Charlie braced herself to pass the bodies of the guards who had been killed and thrown from the bus, but the road was empty. The bodies had already been removed. They did pass a convoy of Jeeplike vehicles heading up the mountain, all running without lights just as they were. It was hard to be sure in the dark, but Charlie assumed they were crammed full of law enforcement officers.

"Virginia State Police SWAT," Brown said, in reply to Charlie's question. "They're heading up to Bob Prager's barn. Word is the bus is holed up in there."

Charlie's heart beat faster.

"Abell and Torres — two of the escapees — will die rather than surrender, and will kill every hostage rather than surrender," she said. "Ware might be persuaded to give himself up, but he's heavily influenced by Abell and Torres. I don't know the other three men." Charlie took a breath and looked at Brown. "I know you're not the person who should be given that information. I need to talk to whoever is in charge of what's getting ready to happen at the barn."

Brown said, "I'm not sure who that is. I can take you to the operations center when we get down to where they're set up. Somebody there'll be able to put you in touch with the right person."

"You need to get checked out by an EMT," Michael told her quietly. "Remember getting thrown out of a moving bus?"

"I will," Charlie promised, slanting a look up at him. His face was close: taking advantage of the darkness, she'd been leaning against him for most of the way down, and at some point her hand had crept into his. Now their fingers were entwined, and the feel of his warm, strong hand holding hers made her both happy and sad. Happy because, miracle of miracles, he was there; sad because having him with her in a physical incarnation couldn't last. "As soon as I talk to whoever's in charge. And I'm really not hurt."

Brown's words had prepared Charlie for a base of operations having been set up, but when they passed through a National Guard–manned roadblock and reached the foot of the mountain, the scope of what they encountered was astounding. The four-lane highway that skirted the mountain had been blocked off, and a large and motley collection of vehicles ranging from patrol cars to ambulances to firetrucks to big green army trucks were parked in and alongside the road for as far as she could see in either direction. There were a number of people moving around inside the cordoned-off area, but it was too dark for her to see much detail. Low-level lanterns had been strung up on ropes stretched between tree trunks along the area's perimeter. Two large military-style tents had been erected in the middle of the road, and these were lit by electricity powered by portable generators. Charlie knew the squat black boxes were generators because she could hear them rumbling as the truck stopped and Michael opened the door and got out. With their flaps closed, the tents glowed as brightly as paper lanterns in the dark.

With a thank-you to Brown, Charlie got out, too, and looked at the closest tent, which he had pointed out as the operations center. It was busy, with uniformed law enforcement personnel, the National Guard, and others in civilian clothes flitting in and out. She could see tables set up inside through the opening created by one tent flap that had been pulled back and secured in place. A group of uniformed cops were clustered around a large chalkboard near the entrance. While Michael closed the door of the Jeep and Brown drove off, Charlie shook off her exhaustion one more time and headed purposefully toward that tent. She'd gone only a few steps when her eye was caught by a short, stocky man with buzzed blond hair who'd just emerged from the second tent, which was maybe some fifty feet away. He was wearing the blue uniform of a prison guard, and what had attracted her attention in the first place was that he had walked out right through the canvas covering the closed side of the tent.

Charlie recognized him with a sinking feeling in the pit of her stomach.

"Oh," she said, and only realized that she'd stopped walking when Michael, who'd been behind her, caught up and stopped, too. It didn't take more than a glance at her for him to follow the direction of her gaze.

"Shit," Michael said. From that, Charlie knew that despite being in Hughes's body Michael was still able to see the same spirits she did, and that he'd also recognized the second of the two prison guards who'd been shot on the bus. The guard was in spirit form now.

". . . need a ride home," the guard called plaintively. "Can anybody give me a ride home?"

He looked around without appearing to see anyone, then turned and walked back through the closed canvas wall of the tent.

The back of his head was missing. From the neck up there was nothing but a mass of bloody red pulp.

Charlie's stomach churned. Her fists clenched as she fought the rush of sorrow that hit her as she remembered the man pleading that he had a wife, children. He would never see them again, never go home. The instant nausea, the deep pity for the victim — they were what happened to her in the close presence of spirits, her crappy life as usual. Her face must have given away some of what she was experiencing, because Michael muttered "Shit" again and pulled her into his arms. Clutching at his shirtfront, she rested her forehead against his chest, shut her eyes, and breathed.

For a moment, just a moment, she let herself be weak.

A sharp sound popped her eyes open again, and she looked up to see the tent flap being thrown back and a man in a white coat stepping out. From his attire, Charlie guessed that he was either the medical examiner or the county coroner or an assistant to one or the other. Beyond him, through the now open flap, she saw gurneys with sheet-covered corpses on them neatly lined up in a row. Grimacing, she realized she was looking at a makeshift morgue. Probably one of the generators was providing refrigeration.

"That must be where they're keeping the bodies until they're taken away to wherever they'll be autopsied," she said, careful to keep her voice even. Inside the tent, as she watched, another spirit sat upright, rising through the sheet covering his gurney as if it wasn't there. Charlie recognized the police officer Abell had shot.

"Come on, babe, you don't need to see this." Michael's arms tightened around her, and he half turned with her as though he would walk her away from the scene. Charlie didn't resist: there was nothing she could do for the dead. Before they could move away, another of the small trucks purred past them and stopped in front of the tent. It was parked so close that Charlie could smell the exhaust wafting toward them.

Two National Guard officers got out of the truck, said something to the man in the white coat, and walked toward the rear of the vehicle. Even before they opened the closed bed and started to remove the blue-tarp-wrapped bundle in the back, Charlie's stomach turned inside out.

". . . shot me in the back!" the kid who sprang out of the truck bed screamed. It was the tall, skinny boy with the stringy brown hair and black hoodie who'd gotten hit in the face for talking to Bree, Charlie saw with a burst of horror. And the horror was because what was screaming at her was the kid's spirit. His body was wrapped in the tarp: he was no longer alive. Usually the dead couldn't see the living, but this boy could. Charlie realized that he saw her even before he came rushing toward her, his eyes wild. "I went out the window just like you said, but they shot me! I was running away and I got hit! It hurts! It hurts!"

He started to scream.

"Holy hell," Michael growled, taking in the hair-raising scene. He whirled with Charlie so that his back was between her and the spirit as the kid reached them, but the spirit, shrieking, ran right through both of them before vanishing.

Charlie was instantly drenched in cold sweat. Her stomach went into full revolt. Shoving away from Michael with both hands, she barely made it to the edge of the pavement before dropping to her knees and vomiting in the scruffy grass.

"Goddamn it." Michael leaned over her, pulling her hair back away from her face, holding it for her and adding a string of choice curse words as she vomited again.

"You know that — spirits affect me like this sometimes," she managed when she was done.

Michael was still leaning over her, keeping her hair back out of her face. "Yeah, I do fucking know. Take a couple of deep breaths."

Charlie did.

"Here." Michael thrust something at her. "Dude had some napkins in his pocket."

Charlie accepted what she discovered was a wad of paper napkins and wiped her mouth.

"I don't suppose you have any water?" she asked over her shoulder. To her consternation, her voice sounded shaky.

"Sorry, babe. We can probably get some around here somewhere."

Charlie nodded. A moment later, she felt recovered enough to let Michael pull her to her feet.

"He was just a kid." Charlie leaned tiredly against him. It felt good to rest her cheek against the solid warmth of his chest.

"I know." Supporting her with an arm around her waist, Michael tucked her hair behind her ears as she tilted her face so she could look up at him.

The dead cop walked out through the tent again. With a muttered "Oh, God," Charlie turned her face away — and found herself looking right at a tall man in a dark suit who emerged from the operations center. He hesitated for a moment, as if he was surprised by what he was seeing, and then came striding toward them. The light was behind him, but —

"Charlie?" His voice was sharp.

She'd known who he was even before he spoke. The lean build, the black hair — "Tony!"

Chapter Fifteen

Charlie didn't know why she was even surprised. Of course Tony had heard about what had happened. Of course he had come. First of all, he was her friend, and he was that kind of guy. Second, he was as serious about his work as she was, and catching serial killers was his job. For this, he would have reactivated himself from sick leave without a second thought. At this moment, there were three of the most notorious serial killers in the country loose on the mountain behind them. When he'd set out, there would have been five of the human predators at large. With hostages, including eight teens and — her.

"Is everything all right?" Tony's voice was still sharp. Charlie realized that she was leaning against Michael with her arms wrapped around his waist and his arm tight around hers. His hand that had just finished tucking her hair behind her ears now rested on her shoulder. He'd stiffened when Tony had called her name, and was now looking at Tony just as she was, although she imagined his expression was very different. The two of them presented an unmistakably intimate picture, she was sure. If her world had been as normal as everyone else's, this wouldn't have been a problem. Michael would have been Michael, the man she was in love with, her guy, and she would have introduced him to Tony as such and that would have been that. Unfortunately, Michael was dead and inhabiting Hughes's body. More unfortunately, Tony was well aware that she had met Hughes only the day before and that she suspected him of being a serial killer. The reason he was aware of all that was that she had told him so herself, which if she had foreseen the turn events would take she might not have done, but what was it they said about hindsight? She was also almost certain Tony knew what Hughes looked like and was thus able to identify him now. A photo would have been part of the investigative file she'd asked him to put together for her.

Which made the fact that she was clinging like a barnacle to a boat to the man who Tony thought was Hughes a little hard to explain.

"She's sick," Michael said, exhibiting more presence of mind than she possessed at the moment in coming up with such a semi-reasonable explanation for their embrace. Charlie could feel the increased tension in his body — he had some issues concerning her relationship with Tony — but his voice was even. "She's had a hell of a day. For starters, she was pushed out of a moving bus and hit the pavement hard. She needs to be checked by a doctor."

"You're Rick Hughes," Tony said, approaching. His left arm was in a sling, Charlie saw, a reminder of the bullet wounds that had nearly killed him. The darkness made his expression — and Michael's — impossible to read. There was no inflection at all in Tony's voice. Which told her a great deal: he didn't like seeing her in the supposed Rick Hughes's arms.

Why was nothing in her life ever simple?

"Yeah," Michael replied as Charlie pushed away from him. He made no attempt to keep her.

"Tony Bartoli, FBI," Tony introduced himself, and the two men exchanged a perfunctory handshake. Michael knew exactly who Tony was, of course, and also knew way more about Tony than Tony probably would be comfortable with if he was aware of it. As the handshake ended, Tony slid a hand around her elbow, deliberately drawing her away from Michael.

"Are you okay? You shouldn't have come." Charlie looked up at Tony reproachfully. He was six-one, one-ninety, and handsome, with a lean, expressive face, even features, and coffee brown eyes. It was hard to tell through the darkness, but she thought he looked tired and kind of drawn around the eyes and mouth. No surprise, given the wounds he had suffered, but still she hated this evidence that he hadn't yet recovered. She and Tony had been through a lot together, and she was immensely fond of him. She hugged him. "How are you feeling?"

He returned her hug with his one good arm. "A lot better as of about twenty minutes ago, when we got the call that you'd been found alive. You got pushed out of a moving bus? Are you hurt?"

"I'm fine. I'll tell you all about it later."

Charlie wasn't looking at Michael, but she could feel him watching the two of them. Because he'd been there throughout the whole thing, he knew every detail of her relationship with Tony, and she was pretty sure he also knew that as much as she might wish it were otherwise, he had nothing to worry about: Tony was not the man who could make her heart go pitter-pat on sight. Still, she was picking up a vibe from Michael as he watched her with Tony that she couldn't quite interpret. Not anger, not jealousy, but — something. What?

"I'm actually really glad you're here," Charlie said to Tony, choosing to ignore the crosscurrents in the air in the interest of passing on the information she possessed as quickly as possible. "You can cut through the red tape for me."

"Red tape?"

"Red tape," she confirmed. "There's no time for me to go through half-a-dozen different people." The exhausted heaviness in her legs made moving an effort, she discovered, as she pulled away from him to head for the tent, but she moved anyway. She threw a quick "Come on" over her shoulder at Tony as she went.

He caught up with her. "Where are we going?"

"The tent," she replied, adding, "I have information for whoever's in charge of trying to rescue the hostages. Three of the men being hunted are my research subjects: I know them well. Two of them — Abell and Torres — will die and kill any hostages they're holding before surrendering. The third, Ware, will do whatever they tell him. A full-out assault on the barn where they may be holed up will almost certainly result in everyone inside being killed. They need to try something else first. Negotiations, snipers, I don't know, but something else."

She was still slightly nauseated and her knees were wobbly and her mouth felt like it was stuffed with sour-tasting cotton balls, to name only the most immediate of her physical concerns, but this information couldn't wait any longer, because if it did it might be too late to do any good.

It might already be too late to do any good. But she had to hope that if the hostages were in the barn, they were still alive, and that it would take a little time for the rescue force to get set up.

"Are you sure you're okay? Because you don't look okay." Tony's hand slid around her elbow again as he looked at her in concern. They were just walking into the rectangle of light that was spilling out through the open tent flap, and he was getting his first good look at her. This close to the tent, the jumble of voices emanating from it was audible. There was a lot of activity in the parking area around them, and she could hear that, too.

"She needs to see a doctor," Michael said

for the second time from a few paces behind them. "She was puking her guts out back there in the grass."

Charlie's lips tightened. Of course, Michael knew that the reason she'd just vomited wasn't anything a doctor could do anything about, but he thought she needed to see one and was using that as an excuse to get Tony to pile on with him. Not that she would explain any of this to Tony.

"I'll see a doctor as soon as I make sure this information is given to the right people," she said. It occurred to her that she wouldn't be quite that impatient with Hughes, whom she barely knew, but it was too late. She moderated her tone. "It might not make a difference, but . . . it might."

The thought of what could be happening to the remaining hostages at that very moment was enough to make her want to jump out of her skin. Any slight help she could give them, she meant to provide.

"Lee Hintz with the Virginia State Police is in charge here. I'll take you to him." Tony's hand tightened on her arm, and he swept her into the tent and over to the chalkboard surrounded by cops she'd spotted when she'd first looked through the flap. It was still surrounded by cops, but it wasn't a chalkboard, she discovered as they reached it. The angle and the uncertain lighting had misled her. It was a dry-erase board with the pictures of everyone who'd been on that bus affixed to it. Her picture, labeled DR. CHARLOTTE STONE and captured from her driver's license, wasn't particularly flattering. Hughes's picture was beside hers. It, too, appeared to have been taken from his driver's license, but because he looked exactly like Michael except in a jacket and tie, the picture was hot. The next picture was of Paris, whose last name, Charlie learned from its label, was Troyan. The three of them made up the first vertical row to the left. In the center, a larger group started with the chaperone. Her name was Tabitha Grunwald. The bus driver's picture was beside hers: Larry Carter. After that came Bree Hoyt. Then the boys, one after the other: Trevor Frost (the small, scared-looking kid), Blake Armour (he was the one who'd looked under the bus seat and told Paris she was too big to get out a window), Josh Watkins (the kid with the carroty hair), Kyle Miller (the heavyset kid), and Chris Thomson. Charlie frowned as she saw that the picture of the sixth boy, Ben Snider, had been moved to the other side of the board. Dead now, his picture had been grouped with those of Frank Macy, the buzzed blond prison guard, and Rob Weise, the other prison guard.

Photos of six of the eight escapees were in a row across the bottom of the board: Charlie mentally categorized that grouping as *still at large.* The two pictures that were together on the lower right side — Fleenor and Sayers — she knew were dead.

"Charlie, this is Major Lee Hintz," Tony said. "Dr. Charlotte Stone."

Charlie turned to see a compact man in his mid-fifties wearing a state police uniform, who extended his hand toward her.

"Glad for your safe recovery, Dr. Stone," Hintz said as they shook hands. "This is a bad business." He looked past her and added, "Glad to see you safe, too, Mr. Hughes."

"Glad to be safe," Michael replied, and they shook hands, too.

Charlie quickly told Hintz what she had come to say. He nodded. "I'll pass that on to my men up there now," he said, and left them, presumably to do just that. Glancing around, Charlie saw that Michael was gone, and frowned. Where could he have . . . ?

"Feel up to telling me what happened?" Tony asked. The tent was packed with people coming and going. It was noisy and slightly chaotic, but where they were, a little to the left of the board with the pictures, was a small oasis of privacy. Charlie spotted Michael on the other side of the tent, felt a flutter of relief, and leaned against the nearest table for support — there were no chairs — as she gave Tony a lightning recap of events. Everything to do with Michael, of course, she left out, along with most of the unnecessary details, including her confrontation with Abell and that she had punched Fleenor. While she spoke she kept track of Michael as he moved around inside the tent with the spidey-sense she seemed to have developed where he was concerned.

"Jesus. I can't begin to fathom how something like this could have happened." Tony rubbed a hand over his forehead when she finished. "Hughes saved your life?"

Charlie nodded. "And Paris Troyan's."

Tony frowned at her. "You still thinking he might be a serial killer?"

Charlie shrugged. Well, actually, yes, she did, but Michael was not Hughes, and for right now it might be better to skirt the issue.

"All I know for sure is he saved my life," she replied.

Tony continued, "Because I went ahead and sent the coffee cup in your office to the lab. At least, I'm presuming the one on the outside corner of your desk was the one with his DNA on it."

Charlie looked at him in surprise. "Yes, but — how in the world were you able to do that?"

Tony shrugged. "When I got to town, first place I went was the prison. See, all I knew at that point was that on the one hand, there'd been a mass escape from Wallens Ridge, and on the other hand, you, having been inside Wallens Ridge at the time, were missing. Those two things might or might not be connected. The last person you'd been seen with was Hughes, who I knew you had suspicions about. It was always possible that Hughes had done something to you under the cover of the fire and the prison break. I went to your office, which wasn't damaged, by the way. The fire in that wing was confined to the library. Anyway, I was in your office looking for anything that might provide a clue as to what had happened to you and was told that a messenger had arrived to pick up some DNA evidence you had made arrangements to send off. Remembering you telling me about it, I bagged up the cup and gave it to him, still thinking that possibly Hughes had abducted you and we might need to know real quick if there was a possibility that you were right about him being a serial killer. But then Hughes's car was found in the prison parking lot, and your car was found in the parking lot, and finally a witness was interviewed who thought he'd seen you getting on the school bus with the Scared Straight kids. When it turned out the witness was right, I almost found myself wishing you'd been grabbed by Hughes."

Before Charlie could reply to that, Buzz and Lena — FBI Special Agents Buzz Crane and Lena Kaminsky, who made up Tony's team — came rushing toward them.

"Charlie! Thank God you're okay!" Buzz exclaimed. Five-ten and wiry in his FBI standard dark suit, with springy brown curls, a thin, sharp-featured face, and bright blue eyes beneath black-framed glasses, he was cute in a geeky kind of way. He enveloped her in a hug. Charlie hugged him back. "The boss here was freaking out."

"I was a little worried," Tony corrected, smiling at Charlie as Buzz released her. She smiled back. God, she really did like him so much! But the operative word there was *like*, not *love*. She now absolutely, positively, and without a doubt knew the difference, God help her.

"Bartoli rushed us down here so fast I forgot and left the iron on. I had to call my sister after I got here to turn it off." Lena was giving her a frowning once-over. "You look like crap."

Despite everything, Charlie had to smile. That was so typically Lena.

"Thanks," she said. Lena looked as exotically lovely as always. Her chin-length black bob was smooth and shining, deep red lipstick outlined her full mouth, and, because she was working and Lena loved her job, her slanting brown eyes were as bright and alert as a terrier's on the hunt. Five-two barefoot, she was sensitive about her height and routinely wore four-inch heels to compensate. Her figure was curvy, and she preferred fitted skirt suits to pants. The one she wore at the moment was deep green, with a matching blouse and nude heels.

Next to her, Charlie was pretty sure she did look like crap.

"She means you look like you've been through an ordeal," Buzz said.

"I mean what I said. Don't put words in my mouth, Crane." Lena gave him a dark look.

"Sorry." Buzz held up both hands in an appeasing gesture.

Charlie took from that exchange that the off-and-on romance the two had going was currently in “off” mode.

Lena scanned Charlie again. “You basically look like you got run over by a train, but that’s not what I’m talking about. You’re skinny, you’re pale, you’ve got dark circles under your eyes. All of this in the past two and a half weeks. What on earth have you been doing since we last saw you?”

Charlie was speechless. She hadn’t realized that what she’d been through with Michael’s absence had left such a noticeable imprint on her appearance.

“Okay, enough with the small talk,” Tony said. Charlie was grateful for the interruption. Impossible to explain that she’d spent the last seventeen days racked with grief. “You two get preliminary cause of death on our fatalities?” he asked Lena.

“Four victims suffered fatal gunshot wounds, one suffered gunshot wounds but expired from blunt-force trauma thought to be the result of a car crash, and two had broken necks,” Lena replied promptly.

“The gunshot wounds were of different calibers, which means multiple shooters and/or weapons,” Buzz said. “The two corrections officers were shot once in the head each with the same caliber bullet, probably the same weapon; the police officer was hit multiple times in the torso, which means multiple weapons and probably multiple shooters; and the teen was shot twice in the back. Same caliber bullet, probably the same weapon and shooter, but we won't know definitively until the test results are back."

"First question: Where did the escapees get the guns?" Bartoli said, and looked at Buzz.

"Working on it, boss," he said.

Charlie folded her arms over her chest. She was so tired that she was practically sitting on the corner of the table by this time. "While I was on the bus, I heard Torres say something about one of the librarians smuggling guns into the prison library. Torres described the librarian as male and fat."

"That should narrow it down," Tony said, and looked at Lena.

Lena grimaced. "I know. Find the fat male librarian."

Tony nodded.

"Heads are going to roll." Buzz shook his head. "Security at that prison must have been off-the-charts lax."

Tony said, "So tell me about the two deaths that weren't by gunshot. Broken necks, you said?"

Buzz nodded. "Both were broken by manual force in the same style. Those were our two deceased hostage takers."

Tony asked something else, but Charlie missed it because she realized with a tiny flutter of alarm that she'd lost track of Michael.

And that would be because he was right behind her, she discovered a second later. She felt the brush of his body against hers even as she anxiously skimmed the knots of people surrounding her, trying to locate him. She couldn't see him, but still she knew who it was instantly, identifying him on what she thought had to be a cellular level, even before he said "Here" in that still too-gravelly voice and handed her a bottle of water.

She knew it was him because when he touched her the air went out of the room.

You've got it bad, she told herself. But she was also resigned to it. She'd come to terms with the fact that apparently, by some inexplicable quirk of fate, he was it for her.

"Thank you." Accepting the water with gratitude, Charlie kept her voice cool and crisp, like everything around her hadn't just taken on a little extra vibrancy just because he was near, like she wasn't barely resisting the urge to lean back against him, to touch him in some way. Unscrewing the cap, she took a long, appreciative drink while Tony,

Buzz, and Lena looked past her at Michael. Tony frowned, Buzz's expression was assessing, and Lena's eyes widened.

"This is Rick Hughes." Tony made the introduction. "Lena Kaminsky, Buzz Crane."

Of course, Michael knew them almost as well as he knew Tony, but they didn't know that.

As Michael stepped forward to shake hands with Lena and Buzz, Tony asked him, "You ever serve in the military?"

Michael met his gaze. "Why do you ask?"

"Haven't met many people who could break a neck like that."

Michael smiled. "I've had some martial arts training."

"I see."

While they were talking, Charlie found herself looking from one man to the other. It was, she thought, sort of like comparing a French rapier to a Viking broadsword. Tony was tall and leanly muscled, the quintessential FBI agent in his dark blue suit, pale blue shirt, and red tie. His black hair and handsome face turned women's heads wherever he went. Wearing a dirty, torn, untucked, and open-collared white shirt (he'd apparently lost the tie somewhere) with stained gray suit pants, Michael was inches taller and more powerfully built. With his lion-colored hair, golden tan, and beautifully cut features, he was outrageously good-looking to the point that the same women who would turn their heads for Tony would trail panting at Michael's heels. There was a hardness around Michael's eyes and mouth, a hint of aggression in the set of his shoulders that, surprisingly, made him the more formidable of the two, despite his sun-god looks. One looked like the kind of man you could bring home to mother, settle down with, and depend on, and that was exactly what Tony was. The other looked dangerous and dirty-minded, pure sex on the hoof, and that described Michael perfectly.

Charlie absolutely knew which man she *should* want.

Maybe Michael's right was the rueful rejoinder that popped into her head. *Maybe I do need a shrink.*

Michael turned to Charlie and said, "I've been sent to fetch you. There's an ambulance pulled up right outside with a crew that's here to check out us rescued hostages."

She met his gaze. His eyes were still black, and she trusted that it would go unremarked in the jerry-rigged fluorescent lighting. Anyway, it was unlikely that anyone here was familiar enough with the normal color of Hughes's eyes to notice the difference.

"Go," Tony said to her. Deciding to go ahead and get it over with, Charlie nodded, and Tony added to Lena, "Kaminsky, go with her."

That told Charlie everything she needed to know about how Tony felt concerning the supposed Hughes: he didn't trust him. Well, fair enough. Given the information Tony had, she wouldn't have trusted him, either.

Michael was already heading for the open tent flap. Swigging thirstily from her water bottle, Charlie started walking after him, and Lena fell into step beside her.

"He's *pretty,*" Lena said under her breath, her eyes on Michael's broad back. "Tell me you're not calling dibs."

Well, actually, she was, but —

"What about Buzz?" Charlie replied, indignant on Buzz's behalf.

"Forget Crane. Plenty of fish in the sea that *weren't* once engaged to my sister." Lena had been looking Michael over. Now she frowned and glanced at Charlie. "Is that Hunky Guy's jacket you're wearing?"

"We were stuck on a ledge. It was cold."

Charlie knew she sounded defensive: ridiculously, she felt defensive.

"So he gave you his jacket, which means he's a gentleman." Lena's speculative gaze, which had returned to slide over Michael again, sliced back to Charlie. "Or else it means he likes you. What is it with men and liking the helpless types, anyway?"

That ruffled Charlie's feathers. "I am not helpless."

"I know. You're not helpless at all. That's what's so damned unfair about it. Men just think you're helpless." Lena shook her head in disgust. "It's that big-eyed, fine-boned thing you have going on. They all want to protect you."

"That is a total crock."

"Uh-uh. Look at the boss. The minute he heard you were missing, he rounded up Crane and me and had us all heading to the rescue so fast the plane practically broke the sound barrier."

"Thank you for coming, by the way."

Lena shrugged. "You showed up for me, I showed up for you."

Charlie looked sideways at Lena. "You know what? I think that makes us friends."

Lena said sourly, "Oh, gosh, should we go shopping or something? Or, I know, maybe we can get a mani-pedi together. That would be fun."

"Shopping would be nice," Charlie replied, her voice deliberately bland. Lena gave her a sharp, aren't-you-funny look. Then they were outside the tent, and what with the sudden darkness and the distracting bustle of activity as vehicles moved in and out of the parking area, the conversation lapsed. Charlie cast a compulsive glance at the tent where the bodies were being held — she was contemplating sneaking in and telling whichever of the spirits could see and hear her to look for the light — only to discover that it was empty: the bodies apparently had been taken away for autopsy.

So. No more to be done there, so put it out of your mind. And keep walking. Because her step had faltered a little.

"Something wrong?" Lena asked.

"No," Charlie replied, and pulled Hughes's jacket more tightly closed against the brisk wind. Being down in a valley as they were with the jagged black peaks of the mountains towering all around made her feel small and isolated, as if the rest of the world were a million miles away. Thinking about what might be happening on the mountain behind her got her so antsy that her pulse started to race and her breathing quickened. Instantly labeling those thoughts as unproductive, she forced them from her head. An ambulance was parked nearby. The rear doors were open and the interior had a faintly greenish glow in the darkness. A couple of EMTs sat with their legs dangling in the open doorway, looking out toward her and Lena as they approached. Michael had gotten there just ahead of them, and he turned around to watch them, too.

They reached the ambulance. Because Michael insisted she go first, Charlie was helped inside.

A couple of ibuprofen, some antiseptic wipes, a turkey sandwich — Michael wolfed down three, courtesy of a catering table that also held coffee — and a trip to a nearby porta-potty later, Charlie was just walking back inside the tent with Michael and Lena when a sudden commotion drew their attention to a table near the dry-erase board. Everybody was rushing in that direction, so they walked over, too.

"What's going on?" Lena asked Buzz as they stopped beside him and Tony, who were in front of a table on which an open laptop computer had been placed. Surrounding them was a crowd — a couple dozen cops mixed with some National Guard types, a contingent of local FBI agents in blue windbreakers, and a few random others who weren't wearing uniforms and thus were difficult to identify. It was worryingly quiet as they all leaned forward almost as one to try to see the computer. Grainy images of something Charlie couldn't quite make out filled the screen. Her hand tightened on the Styrofoam cup of coffee in her hand.

"SWAT's inside the barn," Buzz replied in a hushed tone. "They're just reporting in. What you're looking at are pictures from one of their body cams."

Armed with that knowledge, Charlie felt her heart beat faster as the images resolved themselves into the school bus, its back door open, parked inside what looked like an old tobacco barn. It was darker even than the night toward the outer edges of the screen. The lighting focused on the bus seemed as if it was being supplied by lanterns and flashlights, which made it swoopy and uncertain.

A man appeared on the screen. He was in full SWAT riot gear, with a helmet and a blackened face.

"We've got three victims inside the barn," the man reported, and Charlie felt a chill slide down her spine. "They were dead when we got here. No sign of anyone else. No pickup truck. Just the bus, with one dead inside and two dead on the ground."

A murmur of dismay ran through the group crowding around the monitor.

"Can you identify the dead?" Hintz asked. Along with a quartet of fellow Virginia State Police officers, he was the closest to the laptop, leaning toward it with his hands flat on the table on which it rested.

The man on the computer looked around and said, "Grell, get me a visual on the female. Lane, get me the males."

As Charlie heard the word *female,* her heart sank. Only two females had been left on the bus. That had to mean that either Bree or the chaperone, Tabitha Grunwald, was dead. Blindly she reached out and set her half-empty coffee cup down on a nearby table: she'd just managed to catch herself before her fingers crushed the flimsy Styrofoam.

Chapter Sixteen

Tabitha Grunwald was curled in a fetal position in the aisle near the front of the bus. Seen by the white glow of the lantern that had been placed on the seat nearest her, her short gray hair was shiny red with blood. Her flowered dress was soaked with it. The paper bag Charlie had given her was still clutched in her hand.

Her face had been blown away.

Hintz identified the victim for the man in the barn, who repeated her name to someone who was out of camera range.

As the camera panned Tabitha Grunwald's body, Charlie dropped her head and closed her eyes. Her chest felt tight. It required an effort to breathe. Remembering the chaperone's helpless terror, she shuddered.

A strong masculine arm came around her shoulders; she knew immediately that it belonged to Tony rather than Michael. She also knew that she must be looking bad if

Tony was offering her that kind of comfort and support in such a public setting, because, like her, he always tried to keep it professional when he was on the job. When she opened her eyes, though, she couldn't even look at him or at Michael, who stood silently on her other side, or anyone else, because the computer screen instantly caught her attention again. Her throat closed up as she saw that the kid with the carroty hair, Josh Watkins, was on there now. He was sprawled on his stomach in the dirt on the barn floor and it was obvious that he was dead. His back was a bloody mess. He looked like he'd been shot while trying to run away.

As Hintz identified Watkins to the man in the barn, Charlie's knees wobbled. She felt as if every ounce of strength she had left in her had just drained away.

Tony's arm tightened and he pulled her close against his side.

Leaning against him because she really did need the support to keep from folding like an accordion, she dropped her head forward again and concentrated on regulating her breathing.

As many times as she had seen death, it never got easier. And she'd known these victims, had been a hostage along with them. She had shared their terror.

She felt responsible for them.

Yet she had lived and they had died.

I failed those kids.

Guilt mixed with sorrow mixed with outrage that such terrible things could even happen.

"That's Larry Carter," Hintz said. From that, Charlie knew that the third victim was the driver. She didn't look at the screen again. She had just officially reached her limit: she'd seen too much death for one day.

"The rest of them are still up there on the mountain somewhere, Major," a man said, and Charlie opened her eyes to find that a National Guard officer was talking to Hintz, not via computer but there in the tent. The police contingent was still in front of the computer, but was looking at the guardsman rather than the screen now.

"I want them found," Hintz said. His voice was calmly authoritative, but his one hand that still rested on the table was clenched into a fist and there was fire in his eyes. "I want the rest of those hostages brought out of there alive."

The guardsman nodded. "We've got the mountain surrounded. Every road blocked. A fly couldn't get off there without us spotting it. Give us some daylight and —"

"We can't wait for daylight." Hintz's face was grim. "Physically search every inch of that mountain *now.* Start at the bottom and sweep upward. Grid by grid, everybody no more than arm's length apart. Continue the high-tech stuff: Use every piece of equipment you have. Use everything you have. We've got six murderers up there, and five kids, and we need to find 'em. Let's go."

"Yes, sir."

The crowd around the computer scattered, with everyone moving purposefully to do their jobs. A uniformed state trooper walked up to the little group consisting of Charlie, Michael, Tony, Lena, and Buzz, and said, "Excuse me, Dr. Stone?"

"Yes?" Charlie replied. She'd straightened away from Tony's side the second she'd felt recovered enough, as much for the sake of his professional reputation as her own. His arm was no longer around her, but they were still close. His face impassive, Michael had been watching her and Tony, but he glanced toward the trooper as the man spoke. Lena and Buzz, who'd been talking, broke off.

"I'm Eddie Plank. Major Hintz sent me to drive you and Mr. Hughes back to Big Stone Gap if you're ready to go."

"I am," Michael said, and looked at her. His eyes said *You are, too.* "Dr. Stone?"

Charlie frowned at him. "I can't leave."

"Yes, you can," Tony said, and Charlie switched her attention to him. "There's nothing more you can contribute to this tonight. The situation is contained to the mountain, and there's a search-and-rescue operation in progress. You're not needed for that. You go home, get some sleep, and by tomorrow hopefully everything will be resolved here and we'll be back in Big Stone Gap ourselves trying to determine how the hell this happened. We've got rooms in the Best Western there, so you can expect to see us at some point." He looked at Lena. "Kaminsky, go with her."

Charlie and Lena both stiffened and said "No!" simultaneously.

"I don't need her."

"I'm not a babysitter!"

The women's gazes clashed. For an instant, they glared at each other. Then recognition of the mutual enemy struck, and they transferred those glares to Tony.

"No," Charlie said again. Quietly but firmly. Tony was right, there was nothing more she could contribute to the situation here. All her knowledge of serial killers in general and three of the search subjects in particular could add nothing to the efforts already under way. If the situation changed, her files and notes on Abell, Torres, and Ware were on her laptop, which (thank goodness!) she'd left in her office at home and in her file cabinet in her office at the prison. She was so exhausted and emotionally and physically wrung out that she was becoming more of a liability than an asset with every passing moment. Plus there was Michael. He had only a short time in Hughes's body. If she could help save even one life she wouldn't let that weigh with her, but the truth was her expertise was of no help to anyone now. And she needed — not wanted but *needed* — to be with him. "I'll go, but I'm not taking Lena."

"Damn right you're not," Lena seconded, and scowled at Tony.

Tony slid a hand around Charlie's arm. "Can I talk to you for just a second?" he asked.

Michael's face revealed precisely nothing as he said, "I'll be at the car," and walked away with the trooper while Tony pulled Charlie aside.

"Hughes," Tony said, quietly enough so that only she could hear. He didn't have to say anything else: she knew what he meant.

"He had plenty of time to murder me

while we were stuck on that ledge if he was going to do it. I think I'll survive a car ride with him with a state trooper as an escort." Charlie's reply was equally quiet, and also a little tart. "And he'll know you and Buzz and Lena and the state trooper and no telling who else know he's with me, so I'm betting I'm safe."

Tony frowned. "I'd feel better if Kaminsky went with you."

"Lena wouldn't. Neither would I." Charlie squared her shoulders. She was so tired it was hard to think straight. "This is my decision, Tony, and I'm making it."

His jaw hardened. Then he said, "You're right, it is your decision. I'll walk you to the car." His tone was cooler and more formal than it had been previously.

"Thank you," she said. Then, as they started walking, Charlie flicked a sideways look at him and sighed. "You know I appreciate your concern."

His jaw was still set. "But you don't want it."

"It's not that I don't want it, it's that I don't need it. Right now, for this. I'll make it back to Big Stone Gap in one piece, I promise." She flicked another look at him. "But I am so, so grateful that you grabbed Lena and Buzz and came here. I know you did it for me. You're a really good friend, and I appreciate it."

They were outside now, walking through the dark. The police cruiser waited a few yards away, its lights on, its motor running. Charlie couldn't see who was inside, but she assumed it was Michael and the driver.

Tony stopped her with a hand on her arm. She looked up at him.

"Just so we're clear, I don't want to be your really good friend," he said, and kissed her.

The kiss was quick. Hot on Tony's part, not on hers. Charlie had no idea if it was visible to the occupant of the cruiser's rear seat. The thought that Michael might be watching Tony kiss her made Charlie's pulse give a nervous flutter. Tony lifted his head before she could react in any significant way, leaving Charlie to blink up at him.

"Don't say anything," Tony said, drawing her toward the front passenger door of the cruiser, which he opened for her. "Not right now. Think about it."

Charlie's lips parted to say something along the lines of *I don't need to think about it,* but then she closed them again. There wasn't enough privacy, or enough time, to have the conversation they needed to have.

The cruiser had a metal grid between the

front and rear seats that was designed to protect the officers in the front from prisoners in the back. As she slid into the front passenger seat, Charlie shot a look through the grid at Michael, who was indeed in the back. His face was impossible to read in the brief flash of light she got from the open door. His body language was equally opaque.

But there was something in the air — she thought he'd seen.

Tony leaned across her to tell Plank, "Walk Dr. Stone to her door and make sure she gets inside safely."

Plank nodded and said, "I'll do that."

What was it with all these alpha males? Because clearly that was the type that was attracted to her, and to whom she was attracted. More fodder for her next session of self-analysis, if ever she succumbed to one, Charlie thought. She didn't get a chance to respond to that high-handed and totally unnecessary instruction to the driver before Tony said, "I'll talk to you tomorrow," and shut the door. A moment later the cruiser pulled away.

As they exited the cordoned-off area, Charlie was startled to discover that the media was out in force: satellite trucks crowded the road beyond the barricade, and the bright lights of camera crews made it look like a movie premiere was in progress. Charlie suspected that only direct orders from some high-level authority in combination with the thickening fog kept news helicopters from strafing the mountain. On second thought, though, she wasn't surprised: of course the kidnapping of a school bus full of people including eight teenagers by convicted murderers escaping from one of the most secure prisons in the country would be a lead story on every TV channel in existence.

Vehicles must have been entering and exiting the protected zone fairly steadily, and word must not have leaked that two of the rescued hostages were in the state police car driving sedately through their midst, because they weren't bothered as they nosed through the circus and escaped into the dark.

After a few desultory attempts at conversation directed at Michael, who basically grunted in response, and a few polite remarks aimed at Plank, whose equally polite replies soon left them both at a dead end, Charlie gave up on the whole talking thing and lapsed into silence. The next thing she knew the cruiser was crunching over gravel, and she sat up to find that they were pulling up the driveway to her house. It was dark, not a light on anywhere. Except for the fuzzy glow of a couple of porch lights down the block, the entire street was dark.

Blinking, she realized that she'd fallen asleep and had slept the whole way home. A glance at the dashboard clock told her that it was after one a.m. The nap had helped: physically at least, she felt better.

"I'll walk from here," Michael said as the cruiser stopped. Charlie slewed around to frown at him through the grid. She could see no more of him than a dark shape. "The place where I'm staying isn't far."

"Where are you staying?" Impossible to keep the surprise out of her voice, because of course Michael was staying with her.

"The Pioneer Inn."

It was a small place on the edge of the town square. Trying to figure out how he was even aware of its existence, much less where it was, she was flummoxed. As far as she knew, he'd never been there.

"You're staying at the Pioneer Inn?" Okay, she had to quit talking. She was sounding way too interested in his plans, given their audience.

By way of an answer, Michael silently held up what, when she squinted at it, she perceived to be a plastic key card. Then she got it. Of course *Hughes* was staying at the Pioneer Inn. He must have found the key card in his pocket. But —

"I'll be glad to give you a ride as soon as I see Dr. Stone to her door," Plank replied, getting out. By the interior light that flashed on as the door opened, Charlie met Michael's eyes.

"You aren't really —" There was a touch of panic in her voice at the idea that he was going somewhere else. The door closed, and the visual she had on him was largely lost as he was swallowed up once again by shadows.

"I'll be back in ten minutes," he said. "You barely know me, remember? I can't just go inside with you. Word got back to Dudley Do-Right back there, he'd drop dead."

From the tone of that, she knew Michael had indeed seen the kiss.

She sighed.

Plank opened the door for Michael, who got out. By the time Plank reached her door, Michael was walking away into the night. Having lost her purse, along with her cell phone and keys, Charlie was only glad she had a means of letting herself into her house. Plank escorted her to her front porch and followed her up the shallow steps. Except for the creak of the wood beneath their feet and the brief, distant tinkling of a neighbor's wind chimes, everything was quiet. Hers was the kind of street where even on the weekends people were in bed by one a.m.

"You want me to check your house for you?" Plank asked as she walked down the porch and felt along the ledge over the living room window to find the spare key she kept there.

"Thanks," she replied, locating the key and heading back toward him. Michael would be there in a few minutes, but given the events of the day it was difficult to imagine being too cautious. "And thanks for driving me home."

"You're welcome," he said, waiting for her to get the door open. It was so dark that she had a little trouble fitting the key into the lock, and as she stepped inside she had to slide a hand along the wall to find the switch for the entry hall light. When she found the light switch, she hit it and stood back as Plank entered. Ordinarily she would have turned the porch light on if she was coming home so late, but of course when she'd left the house she'd had no idea that it would be the early hours of the next day before she made it home again.

As she accompanied Plank on a quick walk-through of her house, Charlie felt cold all over. Tabitha Grunwald, Ben Snider, Josh Watkins, the rest of the dead — their faces flashed unbidden into her mind's eye. They'd had no idea when they'd left home the previous morning what their day would hold, either. That yesterday would be the last day of their lives.

The thought brought a lump to her throat. She muttered a quick prayer for them, and for the teens still out there on the mountain.

But as she'd learned over the course of most of a lifetime spent in the close proximity of violent death, making herself sick over the things she couldn't change did nothing but make her sick.

With the house inspection complete, she walked Plank back to the door and said goodbye to him.

When Plank left, she locked the door and shed Hughes's jacket, which she hung up in the closet that was right there. Then she went into the small bathroom off the hall to down two more ibuprofen before her scrapes and bruises could start making themselves felt again. The nap must have given her a second wind, because she felt reasonably rested. A glance in the mirror shocked her by how pale and nervy her reflection looked. Quickly she washed her face, splashing it with icy water in hopes that it would wake her up further as well as put some color back in her cheeks, then brushed her teeth, brushed her hair, and used the cosmetics she kept in the cabinet to apply a vitally necessary little bit of makeup.

Michael's quiet tap on the door came just as she was eyeing the new and deeper neckline of her shirt. As long as she didn't move suddenly, the gap created by the two missing buttons stayed closed, not that it really mattered at this point: there was no one to see but Michael, and he'd already seen that and far more. A final glance in the mirror reassured her that she was looking almost normal, and for that she thanked the miracle of blush. Restoring her things to the cabinet, she hurried to let him in.

"Hey," he said as she opened the door. It was only as she saw him standing there on her porch in the spill of light from the hall that she realized that he had never before been to her house in human form. Tall as he was, he cast a long shadow back down the steps.

Wordlessly, she stood back to let him in.

Having him step through the front door did something to the atmosphere inside the house. Before, it had felt cold and empty. As she shut the door behind him, locked it, and turned to look at him, the place crackled to life.

Now that he was back she was able to inhale inside her own house without the air feeling so thick it threatened to choke her.

He wasn't looking at her. Before him, she'd lived alone for a long time, and she'd decorated the house the way she liked: with pretty furniture and airy fabrics and light, feminine colors. He was entirely too masculine for it. He was glancing around, at the slice of living room he could see through the doorway with its pale linen couch that he'd stretched out on countless times, at the old-fashioned staircase, down the hall toward the kitchen. In that brief moment in which he didn't realize she was watching him, his expression was unguarded.

In it she could read what he was thinking as clearly as if he'd said it out loud.

It's good to be home.

Her throat was suddenly tight.

She went to him, wrapped her arms around his waist, and rested her forehead against his chest. He felt warm, and solid as a wall against her. Being so close to his broad-shouldered, powerful body felt as right and natural to her as breathing. Then she caught a whiff of that fresh woodsy smell she'd noticed on him before and reminded herself that the body wasn't his and certainly wasn't his to keep.

It didn't matter. However he'd gotten here, he was home. However he was able to stay, she would take him.

He'd said *You're mine, Doc.* Well, that worked both ways. He was hers now, too.

God help them both.

Chapter Seventeen

Michael's arms circled her as she hugged him. He pulled her more tightly against him, his hold on her hard and possessive. Charlie felt the brush of what she thought were his lips in her hair.

"So what is it Dudley wants you to think about?" he asked.

Still in his arms, she tilted her face up to consider him. The top of her head didn't quite reach his chin. From the angle at which she was looking at him she could see the darkening shadow of stubble on his square jaw, the beautifully cut, unsmiling mouth, the straight nose, the flat planes of his cheeks and the hard curves of his cheekbones, the sweep of his forehead. His eyes were still coal black as he met her gaze. For all she knew, they would remain black for as long as he stayed in Hughes's body.

There was absolutely no expression on his face.

"He'd like us to have a relationship," she said.

"He looked pretty serious."

"*He* kissed *me,* not the other way around."

"I caught that."

"You are not jealous."

"No man likes it when some other guy kisses his girl. I'm trying to rise above it."

His girl. She was a grown woman, thirty-two years old. A self-supporting, highly successful doctor. How stupid was it that her heart skipped a beat when Michael called her his girl?

She said, "He and I are going to talk. And I'm going to tell him I'm not interested in being anything but friends."

Michael looked at her for a long moment without saying anything. Then he grimaced and said, "Dudley's a good guy."

That was a surprise. "Tony *is* a good guy. I like him a lot. What's your point?"

"You might not want to be so quick to turn him down."

That was wrong in so many ways that Charlie pulled back to frown at him. "*What?* Seriously?"

"Yeah."

"You're encouraging me to have a relationship with Tony?"

"Babe, if I wasn't dead things would be

different, but I am dead, so there you are. You want a *life,* you're not going to be able to have it with me. I'm just saying Dudley's not a bad choice."

Charlie knew she had to be gaping at him.

"I'm hungry," he said, before she could find the words with which to respond to *that.* He wasn't looking at her anymore as his hands found her upper arms and he put her away from him. "I'd almost forgotten what that feels like. You got anything to eat?"

She frowned after him as he started for the kitchen.

What on earth . . . ?

"Eggs. Cheese. Cereal." She did a quick mental review of the contents of her refrigerator and cabinets as she trailed him down the hall. She continued, "Wait, there's no milk. Protein bars. Peanut butter. No bread."

"No bread?"

"I haven't even been back three days. I haven't had time to go to the store."

He was in the galley area of her kitchen, and as she watched from the doorway he delved into the cabinet where she kept her nonperishable staples, i.e., peanut butter and cereal and protein bars. He pulled out a protein bar.

"Want one?" he asked over his shoulder.

Charlie shook her head. "No."

She hadn't pulled the shades closed before she left, because she'd expected that it would still be daylight when she returned. Outside the kitchen windows, the night was black as ink. She couldn't see the sunflowers or the mountain rising behind them, or anything. Remembering how easy it was for anyone outside to see in, she shivered, crossed the kitchen, and pulled the shades down, then headed for the breakfast bar. Perching on one of the stools, she eyed Michael across the counter as he filled a glass with water from the sink just a few feet away. His back was to her, and in the grimy white shirt his shoulders looked impossibly broad. The well-cut gray pants hugged his tight athlete's butt and the long, strong muscles of his legs. All that was left of the protein bar was a wrapper on the counter. She assumed he'd eaten it.

"Okay, enough with the cryptic stuff," she said. "I want to know what's going on with you."

Turning off the water, he turned around to look at her.

"What are you talking about?" Resting his hips back against the sink, he chugged about half the glass of water.

"What happened to you in Spookville?"

"I told you: nothing worth talking about. Spookville is what it is: purple fog, monsters. Jesus, you can't just let things lie, can you?"

"You were gone a long time."

"It's getting harder to get back."

"There's something you're not telling me. I need you to tell me what it is right now. We're both in this together, you know."

"What, do you want me to write it in blood? There's nothing. Look, could we talk about something else? What happened with you while I was gone?"

She looked at him thoughtfully and lied, "I slept with Tony."

That got to him. She saw it in the sudden rigidity in his body, in the tightening of his jaw, in the narrowing of his eyes as they lasered in on her face. Then his mouth twitched. The fierce gleam in his eyes went away and the tension left his long muscles. He took another drink of water. "How was it?"

"Fantastic."

"Uh-huh."

Okay, he didn't believe her. Of course he didn't. She'd known he was going to know she was lying when she said it. She didn't want him to believe her. She just wanted to try to gauge his reaction. Conclusion: for the briefest of moments there, before his brain had actually kicked in, he'd been pissed.

"It's obvious from your reaction that you don't want me to sleep with Tony. So why are you trying to push me into a relationship with him?"

"We've been over this. I'm dead. Body's a loaner. You can't have one with me."

"Let me get this straight: I'm going to have a relationship with — as in, have lots and lots of sex with — Tony, and you're going to hang around and watch?"

He swallowed the last of the water, then turned to put the glass in the sink. Without replying.

"Michael —"

"What are you, part bulldog?" On that exasperated note, he was turning back to face her when his attention was caught by something on the refrigerator. Following his gaze, Charlie saw that he was looking at the letter she'd received from NARSAD. She'd hung it up there with a clip-on magnet so she wouldn't forget to RSVP to the awards dinner invite by the specified date. The bright gold letterhead had apparently caught his eye. It gleamed in the overhead light — and he was looking for something to change the subject.

He wasn't getting out of the conversation

that easily, but . . . she still felt a warm little glow as she remembered what the letter said. Until that moment, she'd forgotten all about it, which said way too much about the chaotic nature of her life.

"You won a prize?" Having clearly read the letter, he was looking at her now.

Charlie nodded. "A NARSAD." She could feel the smile spreading over her face. Whatever miracle it had taken to bring him back, the one person she'd wanted to share the news with was here. "It's a big deal."

"Tell me." He came to stand on the other side of the breakfast bar directly across from her. Leaning toward her, he placed his hands flat on the counter and fixed his eyes on her face.

"I won the Goldman-Rakic Prize for Outstanding Achievement in Cognitive Neuroscience." Even saying the words gave her a thrill. She told him all about it, not holding anything back, no false modesty, no downplaying the magnitude of it, because the thing about their relationship, she realized as she talked, was that with him she felt like she could be totally herself. After all they'd been through together, he knew her better than anyone else in her life. As she finished, he was smiling broadly at her. Then he came around the breakfast bar and caught her around the waist and plucked her up off the stool like she weighed nothing at all, making her squeak with surprise and grab on to his shoulders for balance.

"That's great." His arms were tight around her waist as he swung her in a series of wide circles. Her feet weren't touching the ground, and she wrapped her arms around his neck and hung on, laughing a little at his exuberance and at the sheer unexpectedness of finding herself being twirled around her own kitchen. His hard, handsome face was alight with pleasure in her achievement. "I am so damned proud of you. You're a remarkable woman, Charlie Stone."

Their eyes met, and everything he was flashed into her consciousness in a single burst of absolutely clearheaded awareness. A dead man in another man's body. A spirit who'd apparently done something so terrible in life that the universe had decreed his soul should be destroyed. A man who'd wound up on death row in the earth plane because he'd been convicted of murdering multiple women. Sometimes short-tempered. Occasionally scary. An intermittent jackass who was smart and funny and caring and, yes, sexy as hell. A badass protector who'd saved her life a number of times. A friend. A lover. Someone she could confide in. Someone she could count on. *The* someone she could count on.

In a word: Michael.

She was smiling at him and he was smiling back, but she guessed he must have been able to read something of her thoughts in her eyes — he could always read her eyes — because his expression changed. The broad smile died, and his face tightened fractionally and he stopped twirling her.

As he set her back on her feet she kept her arms around his neck and her face lifted to his. Still faintly breathless, she said, "I haven't told anybody else. I — when I opened the letter, the one person I wanted to tell was you. But you weren't here, and so —"

She didn't get to finish. He bent his head and kissed her. It was an achingly tender kiss, a careful molding of her mouth that made her heart lurch, that made her return his kiss as tenderly. Then his lips hardened in a way that had her tightening her arms around his neck, that had her going up on tiptoe to fit her mouth to his and her body to his with an ardency that was her own silent acknowledgment of how she felt about him. His tongue came into her mouth, and she answered it with her own. The fire that was always there between them blazed up so fast and hot that she could feel the scorching heat of it blistering her skin and turning the air around them to steam. Her heart pounded and her pulse raced and her body quickened, conditioned responses to him now that had her melting like superheated plastic in his arms.

Kissing him, she faced the terrible truth: she was absolutely, irrevocably his. Nobody else had ever been able to make her feel like this, and she was as sure as it was possible to be that nobody else ever would.

When he lifted his head she looked up at him. She was tingly, fuzzy-headed, plastered against him like peanut butter on bread — and she had a terrible feeling that her heart might be in her eyes.

So be it. Truth was truth, and sometimes you just had to face up to things.

"I love you," she said.

He took a breath. She could feel his body tense. His arms around her were suddenly as taut as iron bands. Those unholy black eyes blazed down at her.

He said, "I know."

Charlie blinked. Not exactly the words of deathless romance she'd been longing to hear. Then she waited, thinking that it might take him a moment to build up to it, to get his act together. Nothing.

He was still breathing unevenly, and there were dark slashes of color high on his cheekbones. She could feel the rise and fall of his chest against her breasts. His body was hard with wanting her: there was no mistake about that. He stood very still.

Her eyes searched his.

" 'I know'?" she repeated. Quietly. Calmly. Not ominously at all. "What kind of response to 'I love you' is that?"

His face hardened into brutality. "The only one I have."

Because she hadn't seen it coming, the pain blindsided her. It was sharp and physical, and it lodged squarely in the region of her heart. If he hadn't been holding her, she might have doubled over with the intensity of it.

Her instinctive, thankfully silent response was a pitiful: *You don't love me?*

She had her pride. She refused to let him see that he'd just burst the magical bubble she'd been living in since his return. She refused to let him see that there'd been a magical bubble at all.

Grow up, Cinderella. When you lose your shoe at midnight, you're not getting it back.

She managed *not* to take a deep breath.

"Really? Good to know." Her tone was even borderline polite. A little chilly, maybe, but she couldn't help that. Oh, God, her arms were still around his neck. She lowered them, shoved — not angrily or anything; actually, in a very controlled way — against his chest in a silent demand to be released. "Excuse me, I'm going to go take a shower and go to bed."

He let her go without a word.

If he watched her leave the kitchen, she didn't know it, because she didn't look back.

Head high, back straight, she climbed the stairs and walked through the bedroom into the bathroom and stripped off her ruined clothes and got into the shower. It was a large unit that she'd had built into a corner of the bathroom when she'd remodeled. Glass doors took up the entire side facing the bathroom, while the other three sides were tiled. It was separate from her big claw-foot tub and she actually used it a lot more, because she was usually in a hurry. It had lots of small nozzles that shot spray in every direction and a big central shower-head that sent torrents of water cascading down.

She made the water as hot as she could stand it and then stepped under it, soaping herself, vigorously washing her hair with her floral-scented shampoo, enduring the sting of the water and soap and shampoo sluicing over all the scratches and scrapes the day had left her with.

Barely feeling any of it.

I'm gonna wash that man right outta my hair: the showstopper from *South Pacific* rolled through her head. Song or no song, though, it wasn't working.

She was hurting so badly inside that there was no room for anything else.

What she was not going to do was cry. Not over him. Not ever again.

The thing about letting yourself fall in love with a jackass was — you might be in love, but he was still a jackass.

With the power to break your heart.

I'll be damned if he's going to break mine, she told herself fiercely.

Even as she was thinking it, she heard a *whoosh* from the shower door. A rush of cooler air penetrating the steam reinforced her interpretation of the sound: the door had just been yanked open.

Her eyes popped open. Water tinged with soap ran into them, making them burn, blurring her vision. Instantly she shut them again — but not before she saw Michael standing in the shower's open doorway, scowling at her. *Scowling* at her. While, startled by his advent, she was stark naked and cringing in an instinctive pose of classic female modesty under the spray, and he stood fully dressed, with billows of steam escaping around him, inches away in her bathroom, watching her shower. She'd shut the bathroom door. Had she locked it? She couldn't remember, but obviously not. Growling, she opened her eyes again just enough to allow her to see and snatch at the towel she'd flung over the top of the door.

"You really are self-destructive, aren't you?" he bit out before she could say anything.

She'd been scowling right back at him even before she'd opened her eyes.

At that, her scowl deepened into a full-blown glower.

She snapped, "Get out of my shower."

Stepping sideways, which took her out from under the full force of the spray, Charlie swiped the towel over her face, then clasped it to her body so that it at least covered the vital full-frontal view that she had no intention of allowing him to keep looking at. It was a pale blue towel, plush and pretty. A hand towel, positioned over the door so she could use it to dry her eyes if she needed to, while her bath towel remained safely tucked away from the spray over the towel rack just outside the shower.

Water soaked the towel almost instantly; she could feel the thick terry cloth getting heavier because it was wet.

"You say 'I love you' to me. What, were you thinking I was going to say it back?" He looked mad. He sounded mad.

Well, welcome to the club.

Her chin came up. Her voice stayed sharp. "We had an agreement. You stay out of the bathroom while I'm in it."

His eyes swept her. "That's what you want. Admit it. You want me to say it back."

That stung. Because it was true. *"Go the fuck away."* Her voice had risen in volume until it was perilously close to a shout. Only she never shouted. Plus, he was the one who was always saying "fuck." She never did that, either. Except now, when she was suddenly furiously angry with him.

His face was hard. His mouth was ugly. "What's the point? How do you think this whole thing's going to end, huh?"

Stomping her foot in the inch or so of water swirling on the shower floor, Charlie tightened her grip on the towel, pointed a finger at him, and yelled, *"I want you out of this bathroom. Now."*

"Fuck that." He stepped into the shower with her. Fully clothed. All hard-eyed and hard-jawed and badass, radiating attitude at her. Hot water poured down over him, soaking his hair, his clothes, running in rivulets down his face. In that confined space he looked huge. Intimidating. Menacing, even. The skin around his eyes was tight with anger. His mouth was grim with it. She could feel the aggression coming off his big body in waves.

Cool, calm, and collected, that was her. In control of her emotions. Reserved. Self-contained. At least that was her before him. Now it was not her. Anger and hurt and a whole constellation of other emotions surged through her veins, and she shoved her pointing finger smack-dab into the center of his infuriatingly wide, honed chest with the soaking-wet white shirt plastered to it that of course revealed rather than concealed every single sculpted muscle, screwed up her face at him, and shrieked, *"Get. Out."*

Grabbing her with a hand on either side of her waist, he shoved her back against the slippery-wet tile wall and held her there, looming over her, his long fingers digging into her bare skin just above her hipbones, giving off dangerous vibes like the atmosphere does right before a lightning strike. She glared up at him, all but spitting with rage, and he bent his head to hers until they were practically nose to nose and snarled, "So you get me to say it. Then what? What do you see happening, exactly? You want to marry me and have my babies?"

What? Charlie's heart stood still. Not even the savagery in his face or the sneer in his voice could take away from the unexpected chord that his words touched inside her.

Yes, that's what I want. Her silent answer was instant, instinctive, and absolute. And shattering in its impossibility.

Bitterly, he said, "Goddamn it. You got no business looking at me like that."

Then he kissed her.

Chapter Eighteen

Hell itself couldn't have burned hotter than that kiss. It was incendiary, explosive, combustible. A blast wave of heat igniting everything in its path. His mouth took hers, *took* it, a harsh possession that surprised a sound out of her, that had her grabbing at his wide shoulders for balance, that rocked her with its intensity. He kissed her fiercely, his tongue invading her mouth, his lips hard and insistent as they commanded her response. He slid a hand along her jaw, holding her head still for him. Leaning his considerable weight against her, trapping her in place, he kissed her as if he was the one calling all the shots, as if she had no say in the matter at all.

And instead of protesting, instead of pushing him away, instead of going all cold and rigid or, alternatively, punching him or kicking him in the kneecap or doing something to drive home her assertion that she wanted him to leave her alone, which she absolutely should have done, she went up in flames like the total sucker for him she was and closed her eyes and kissed him back.

As if she would die if she didn't.

At her response, she could feel the shudder that racked his big body, feel the rocketing urgency of his passion in the steeliness of the strong arm that snaked around her waist to pull her even closer against him, feel the unmistakable evidence of how aroused he was in the enormous erection he was holding her so tightly against.

When he lifted his head, electricity sizzled in the air between them. She could feel the charge of it even as she fought to breathe.

"You want me to say it? Fine," he grated in a thick voice that barely sounded like his at all. "I love you. There. Is that what you wanted to hear?"

No, not like that, the tiny part of her brain that was still capable of coherent thought protested. Not hurled at her in a brutish growl that vibrated with suppressed violence and a whole host of other charged emotions that that blistering kiss had left her too shaken to try to sort out. Dazzled, disturbed, and angry all at the same time, she opened her eyes and looked up at him. His body was curved over hers like a predator's. His handsome face was hard with passion. His eyes were fierce with it. His mouth was cruel.

Yeah, well. Under the right circumstances, she could radiate some attitude, too.

"Hey, Goldilocks? You know where you can stick that," she said, meaning every word.

For a second, surprise flickered in his eyes. Then they blazed down at her. She glared right back at him, not giving an inch.

In that same thick, harsh voice, he said, "Just so you know, I'm getting ready to fuck the hell out of you."

Oh, God.

Fire rolled through her. Her heart thumped. Her bones dissolved. Deep inside, her body went all shivery and tight. She was just mad and hurt enough that she might have been able to resist him, that she might have been able to shove past him and walk on out of there. What she couldn't resist was her burning desire to have him do exactly what he'd said. Her body hungered for him almost as much as her heart did. The really sad thing was he knew it. She could read the knowledge in his face, and that upped her anger quotient considerably. It was embarrassing, annoying, and — face it — hot. She was still glaring up at him, angry and conflicted — and yes, so turned on that she was already breathless — when he bent his head and kissed her again, licking into her mouth before taking full possession, his tongue and lips hot and insistent, making her instantly dizzy, making her cling to him, making every rational thought in her head go away.

She kissed him back like she was a junkie and he was her drug, which in all honesty she supposed he was. However it had happened, she needed him now in a way that was as elemental to her as her need for air to breathe. The steam rising around them was nothing compared to the steam gushing through her veins. He kissed her, and ribbons of desire snaked over her skin like the droplets of water that splashed them from the cascading torrent inches away, making her so hot that her mind clouded over, that she could scarcely breathe.

She gave herself up to kissing him, to the urgency of her own desire, to her certain knowledge of the way he could make her feel and her absolutely primal need to feel that way again. Her heart pounded. Her pulse raced. That tight, shivery feeling he'd awakened escalated until she was on fire with it. Deep inside, her body clenched and burned.

Whatever sexual attraction was, it sparked between them always. Now it was a monster of an electrical storm raging around them, sending firebolts cascading to earth that trapped them both in the resulting flames.

Still kissing her, he pulled the wet towel out from between them. Then his hand slid down from her jaw to find her breasts, caressing the soft globes, squeezing and fondling, a little rough, possessive, his fingers teasing her nipples until they were pebble hard and she was arching up against him and kissing him back with shameless abandon while her toes curled into the eddies of water at her feet. His clothes were wet but there. The knowledge that he was fully dressed while she was naked, the slight friction of his clothes against the silkiness of her bare skin, excited her more than she'd ever thought something like that could. The thought of him naked excited her even more. Her hands slid down to the buttons of his shirt. As she started to unfasten them she discovered that her fingers were unsteady. He lifted his head, looked down at her for an instant with eyes that smoldered, then let go of her to unbutton his cuffs and pull his shirt over his head. Even as she registered the utterly masculine beauty of his heavy shoulders and corded arms, of his wide chest and taut abdomen, even as she slid her hands over the warm, firm muscles covering his rib cage and thrilled at how sleek and taut they felt, he dropped the shirt. It landed with a wet slither in the swirling water on the floor.

With her hands still moving sensuously up the hard wall of his chest, she looked at him standing there bared to the waist, skin glistening wet and golden bronze, and her breathing suspended. He was tall enough, and close enough, that she had to tilt her head back to meet his eyes. His jaw was set. His mouth was tight. His broad shoulders were wide enough to block her view of the glass doors behind him. His muscular frame looked impressively athletic. He was impossibly sexy, and looking at him, touching him, made her go all light-headed and tremulous with desire. At least a hint of what she was feeling must have shown in her eyes, because as he met them something raw and primordial flashed across his face.

"I want you more than I've ever wanted anything in my life," he said, husky and low. As her heart shuddered in response, he kissed her again. Senses reeling, she kissed him back, wrapping her arms around his neck, intoxicated by the feel of his wet skin against her breasts, by the warm resilience of his muscles. The instant reaction of her nipples to being pressed so tightly to the unyielding wall of his chest made her insides quiver.

He was so much bigger than she was, so much stronger than she was, that there was no way she was getting away from him unless he chose to let her go — but she didn't want to get away. She loved his hands on her, loved the way he kissed her, loved how excited he was getting her. He knew it, he could always read her. She could tell, from how heavy-lidded his eyes had become, from the way he was breathing like he'd been running for miles, from the increasing tension in his muscles, that her skyrocketing arousal was acting on him like a match to gasoline. The thing was, she'd never burned as hot for anyone but him.

His hands found her bottom, splayed over the taut curves, tightened and pulled her even closer, fitting her to him like two pieces of a puzzle, moving her against his hardness in a blatant way that sent shock waves of desire shooting through her. Her stomach quivered. Her mouth went dry. Then one hand slid down even farther and his fingers slipped all the way between her legs to stroke her there. She gasped at the intimacy of it, at the sheer sensual delight of having him touch her like that. Melting against him, breathing in the warm, wet smell of his skin along with the faintly floral scent that rose around them in the steam, she instantly went all hot and liquid inside. Losing herself in a long, drugging kiss that was rendering her officially mindless, she clung to him as her head spun and electric little shivers raced over her skin. He touched and stroked the velvety delta between her thighs until her knees threatened to buckle, until she was lying bonelessly against him and moaning into his mouth. Then he pushed two long, hard fingers into her. At the unexpected jolt of pleasure, she cried out.

Then he did it again. And again.

A man with a slow hand. Words from a song, they fit him perfectly.

"Oh. *Oh.*" Her little cries of excitement were accompanied by an urgent pulsing tension that wound ever tighter. Each thrust of his fingers made the hot quickening inside her intensify until she was burning with passion, mindless with it, absolutely his to do with as he would.

"See, I know what you like." It was a guttural murmur uttered as he kissed her ear, slid his mouth down the sensitive column of her neck.

She was so turned on by what he was doing that she was trembling. Her pulse drummed in her ears. Her breasts swelled eagerly against the hard wall of his chest. Her body burned and throbbed and moved for him.

"Michael —" Her voice shook. She pressed intoxicated little kisses to the section of his chest that was closest to her mouth. He tasted of water, of man.

He lifted his head. She felt him inhale. Hanging on to him like he was the only solid thing in the world, plastered against the firm muscles of his chest and pressed so close to his powerful thighs and the tantalizing rigidity of his erection that she could feel their imprint like a brand even through the soaked wool of his pants, she left off kissing his chest and opened her eyes to find that he was looking down at her once more. His eyes gleamed with lust. His face was dark with it.

"Look at you. Look at how much you like this." Holding her gaze, his hand big and warm between her legs, he stroked her most intimate flesh and caressed the tiny nub that quivered and throbbed at his touch. She reacted by gasping and writhing against him with helpless pleasure. Then he pushed his fingers inside her again, and every fragment of rational thought that remained to her was lost in the resulting wave of blistering heat. She cried out, shuddering, and his face suddenly turned so fierce and primitive that it made her breath catch. Heart thundering, closing her eyes in the only act of self-preservation she had the willpower left to summon, she let her head fall back against his shoulder in abject surrender as he bent his head and took her mouth.

Dropping a series of sizzling kisses on her mouth, on her neck, on her shoulder, he watched her between kisses while he fondled her breasts and played between her legs. Her body was on fire, burning up with readiness, and he knew it. He knew his way around a woman's body and, as he'd said, he knew her. Even with her eyes closed, she could feel the smoldering weight of his gaze on her as he deliberately brought her to fever pitch. She might have been embarrassed at the thought of what she must look like, all flushed and breathing hard and moving under his hands, if she'd been capable of any coherent thought at all. But she wasn't, she was mindless with need, so shivery and hot she thought she must climax at any second. Then his fingers left her, trailed provocatively across her one last time and were gone, and she squirmed in protest.

"Michael." Her eyes shot open and she

shuddered with frustration because she was absolutely on fire, so close to coming that she was shaking with it. Her arms tightened around his neck. “Don’t stop.”

“Patience, grasshopper.” He repeated the words she’d said to him previously in a low-pitched rasp that made butterflies take flight in her stomach. Charlie thought she probably would have smiled in response if she hadn’t been so consumed with lust for him that smiling, or anything that was much beyond panting and squirming and begging, was impossible. His hands were on her hipbones now. He pressed her back against the slick tile wall, holding her still and a little away from him when she would have clung, and bent his head so that she found herself looking down at the flexing muscles of his broad back. He kissed her breasts, trailing fire over the soft slopes, licking at the hard little points of her nipples until he had her gasping and spiraling even higher and forgetting every complaint she’d had. He said in that same gritty voice, “I’m trying to make a point here.”

“What point?” Oh, God, she was so hot for him she could barely talk.

He straightened to look at her. She clung to his shoulders, trying to keep at least a tiny portion of her head in the game, which was hard to do when she was throbbing and quaking inside and her skin sizzled everywhere they touched and her body burned for him and the intensity of the voltage between them practically crackled in the air.

"You like sex, babe. That whole cold, repressed Dr. Stone thing you do? It's not who you really are."

I only get this turned on with you. She didn't say it, because after the I-love-you debacle she would be damned before she'd give that much away. Or maybe she did say it, because his eyes suddenly blazed at her like twin flamethrowers. Or maybe, terrifying thought, he was once more reading her thoughts in her face.

"You like *this,*" he told her in a hoarse voice just before his mouth closed over her nipple. She gasped at the feel of the hot, wet suction pulling at the aroused peak, and dug her nails into his shoulders and arched her back to give him better access and moaned. His mouth on her breasts went all greedy and hard, and it made her pulsate with excitement. Her body was so tight and hungry for release now that she couldn't wait any longer, that she needed — *needed — him.*

She reached for his belt buckle, but it was

too far away for her to properly grasp. Like the rest of him, his abdomen was firm with muscle. Her fingers just brushed his warm, taut skin —

His mouth left her breasts to trail down over her rib cage, over her belly button and flat stomach in a hot, wet slide. At the enthralling sensation, Charlie sucked in a lungful of steamy air and forgot all about undressing him. Her heart thundered as he crouched in front of her and she realized where he was going. Long tremors of desire snaked down her thighs. His fingers dug into her hipbones, holding her in place against the wall as her legs trembled and threatened to give way. She grabbed on to his hard arms for support.

His wet, tawny head nuzzling into her sex was the most erotic thing she had ever seen in her life.

Dry-mouthed, she watched as he kissed her there and then licked into the cleft between her legs. The fiery thrill of his mouth on her started a series of hot rhythmic contractions deep inside her that made her shiver and gasp and burn.

He flicked another of those blazing looks up at her, and she realized that she must have made some tiny, bedazzled sound.

"And you like *this,*" he growled.

He put his mouth back against the notch between her legs, kissing her, licking into her with long, wet strokes, and her loins clenched as pleasure shot through her like a flash fire. She moaned. Then, shaking, she closed her eyes. His lips and tongue felt scalding hot as they caressed her tender flesh. The sensation was mind-blowing, a million tiny lightning bolts of pure bliss. She let go of his arms to stroke his head, clutch it close. Without his hands on her, she would have been slipping down the warm, wet tile.

The rhythmic contractions inside her were suddenly impossible to resist. Wave after wave of cataclysmic heat hit her as the fiery thrill of what he was doing broke over her. Crying out, she came hard against his mouth, her eyes closed, her hands buried deep in the coarse, wet strands of his hair.

She was still trembling and breathing hard in the aftermath when he pressed one last hot, lingering kiss on her and then abruptly stood up. Her hands dropped to his shoulders as she swayed against him. He felt big and muscular, and he was radiating heat like a furnace. Still caught up in the last lingering throes of passion, she opened dazed eyes and looked at him. His face was dark and dangerous.

Before she could say anything he kissed her lips, his mouth both tender and nakedly hungry. Wrapping her arms around his neck, she kissed him back, melting against him, totally pliable now because her bones and muscles had been reduced to the approximate consistency of jelly. She didn't even realize that he was shucking his pants and everything else he was wearing at what must have been warp speed until his arm curved beneath her bottom and he lifted her clear up off her feet.

Surprised, she broke the kiss and looked at him to find raw carnality blazing at her from his eyes. Her heart, which had been gearing down, lurched and started to pick up the pace again as she realized what he had in mind.

"Really?" she murmured, and he nodded. Her breath caught as his arms hardened into iron bands and he jockeyed her into the position he wanted. Responding to the pressure of his hands and body, she opened her legs for him, then gasped and wrapped her legs around his waist as he penetrated her instantly. Huge and hot and hard, he pushed deep inside her, letting her feel him, filling her to capacity, claiming her. Instinctively her body clenched around him, and then there it was again, the shivery tightening, the delicious heat, the sweet undulations of desire that seemed to belong exclusively to him.

Their eyes met. She didn't know what he read in hers, but something infernal gleamed at her from his.

"Michael," she breathed, arrested by that glittering look, and frowned as the smallest flicker of unease slithered through what little consciousness she had remaining to her.

"You like getting fucked, babe. You remember that," he said. Then he kissed her, a ragingly torrid kiss, and as she kissed him back she was once again lost in a haze of white-hot passion. He pressed her back against the wall and thrust into her with what felt like careful calculation until he had her burning for him again and crying out and clinging to him. Then he went all savage and uncontrolled, taking her with a ferocious intensity that made her wild, that turned her into someone she didn't even know who did things and said things and felt things that were as far removed from her usual calm and careful self as it was possible to be.

When she came this time, it was with a rapturous abandon that was like nothing she'd ever experienced. Blowing through her in long, explosive spasms of heat that rocked her to the core, that climax belonged to somebody who was hot-blooded and uninhibited and primitive. In other words, not her. Or at least not her with anyone else but him.

"Oh. Oh. Oh. Michael," she moaned, her arms tight around his neck, her face buried against the hard shelf of his shoulder, shuddering in his arms as her body convulsed around him.

He groaned in answer and thrust deep inside her one final time as he found his own release. Then he leaned against her, heavy as a brick wall, buried to the hilt in her body, holding her like he was never going to let her go, as the world spun away around them.

Chapter Nineteen

A few moments later Charlie slid down Michael's body and her feet splashed into water that wasn't as hot as it had been earlier. In fact, it wasn't hot at all.

Until then, she'd been so dizzy and replete with physical satisfaction that she'd had no room left in her head for anything except him and how pleased with him and herself she was in the aftermath of what had been some truly phenomenal sex. But the cooling water swirling around her feet brought her back to reality. The shower was still on: it sounded like a waterfall in that enclosed space. Abstractedly, she took in other small, unimportant details: his clothes, including maroon boxers that did indeed appear to be made of some kind of silky material and an expensive pair of black leather shoes, soaked through on the shower floor. Streams of water still pouring down her own body from the tails of her wet hair. How round and pale her breasts looked pressed against his chest, and how dark and puckered her nipples still were. How firm and solid his chest felt. That he was absolutely hung. That the fact was still apparent even now, when he was at half-mast.

That she was getting cold.

She would have pushed away from him, except she was absolutely spent, and her legs were showing an alarming tendency to refuse to support her. So, naked and wet, with the no-longer-hot shower sprinkling them with lukewarm droplets, she leaned against his equally naked and wet, yet warm-as-toast-anyway body, let her hands slide down until they were flat against his muscular chest, and looked up at him with a gathering frown.

He wasn't looking at her. He was looking around at the torrent pouring down from the showerhead, but he must have felt her gaze on him because he said, "Water's getting cold," without glancing her way as he reached over to shut off the shower.

Then he looked back at her, saw the way she was looking at him, and his eyes narrowed.

"We need to talk," she said grimly.

For an instant, his expression went all guarded and wary. Then it changed. He dropped a quick, possessive kiss on her mouth, making her tingle despite the fact that she should have been officially blissed out by that time, then lifted his head and cocked a sardonic eyebrow at her.

He said, "As in, was it as good for you as it was for me?"

"Ha, ha." Although she had returned his kiss — she couldn't help it — she didn't smile at him. Instead, the look she gave him was severe. She was worried, and it was manifesting itself in a growing tightness in her chest. Exhaustion was beginning to kick in big-time, but there was something there, something going on with him, that she needed to get to the bottom of. She knew it with every atom of intuition she possessed.

" 'Cause I gotta say, for me it was fantastic. Incredible. Bombs-bursting-in-air good. You rocked my world there, babe." Hooking an arm around her waist, he pushed open the shower door, hauled her out to stand shivering on the cozy white shower mat, snagged the plush blue towel hanging there, and started toweling her hair for her while she stood there naked and weak-kneed and shivering, grabbing for the towel.

"Would you be serious?" She succeeded in snatching the towel from him, shook her tangled hair back from her face, and summoned her last reserves of strength to stay upright and frown direly at him.

"What, bombs didn't burst for you?" He was already pulling two more of the pale blue towels from a shelf. As he did she had a moment to appreciate the absolute eye candy that was him naked. He was tall and built and gorgeous. Tan except for the bathing suit area, which was pale. Absorbing that detail, which was different from Michael's all-over golden bronze, she was reminded that the body she was viewing was not Michael's. Hughes was leaner, with less muscle mass in the shoulders and chest and arms. He also, she saw as he turned toward her, was missing the cobra tattoo that adorned Michael's ripped biceps.

But except for the tattoo, the rest was a matter of degrees. Essentially, the man she was looking at was Michael. The man she'd just argued with, had the best sex of her life with, and was currently trying to prise information from was Michael.

Vibrantly alive, naked in her bathroom, being his usual heartstopping, aggravating self.

It shook her to realize how much she wanted him to stay that way.

"Nope," she replied, just to be aggravating, too, her hands tightening on the towel she held.

"Liar," he said softly. He smiled at her and added, "You're beautiful, by the way, in case I forgot to mention it." As he handed her a second towel, she realized that he'd been checking her out that whole time, too.

"Thank you." Her voice now sounded blessedly composed. Okay, good, her emotions and thought processes and everything else associated with her cognitive functioning seemed to be getting back to normal. Wrapping that towel around herself, she finished blotting her hair with the other towel and moved over to the white pedestal sink, covertly watching him — he was toweling off — all the while. In the weeks before he'd disappeared, she'd grown accustomed to living with him, but there was, she discovered, a subtle difference between sharing space with a ghost and a living, breathing man. Being together like this with him in real live human form was new for them, but it also felt utterly right. It hit her that this was the relationship she'd been waiting for all her life without even knowing it — and it couldn't last. The realization made the tightness in her chest worsen.

Time to get to the bottom of what was up with him. "Michael —"

"Got a spare toothbrush?" he asked, cutting her off. She was quite sure he'd done it deliberately.

"You know I do. In the medicine cabinet."

The pale blue towel was hitched around his hips now, and he looked so sexy in it as he walked toward her that, despite her determination to have a very serious talk with him, she succumbed to a wry inner smile. All her life, when she'd tried to picture the man who would ultimately be "the one" for her, her thoughts had run toward academic types, physicians, scientists, nice-looking nice guys with whom she could have a nice life. Conventional. Straight arrows. Good potential family men. Never in her wildest dreams had she imagined that she could possibly fall crazily, head-over-heels in love with somebody like him.

"You are so not my type," she said, eyeing his surfer-god magnificence ruefully as he joined her at the sink. Her nightly pre-bed ritual was simple, and she had started in on it automatically, picking up the bottle of moisturizer from the shelf over the sink and squeezing some into her palm, then smoothing the light lotion into her skin. He'd watched it many times before, so doing it in front of him now was as natural as breathing.

Reaching past her to open the medicine cabinet, he slanted a look down at her.

"Right back at you, Doc. But here we are. What're you gonna do?" He extracted one of the extra toothbrushes she always kept on hand from the cabinet. Popping it out of its plastic wrapper, he grabbed the toothpaste. It was ridiculous that she could still be picking up an electric charge from the proximity of his body to hers, but she was. "Isn't there some quote, something like 'death makes strange bedfellows'? That's us."

"I think it's 'misery.' Misery makes strange bedfellows. It's from Shakespeare." At first she'd been surprised to discover how intelligent he was, and how widely read, which, she'd later realized, was as much stereotyping on her part as was the apparently common male assumption that a woman with her credentials would be unattractive. Now she just accepted it as one more way in which he wasn't what she'd expected. Finishing with the moisturizer, she rubbed the residue into her hands as she spoke, and picked up her own toothbrush.

He gave a slight shrug. "You'd be the one to know. You're the brainiac."

Through the mirror, she gave him a slightly indignant look. "I am not a brainiac."

He passed her the tube of Crest and stuck his toothbrush in his mouth. "You just won a big ol' whopping prize that says otherwise, babe," he said around it, and grinned at her. " 'Nuff said."

She met his gaze through the mirror, and suddenly she became pretty sure that she knew the answer to at least one thing she badly needed to know: how he really felt about her. There was too much pride in his face when he talked about her achievement to allow her to reach any other conclusion than that he loved her, no matter how reluctant he might be to admit it or to tell her so.

Then she took in the bigger picture that the mirror framed, took in their side-by-side reflections as they stood together sharing the tube of Crest and jockeying for position in front of the sink. Watching him brush his teeth was new for her, and she loved the hominess of it, loved how easy they were together. His tawny hair was already almost dry, while her dark hair hung in a damp and tangled cloud around her face. His eyes were still Spookville black and his square jaw was shadowed with stubble, but he didn't look particularly tired, while it was easy to read exhaustion in the pale oval of her face. His strong neck, broad shoulders, and wide chest formed a marked contrast to the slender column of her neck and her narrow shoulders above the towel. Her head didn't quite reach his chin, and he took up about twice the amount of horizontal space she did. To use Lena's description of him, which she was going to have to repeat to him one of these days just to see his reaction, he was pretty, prettier than she was. But they looked right together. Like a couple.

The thought was so enthralling, and at the same time so shattering, that the tightness in her chest was suddenly almost painful.

He rinsed and spit.

Forget the mirror. Toothbrush in hand, she fixed him with a direct look. "What exactly did you mean when you said *'You like getting fucked . . . Remember that'?*"

Glancing sideways at her, he responded, "That you like getting fucked?" Rinsing his toothbrush, he put it on the shelf over the sink.

"Uh-huh."

"Which, by the way, you do." Dropping a kiss on her shoulder and giving her a wicked smile through the mirror — despite the shiver that both the kiss and smile sent through her, she responded with a narrowing of her eyes — he headed toward the bedroom.

Charlie watched him go with a deepening frown. He might be beating a strategic retreat, but it wasn't going to help him long-term: they were going to talk whether he wanted to or not. Quickly she slapped on a little cherry ChapStick and did the world's fastest blow-dry of her hair because she hated going to bed with it damp. Then she picked up his watch from the back of the toilet where she'd deposited it on her original march to the shower, slid it onto her arm — it was the one piece of jewelry she was never without now — and followed him, turning off the bathroom light as she went. She'd left the overhead light on as she'd stalked through the bedroom earlier, but now only the bedside lamp was lit. The warm glow it cast over her pristine white bed faded the farther it stretched out into the big, high-ceilinged room with its white walls and dark wood floor. The ornate fireplace with the painting of a waterfall over it and her large mirrored dresser, at opposite ends of the room, were in shadow.

"It was the *'remember that'* part of what

you said that I was specifically referring to, and you know it." She paused in the bathroom doorway to look at him. He stood with his back to her in front of one of the long windows that flanked the fireplace, one hand pushing the drawn curtains a few inches aside as he looked out at the darkness that lay over her front yard and the street. The darkness that hid the serial killers she'd left behind on the mountain and — no, she wasn't going to think about that. Not now. Now dealing with that was someone else's responsibility, and she had other priorities — *an* other priority — that was hers alone. At her words, he let the curtain drop and turned to face her. Under different circumstances, a smoking-hot guy wearing nothing but a towel in her bedroom would have equaled distraction. "That sounded like you don't expect to be around to remind me. Then there was the *'Dudley's a good guy'* bit, when you've always been jealous of him." When he looked like he was going to protest, Charlie pointed an admonishing finger at him and added, "Don't even bother denying it. And the whole obsession with me finding a new line of work?" She paused and her eyes widened as she put it all together. "It's like you're trying to get me squared away for life without you." He said nothing, just folded his arms over his brawny bare chest and looked at her. His face was shuttered, unreadable. "That's it, isn't it? That's what you're doing. *Why?*"

Michael's lips compressed. "You know why." The tacit admission that she was right sent a bolt of fear through her.

"I know you can't keep this body. But you can still stay here in spirit form and we can —" Something in his face stopped her. The memory of the last time he'd possessed a body and how that had ended sent a shiver down her spine. "You're thinking you're going to be jerked straight back into Spookville when you have to leave Hughes's body, aren't you? And you're afraid you're not going to be able to get back again. But you got back this time. What makes you think you can't do it again?"

"I told you, it's getting harder." He started walking toward the bed. "Can we drop this? It's after two. Come on, let's go to bed. You've got to be out on your feet."

She headed toward him, bare feet padding across the smooth floor. No way was the conversation ending there. He was right, she *was* out on her feet, or at least she had been out on her feet until her fear for him had sent a spike of adrenaline shooting through her system. Now she was too anxious to be sleepy.

He was pulling the fluffy white comforter down, reaching for the top sheet, on his side of the bed. It jolted her to realize that there was a "his side of the bed." But since he'd started living with her, they'd developed a routine, even though in his ghostly state he'd usually stretched out on top of the covers and she'd been the one snuggling in between the sheets. There *was* a "his side of the bed," and she was just now discovering that she loved that there was. Her heart stuttered as she remembered the last seventeen days when she'd gone to bed alone, and how bereft she'd felt, then looked at him getting ready to climb into bed with her now. *This* was what she wanted. *He* was what she wanted.

And she couldn't have it. Couldn't have him. Not for keeps.

Her chest felt like it was being squeezed in a vise.

Reaching him, she put a gentle hand on his back as he pulled the top sheet down. She felt the warm sleekness of his skin, the flexing of the powerful muscles beneath.

"Michael. What happened in Spookville?"

He rounded on her, catching her wrist. His hand was big enough that it could circle her wrist with inches to spare, and strong enough that it felt as immovable as a shackle. A few inches farther up the arm he held, the heavy silver of his watch circling her slender forearm caught the light.

"Holy fucking Christ, you *are* a bulldog. You can't ever let anything go, can you?" His face looked tighter, his features more chiseled now with anger. "I already told you. A couple of times." Their eyes met, and his face softened fractionally. "All right, yes, unlike one of us who seems to be living in a damned Disney movie, I'm facing the reality that the next time I get sucked up in there I might not be able to get back. If that happens, *when* that happens, I want you to be able to go on with your life. I want you to be happy. I want you to be fucking *safe.*"

Her eyes widened. "You're being *noble.*"

He looked mildly revolted. "I am not being noble."

"Yes, you are. You're being noble." She drew in a breath as she zeroed in on an underlying truth that, now that she saw it, made perfect sense. "When I told you I loved you down there in the kitchen, it would have been easy for you to say it back. From your point of view, it would have been the smart, expedient thing to do. It would have made me happy, it would have gotten you laid." She paused, remembering that he had, in fact, ended up getting laid, before adding, "More quickly, and it wouldn't have cost you a thing. But you didn't say it, and the only reason I can see that you wouldn't have said it back was because you're being noble and you *do.*"

"Would you cut the 'noble' crap?" His voice was savage. His hand around her wrist had tightened, and his face was hard and dark. "I already told you I love you. What, did you miss that back there in the shower? I might not have twisted it all up in a pretty package with hearts and flowers, but that's because falling in love is such a stupid thing for you and me to do. You want the truth? I love you so fucking much it kills me to know that I can't have you, that I can't give you the life you want, that I can't do anything except make you miserable."

Her heart was suddenly thumping so hard that it felt like it was trying to beat its way out of her chest. Her mouth went dry. Her eyes were glued to his face. "You don't make me miserable."

"I will. When I go. And we both know I can't stay."

She took a breath. "You're here now."

His eyes were blacker than the blackest midnight as they held hers. Some indescribable emotion flickered across his face and was gone too fast for her to even try to identify it.

"I'm here now," he agreed.

Pulling her wrist free of his hold, she took the half-step forward needed to close the distance between them, slid her arms around his neck and kissed him, a slow, tender kiss with an eternity's worth of yearning in it. He kissed her back, his lips equally tender and slow — until they weren't. Until he made a harsh sound under his breath and his hold on her tightened, until he was crushing her against him, until his lips hardened, until he was kissing her like it was the most vital thing he'd ever done or ever would do. Then they went up in flames, both of them, and he took her to bed, where he said all the mushy things she was longing to hear and she said equally mushy things back, and he made love to her until at last, somewhere deep in the darkest stretch of the night, she fell into an exhausted sleep in his arms.

When Charlie awoke, she was alone in bed. Coming instantly alert as alarm slammed through her system, she sat straight up, looking around. The clock beside the bed read 5:47 a.m. She was naked and cool air whispered over her body, reminding her of that fact, and also that it was October and she hadn't yet turned on the furnace, which she needed to do. The room was no longer the pitch dark that it had been after he'd turned out the light. Instead, it was a shadowy gray that spoke of daybreak. Gauzy fingers of light probed around the edges of the curtains, crept across the floor. Michael was nowhere in sight. The bathroom was dark and still. She was almost positive that he wasn't in there, either.

"Michael?" No answer.

Where was he? Oh, God, had he been snatched away during the night?

The beginnings of panic started to curl through her system, and Charlie realized that this kind of sudden-onset fear was going to be a staple of her life until, inevitably, one day what she feared most would happen and he would be gone.

But that day was probably not today, not right now. He was almost certainly somewhere on the premises. They still had time.

Please God, let us still have time.

Having just sent that fervent plea skyward, she was swinging her legs over the side of the bed to go in search of him when the unmistakable smell of coffee reached her.

Inhaling, she felt an immediate easing of tension: the kitchen. He was in the kitchen. She got out of bed, snagged her blue terry-cloth robe from the hook inside the closet door, pulled it on, and went into the bathroom, where she washed her face and brushed her teeth and hair. Looking at herself in the mirror as she quickly applied a little blush and a slick of lip gloss, she compared her face now with her face last night. Last night she'd looked pale and tense and exhausted. This morning, despite the limited amount of sleep she'd gotten and the lingering images of yesterday's horrors and all she had coming up today, she was bright-eyed and glowing. In fact, she looked like — a woman in love. Which was what she was, completely and irretrievably. A total disaster, and she knew it, and she was so idiotically happy anyway she wanted to kick herself.

Leaving the bathroom, she quickly put on jeans and a loose black pullover to look for Michael.

"Michael?" she called as she went down the stairs. No answer. She frowned.

The rest of the house was as dark and shadowy as the bedroom, but the smell of coffee drew her straight to the kitchen. The shades were open, filling the kitchen with the muted light of a fresh dawn, and there was coffee brewing in the coffeemaker, plus an empty cup and a new PowerBar wrapper on the counter. But no sign of Michael.

The sense of rightness that seeing those simple things gave her was just wrong, she knew. But knowing that he'd made himself breakfast in her kitchen felt right anyway.

She was getting ready to check the other downstairs rooms when she glanced out the window and saw him.

He was standing near her tall sunflowers with his back to her as he looked at the heavily wooded mountainside rising steeply beyond the fence. There was dew on the grass and a little bit of mist rising up from the ground. He was dressed in the same white shirt and gray suit pants as yesterday. They looked rumpled but dry, and she could only imagine he'd thrown them in the dryer after she'd fallen asleep. Something about the way he was standing there, with his hands thrust deep into his pants pockets and a slight slump to his broad shoulders, made her feel anxious all over again. Whatever he was thinking about, it clearly wasn't anything good.

Charlie slid her feet into the garden clogs she kept near the back door and went outside to join him. He didn't hear her, or if he did he didn't turn around. The air was fresh and crisp, bordering on cold, and she shivered a little as she walked across the grass. The yard was still shadowy. Shades of pink and orange were just beginning to streak the sky, which was turning from gray to lavender. From the corner of her eye she caught a glimpse of Pumpkin, tail swishing, crouched on the Powells' back porch. A rooster crowed on the other side, in Mrs. Norman's yard. The noise was unexpected enough to startle her.

She must have made a sound then, because Michael turned around and spotted her. Unsmiling, with shadows lying all around him and mist rising at his feet, he looked big, powerful, and a little bit dangerous. And so handsome, so just exactly what she had always wanted, that it made her breath hitch.

Then she saw that he had one of her big yellow sunflowers, which he'd obviously just picked, in his hand.

As she reached him he held it out to her. Her heart turned over.

She took it, met his eyes, raised it to her nose, and smiled at him over it.

"You threw your clothes in the dryer?" she asked, and he nodded.

"Shoes are squelching wet, though," he said.

"Oh?" she asked as he reached for her. She was already lifting her mouth to meet his as he drew her into his arms.

They kissed like they never meant to stop until Charlie sensed that they were not alone, a split second before a female voice gasped, "Charlie?"

Pulling her mouth from Michael's, glancing around in surprise, Charlie discovered Tam staring at her in horror from right inside the backyard gate.

Chapter Twenty

"Tam!" Still wrapped in Michael's arms, Charlie greeted her friend with a combination of surprise and delight, while Michael stiffened and muttered, "Holy hell, the voodoo priestess," just loudly enough to reach Charlie's ears. Ignoring that, Charlie continued with, "What are you doing here?"

Tamsyn Green was a young, strikingly glamorous thirty-five. One of the few who knew about Charlie's ability to see the newly, violently dead, she not only knew *about* Michael, she actually knew him. Not so long ago, she had brought him back from the brink of being terminated, despite deep misgivings, and had warned that it wouldn't be possible to do again. Her deep red hair hung in long, loose waves just past her shoulders and she had big brown eyes, alabaster skin, and a va-va-voom figure that combined voluptuous breasts with a tiny waist and long, shapely legs. Her slim, attractive face with its high cheekbones, aquiline nose, and full mouth looked as tired as Charlie had ever seen it. In a chic, waist-length wool jacket in a vibrant mustard hue, a clingy orange top, chocolate slacks with high-heeled boots, and a ton of gold jewelry, she looked as vivid as the sun despite the purplish shadows that still hung over the backyard. As Charlie looked at her, she felt a flutter of wild hope. If anybody could help keep Michael out of Spookville, it was Tam. While she wasn't the voodoo priestess Michael called her, she was actually the daughter of an extremely powerful voodoo priestess, whom Charlie had seen work incredible spells.

Ignoring Charlie's question, Tam abandoned a roller suitcase that Charlie had only just noticed and strode toward them, her eyes fixed on Michael.

"Spirit!" Tam's voice was harsh. Her subsequent expression made it clear that any doubts she might have harbored concerning Michael's identity were instantly erased by his answering frown, and her alarmed gaze shifted to Charlie. "Cherie, something is very wrong. This isn't possible. He can't be here."

As she spoke, she was stretching out a hand to Charlie as if to grab her and pull her away from Michael.

"Hello to you, too," Michael said, while Charlie disengaged herself from his arms and, careful not to crush the sunflower she still held, gave Tam a hug, only to immediately find herself engulfed in a subtle sandalwood-based perfume.

"I'm so glad you're here," Charlie told her as Tam returned her hug without ever taking her eyes off Michael's face. "You're the person I most wanted to see."

"In the After, he was nowhere where I could find him." Tam was sounding faintly stunned as Charlie let her go, and was looking at Michael as if he was seriously freaking her out. "He was being terminated. He should have been terminated by now. That's the only reason I wouldn't have been able to sense him."

"So that would make me, what, the ghost of a ghost?" Michael's voice was dry.

Tam was looking at him like he'd grown a second head. "There is no such thing!"

Knowing humor wasn't big on Tam's list of virtues, Charlie rushed to try to explain the situation. "He was able to get away. He has a twin brother — Rick Hughes. Michael borrowed his body to save me from a — bad situation."

"Another serial killer," Michael explained.

As Tam frowned — she and Michael were on the same page about Charlie's work with serial killers — Charlie continued as if she hadn't been interrupted. "And now he's afraid that he'll be sucked back into Spookville when he has to exit the body and he won't be able to get out again." She caught Michael's hand and tugged him forward to stand beside her as she looked at Tam beseechingly. "Can you help us? Keep him here, I mean? I know the body probably has to go, but if we could just find a way to keep him out of Spookville . . ."

She had said "probably" because it occurred to her that the ideal solution would be for Michael to stay in Hughes's body. What did it say about her moral compass that she was even willing to entertain the possibility? Charlie didn't care to look too deeply. But at that point, the terrible truth was she was so desperate to keep Michael with her that the morality of whatever it might take to get the job done barely entered into it.

Michael said, "Babe, there's nothing she can do."

Charlie shot him a fierce look. "You don't know that."

Tam finally tore her eyes from Michael's face to look at Charlie. She shook her head.

"Cherie, he may be right. I can possibly keep him from getting borne away into the Dark Place. But now that he's been slated for termination his situation is very different than it was when all we had to do was close the portal. Since he obviously somehow escaped from the *executeurs,* his best hope is that they won't come looking for him. But if they do . . ."

Her voice trailed off.

Charlie felt her lungs constrict. She worked hard to keep breathing. Until that moment, she hadn't realized how much she'd counted on Tam being able to help. But the realization that Spookville might not be the worst of Michael's problems made her blood run cold. Something of what she was feeling must have shown in her face, because Michael's hand tightened on hers. He stood close enough to her that their bodies brushed, and the electric tingle that his touch always engendered in her arced from his body to hers. It was suddenly bittersweet.

"It's okay," he told her, and as she glanced up at him in instant rebuttal — *it is not okay* — he carried her hand that was entwined with his to his mouth and kissed the back of it. Charlie felt the warm brush of his lips on her skin all the way down to her toes. It was such a romantic gesture, and at such odds with his tough-guy persona, and done in front of Tam, too, that Charlie was knocked a little sideways. She looked at his handsome head bent over her hand, and her heart skipped a beat. No, a whole series of beats. *Oh, my God, I am so in love with him.* Panic threatened to consume her at the thought, and she had to work to beat it back. He said, "Don't worry about it. We're fine for now."

For now.

The words were both comforting and terrifying. Charlie took comfort in reminding herself, *We still have time.* And refused to allow herself to even dwell on the question of how much.

Tam was watching the pair of them with a troubled expression. "I'll look into this and see what I can do," she said, catching Charlie's eyes. By "look into it," Charlie knew Tam probably meant that she would talk to her mother. "You know that I think your feelings for him are insane. He's one thing, you're another. The dead and the living don't mix. And now he shouldn't even exist. But you're my dear friend, and you" — she speared Michael with a glance — "saved my life. I don't forget that, believe me. If there's anything I can do to help you, I will."

"I'd be grateful," Michael said, and he and Tam exchanged measuring looks while Charlie said, "Thanks, Tam," with a renewed spurt of hope.

"Don't thank me yet." Tam was still looking at Michael.

"Come on in." Recalled to a sense of where they were by another exuberant cock-a-doodle-doo from Mrs. Norman's yard, Charlie dropped Michael's hand to usher Tam toward the house. "Not that I'm not glad to see you — actually, I am, I'm thrilled — but, once again, what are you doing here?"

"What do you think I'm doing here? I'm here because of you, of course." Tam's tone was acerbic. "I've never seen anybody get herself in so much trouble, by the way. It's ridiculous. And terrifying. One thing after another, all the time."

"Yep," Michael chimed in, on his way to picking up Tam's suitcase. Charlie sent an evil glance his way.

As they entered the house Tam continued, "I've been having a bad feeling about you for the last few days. Yesterday it got much worse. I saw a black cloud around you, and I felt you were in terrible danger. I tried to call, but your phone kept going to voice mail. The bad feeling kept getting worse and worse, and then I turned on the TV only to learn that you'd been taken hostage in a prison escape."

"Oh, no." Charlie winced at the thought, had another one — *I have to call my mother and let her know I'm all right* — and then concentrated on listening to Tam, who kept talking as Charlie headed into the kitchen.

"So I hopped a red-eye flight that landed about an hour ago, rented a car, and here I am." Tam finished by fixing Charlie with a frowning look.

"You must be exhausted," Charlie sympathized. "Did you get any sleep at all?"

"No. And I'm still having that feeling about you, by the way. That black-cloud feeling. You seem perfectly safe, and yet it hasn't gone away."

Giving it a discreet sniff — sunflowers really have no smell, but it was big and beautiful and Michael had given it to her, which was the part that gave her butterflies in her stomach — Charlie put the sunflower in a glass of water and snagged a couple of cups from the cabinet as she listened.

"Maybe it's a residual feeling," she suggested, pouring coffee in both cups. "Left over from me being held hostage yesterday."

"Or maybe it's because of Gorgeous Ghost Guy." Tam's tone was sour as she hitched herself onto a stool at the counter and curled her fingers around the cup of coffee Charlie handed her. "FYI, that sappy smile that's been on your face ever since you smelled that flower makes me want to hurl."

Checking herself, Charlie discovered that she was indeed smiling. Probably sappily. Over the flower. Okay, now she'd stopped. "I'm not in danger from Michael."

Tam paused in the act of chugging coffee to make a skeptical sound. "Maybe not physically. Cherie —"

She broke off as Michael stepped through the back door with her bag. The silence, coupled with Charlie's or Tam's or both of their expressions, must have been telltale, because Michael looked from one to the other of them, raised his eyebrows at Charlie, and said, "You talking about me?"

"Maybe," she said, and smiled at him.

"Oh, my God, I *am* going to puke," Tam muttered, and Charlie shot her a look. Then Charlie said to Michael, "Would you take that up to the guest bedroom, please?" before confirming with Tam by asking, "You're staying here, right?"

Grimacing at her where Michael couldn't

see, Tam nodded. Then, as Michael headed down the hall with her suitcase, Tam added under her breath, "Unless I'm interrupting the honeymoon."

Charlie made a face at her.

After she'd filled Tam in on everything that had happened with help from the occasional, usually annoying-to-Charlie interjection from Michael and he'd told Tam about the NARSAD and Tam had exclaimed over it and they'd all eaten scrambled eggs — "No bread?" Tam had protested — and PowerBars and coffee, and Charlie had left her mother a voice-mail message and they'd moved to the living room and turned on CNN to discover that the prison escape was, indeed, headline news and what was described as the "exhaustive search" of the mountain was still ongoing, Charlie called Tony. It wasn't quite eight a.m. She was afraid that if he'd been up most of the night in conjunction with the search she would wake him, which was why she hadn't called earlier. But he sounded completely alert, and Charlie learned that he, Lena, and Buzz were in fact in a car on their way back to Big Stone Gap.

"On TV it says the search is ongoing," Charlie said. "Have they found anybody?"

"Creech and Ruben have been recaptured,

and two of the teens rescued," Tony replied. "They both credit you with telling them to climb out a window and run when they got the chance, by the way."

It wasn't much of a counterbalance to the knowledge that the same advice had gotten Ben Snider killed, but it was something.

"What two teens?" Charlie asked. She could feel tension rising inside her.

Tony named two of the boys. "We're still hunting for Bree Hoyt, Trevor Frost, and Blake Armour. And Doyle, Torres, Ware, and Abell."

Trevor Frost was the small, scared-looking boy, Charlie remembered. Blake Armour was the kid who'd told Paris she was too fat to make it out a window.

"Do you think they're all still on the mountain?" Charlie felt sick at the idea that those kids were somewhere at the mercy of the animals she knew the three missing serial killers to be. Or worse, they were dead.

"It's possible," Tony replied. "The locals tell me that there are lots of caves, lots of nooks and crannies where their thermal imaging equipment and the rest of that high-tech stuff might not be effective, so they're searching on foot, too, which is what's taking so long. And if anybody's dead, thermal imaging would be ineffective.

But it's equally possible that at least one or two of those guys managed to escape the net."

"What about the pickup truck? Has anybody found the pickup truck?" she asked.

"No sign of it. Which is another reason why I think they might have made it past the roadblocks. The search is being expanded, and I'd have a BOLO out on the pickup except we have no idea what it looks like. Think you have anything in those files of yours that could help us pinpoint where the serial killers in the group are likely to head?"

"Yes," Charlie said, trying to recall as much of the three men's files as she could. Doyle she knew nothing about.

"Thought so." Tony was smiling, she could tell. "We're meeting Warden Pugh and a team of investigators in the prison library at ten. You could meet us there, give us your insights."

"I'll be there," Charlie said. "Did you get any sleep at all?"

"They set up some cots. Crane, Kaminsky, and I took turns sacking out. What about you? No trouble with Hughes?"

"No, no trouble," Charlie answered. In fact, she was looking right at "Hughes." She was in the kitchen, talking on the landline because her cell phone was sleeping with the fishes, and he'd just walked in from the living room, where he'd been watching more of the escape coverage on TV. Crossing his arms over his chest, he leaned a broad shoulder against the refrigerator and frowned as he listened to her. "I'll see you at ten. Bye."

When she hung up, Michael looked at her.

"I'm meeting Tony at the prison library at ten," she told him, and repeated the gist of what Tony had told her.

He didn't say anything.

"What?" she asked defensively.

"You know what," he said.

She sighed. She did know what, and it wasn't jealousy over Tony. It was the serial killer thing.

"I'm thinking about it," she said. "But this is important. I can use what I know to help people. I can save lives."

"You can also get yourself killed." The look he gave her was stone-cold serious. He straightened away from the refrigerator to grasp her upper arms. "Babe, I know you suffered a childhood trauma. A bad one. But you get over it, you move on. You don't spend your whole life wallowing in it, replaying it, trying to make it right. The hair of the dog that bit you? Forget that. The important thing to remember there is that the dog bit you. Sooner or later it'll do it again."

"Hear, hear," Tam said as she entered the kitchen in time to overhear, and gave Michael an approving look. "Really, cherie, much as it hurts me to say it, Ghost Boy's right."

"You're double-teaming me," Charlie protested, frowning from one to the other of them. "Not fair!"

"Yeah, we're double-teaming you," Michael said. "Which should tell you something."

"It should," Tam agreed.

Charlie rolled her eyes. "It does, all right? When I get this project wrapped up maybe I'll take all my research and write a book on serial killers or something. That sound safe enough for you?"

"Gets my vote," Michael said, and Tam said, "Mine, too. Although the frequent-flyer miles involved in me rushing to your rescue are nice."

Charlie made a face at Tam. "But in the meantime I'm supposed to be at the prison at ten because armed killers with child hostages are out there on the loose somewhere, and I can help find them. I'm going to go upstairs and change clothes now, and then if you'll give us a ride, Tam, we'll take Michael by the inn where his body has a room so he can change so that everybody won't realize he spent last night with me. Then if you would drive us both up to the prison, we can get our cars. Well, I can get mine, and Michael can get the Mustang Shelby GT that Hughes drives."

"A Shelby?" The look on Michael's face was pure masculine appreciation for a cool car.

"Yes," Charlie replied, while Tam said, "Fine by me. As long as I can nap after that."

"Absolutely you can nap," Charlie told her.

At some point during the conversation her hands had come to rest flat against Michael's chest without her even really being aware of it. Now Charlie closed her fingers around the slightly stiff, slightly crumpled shirt, went up on tiptoe to plant a quick kiss on his hard mouth, then pulled away from him and left the kitchen, calling, "Back in ten," over her shoulder at them as she went.

Her kiss lingered on his mouth like honey.

Michael watched Charlie head down the

hall with an automatic stir of appreciation for the sweet curve of her ass; for her long, slim legs in their jeans; for the slender lines of her back; for the utterly feminine way she moved. The copper highlights in her hair glinted in the first beams of sunlight coming through the windows before she disappeared from his view.

By then his pulse rate had jacked itself up, his gut had tightened, and his heart felt like it was being impaled on a skewer.

He was crazy about the woman, so stupidly smitten that he would have laughed and jeered if he'd watched it happen to somebody else.

Just as he'd always suspected, being "in love" blew.

He didn't want to lose her.

There wasn't any choice.

He was still looking after Charlie and harboring increasingly grim thoughts when he felt the weight of someone's gaze on his face. Turning his head sharply to seek the source, he found the voodoo priestess watching him.

Damn, he'd forgotten she was even there.

"She'll be twenty minutes at least," he said easily. He'd always been good at keeping his thoughts hidden, and he wasn't about to start being bad at it now.

The voodoo priestess — Tam — nodded. Her eyes were fixed on his face, and they were getting a kind of glazed look in them that he didn't much like.

"I'm going to walk on over to the Pioneer Inn and change while Charlie's changing," he said, coming around the edge of the counter to head toward the back door. "If you can wait for her, then drive over and pick me up there, that'd be good."

Tam was perched on the stool at the end of the row, and to get out of the kitchen he had to walk right by her. She never took her eyes off him the whole time, and as he headed past her she reached out and grabbed his arm.

"Wait," she ordered in a throbbing voice. He was so surprised that he stopped to look down at her. Her grip tightened until her nails dug into his skin. Her eyes blazed at him. "*Mon dieu,* Spirit, what have you done?"

CHAPTER TWENTY-ONE

Michael jerked his arm free of her hold. The look he gave her was both alarmed and borderline hostile.

"You were in the *lieu de la mort,*" Tam said. Her eyes were as shiny as glass as they met his. "You were in terrible pain, excruciating pain, being tortured endlessly. It felt like your flesh was being flayed from your bones. Like you were being burned alive. They were to terminate you, but they had to wait. Oh, you suffered! *I love you.* A whisper — the whisper is a shield. *Charlie. Don't hurt Charlie. I'll do anything. Please.* You're begging." Her words had become disjointed. She was speaking quickly, breathlessly, and he got the impression that she was seeing, not him, not Charlie's kitchen, but the icy horror of the place where he'd been imprisoned. "You made a bargain. You got to come back here, to her. For a little bit of time. To save her. In return, you gave up the shield. You have no defense against them now. They will come, and when they do you will be taken back to the *lieu de la mort* and instantly terminated. They have put on you *un mouchard* — a tracker. You have been injected with an *incendiaire* that will self-combust at the appointed time. It will destroy you. There is no possibility of escape."

She blinked, and the focus returned to her eyes. She was still looking at him wide-eyed, but the glassy blankness was gone.

The accuracy of what she'd said stunned him. Then he remembered what she was.

Damned psychics.

"There's nothing I can do," Tam said. It was her normal voice, maybe slightly breathless. She was fully focused on him now, and aware. Her eyes were dark with horror. "There's nothing anyone can do for you. You're done."

Well, he'd known it. He believed in miracles about as much as he believed in the Tooth Fairy.

"Stay the fuck out of my head," he told her, almost politely.

The snort she gave wasn't polite at all.

"I thought you couldn't read dead people," he said.

"You're in a body now. That gives me access. I still can't read everything, but an experience that strong, that powerful, that recent — I saw that."

"So you saw it. Keep it to yourself." His voice was gritty with warning.

"You must tell Charlie."

His Achilles' heel. He didn't want Charlie to know. He folded his arms over his chest, took a step back. "What makes you think I haven't?"

The look she gave him was scornful. She tapped her temple with a forefinger. "Hello, psychic here? Besides, she's too happy. Too hopeful. If she knew —"

The shudder with which she finished that sentence echoed his thoughts on the subject. If Charlie knew, she would be frantic. Pulling out all the stops to try to save him, which couldn't be done. And once he was taken, once he was terminated, she would be wild with grief. Beside herself. Inconsolable.

The thought of how she would grieve for him was worse than any torture. He'd felt her pain before. There wasn't much he wouldn't have done to spare her from it then, and there wasn't much he wouldn't do to protect her from it now. He might not be able to change what was going to happen to him, but he could keep her from ever finding out the full extent of it.

He said, "I don't want her to know."

She frowned. "I think she's going to notice when you aren't here anymore." The tinge of sarcasm in her voice faded as she looked at him. "She was — upset — the last time you disappeared. She had me searching all over the Beyond for you. This is going to hit her, oh, very hard."

"I know." He wasn't big on asking for favors. In fact, he never did it. But this was for Charlie. "I want her to think I just got sucked into Spookville again and can't get back. She'll miss me, but she'll get over it, and it won't be as hard on her as knowing I've been snuffed out of existence. If you wouldn't tell her any different, I'd appreciate it."

She was watching him closely. "You would spare her pain."

"Yes."

"You love her."

He didn't answer that. What he did or didn't feel for Charlie was between him and Charlie. Period.

Tam didn't push it. Instead she said, "You're not just going to vanish on her, are you? You do plan on telling her good-bye?"

He nodded. "When the time comes, I'm going to tell her I can feel that I'm getting ready to go, and I don't think I'll be coming back."

The thought of how she was going to react to that made his gut clench. But he couldn't just disappear without a word, and it was better than the truth. Even he, as inured to the idea of his own destruction as he had become, was having a hard time with the truth.

He wanted to stay.

Tam sucked in a breath. "How much time?"

He understood that to mean *How much time do you have left?* "They ain't real up on the fine points of time in the Dungeon of Doom, but I think about two more days."

"So soon." Her face clouded.

He knew just how she felt. "Will you keep my secret?"

She looked at him thoughtfully. She didn't like him, didn't trust him, didn't approve of him, but they'd had a meeting of the minds over Charlie: they both cared about her.

"Yes," she said. "I agree that it would be easier for her to believe that you're trapped in the Dark Place than to know that you no longer exist. But it's still going to be very difficult for her." She frowned at him. "You should not have made her care about you."

Like he'd seen it coming. Like he'd meant

to. Like he'd intentionally waited until after he'd died to fall in love. Whoever it was who'd said life's a bitch didn't know the half of it. Death was the bitch's bigger, badder sister.

"I'm heading over to the Pioneer Inn now," he said.

The voodoo priestess didn't say anything else, but he could feel her eyes on his back as he walked out the door.

Tam was in the downstairs bathroom when Charlie reached the bottom of the stairs. Dressed in her workwear staple of black pants and a black blazer with a color-of-the-day blouse — today's was sapphire — and tiny silver hoops in her ears that were her only jewelry besides Michael's watch, she was a little stiff as she waited for the Advil to kick in; a lot saddened by the loss of so many lives yesterday; terrified for the still missing teens; resolved to do everything she could to help locate Abell, Torres, and Ware; worried about Michael — and still so fricking happy it was embarrassing.

Because she was in love with a dead man, and he loved her back.

Professional diagnosis: *They make padded rooms for people like you.*

Tam must have heard her in the hall,

because she called through the bathroom door, "Triple G decided to walk to the inn to change. We're supposed to pick him up there. He just left, so we've got a few."

"Triple G?" Charlie asked before she got it.

"Gorgeous Ghost Guy," Tam replied, confirming.

"Okay," Charlie called back, and went on into the kitchen, debating the wisdom of consuming one more cup of coffee. Once again she'd gotten very little sleep, but this kind of lack of sleep she could live with. Definitely. Long-term. Like, say, forever. She was smiling — probably sappily — at the sunflower bobbing in its glass when her attention was caught by the ongoing drama in her backyard.

Mrs. Norman's prized white hens were scratching for food under her sunflowers again, and Pumpkin was crouched maybe six feet away, watching them.

Charlie hurried outside to prevent catastrophe while she could. Scooping up Pumpkin before he could succumb to what she could only feel were his regrettably violent tendencies, Charlie was just saying, "What, did they lock you out for the day?" to him in a commiserating tone when a hand clamped down over her mouth and she was jerked back hard against a hulking male body.

Terror and shocked recognition stabbed through her even before Pumpkin tumbled from her arms, even before a horribly familiar voice said with false affability, "Morning, Dr. Stone."

Abell! She was instantly icy with dread. Her stomach dropped like an elevator in free-fall. Her heart seized up.

A gun poked into her rib cage.

Her pulse leaped to instant warp speed as he shoved her ahead of him toward the gate.

"We're going next door," he said. "Walk, or I'll shoot you right here."

Charlie knew Abell, knew what he was capable of. She had no doubt whatsoever that he meant it. The "next door" he was pushing her toward was the Powells'. She walked through her gate and another one, into the Powells' backyard and up their steps, while her heart pounded and her insides jellied and her mind raced. A thousand thoughts and images fought for supremacy — Pumpkin out on the Powells' back porch so early that morning: *Should have realized there was something odd about that;* Glory Powell with her new braces: *Don't let him have hurt her;* Abell shooting the guards on the bus through the head; *Mi-*

chael, Michael, Michael — but she thrust them aside as she frantically searched for something, some tidbit of information or ace-in-the-hole survivor maneuver that she could use to save herself.

Her heart palpitated as she realized she was coming up with zilch.

Tam would miss her almost right away. Tam might even have seen — no, if Tam had seen her being grabbed and taken away, Tam would have come bursting out the door yelling at the top of her lungs and would probably have gotten herself, and Charlie, too, killed on the spot. But Tam was psychic.

Help. Concentrating as hard as she could, Charlie tried beaming a message to Tam.

"Keep walking," Abell growled as he forced Charlie through the Powells' back door into their warm, bright, surprisingly noisy kitchen. A single half-eaten bowl of cereal sat on the table, a small TV on the counter was turned to CNN, and the kitchen curtains were open. Charlie saw at a glance that whoever had been eating the cereal at the table would have had a view of her backyard that was obstructed only by the fence between the properties. It wasn't much of a stretch to assume that the person eating at the table had been Abell, and that he had seen her come outside after

Pumpkin. A knot formed in her chest as she realized that there was no sign of the Powells. Any of them.

"Please don't kill me, please don't kill me, please don't kill me." The shriek came from behind Charlie, and as it tore through the TV's noise she jumped reactively in Abell's hold. His gun jabbed harder into her rib cage in retaliation for her sudden movement, but she scarcely noticed it.

The spirit of the chaperone from the school bus — Tabitha Grunwald — appeared out of nowhere, dropping to her knees in the middle of the kitchen floor, clasping her hands in front of her as she begged for her life. Her crisp gray curls and attractive, middle-aged face, pale and drawn now with fear, her flowered dress, the paper bag still clutched in her hand, were as vividly real as they had been in life. She was crying, her face tilted up in supplication — and Charlie could only watch in horror as her face disintegrated into a red, pulpy mass that was the stuff of nightmares between one second and the next. Then she disappeared.

By the time she did, Charlie felt as if her nerves were trying to jump through her skin.

Tabitha Grunwald had clearly attached

herself to her killer in the moment of her death.

"I said *walk.*" Voice harsh with impatience, Abell, who of course had seen nothing spectral, shoved Charlie toward a closed door at the far end of the kitchen. Oh, God, Tabitha Grunwald's appearance had distracted her, robbed her of vital seconds when she should have been trying something, anything, to attract attention or get away. Like, say, snatch up the cereal bowl and hurl it through the window? Who'd notice? Punch Abell in the nose and try to bolt? He was holding her too tightly for her to even attempt it, and if she did attempt it he would blow a hole through her before her fist could begin to connect. A set of knives in a wooden block on the counter near the door caught her eye. But they were too far away now. Why hadn't she noticed them when he'd first pushed her inside? Why — ?

Tam. Help.

They were at the door. Abell said, "Open it."

Hands shaking, Charlie did as he said.

The door led to the basement. The Powells' house was newer than hers, a 1950s-era bungalow, but the basement had that damp, musty smell of old basements everywhere, and that was what hit her first. Second, it was dark, not pitch black but gloomy, especially in contrast to the sunny kitchen. Abell's hand dropped away from her mouth to fist in the back of her jacket as he pushed her into the stairwell. Trying to break away and run for it wasn't an option. He blocked the doorway behind her, and he was the approximate size of King Kong. Her heart hammered like it was trying to knock its way out of her chest. She could hear her pulse thundering in her ears.

The only semicoherent thought that flashed through her head was: *Basement bad.*

"Move," he said, and shoved the gun into her spine.

With her mouth sour with fear, she went down the stairs.

They were gray-painted planks, no risers between them. The floor she was approaching was poured concrete. The walls were raw concrete block. It was, she saw as she reached the lower steps, one room about half the size of the footprint of the house, with a furnace and a washer and dryer and boxes and — Melissa and Glory Powell, each tied to one of the separate metal poles that supported the unfinished ceiling. Their mouths were sealed with duct tape, and they were sitting on the floor with their hands zip-tied behind the pole against which they leaned. Melissa was wearing a blue nightgown, Glory pink pajamas. Melissa's short hair was standing on end. Glory's hair was in twin braids, one of which had unraveled. Their faces were utterly white and exhausted-looking. There was no sign of Brett Powell. Charlie prayed that wasn't a bad thing.

Her eyes slid from Melissa's tense face to Glory's. Thc girl's brown eyes were huge with fright. She had been crying. Tear tracks were still evident on her cheeks.

The air was thick with fear.

Charlie was suddenly freezing, a bone-deep cold that had nothing to do with the basement's slight chill. Her hands fisted at her sides. Her palms were damp, she discovered as her nails dug into them.

I have to help them. I have to help me.

"I explained to your neighbors that I really came here for you," Abell said, shoving Charlie forcefully away from him as they reached the bottom of the stairs. "But you had a guy spend the night at your place, so I had to find accommodations elsewhere."

Charlie pitched up against the washing machine and whipped around to face him, her hands resting on the cool metal surface as she tried to get her bearings. She was breathing too hard, and she tried to control that. *Be calm.* Even if Tam wasn't catching her psychic messages, Tam would miss her. Tam would search, call for help. What Charlie knew she needed to do, first and foremost, was stall for time. The situation was beyond bad. She had no doubt at all that Abell meant to kill her, and Glory and Melissa, too, although if they were still alive it must mean that he had a use for them.

But he'd come here for *her.* To kill *her.*

There was only one way that was even remotely possible.

Ask him about it. Get him to talk.

"You were in the trunk of the patrol car that brought me home last night, is that it?" she asked, trying to sound much cooler than she felt. She could feel goose bumps rippling to life all across the surface of her skin. Her throat was dry with fear. But delay was her friend. *Delay, delay.*

She tried not to remember how quickly and unceremoniously he'd ended the blond prison guard's life. Like now, his gun had been in his hand. He'd simply jerked it up and . . .

Oh, God, please. Tam.

Abell looked at her with surprise. "You're smart. Yeah, I was in the trunk. I was also in the back of that truck that brought you down the mountain."

Melissa and Glory sat perfectly still. Their eyes darted between her and Abell. She could feel their rising terror like a vibration in the air.

Try reasoning with him.

"Are you afraid of what I know about you, Mr. Abell? Is that what this is about? Because everything I know is written down in my files. Even without me, the authorities have access to it all."

He snorted. "You think I don't know how the *authorities* work? They've got so much information on me that it'll take them months to get to your files. But you — you can just tell them. And I need time to grab my daughter and get away."

Charlie felt her stomach twist. "You're going to take Heidi with you?"

"She's my little girl. Of course, that bitch of an ex-wife of mine had her second husband adopt her. She's not even listed on any of the records as mine anymore. But I made a mistake and told you. Once you mentioned my daughter, I wasn't letting you off that damned bus alive. When you got off anyway, I had to track you. I was going to kill you the first chance I got, but you were always with that guy." He frowned. "That guy — who the hell is he? He looks like —"

Charlie seized on that, and was getting ready to say *He's Michael Garland, the guy you knew on death row,* was getting ready to play the a-dead-guy-is-stalking-you card in hopes of rattling him, of throwing him off his game, of at least keeping him talking when he said, "I don't give a shit," and glanced at Glory. "Shut your eyes, cutie pie."

Charlie's heart lurched with horrified realization.

Here it comes.

"No, no, no," she stuttered. Panic surged in an icy tide through her veins as Abell's hand holding the gun jerked up. He aimed right between her eyes and —

Screaming, Charlie threw herself to one side.

But the gun didn't fire. Instead, Abell seemed to freeze. His eyes widened. Then he toppled like a felled oak, pitching forward to smack the floor with his face.

CHAPTER TWENTY-TWO

For a split second Charlie stared at Abell's sprawled body in stupefaction. He lay unmoving, his eyes still open, his gun still in his hand. She was as sure as it was possible to be without actually checking that he was dead. A brown-handled knife stuck out of the back of his neck right below the base of his skull. Blood was just beginning to well up around the blade.

It didn't require an expert knowledge of anatomy to conclude that his spinal cord had been severed.

Abruptly her knees gave out. Legs folding beneath her, she sat down hard on the basement floor.

Michael came down the stairs, stepped over Abell with no more than a cursory glance, bent to pluck the dead man's gun out of his hand, and then headed straight for her, tucking the gun into the small of his back as he came. Glory, who like her mother had been frozen in place, drew her legs back out of his way with a quick scrambling movement that spoke of fear. Her eyes on Glory, Melissa made a muffled sound of distress. Grim-faced and intimidatingly large in that enclosed space, Michael paid no attention to either of them.

"It's all right," Charlie said to them. Her voice was clear, if a little high-pitched. The surprise was that she could talk at all. On the inside, she was shaking like a paint mixer. If she had any muscles, they were concealing their existence well. "He's a friend."

Michael loomed over her, distracting her attention from her neighbors as she tilted her head back to see his face.

"We gotta stop meeting like this," he said. The words may have been jokey, but his tone wasn't. It was grim.

She looked up at him. His mouth was tight with anger. His face was hard with it.

She said, "Was that one of the Powells' kitchen knives?"

He nodded.

"What happened to the gun you took off Fleenor?" She was trying to sound normal, trying to keep it calm and controlled, trying to keep the waves of reaction that were hitting her at bay.

"I left it in the top drawer of your nightstand. Dumb of me not to realize I might need it to shoot a serial killer who was trying to off you in your next-door neighbor's house in broad daylight, I know." The bite in his tone hadn't abated. He hunkered down in front of her, and she got a good look at his eyes. They were leaping with emotion, blazing at her. She could feel the heat of his anger and fear for her coming off him like sun rays.

She would have held out her arms to him except she was pretty sure she couldn't lift them. She wanted to swallow to try to get rid of the tightness in her throat, but she couldn't do that, either. "How did you find me?"

"I was all the way down at the end of the street when I heard Tam outside screaming your name. I ran back, got told you'd disappeared, did the frantic look-all-around thing, saw the cat scratching at your neighbor's back door, and rolled the dice. You came up lucky one more time." His voice was as grim as his face. His eyes were moving over her. She was hoping he couldn't tell what an absolute mess she was inside — but she was pretty sure he could.

She offered him a placating little smile. "Okay, now I am so totally going to write that book."

"You better," he growled, and gathered her into his arms, kissing her cheek and then her mouth with brief hard kisses. Regaining enough control over her muscles to wrap her arms around his neck, Charlie was enjoying being crushed in his arms and kissed until, over his shoulder, she saw the mist that she dreaded start to rise up out of Abell's body. She sucked in a breath, staring. Michael must have registered that, because he looked swiftly around in time to see the vapor form itself into Abell's spirit, which was an exact replica of how Abell had looked in life. Michael stiffened as he saw and recognized Abell, and realized what was happening, but before he could do anything else Abell looked behind him and screamed, an otherworldly shriek that made the hair on the back of Charlie's neck catapult upright. Then Abell bolted across the basement floor as if all the hounds of hell were after him, which they probably were, only to vanish when he reached the far wall.

Charlie shuddered.

"Fucking freak show," Michael muttered in her ear as he scooped her up and stood up with her. His words eased the sudden, reactive spike in her supernatural-exposure-induced tension. God, how great was it to have someone in her life who could actually see the same things she saw? And also, how much did she like the fact that he could just pick her up like that? That last had to be some atavistic female reaction, and she was so going to keep it to herself, she decided as he started walking with her, clearly meaning to carry her out of the basement. Some things he did not need to know.

Melissa and Glory were looking up at the two of them, wide-eyed. To Michael Charlie said, "Wait, you need to free them," meaning the Powells. At the same time she saw Tam, wide-eyed, on the stairs, and heard a commotion as if many people had suddenly burst into the kitchen.

"I called the cops. They're here." Tam sounded breathless. Then Big Stone Gap's finest were clattering down the stairs and the basement was suddenly full of people.

Charlie was recounting her part in what had happened for what must have been the dozenth time, this time to a state police captain at the Powells' kitchen table, when Michael came up the stairs from the basement. As he stepped into the kitchen his eyes touched hers, slid over her, checking in with her, making sure she was all right. She smiled faintly at him in response. Two cops trailed behind him, no doubt asking what he'd seen and how he'd managed to kill Abell, probably for the dozenth time. It was unquestionably justifiable homicide and every law enforcement officer on the scene was full of admiration. The only exception was Tony, and by extension Lena and Buzz, who regarded "Rick Hughes" with barely veiled suspicion. Which was entirely her fault, Charlie knew.

Oh, what a tangled web we weave . . .

Charlie pulled her gaze away from Michael as a state police officer asked her another question.

Glory and Melissa had previously given their statements, and, after accepting Charlie's apology for bringing a serial killer to their door and thanking Michael over and over again for saving their lives, had been taken to the hospital to be checked out. Melissa had pressed a spare key into Charlie's hand and asked her to check on Pumpkin, who was at that moment sitting on the kitchen counter watching the proceedings, if they should be gone overnight. They'd been traumatized and were suffering from shock, but both were going to be okay. Brett Powell, who'd been away on a fishing trip, was rushing home to be with his wife and daughter. Abell's plan, which he'd talked about openly from the time he'd broken into the Powells' house in the small hours, had been to kill Charlie and then to head for Mobile, Alabama, where his daughter now lived. He'd intended to take the Powells' car, holding Glory at gunpoint while Melissa drove. Left unsaid was how soon he would have murdered the pair of them — Charlie bet relatively soon.

"I almost got them killed. I feel so bad about it," Charlie confessed in a low voice to Tam, who was sitting beside her, as the officer they'd been talking to put away his notebook and left the table. Leaving out the part about Tam being a psychic — nobody who didn't already know had been let in on that — they'd pretty much told the truth: that Charlie had gone out into the backyard, been grabbed by Abell, then been missed by Tam, who'd gone outside yelling for her. That in turn had brought Michael, who'd been out for an early-morning walk, running. As far as Charlie knew, no one had thought to ask where Michael had been walking from or to, and the fact that he was wearing the previous day's clothes, something that would only be apparent to Tony, Buzz, and Lena anyway, had seemingly passed unnoticed.

"You're a danger to yourself and others, cherie. Face facts," Tam's voice was equally low, but tart. "Lucky for you, a few of us love you anyway."

Charlie made a face at her. "Lucky for me, you're psychic. I was beaming messages to you the whole time."

Tam nodded complacently. "I know. I got them. Next time, try to be more specific about your location so I don't have to just run around outside screaming blindly for you."

"Got it: next time someone's trying to kill me I will beam you an address."

Tam made a face at her, and then Charlie was distracted by yet one more cop stopping to ask one more question.

In the aftermath of her encounter with Abell, Charlie was still feeling shaky. She had her hands clasped together on the table in front of her (the better to make sure that no one could see them tremble) and she'd been sitting at the table for longer than she normally would have done because she didn't quite trust her knees yet.

The house was crowded with law enforcement officers from so many agencies she couldn't keep them straight. The Virginia State Police were there in force, as were representatives from the local FBI along with what seemed to be most of the Big Stone Gap Police Department. Tony, Buzz, and Lena were in the basement with the local FBI and a couple of the ranking state police officers on the scene as the contents of Abell's pockets were gone through, his clothing was searched, and his shoes were removed so that any residue on the bottom of them could be analyzed in a search for any clue that might lead them to the whereabouts of the other escapees or the hostages. Until they'd gotten the call that he was in the Powells' house and dead, the cops had feared that Abell had one or more of the missing teens with him. With Abell's death that fear had been eliminated, but now it became more imperative than ever to find the remaining hostages. Bree was the consensus pick as the one Abell would have been most likely to zero in on. Now that he was dead, the possibility loomed large in investigators' minds that he'd left her tied up or imprisoned somewhere, never to be found. That wasn't likely, as Charlie told them: Abell never would have left her behind alive. All anyone could do was pray that Bree had managed to escape, or that one of the other escapees had her. They had the same concerns about the missing boys, although it was felt that Abell would have been less likely to target them. Still, all three teens were out there somewhere, along with the three remaining escapees. More home-invasion scenarios like this one, carjackings, random murders, and hostage takings haunted the thoughts of the investigators tasked with recovering the hostages and bringing the fugitives in.

Charlie had already told them that while she didn't know anything about Doyle, she felt that Torres and Ware would stick together, and that Torres would be the leader and would head for his native Matamoros, Mexico. He'd been jonesing for a Whataburger during their last session, so she felt it was highly likely that he would stop by one of the chain's restaurants. She also told them that she had no doubt that the pair would kill anyone who got in their way, and that she felt sure that Torres would have taken one or more of the hostages with him if it had been possible for him to do so. As a result of her information, BOLOs had been issued along every route heading south, and patrol cars sent to stake out every Whataburger along the two or three most likely routes, even as the search of the mountain continued.

Tony emerged from the basement, followed by Lena and Buzz. Charlie smiled at him, but he wasn't paying any attention to her and didn't see. Instead he was focused exclusively on Michael, who was still talking to the other cops. As Tony stopped beside Michael with Buzz hovering at his elbow, Lena came on over to join Charlie and Tam, whom the three FBI agents knew from a previous case. Michael finished his conversation with the cops. As they moved away, he was left alone with Tony and Buzz.

Charlie was suddenly very interested in listening in on that conversation.

"So where exactly did you learn to throw a knife like that?" Tony asked Michael. Charlie didn't even have to strain her ears to hear him. Tony's voice wasn't loud, but there was a quality to it that made it carry. A hard quality, like he was talking to a suspect.

"It's a hobby of mine. I practice a lot," Michael replied, perfectly bland.

"That's quite a skill set you have. Throwing knives, breaking necks." Tony's body language was all cop. Like Michael, and Buzz and Lena, too, he was dressed in the same clothes he'd been wearing the day before, but unlike Michael Tony had managed a shave. "Quite a body count, too. Three killed in two days."

Michael said, "I'm just glad I was in the

right place at the right time to make a difference."

Charlie couldn't help it: her lips curved a little at that one. He sounded like a beauty contestant proclaiming that her greatest wish was world peace.

Lena was standing beside Charlie. She leaned close to whisper, "Bartoli thinks Hughes has to have had some advanced military training, but we can't find any record of it. And that was before he saw the knife in Abell's neck. Now he's going ape. He doesn't think there's any way a man with Hughes's background should have been able to do that."

"He saved my life. And Melissa and Glory Powell's. And Paris Troyan's," Charlie pointed out, as she had already done to Tony. "However he came by the skill set, I'm grateful."

Still whispering, Lena continued, "The boss says there's something wrong somewhere. He's got people looking into the serial killer angle you suggested. He thinks there's something to it."

Charlie barely stifled a sigh. That was exactly what she wanted, except for the cursed issue of timing.

"Umm," she said. So maybe she wasn't at her eloquent best. She'd had a trauma, damn it. And the Michael/Hughes situation was getting twisted beyond unraveling.

Lena said, "I just wanted to let you know. Because I've seen the way you're looking at him, and the way he's looking back. Not that I'd blame you for tapping that, I totally would, too, but given what we all suspect, you should probably be careful."

Charlie had to fight the urge to drop her head into her hands: she'd thought she was being discreet. Apparently not. Tam's eyes slid her way in silent commiseration. She'd clearly overheard. Denying that she had the slightest interest in Hughes occurred to Charlie, and had the advantage of being absolutely true, but would probably do more harm than good. *Least said, soonest mended* were actually good words to live by, she'd discovered. Lena was warning her out of the purest goodwill, she realized, which she took as another step forward in their building friendship, so Charlie did the only thing she could do.

She said, "Thanks. I appreciate you looking out for me," and smiled at Lena. Lena's brows snapped together, and she frowned back. *Ah, well. Baby steps.*

Tam said to Lena, "That was really nice of him to take your shift as well as his own last night and let you sleep an extra two hours." As Lena's frown darkened and Charlie's eyes widened, Tam's significant glance at Buzz confirmed who she was talking about.

"I didn't ask him to." Lena's voice was no less fierce for being kept low. The glance she shot at Buzz was poisonous. Fortunately for him, he was looking at Michael and thus remained oblivious. "I didn't want him to. He was supposed to wake me up."

Tam said gently, "I can feel that he really cares about you."

As Lena sputtered with indignation and denial, inspiration hit Charlie, and that, coupled with a desire to rescue Michael, had her saying to hell with her unreliable knees and standing up and walking over to Tony. After all, Abell was dead, she was no longer in danger, and there were missing teens out there. She could sit around and be traumatized later. All three men looked at her as she joined them. She consciously did not look at Michael. Still, after what Lena had picked up, she was afraid that she might be sending *I'm-so-in-love-with-you* vibes in his direction. God, she hoped not. How absolutely lame and embarrassing would that be?

"You know, Tam might be able to help locate some of these people," Charlie said to Tony.

Officially, the FBI did not authorize the use of psychics. On their last case, Tony had taken a gamble and Charlie's word, and turned to Tam for help when time was of the essence and the situation was desperate. Tam had more than established her bona fides with this team, and both Tony and Buzz looked at Charlie with approval.

"Good idea," Tony said, glancing at Tam, who was still talking to Lena. As if she felt their eyes on her, Tam looked at them. Charlie smiled and beckoned. Tam looked wary, but stood up and joined them. Her face like a thundercloud now, Lena came with her.

Tony told Tam about Charlie's suggestion.

"I can try," Tam said. She was absolutely confident in her abilities, her face and voice serene. "It would help if I had something that belonged to the subject or that the subject had some contact with."

Charlie, Tony, Buzz, and Lena looked at each other.

"Torres, Ware, and Doyle will have personal belongings at the Ridge," Charlie said.

"I'm better with past events," Tam warned. "More accurate and detailed. For present and future events, I tend to get mostly feelings and impressions. For example, I can feel danger hanging over someone, but I can't see exactly what that danger is."

The five people standing around her nodded their comprehension. Charlie had already told Tony and company that Tam had arrived in Big Stone Gap unexpectedly because she'd felt Charlie was in danger and had then seen more danger even after Charlie had survived the ordeal in the school bus, and Michael had firsthand knowledge because he'd been there. Clearly, the horror with Abell had been the additional danger Tam had foreseen. Looking at Tam, Charlie thought, *Accurate again.* Actually, in Charlie's experience, Tam had never been wrong. Sometimes muddled, but never wrong.

"Any help you can give us will be appreciated," Tony told Tam, and smiled at her. Tam smiled back. Then he looked at Lena and Buzz. "When we get up there, I want you two to interview as many people as you can while their memory of what happened is fresh. Our meeting got blown out of the water, but you can talk to Pugh and whoever else is available. We need to try to nail down exactly what happened in that prison. The who, how, and why of how a bunch of death row convicts were able to break out of a supermax."

Charlie frowned as a memory surfaced. Speaking slowly as she tried to dredge up the exact words she was remembering, she said, "While we were on the bus, Abell said something to Ware. It was along the lines of if Ware had a problem with what they were doing he could have stayed in his cell and taken a chance on being the next one hit."

Although she was still being careful not to look at him, Charlie happened to catch the expression on Michael's face from the corner of her eye as she said that. His eyes sharpened with interest.

Crap. Was deliberately not looking at him even more obvious than looking at him? Who knew?

"Next one hit?" Buzz frowned at her. "You have any idea what he meant by that?"

Charlie was glad of the distraction. "Three death row inmates have died violently while in custody at the Ridge within the last few months. One was a supposed suicide, one was stabbed by another inmate" — that death would have been Michael's; still deliberately not looking at him, she glanced from Tony to Buzz instead — "you two were there for that — and the last one was Walter Spivey, who died in mysterious circumstances in the infirmary after attacking me."

Everybody except Tam nodded. They all remembered that one, and Tony and Buzz — and Michael — clearly remembered Michael's death as well.

"You think someone's killing death row inmates up at the prison?" Tony asked.

Charlie said, "I think someone's killing convicted serial killers who are on death row at the prison, and I think that's why the remaining serial killers on death row were motivated enough to figure out how to pull off a break out. People tend to forget that, despite their psychopathology, serial killers are generally highly intelligent and resourceful."

The rattle of a gurney coming through the kitchen distracted them. It was being wheeled purposefully toward the basement door, and Charlie realized that they would be using it to carry out Abell's body.

She shuddered inwardly. She so did not want to be here for that.

Totally by accident, her eyes met Michael's. His expression was inscrutable, but she was sure he could read what she was feeling in her face.

"If you're heading up to the prison, I could use a ride," Michael said easily to Tony. "My car's up there." His gaze shifted to Charlie. She looked back at him, hoping that her expression was as impenetrable as his, but fairly certain it was not. "Plus *you* owe me some files. I'll collect them while I'm there."

Chapter Twenty-Three

The logistics involved in getting all six of them up to Wallens Ridge were enough to make Charlie long for more Advil to combat the resulting headache. First, they had to get past the TV crews and journalists going nuts over the home invasion and Abell's subsequent killing that were camped out en masse in front of the Powells' house. Then, in ways that she feared would abruptly get much less subtle if she ignored them, Michael made it clear that he wasn't about to leave her side, not that she wanted him to. But what caused that to be awkward was that Tony made it equally clear that he wasn't about to leave her in Michael's company without his — Tony's — protection. Clearly the knife-throwing, neck-breaking thing had put Tony on edge about what the supposed Rick Hughes was capable of, and he didn't trust even Lena or Buzz to stand between Charlie and an increasingly viable-seeming serial killer suspect whose company she didn't seem to have the good sense to avoid. Since Charlie emphatically didn't want to be in a car with only Michael and Tony — think ping-pong ball between two paddles, mouse between two cats, that kind of thing — she locked her hand around Tam's elbow and announced that she was riding with Tam to the prison. Michael promptly said he'd come with them, which led to Tony opting for Tam's car, too. Then when that was settled and they'd snuck through the backyard to her driveway and were getting ready to pile into the small white Kia Tam had rented, Tam automatically headed for the driver's seat, Tony held the passenger-side door open for Charlie, and Charlie was faced with the horrifying prospect of two large and deadly men who didn't like each other crammed into a tiny backseat. Her eyes met Tam's over the roof of the car as they exchanged some urgent nonverbal communication. The upshot was that Tony ended up driving, because his badge was the golden ticket that would get them through the prison gate, Charlie was in the front passenger seat because Tony showed an alarming tendency to get all stony-jawed at the idea of Charlie getting in back with Michael, and a surprisingly zen Michael and Tam sat in the back together and, equally surprising, appeared perfectly companionable despite the close quarters. Conversation was sparse for the entire winding road trip up to the prison as each one of them seemed lost in thought. But no wars broke out, and Charlie counted that as a win.

Left by default to drive up in the big black Bronco Tony had rented, Lena and Buzz pulled in beside them as they were getting out of the car in the prison lot where Charlie always parked. Her car, she saw at a glance, was right where she had left it, and she was experiencing a moment of thanksgiving for the spare key she always kept in a magnetic case under the bumper when Lena sprang out of the passenger seat of the Bronco. Shouting, "No!" through the open door at Buzz, who was driving, Lena slammed the door so hard the Bronco shook. She stalked away toward the prison, totally ignoring the rest of them, her face aflame.

Climbing out of the Bronco a second later, a scowling Buzz met four sets of interested eyes and grimaced.

"What the hell?" Tony asked him, throwing out his hands in a gesture of mystified inquiry. "You two were fine fifteen minutes ago."

Buzz's jaw worked. "I asked her to marry me, all right?" he said, and, thrusting his hands deep in his pants pockets, dropped his head, said something indecipherable under his breath, and kicked the Bronco's rear tire.

"Oh, for God's sake," Tony ground out, rounding the Kia to glare at Buzz. "Shake it off and move your ass. We have work to do." As Charlie was already scooting after Lena, who was booking it toward the glass double doors where two corrections officers stood guard, Charlie barely caught Tony's next remark, uttered as he shoved a hand into Buzz's shoulder to urge him forward. "You ever hear of candlelight and flowers, numbskull?"

"Lena." Charlie looked at the other woman as she caught up with her. Lena's jaw could have been carved from granite. Her eyes focused dead ahead. "Want to talk about it?"

Lena shook her head. They reached the door, which was the main outside entrance to the administrative wing and was located maybe fifty feet away from the stairwell exit that had been used to evacuate the building when it caught fire. The building was not yet back in use and access was restricted, as evidenced by the guards stationed outside the door. Lena flashed her cred pack at the guards to gain admittance and Charlie, who they already knew, nodded as she was allowed to pass as well. Once they were inside and walking through the gray-walled, terrazzo-floored visitor admission center, Lena said in a furious undertone, "I cannot believe he did that."

"Proposed?" Charlie questioned cautiously as she trailed Lena toward the elevator banks. A glance over her shoulder located Michael and Tam, who, not possessing the necessary credentials, were being forced to wait outside the glass doors for Tony and Buzz to catch up to them. Michael was looking at her hard, and Charlie got from his expression that he didn't want her getting out of his sight.

Considering the number of times she'd nearly died in the last twenty-four hours, this was not exactly paranoia. She reassured him with a little, stop-worrying wave.

"Who does that?" Lena gave the up button a savage jab.

"Somebody who's in love with you?" Charlie tried.

"He doesn't know who he's in love with. He spent years being in love with my sister.

He proposed to her, too," Lena snapped. The fact that Buzz had once been engaged to Lena's older sister, Giselle, was a major stumbling block to their relationship.

"He's acknowledged that he made a mistake." Charlie could feel herself slipping into professional mode. "The question you need to be asking yourself is: What do you want? Are you in love with him?"

Lena gave her a startled look, but the nearly simultaneous arrival of the elevator and the other four members of their party kept her from replying. Lips thin, Lena said not a word to Buzz or anyone else as they all rode up the elevator together. What with one thing and another, the atmosphere in the elevator was so thick Charlie was surprised any of them could even breathe.

The minute they stepped off, Charlie was hit by the smell of smoke. Although the wing was nonoperational in the wake of the fire, a surprising number of people were present on her floor: investigators from the Bureau of Prisons and the FBI, identifiable by their windbreakers and badges, corrections officers, construction workers, cleaning crews, random strangers about whose function she had no clue. There was no visible damage to the hall, but as they walked toward Charlie's office and the library beyond it the smell of smoke grew stronger.

Charlie shuddered to think about what had happened in that library. The closer they got to it, the colder she felt. That signified the presence of the dead. In significant numbers. She was glad to see the library blocked off and guarded.

One of the guards stationed in front of the library raised a hand in greeting as he saw her. It was Johnson, and as Charlie waved back she remembered something.

She slowed her step, purposefully falling a little behind the group, and a flick of her eyes at Michael had him falling back with her.

In a quick whisper she told him, "When Johnson saw Hughes in my office before the fire, he was obviously rattled by how much he looked like you. He asked me if I thought we had something like a *High Plains Drifter* situation going on. I know it's a Clint Eastwood movie, but other than that I'm out. I have no idea what that means. Do you?"

Michael looked down the hall at Johnson. His face darkened and hardened. His body tightened. Instinctively, she put a hand on his arm only to feel aggression coursing through his muscles. Whatever a *High Plains Drifter* situation meant, clearly it was bad.

He said, "Yeah, I do."

Charlie would have demanded an explanation, but they reached her office just then, which was where they were going to have Tam do her thing and where Tony had called ahead to have objects belonging to Torres, Ware, and Doyle sent. Tam, Lena, and Buzz walked on inside while Tony stopped at the door and looked around to see where Charlie was.

Of course he caught her with her hand on Michael's arm. Charlie let her hand drop instantly, but it was too late. Tony's eyes narrowed on the point of contact and then rose to her face. Ridiculous as it was, Charlie felt a pang of guilt as she met his incredulous gaze.

For once Michael was oblivious to what was going on with her. "I'm just going to the men's room. I'll join you in your office in a few minutes," Michael said, without even looking at her. His focus was all on Johnson, and his voice was loud enough to be heard by Tony, too. Then he seemed to recall his surroundings, because he looked down at her and murmured for her ears alone, "Hang with Dudley for a few, babe."

With Tony's eyes on her, Charlie couldn't answer, and she didn't feel up to even trying to sort out what Michael was planning.

She nodded, and as she walked past Tony into her office Michael strode on down the hall. Tony looked after him briefly, but then he followed her inside her office, too.

By the time Tam was finished doing her thing, they had learned that she saw Torres, Ware, and Doyle together in a green Dodge Ram pickup truck that was old and had engine trouble, thus filling the escapees with anxiety. That they had a small, scared-looking boy and a bigger but equally scared-looking boy bound and gagged and tucked away inside the camper attachment that covered the truck bed, that the teens were injured but alive, although that could change at any moment as a feeling of acute danger enveloped them. Doing her best to project herself into the truck, Tam was able to get a quick glimpse of the four lanes of a section of interstate highway falling away in front of the truck, and a sign it was passing that said *Mobile, 52 miles.*

No sooner had Tam finished than Tony was on the phone relaying the information to the FBI or the Alabama State Police or whomever it was he relayed that kind of information to. A sense of excitement was palpable in the room; if Tam's information proved accurate, which of course Charlie knew it was, and the pickup could be intercepted, two more hostages would be saved, and the remaining escapees would be recaptured. Only Bree would remain, and Charlie said a silent prayer for her. If she wasn't in the truck with the remaining escapees, and she hadn't yet been found, all of them knew that chances were slim she would be recovered alive. But no one was prepared to give up hope yet. An object belonging to Bree was being driven to Big Stone Gap for Tam to use in trying to locate her. Until it arrived, Tam was going to go back to Charlie's house and nap.

Charlie had made coffee. Having a coffeemaker in her office was surprisingly handy; she couldn't believe that getting one hadn't occurred to her before she'd needed one to collect DNA from Hughes. Tam rose from the comfy chair behind Charlie's desk, sipping slowly at a Styrofoam cup of the brew as she got ready to leave. Lena was on her way out the door, followed by Buzz, neither of whom looked very happy. As far as Charlie was aware, they hadn't exchanged a word since Lena had slammed out of the Bronco. Charlie was just starting to worry about what had become of Michael when she spotted him outside the door that Lena had just opened. He'd apparently been on his way back to her office and had stopped as the door opened.

"There's a big-time confession going down in the room next door," Michael said to the group at large. "I figure there needs to be some FBI agents there to make it official."

Lena, Buzz, and Tony, suspending his phone conversation, looked at him sharply.

Michael continued, "Officer Johnson apparently feels the need to get something off his chest. Seems like some of the guards conspired to murder prisoners. He started spilling his guts to a couple of Bureau of Prisons investigators, but I thought maybe you folks might want to get in on it while the getting's good."

Tony ended his conversation with a terse "Call me when you hear" and, following Michael's jerked-thumb gesture, rushed next door with Lena and Buzz.

Charlie automatically started to follow, but Michael stepped inside her office to block her path.

"Not you, Doc," he said, and at the look in his eyes Charlie realized she wasn't an FBI agent and didn't really need to hear any confessions at all.

"I'll be at your house if you need me," Tam said dryly as she stepped around them.

"I really need some sleep before I try that again."

Charlie looked at her and smiled. "*Mi casa es su casa.* I see a lot of work consulting for the FBI in your future, by the way."

"Cherie, the FBI can't afford me." That was true — Tam made a great living doing readings for movie stars and other celebrities. But Charlie also knew that Tam would never turn anybody in real need down. Tam and Michael exchanged glances in a kind of silent acknowledgment of each other, and then Tam pulled the door closed behind her and was gone.

"So you want to explain what's happening next door?" Charlie asked.

"In a minute," Michael said, and kissed her.

She melted against him instantly, sliding her arms around his neck, kissing him back, luxuriating in the feel of his lips on hers, in the scalding heat of his mouth, in the feel of him, so solid and *alive,* against her.

But then she pulled her mouth from his and said, "Spill."

He made a face at her. "*High Plains Drifter* is a movie about a man who's murdered and comes back in human form to seek revenge on his killers. As soon as I heard Johnson was worried about that, I knew that what I suspected was true and that he was in on it. So I went up to him, and I told him who I really am, and I told him enough details about some things that had happened on the Ridge while I was here to convince him. Then I told him that I was going to drag him to hell with me if he didn't confess everything he knew." Michael grinned. "He was about ready to crap his pants. One of the few times I've ever really enjoyed being a ghost. He told me everything, and I told him he had to tell the cops. That's what he's doing now."

"But he'll tell them about you," Charlie said in horror. "About you being in Hughes's body, I mean."

"First off, who's going to believe that? And anyway, I told him if he did he'd go to hell. Today."

Charlie looked at him. "I cannot believe that worked."

"Babe, most people are afraid of ghosts. Especially walking, talking ghosts who know lots of things they shouldn't. And they're really, really afraid of going to hell. Of course it worked." His face darkened. "I only wish I could pay a visit to Nash" — Nash was the inmate who had murdered him — "while I'm here. But the rest of the prison's on lockdown, and I doubt they'll let me through."

"I'm sure they won't." Charlie's hold on him tightened. On that terrible day when Michael had bled out in her arms, Nash had taken him unawares; no way could he have killed Michael otherwise. But she still didn't like the idea of Michael going anywhere near his murderer. Then she had a thought and frowned at him. "Nash stabbed you, not a guard. There were witnesses. Lots."

"The guards hired him, apparently. They had a thing going where they got rid of death row inmates that they really didn't like or that were special pains in the asses. Figured nobody would care and they'd save the state a bundle, so why not? Staged suicides, inmate-on-inmate attacks, accidents, anything they could come up with. Been going on for a while, apparently."

"Oh, my God, and no one noticed?"

"Who's going to notice? Prison's a jungle, babe." He kissed her again, then smiled down into her eyes. "Let's get out of here. Come spend the rest of the day with me."

"What?" The suggestion startled her.

"We can go for a drive. Grab dinner. Whatever you want. You realize we've never been on a date?"

Charlie's eyes widened. That was true, and was also mind-boggling and heartbreaking at the same time. He was so outrageously handsome he stole her breath — and she loved him. Her heart beat a little faster every time she looked at him. Her body tingled from his slightest touch. As much as she hated to think about it, the fact was that his time in Hughes's body was limited. Once he was out of Hughes's body, Michael would, she hoped, still be with her in spirit form, but going for a drive or grabbing dinner with a spirit was not the same thing as doing those things with a living, breathing man. There was nothing she could do to help the missing teens, and — she wanted to be with him.

"Yes," she said.

"Yes, you realize we've never been on a date?" He was teasing her.

"Yes, I'd love to go for a drive or to dinner or whatever."

He was smiling down into her eyes when a sharp rap on her door was followed by the door, which had obviously not been shut all the way, being pushed open.

"Char—" Tony was already walking through the door when he saw them. He broke off abruptly and stopped walking at the same time. Charlie realized what he was seeing: she and the supposed Hughes, a man she'd only met two days previously that they all suspected of being a serial killer, their bodies pressed close together, her hands on his shoulders, his hands on her waist, obviously intimate. She winced inwardly. Anger, astonishment, and pain blazed at her out of Tony's eyes for the briefest of moments, and then his face shut down, became hard and distant. "I'm sorry, I didn't realize you were busy. I have some news for you. I'll come back."

She knew the exact moment when his gaze and Michael's collided, because Tony's eyes narrowed and went stony, while Michael's body tensed. She could feel his hands hardening on her waist.

"No, Tony, come in, please." Charlie stepped away from Michael as she spoke. Tony looked at her warily. Michael frowned at her. To Michael she said, "If you'll give Tony and me a minute, I'll be right out."

Michael didn't move. His eyebrows went up. "Now?"

"I don't think —" Tony began stiffly at the same time, making no move to come farther into the room.

"Oh, my God," Charlie snapped, losing her patience. Walking forward, she grabbed Tony by the arm and dragged him into the room. Really, she'd had a trying couple of days. No, make that a trying couple of weeks. Or actually, now that she thought about it, make that a trying couple of months. To Michael she said, "Out. I'll meet you at my car."

Michael hesitated, and she made a shooing motion with her hand. His lips compressed.

"I'll be in the hall," Michael replied, shot a look at Tony, whose arm was rigid under her hand and whose face was so hard it could have broken rock, and walked out the door.

Following him, Charlie closed the door firmly behind him, then turned to look at Tony, who was standing thin-lipped and remote in the middle of the room. Advancing toward him, she considered her options.

"Tony —"

"You don't have to explain yourself to me. None of my business," Tony said in a cold, clipped voice. Then he turned around, took a hasty couple of steps toward her desk, turned back to face her, and burst out with, "How the hell is it possible for you to have a thing for that guy? You know what I was coming to tell you? I just heard from the lab, which, since they couldn't reach you, called me. The DNA's a match. That guy may very well be the Southern Slasher."

Chapter Twenty-Four

Charlie felt a surge of excitement. "That's wonderful! I knew it."

"What?" Tony looked at her like she was insane. Which, Charlie supposed, she might very well be. Just not in the way he thought.

"Tony, listen." She moved toward him, stopping when she was only a few feet away to look at him earnestly. "You asked me to think about whether we can be more than friends. And the answer is we *are* more than friends. You're one of the few people in my life that I can turn to when things go wrong, that I can call and you'll come running, that I can be honest with, and I hope you feel that way about me. That means so much more to me than you know. That makes us important to each other. That makes us family. I don't know about you, but there aren't many people in my life like that."

Tony gave her a hard look. "You know, if this is designed to let me down easy, don't bother. I get it."

Charlie made an impatient sound. "No, you don't get it," she said. "There's something going on here that you don't know about. That I trust you enough to tell you the truth about. And for me to trust you that much is a really big deal."

He crossed his arms over his chest and said, "You've got my attention. Go on."

Charlie wet her lips. "Remember that guy I told you about, the one who died and I was still getting over, which was why I couldn't start a relationship with you?"

"I remember," he said.

"When I was in that school bus, I thought I was going to be killed. I would have been killed, except" — she broke off, took a breath, and came out with it — "that guy — the one I love — came back in spirit form, and, since Rick Hughes was unconscious, took over his body to save my life. He's in Rick Hughes's body now."

No need to tell Tony exactly who that guy was. No need to mention that Hughes's body was now occupied by the man convicted of being the Southern Slasher, Michael Garland. All that, in her opinion, fell under the heading of TMI: too much information.

Tony stared at her. He took a faltering

step back, bumped into her desk, and sank down on the corner of it. His eyes stayed glued to her face. "You are seriously telling me that you think Hughes — that guy out there — isn't Hughes? That he's a damned *zombie*?"

Charlie sighed. "Not a zombie. I think the correct term is *revenant.* According to Tam."

He looked even more gobsmacked. "According to *Tam? Tam* knows about this?"

"Yes. Tam knows. In fact, you and she are the only people who know. And I'd appreciate it if you'd keep it like that."

He made a gesture indicating that she could count on that. "You actually believe what you're saying."

"No, I lie to myself on a regular basis just to see if I can tell when I'm doing it." She narrowed her eyes at him. "Yes, I believe what I'm saying. Because it's true."

"Let me get this straight: You're saying you're in a relationship with a dead guy. Who has come back to earth and taken over another man's body."

"Yes." Charlie gave up on trying to ease him into it. Apparently, easing wasn't going to be possible. "Although the body is temporary."

"He's in Hughes's body *temporarily*? Where the hell is Hughes?"

"I don't know. But he'll be back, probably in another day or so."

"He'll be back." The fact that Tony was repeating practically everything she told him was a measure of how dumbfounded he was, Charlie knew. She sighed inwardly. Somewhere, somebody had a life that was simple. Too bad it wasn't her. Tony continued, "So the serial killer suspect is going to return to his body. Then what? Are you still going to hang all over him?"

Charlie folded her arms over her chest and gave him a look. "You know, considering that I've given you ample demonstration of my ability to see and talk to the newly, violently dead, given that Tam has more than proved to you that some psychics are the real deal, given that we've both provided you with consistent evidence that there are whole other dimensions out there that most people have no clue exist, you'd think you'd be a little more open to the idea that the dead can and do walk among us and can, on occasion and under extreme provocation, possess a human body. Temporarily."

He said, "You're accusing me of being narrow-minded."

"There are only two ways this can go: You either believe I'm crazy or believe I'm telling the truth."

They locked eyes. Tony stared at her, then said slowly, "He can break necks. He can throw kitchen knives with enough precision to kill. Those skills aren't easy to come by, and there's nothing in Hughes's background to suggest he should possess them."

Charlie lifted her eyebrows at him, waiting.

"Fuck," Tony swore, which unlike some people he almost never did, and Charlie knew he'd seen the truth.

She nodded, then watched him as he continued to process. Finally he shook his head and said, "You are a *hell* of an interesting woman, Charlie Stone."

That surprised her. That made her smile and remember why she liked him so much. "*You* are a great guy, Tony Bartoli."

"Yeah." His voice was dry. He slid off her desk, walked over to her, and when he reached her shoved his hands in his pockets without touching her. Looking down at her, he hesitated, then said, "You're sure Hughes isn't this super con artist who's somehow convinced you of this? Because —"

Charlie shook her head. "No backsliding," she warned him. "Think broken necks. Thrown knives."

"Right." He grimaced. "So what now?"

She sighed, outwardly this time, and went

for the truth once more. "Now I'm getting ready to go spend the afternoon with a revenant and you are going off to find the remaining hostages and the escapees, preside over the arrest of a bunch of murderous prison guards, and, hopefully, investigate the hell out of the Southern Slasher murders. Oh, and see if you can get Lena and Buzz to make up."

That brought a glimmer of humor to his face. "The last thing may be beyond me."

"The rest, then." She smiled at him. "I better go."

"Wouldn't want to keep your revenant waiting."

She gave him a look that said *Don't be sarcastic,* and he smiled wryly at her. And she was reminded one more time of what a good-looking guy he was, and how perfect for her in just about every way he was. It was, she reflected, a crying shame that her heart didn't see it the same way.

"Charlie," he said. She was on her way to the door, and she looked back over her shoulder at him. "Friends."

Shaking her head at him, she corrected, "Family."

He looked at her, then nodded. "Family," he repeated solemnly.

It felt like they were sealing a pact or

something.

She smiled at him, then opened her door and walked out into the corridor where Michael waited. He was leaning against the wall directly opposite her door, arms folded over his chest, not looking particularly patient. As she came toward him he straightened away from the wall, greeting her with a quizzical look that changed as it moved past her to Tony, who was behind her. She looked around at Tony too to see what exactly about him was prompting Michael's suddenly coolly watchful expression.

But Tony's gaze slid to her as she turned toward him, so she got no chance to judge. All she got was a glimpse of the jaw-jut thing guys did sometimes in a kind of silent warning to other guys.

"Check in this afternoon," Tony told her, then flicked another look at Michael that was too brief for her to read and moved away toward the group that was emerging from the interview room. Johnson, now in handcuffs and clearly about to be escorted away, was in their midst. Tony said something to the group and disappeared into the interview room. Meanwhile, with a guard at each elbow, Johnson headed their way.

They were all walking in the same direction, but the guards were hurrying Johnson along. As Johnson came abreast of them, Michael gave him the stink-eye. Johnson visibly quailed. Then they were past each other, and a moment later Johnson and his escort rounded a corner and were out of sight. Michael and Charlie reached the elevators and stopped.

Charlie said under her breath, "You know, you just made life a whole lot safer for everybody on death row, except, wait, there is no one left on death row."

One corner of Michael's mouth quirked up. "I know, right?"

Then the elevator arrived, and on the ride down they discussed logistics and came to a consensus: Charlie would drive her car, Michael would drive Hughes's — Hughes's keys were in his pocket — and they would go first to the Pioneer Inn, where Charlie would leave her car and Michael would change clothes. Then they would head out in Hughes's Shelby, the thought of which sent an anticipatory smile curling across Michael's lips.

Nothing of importance was said until they were out of the building and heading across the parking lot. It was a beautiful Indian-summer day, sunny and just cool enough to call for a long-sleeved shirt or the lightest of jackets. On such a perfect day it was hard to imagine that such evil as they had been dealing with existed. Sadly, though, it did, and Charlie said one more prayer for Bree and the two boys who had yet to be found, then another one for the dead.

"So are you going to tell me what you and Dudley talked about?" Michael asked as they walked toward her car. The Shelby was parked all by itself in a far corner, presumably so it wouldn't run the risk of getting dinged. Michael had already spotted it: she'd seen his face brighten when he did.

Men.

"I told him about you," Charlie said.

Michael slanted a surprised look at her. "What about me?"

"That you're not Hughes. That you're a spirit who's taken over Hughes's body. A revenant."

"What?" Michael gave her an astonished look. "What did he say?"

"He was surprised."

"I bet he was. Don't tell me he believed you?"

They reached her car. Charlie retrieved her spare key and turned to face him. "Of course. I'm extremely believable. Are you telling me that if I'd told you something like that, you wouldn't have believed me?"

"Babe, if you'd told me something like that back before I died, I would have thought you were bat-shit crazy." Michael caught her chin, turned her face up to his, and bent his head to drop a quick kiss on her mouth. When he lifted his head, he grinned down at her. "Cute, but bat-shit crazy."

"Obviously Tony is more perceptive than you are," Charlie said with dignity as she opened her door and got ready to slide inside. "He did have a brief moment there when he wondered if maybe you were a really slick con artist trying to pull a fast one on me. But we got past that."

"No wonder he was looking at me like he wanted to break out the handcuffs."

"That wasn't the only reason. The DNA results came back and the lab called Tony because I no longer have my phone: Rick Hughes *is* your identical twin brother, which means he's probably also the Southern Slasher."

"So this body I'm in belongs to my identical twin brother. Who wears silk boxers and some kind of girly-smelling aftershave and is a lawyer." Michael stood in Hughes's room at the Pioneer Inn in said silk boxer shorts, halfway through changing his clothes. Charlie was ensconced in the surprisingly comfortable armchair in the corner, admiring the view.

The room itself was nice: large, lots of dark wood, green-striped wallpaper, heavy forest green draperies that were open to allow the afternoon sunlight to flood the room, a king-size bed. Hughes had not brought many personal items: a few changes of clothes, toiletries, a laptop. His briefcase had been on the bus, and Charlie had no idea what had happened to it. Presumably it had been logged as evidence somewhere. But Michael looked around as if trying to get a sense of who Rick Hughes was. As far as Charlie was concerned, he was the monster who had murdered seven women and gotten Michael killed. But Michael seemed to be having trouble getting his mind around that.

"Yes," Charlie said, trying not to let herself get distracted by broad shoulders and brawny arms or a wide chest that tapered down into narrow hips. Or six-pack abs bisected by trim-fitting silk boxers in a sexy shade of maroon. Or long, powerful legs — okay, she'd just officially gotten distracted. She refocused. "He's also a murderous psychopath who almost certainly killed all those women."

"I don't know." Michael frowned at her. "I can't believe I was followed around by a guy who looked exactly like me and I never noticed. No one noticed. He almost had to have been inside that bar where I picked up Candace Hartnell. Or maybe he was outside and followed us. I guess that's possible: he might not have been seen if he was waiting out there in the dark."

Charlie had seen the security video from the bar that had shown Michael meeting and leaving with Candace Hartnell. From what she could tell, it wasn't a big place, and it was in a fairly rural area, and, yes, one would think somebody would have noticed two identical men, especially when they were as big and heart-stoppingly handsome as Michael. But —

"Then there's the watch." Michael sounded like he was talking at least halfway to himself. "Where did he get the watch? And how could he have known that my watch" — Michael nodded at the heavy silver bracelet dangling from Charlie's wrist — "would be lost by the damned idiots at the Mariposa Police Department, not to be found until after I died?"

Charlie frowned. That *was* a coincidence. A striking coincidence, now that she thought about it. Because if Michael's watch hadn't been lost, then two watches would have been introduced into evidence at his trial. His, with *Semper fi* engraved on the case, and the broken and bloodied one that had been found in Candace Hartnell's sheets. His would have been exculpatory —

"And there's you," Michael's eyes met hers. "Why the hell would he come here looking for you?"

Charlie's new cell phone rang, interrupting before they could explore that thought any further. That she even had a cell phone was due to a pit stop she (well, actually they) had made by Walmart on the way to the Pioneer Inn. They'd done a quick dash in and out because Charlie had felt an urgent need to pick up a temporary phone so she could stay in touch with everything that was going on. Much as she was looking forward to spending the day with Michael, she was discovering that simply totally abandoning a search for missing hostages and serial killers was beyond her. On the drive from Walmart to the inn she'd called Tam to give her the number in case something came up, and she'd called Tony, too, for the same reason. Both calls had gone to voice mail, and her new phone now rested on the end table beside her as she waited for one or the other of them to call back.

This was Tony, calling back. Smiling as she listened, Charlie felt a flood of relief.

"They found the pickup. The two boys are safe, and Torres, Ware, and Doyle are back in custody." Charlie reported what Tony had just finished telling her to Michael, who, having been drawn by the call, was standing beside her, looking down at her as she curled in the chair.

"That's good. I'm glad," Michael said, while Tony, on the other end of the phone, asked sourly, "That him you're talking to?"

Charlie noticed that he didn't refer to Michael as Hughes.

"Yes," she admitted.

"Well, hold on to your hat. I've got some other news for you. I had some state-of-the-art, don't-tell-the-bean-counters-how-much-it-cost testing done, using blood Hughes donated to an office blood drive right before he came up here. I had it compared to blood test results from Hughes's identical twin who was actually convicted of being the Southern Slasher. Hughes never had chicken pox."

Charlie was momentarily at a loss. "What?"

"There were antibodies to the Varicella-zoster virus — chicken pox — in the blood of the twin who was convicted of being the Southern Slasher: Michael Garland. At some point in his life, Michael Garland had chicken pox. Rick Hughes did not. Blood left at the crime scenes by the Southern Slasher had the antibodies in it. Which means the right twin was convicted of being the Southern Slasher: Michael Garland, not Rick Hughes, killed those women."

Chapter Twenty-Five

Disconnecting, Charlie stared at Michael.

He clearly was able to read in her face that something was up, because he frowned down at her.

"Did you ever have chicken pox?" she asked him. Her voice was only a little high-pitched.

His frown deepened. "I think so. When I was a little kid. Why?"

"Hughes never had chicken pox."

"You want to get to the point here?"

"The genetic material left by the killer at the scenes of the Southern Slasher murders contained antibodies to the Varicella zoster virus, which is chicken pox. Hughes never had chicken pox. His blood doesn't have any antibodies to chicken pox in it. You did, and yours does. Hughes didn't do it."

Feeling her chest tighten like it was being squeezed in a vice, Charlie watched as he took that in.

Then his face hardened, his mouth thinned, and his eyes flared at her.

"So I guess that makes me the Southern Slasher, huh?" Not a trace of intonation in his voice.

The evidence was there, and it was damning. The evil-twin thing had been so perfect, just the explanation for Michael's innocence she'd been searching for — but it was wrong. She had wanted it to be true so badly that she'd been guilty of the classic researcher's mistake, using evidence selectively to arrive at the desired outcome. But the cold, hard truth was this: Rick Hughes might be Michael's long-lost identical twin, but the Southern Slasher was not Hughes.

Which left Michael.

Charlie looked up at him, at the beautifully cut mouth, the straight nose, the square jaw, broad cheekbones and forehead, the thick, tawny hair. Eyes that were a hell-born black instead of their usual sky blue beneath straight dark brows. Intimidatingly tall and powerfully built. Outrageously handsome. Demonstrably dangerous. Able to break necks and sever spinal columns with ease. She'd seen him kill without hesitation or apparent compunction, although every time he'd killed since they'd been acquainted it had been to save her.

"Scared of me, babe?" There was a sneer in his voice. And something else, too: bitterness. A trace amount only, but it was there, in his voice and his face.

Charlie decided.

"In your dreams," she said, putting the phone down and standing up. That brought her so close to him that their bodies brushed. She was immediately enveloped by the heat coming off him. His hands settled automatically on either side of her waist. Hers flattened against his chest. For a moment, the tiniest moment, she allowed herself to be distracted by the sleek warmth of his skin, the firm resilience of his muscles. Then she got a grip and met his eyes. "Guess what, pretty boy? I know you didn't kill those women, so you can go ahead and drop this whole badass vibe you've got going on."

He looked at her. His face was still grim. Then one corner of his mouth twitched. " 'Pretty boy'?"

Charlie nodded. "Really pretty. Even Lena thinks so." He was making a face as she went up on tiptoe to kiss him. "Remind me to tell you about it sometime," she murmured, and pressed her mouth to his.

His arms came around her, and he kissed

her back, and the magic that was them, the blazing sexual chemistry, the electric charge that sparked from his body to hers, ignited the air. He kissed her dizzy, and undressed her, and took her to bed. They made love until the sunlight slanting across the bed turned golden, until Charlie was so sated she could hardly move, until just lifting her head from Michael's shoulder where it rested was an effort.

But she did it.

They were lying sideways across the bed. Naked. On top of the fitted forest green bottom sheet, the top sheet and the other covers and pillows having been long since lost to the foot of the bed or the floor. He was flat on his back with an arm folded behind his head. She was tucked against his side. Stroking a hand down his chest, she took a moment to enjoy the tensile strength of his muscles and the damp warmth of his skin as well as the sheer masculine beauty of him. Bottom line: the guy was seriously hot, and she was seriously smitten.

His eyes were open. He was watching her look at him, and all that watching was having an interesting effect on an interesting part of his anatomy. But that was a diversion to be explored later. For now, there was something she needed to know. Propping an arm on his chest, rearing up higher so that she could see his eyes, she met his gaze.

His eyes promptly dipped to ogle her bare breasts that were hanging like ripe fruit just above his chest.

"Hey." She snapped her fingers to get his attention. "Eyes on the face."

He complied. His eyebrows rose questioningly at her.

"I love you," she said.

His eyes narrowed slightly. His hand that had been lightly stroking the curve of her waist slid down to her hip and tightened.

"I know," he said.

The look she gave him then was downright threatening. "That is so not going to be our code for *I love you, too.*"

The grin he gave her was so charming her toes curled. "I just wanted to see what you'd say."

She frowned, pointedly waiting.

"I love you, too," he said.

"There you go. That wasn't so hard, was it?" As he shook his head she regarded him meditatively. "Michael."

He huffed out a breath. "Jesus, there's your we-need-to-talk face. No, we don't. There's lots of other things we can do." His hand slid suggestively over her butt, fondling and squeezing.

"No." Reaching for the top sheet, she dragged it back from the crevice between the mattress and the footboard it was lost in and wrapped it around herself as she wriggled around until she sat cross-legged on the mattress beside him. "I want to know why you ended up in Spookville."

He regarded her unsmilingly. For a moment she thought he wasn't going to answer. Then he said, "Could have been a lot of things. Who knows?"

"You know."

Picking up her hand, he carried it to his mouth and kissed her palm, then let his lips crawl down the sensitive skin on the inside of her arm. "I know how soft your skin is. How sweet it smells. How —"

She yanked her arm away from him. "Just so you know, what you're doing here is classic avoidance. When individuals opt to avoid a subject, it's usually because it's something that carries a great deal of pain for them. Quite often there's shame associated with it, too, and —"

Michael growled and sat up. "Would you stop with the shrink shit, please?"

"Will you tell me why you were sent to Spookville?"

Their eyes warred.

Michael said, "I was wrong. A bulldog's got nothing on you."

"Michael. Please. I need to know."

He looked at her. His face tightened. His jaw grew hard. "Babe, you ever think that maybe you don't want to know?"

She regarded him steadily. "Whatever you did, I know that it wasn't evil. So I'm not worried."

He snorted. "You got any more of those rose-colored glasses you're wearing on you? Because I could sure use a pair."

She just looked at him.

"Fine," he said. Stretching out a long arm, he snagged a pillow from the floor and flopped back down on the mattress with it stuffed behind his head. Catching a corner of the sheet she was wrapped in, he pulled it over himself so that he was minimally decent. He slanted a look at her. "You remember I told you how Sean died?"

She did. As a member of Marine Force Recon in Afghanistan, pinned down by a vicious enemy, Michael had been forced to shoot his mortally wounded buddy to survive.

"Yes," she said. Her hand crept into his. His fingers entwined with hers, but she wasn't sure it was a conscious act on his part. He was staring up at the ceiling.

"After that, our unit was broken up, and I was given another assignment. Black ops stuff. There were a few of us. We worked with military intelligence. Our job was to facilitate the mission by going in clandestinely and taking out high-value targets. Wet work. We'd already been doing some, Sean and Hoop and Cap and me, but this took it to a whole different level." He glanced at her, and must have decided that she wasn't following because he spelled it out. "We were assassins, babe. We killed up close and personal. Sometimes a lot of lives could be saved if a particular leader or bomb maker or someone like that was taken out individually. That's what we did. That's what I did. Went in, eliminated the designated target as quietly and with as little collateral damage as possible, and got out. I was good at it and I had no problem with what I was doing. Remember how you were always asking me if I felt remorse? No, I never did. It was my job. Most of the people I served with, Sean and Cap and Hoop and everybody else, they had people they loved, people who loved them. Families, people they wanted to go back to. I was different. Fundamentally different, do you understand? Like there was a giant coldness inside me. I didn't love anybody, didn't have anybody I wanted to get back to, didn't give a fuck about anybody or anything. I could do what needed to be done, and afterward I could sleep at night just fine. I always wondered if the military knew that about me, and that's why I was given the job they gave me." He looked at her again then. "Just so we're clear, I did that for a little over two years. I killed whoever they told me to kill. No mercy, not a bit. And no, no fucking remorse."

Charlie consciously stopped herself from sucking in air. If her fingers tightened on his, well, that was just reflexive. "You followed orders. You did what you were told to do."

His mouth twisted. He slanted a glance at her. "That excuse won't get you off in a court here on earth, much less the court I'm facing."

"Whoever's in charge of these things in the universe can't decide to hold you accountable because of something the military ordered you to do!"

"I guess whoever's in charge can decide any damned thing they want."

"It's not fair! You never had a chance! Your childhood — you were abused — your mother" — she gave a snort of scornful laughter — "what mother? That woman was not a mother! You —"

"Babe, I'm a grown-ass man, and have been for a while now. You can't go blaming all the shit I've done on a crappy childhood and a bad mother." He brought their joined hands up to rest on his chest. "Truth is, I didn't do anything I wasn't perfectly willing to do. And anyway, that's not the worst of it."

She pressed her lips tightly together as their eyes met. "Tell me," she said.

"Hoop and Cap were with another unit, and that unit — the survivors of that unit, because there was a hell of a firefight first — got captured. There was a lot of noise about what the enemy was going to do to them, that they were planning to make a big spectacle out of beheading them or maybe burning them alive. So a group went in to get them out. It was all volunteer, because it was pretty much a suicide mission, deep in the mountains, deep in enemy territory. Getting in was doable because nobody knew we were coming, but getting out —" He broke off, shook his head, and looked at the ceiling again. "Eight of us went in there, three of us came out. We brought five prisoners out with us. The survivors. They were in rough shape, we were mostly carrying them on our backs. Cap made it out.

Hoop didn't. He was dead when we got there. So there's eight of us hustling through these mountains that make our mountains around here look like a park in Kansas, with half the Afghan army on our tail. We're skirting around the villages, trying to get to a point where some choppers or AMTRACs can get in there and get us, when we walk right into this group of villagers having some kind of meeting in the woods. There's like six of them. Men, most of them old, a couple not. They see us, we see them. Nothing to do. So we round them up, and we have this quick little debate. If we let them go, they'll run straight to their village and we're fucked. If we tie them up, the minute they get loose or are found they'll tell everything they know about us, and we're fucked again. I knew from the beginning that the only thing to do was kill them, but we took a vote and the vote was that we were going to leave them tied to a tree. So we leave them tied to a tree. Every single one of us knows it's a bad decision, that it's going to come back and bite us in the ass big-time. So I make the call, just to myself, don't say a word to the others, and I go back and shoot them. I shot unarmed civilians. The youngest looked like he was maybe fourteen. After that, we made it out, all of us, alive. I looked at it the way it was, us or them."

Listening, Charlie's heart seized up. Her insides quivered. Her throat tightened, all with horror for the fate of those men — and for him. His voice was totally devoid of inflection. His face was as expressionless as a wall.

He continued, "Cap got killed about a month later. IED. I finished my tour three months after that." He must have felt the emotions she was trying hard to keep contained because he looked at her then. "I told you from the get-go I've done some bad things. I'm a killer. I just don't happen to be a serial killer who slices up women."

But despite his denials, he'd been haunted by what he'd done, by those whose lives he had taken, by the villagers, by the thought that he'd killed a teenager. She knew it by the expressionlessness of his face, the lack of intonation in his voice, by his body language. She knew it by the way he reacted to kids who were in danger now. He might say he felt no remorse. He might even believe he felt no remorse. But it was there, buried deep under a ton of denial, eating him alive. He'd never forgiven himself for the things he had done, and her heart turned over at the knowledge.

He was looking at her, watching her, waiting for her verdict, for her judgment, although she knew he would die before he'd admit it. His face was completely unreadable. His hand gripped hers hard.

All kinds of things that she wanted to say to him crowded into her head. Things like: deeds done in the fog of war don't count; surviving at all costs is the oldest human instinct there is; you almost certainly saved the lives of the men you were with that day.

But this wasn't the moment for any of that.

"I love you," she said again, softly. And then she leaned over and kissed him, and crawled on top of him, and proceeded to show him how much.

His stomach growling was what finally got them up and out of the hotel room. He pulled on a pair of black pants and a gray button-down from Hughes's closet, and they went down to the Pioneer Inn's restaurant, which was a small but pleasant combination dining room/bar. They talked, by silent but mutual agreement staying away from anything heavy or distressing, and Charlie watched Michael devour what was possibly the largest steak she'd ever seen, plus sides and two beers. Then they walked outside and down the block to the closed-off streets and town square full of booths and vendors that was the Big Stone Gap Fall Festival. By this time it was full dark, and white Christmas lights had been strung up everywhere. It was beautiful. There were jugglers and fortune-tellers and foam rubber animals on sticks and lots of carnival games and food and music. They laughed and talked and Michael ate two hot dogs and a caramel apple while Charlie picked at some cotton candy, and then he tried to win her a stuffed animal by throwing a baseball at some stacked bottles and failed miserably.

Which made her giggle. Like she was seventeen.

Casting her a glinting look, he shelled out another five dollars (from Hughes's wallet) and tried again.

Watching him hurl the baseball at the bottles, which still stubbornly resisted going down in sufficient quantities, Charlie thought, *I'm happy.*

The thought scared her because she knew *happy* couldn't last.

"Damned game's fixed," he growled as he gave up finally, turning away from the booth and sheepishly presenting her with the six-inch-long neon green stuffed worm that was the losers' consolation prize.

Charlie couldn't help it: she accepted the worm and snickered.

His eyes narrowed dangerously at her. "Are you laughing at me?"

"No." She clasped the worm to her heart, looked at him soulfully and said, "My hero." And snickered again.

"That's going to cost you," he threatened, and wrapped his arms around her and kissed her, right there in the middle of the fall festival.

The ringing of her phone broke them apart.

It was Tam.

"Hey," Charlie said.

"I couldn't find her," Tam said. Her anguish was obvious even through the phone. Charlie knew instantly that Tam was talking about Bree. Michael was looking down at her, and she mouthed *Tam* and he nodded. "They brought me her sweater, and a bracelet, and I picked her up. I felt her. But I couldn't find her. All I got was cold. Cold and dark."

"Maybe that means she's dead." Even saying it was upsetting.

"I didn't get the afterlife. I got the kind of cold and dark that's of this plane. It's like I'm inside her body, but I can't see anything because it's pitch black where she is. And she's so cold. Deathly cold."

"Tam —"

Tam broke in before Charlie could say anything more. "I think she's here, but I think she's dying. And I can't get a read on where."

Charlie clutched the phone. Her whole body went tight with distress. Then the merest glimmer of a possibility occurred to her.

"I have an idea," Charlie told her. "I'll be right there."

Chapter Twenty-Six

With Michael riding shotgun, Charlie drove the short distance from the Pioneer Inn in her car and then had to park a street over and sneak through backyards in order to avoid the media that were still camped out on the street in front of the Powells' house. Letting herself in through the kitchen door, she was slightly taken aback to find that her home appeared to be packed with people. Not only Tam, but Tony, Lena, Buzz, a woman from Child Protective Services, and a pair of uniformed state troopers were in her kitchen.

Behind her, Michael seemed to pause for a moment on the threshold to survey the group. Then he followed her inside.

In the chorus of greetings that ensued, Charlie was introduced to Sarah Combs, the woman from Child Protective Services, and the state troopers. Apparently Bree was a ward of the state and Ms. Combs had been charged with finding items that belonged to her and bringing them to Tony (actually Tam, but the whole psychic thing hadn't been divulged to Ms. Combs). The cops — Officers Huddleston and Rink — were there to drive Ms. Combs back home again.

"I couldn't help," Tam whispered, clutching Charlie's hands with fingers that were cold as ice. Her face was pale and pinched with anxiety. "I can feel her, but I can't find her."

"Tam said you have an idea?" Tony stepped up beside Tam to ask in a lowered voice. He was carefully ignoring Michael, who was right behind Charlie. Lena and Buzz joined the group, focusing on Charlie after giving Michael almost identical hostile looks. Since they thought Michael was Hughes, and Hughes had been cleared of suspicion in the Southern Slasher case, Charlie could only suppose their hostility was because she was apparently dating Hughes rather than Tony, whom they both tended to look out for in the same way that he looked out for them. She took quick note of the fact that Lena and Buzz were standing reasonably close together, and Lena was no longer crackling with anger every time she glanced in Buzz's direction. Charlie could only suppose they'd talked.

At the moment, though, Charlie didn't have the time or the energy to deal with all the undercurrents in the room.

"Yes," she said. "I just need to run upstairs for a minute." She looked at Michael. "You okay with hanging out down here?"

Michael nodded. Charlie looked meaningfully at Tam, who moved to stand protectively at Michael's side. Michael slanted a quizzical look down at Tam. Tam smiled at Charlie. Silent message: *Don't worry, I've got him.*

Charlie ran upstairs, offloaded Squirmy (her name for the neon worm) onto her dresser, grabbed the supplies she needed, and stuffed them in a tote bag. Then she returned to the kitchen.

Ms. Combs and the troopers were gone. Michael leaned against the breakfast bar while Tam perched on one of the stools. Tony, Lena, and Buzz sat around the kitchen table.

"Tam was just telling us about the award you won," Tony said as Charlie entered the room. "Congratulations."

Lena and Buzz chimed in with congratulations, too.

"Thanks." Charlie smiled at them. Her eyes met Tony's. "I'm going next door. You can come with me. The rest of you stay here."

"I'm not staying here," Michael said, straightening away from the bar. Everyone looked at him.

"I didn't mean you," Charlie told him. Remembering how her last trip inside the Powells' house had ended, she was absolutely in favor of having all the protection she could get. She would have let Buzz and Lena come, except the last thing she needed for what she intended to do was an audience of skeptics. And to take Tam would only add to Tam's distress while serving no purpose. Tam got debilitated by the dark side of the spirit world. Tam was a creature of the light.

With Michael and Tony in tow, Charlie headed out the door.

"Why are we going next door?" Michael asked as they crossed the yard. He and Tony loomed on either side of her.

"I'm going to try to summon a spirit," Charlie replied. "And also feed the cat." Then, before Michael could say anything more, because she figured he would object to her plan if he knew exactly what it entailed, she turned to Tony and asked, "So did Lena and Buzz make up? They seem to be being relatively civil to each other."

He snorted. "I told them they were both fired as soon as this case is over. They've been on their best behavior ever since."

Charlie looked at him. "You don't mean it."

"They don't know that."

Sure they do, Charlie thought, but they had reached the Powells' house by that time and her attention turned to the task at hand.

"You stay outside," Charlie said to Michael as she inserted the key Melissa had given her into the back door lock. The porch was dark and shadowy. Given her recent experience in the house, the thought of walking back inside it creeped her out, but it had to be done.

"What?" From Michael's tone he might as well have said *Like hell.*

"I'm going to open a portal," she explained. "I don't know what that will do to you, but I don't think either one of us wants to find out. So you stay out here. Believe me, I'll scream if I need you."

"You're taking Dudley?" He sounded affronted.

"In case there's another bad guy in the house, I need someone to shoot him," Charlie said, exasperated. "Think I didn't get the memo about going alone into dark, scary houses? I did." The lock clicked. Pushing the door open, she looked over her shoulder at him. "Will you just stay here?"

Michael made a sound that she didn't stick around to try to decipher. She went on into the house, then closed the door after Tony, who followed her.

" 'Dudley'?" Tony asked when they were inside. Charlie could see the silhouette of Michael's big body through the glass in the top of the door. He was sticking close, but doing as she'd said and staying outside. As a spirit, he'd had experience with portals and was wary.

"He's bad with names," Charlie lied, then added, as Tony reached for the switch beside the door, "Don't turn on the light."

God, she hated having to say that, she thought as his hand dropped. The house was dark and silent and cold in an otherworldly way that told her that she was on the right track. Already the back of her neck was prickling, which, depending on how you looked at it, could be either a good or a bad sign. She'd already ascertained that the Powell family, too traumatized to reenter their house so soon, had gone to Melissa's mother's to spend the night.

"Jesus Christ, that's the cat," Tony said, sounding startled, as Pumpkin greeted Charlie with a yowl and a rush to rub against her legs. Patting him absently, she remembered the instructions Melissa had given her and said to Tony, who was only a few feet behind her, "His bowl's over there, and his food's on the shelf above it. Would you mind feeding him while I get set up, please?"

Gesturing in the direction she meant, she watched Tony move to do as she'd asked.

"Set up?" Tony asked as he poured kibble in a bowl.

The homely sound of the cat food hitting the dish was soothing as Charlie pulled the jasmine candle that she'd taken from her dresser drawer from the tote bag and placed it on the end of the kitchen table that was farthest from the basement door. The candle was part of her Miracle-Go kit, a collection of objects she'd accumulated over the years for dealing with spirits. Setting the heavy glass she might need to put over the candle beside it, she fished out the lighter that was her last piece of equipment and looked at Tony.

"I'm going to light this candle," she said, "which will open a portal to the Other Side. If Abell is still in the house, he will be drawn to it. When he shows up, if he shows up, I'm going to ask him where Bree is."

It was hard to see Tony's expression in the

dark, but she could feel him staring at her.

"Okay." He sounded only slightly taken aback.

"You're not going to be able to see him. It's going to look to you like I'm talking to thin air," she warned. "All you have to do is be quiet and stay out of the way."

"I can do that."

See, that was why she liked him so much. The man took everything she threw at him in stride. She smiled at him, then picked up the lighter and lit the candle. The tiny flame caught and flickered, growing stronger. The smell of jasmine wafted through the air.

"He can't hurt me, by the way," Charlie said as an afterthought. "Or you, either."

Then she quit talking as Abell's spirit stepped through the closed basement door. Her heart beat faster at the sight of him. The living world dropped away as she focused on him.

Abell looked exactly as he had in life, a big, apelike man in the blue prison guard uniform in which he'd died, his dark hair shaved close to his scalp, his skin waxy pale. A shiny dark streak running down the side of his throat caught the moonlight coming in through the window. Charlie had no doubt that it was blood, from the knife wound in the back of his neck.

For a moment after he entered the kitchen he looked disoriented. He glanced around, fists clenching as he frowned. Then he spotted the candle and his gaze riveted on it. He took a step toward it as if compelled, then another one. Then he seemed to struggle against the invisible force that had caught him and was tugging him forward.

"That suction you feel is going to take you to hell," Charlie told him. At the sound of her voice, Abell's head swiveled toward her. She was standing beside the table within easy reach of the candle, and he was obviously seeing her for the first time.

His face contorted with rage and hate.

"You bitch," he snarled. "This is all your fault. I'm going to kill you." Roaring, he leaped toward her, his body barreling right through the table as if the sturdy wood wasn't even there. Stomach churning, assailed by a sudden blast of cold, Charlie stood her ground, expecting him to make a grab for her and in the process surge right through her. But the suction generated by the opening portal caught him up, throwing him off balance before he could reach her, pulling him toward it. Listing sideways, struggling to resist, he looked toward the candle with sudden fear.

"You can't hurt me, Mr. Abell," Charlie

said. "But I can hurt you. You see the candle? It's creating a vortex that you can't escape. In a minute or so you'll be swept up by it and it'll take you to hell and then you'll burn forever. But I can stop it. If you tell me where Bree is, I will stop it. All I have to do is put this glass over the flame and it goes out and you're safe. You can go to hell in your own time."

"Fuck you," he flung at her. But he was moving toward the candle, pulled inexorably, although he was obviously struggling with all his might against the force of it. Suddenly his face twisted with fear. His voice went shrill. "Where the hell are those screams coming from?"

"They're coming from hell, Mr. Abell. Where you're going in just a minute or so unless you tell me where Bree is." Charlie picked up the glass, her eyes never leaving his face. She could see the whites of his eyes now as he fought to resist the pull. "I can stop it. All I have to do is drop the glass over the candle."

"Oh, God, that hurts. Make it stop hurting." He screamed suddenly, as if afflicted by sudden, acute pain, and Charlie tensed even though she'd known what to expect. He was windmilling, on his tiptoes, barely keeping his balance, as the vacuum created by the

portal sucked at him. "I shot the bitch, okay? She shimmied out a window and took off running and I shot her. She fell over a cliff. *Now make it stop.*"

He was teetering, swaying like an autumn leaf in a high wind, barely hanging on. Charlie held the glass directly over the candle. The flame was almost horizontal now as the suction pulled it, too. Abell's eyes fastened on her hand holding the glass.

"*Please,*" he begged.

"*Where* did Bree go out the window, Mr. Abell?"

"How the hell should I know? It was right after you and Dirty jumped off the bus." He screamed again and started moving forward, step by increasingly rapid step, clearly being pulled against his will despite his frantic efforts to save himself. "I told you what you wanted to know. *Now put out that candle.*"

Charlie set the glass down on the table, leaving the candle burning beside it. "Go to hell, Mr. Abell," she said.

"You fu—" His words cut off as he was abruptly yanked off his feet and hurtled toward the candle. Shrieking, he vanished from sight.

Charlie didn't even realize that her hands were shaking until she picked up the glass and dropped it over the candle, extinguishing the flame.

Then she took a deep breath —

"Did you really just send Abell to hell?" Tony asked in a fascinated tone a minute or so later. They were on their way out the back door, with Charlie's supplies safely restored to the tote she carried over her arm. She'd told him what Abell had said about what had happened to Bree, and he was already punching in a number on his phone.

"I have no idea where I sent him," Charlie answered truthfully. "But hell's definitely where he deserved to go."

Then, as Tony moved away to talk into the phone, Charlie walked quickly in the opposite direction, sank to her knees, and vomited in the grass.

Michael crouched beside her. "Damn it —"

"I'm all right," Charlie told him, taking a deep breath and willing the shakes to go away. After a moment she let him help her to her feet. "That was just — intense."

"No more fucking serial killers," Michael said fiercely. His arm was around her, and she was grateful for his solid warmth as she leaned against him. "Promise me."

Before Charlie could reply, Tony walked up to them.

"Everything all right?" he asked. His eyes were on Michael. He had that guy jut to his jaw again. Charlie could feel a hardening of Michael's muscles in response.

"Talking to spirits makes me sick sometimes," she said. "I'm fine."

Pulling away from Michael, she went home. Neither man said anything, but there was a tension in the air between them that was palpable. Then, as she stepped through her kitchen door, she glanced back to find that they were talking, a brief exchange that was too low-voiced for her to overhear. Her inner alarm went off, but as they followed her inside, neither man's face revealed a thing.

It was a good half an hour before she was able to get Michael alone and ask him what he and Tony had been talking about. By unspoken consensus, they were all staying together as they waited for a call back from Major Hintz about the results of the search his people were currently conducting of the ledges and ravines near where Charlie had been rescued. The others were gathered in the living room. Michael had gone back into the kitchen for a refill on coffee. Charlie followed.

"What did you say to Tony outside?"

Charlie asked him quietly. In the act of taking a sip from the coffee he'd just poured himself, Michael paused and looked at her over the cup.

"What you should be asking is, What did he say to me?" Michael responded. "And the answer is: He told me that if I did anything to hurt you, he'd kill me."

Charlie's eyes widened. Knowing the personalities involved, that didn't sound like a promising start to a conversation. "What did you say?"

Michael swallowed some coffee, then lowered the cup. "I took it that he meant physically hurt you, and I said he didn't have anything to worry about. Then we came inside."

Charlie blinked at him. The whole idea of the two of them talking about her in that way didn't sit well with her. First, how sexist was that? Second, how liable to go wrong was that? But before she could say anything else, the muffled sound of a phone ringing, followed by Tony's voice responding with a terse "Bartoli," sent them both striding toward the living room.

As soon as she entered the room, Charlie could tell from the expression on Tony's face that it was good news.

He was smiling as he listened to whoever

— Charlie assumed it was Hintz — was on the other end of the phone.

"They found her," Tony said as he disconnected. He'd been sitting on the far end of the couch when Charlie had left the room, but he was now standing near the door, having apparently moved to take the call. Charlie and Michael, who were just inside the door, stood closest to him, but everyone had turned to him, focused on what he had to say. "She was on a narrow ledge about twenty feet below the road. She's been shot, she's unconscious, and she's lost a lot of blood. But she's alive, and they think she's going to make it."

"Thank God!" Tam breathed, and the rest of them chimed in with happy exclamations and a ton of questions.

Relief and joy rushed through Charlie in a warm tide. She hadn't realized how terrified she'd been for Bree until now, when something inside her finally relaxed and let go. Listening to the excited conversation welling up around her, she leaned against the wall.

"Tired?" Michael asked. He was standing beside her, his voice pitched so only she could hear. Charlie nodded. He continued, "I don't want Dudley or the others to get the idea that I'm spending the night with you, so I'm getting ready to leave. I'm going to walk around for a little while. After they're gone I'll be back. I already took the key off the hook, so you don't have to worry about letting me in."

Charlie looked up at him. There was no question in either of their minds about whether she wanted him to stay the night: they both just accepted that she did, and he would.

She nodded. Then a terrifying thought hit her, and she frowned, catching his arm. "You won't do something like disappear?"

He shook his head. "I'll be back."

Moving away from her, he said to the room in general, "I'm out of here. Good night, all."

Tam and Charlie were the only ones who echoed his good night. The others kind of looked at him and nodded.

Charlie sighed inwardly. She and Tam were going to have a serious discussion later about whether there was any possible way of keeping Michael in Hughes's body, as awful as she knew it was of her to want to do that. If there was a way, if Tam was able to do it, then she was going to have a talk with Tony, and Lena and Buzz, too, about their attitude toward Michael. But not before then, because if Tam wasn't able to do it, then she wasn't going to have to worry about what her FBI pals thought, because Michael would be once again in spirit form and they wouldn't be able to see him.

Tony, Lena, and Buzz left shortly after Michael. Lena and Buzz were subdued but polite to each other, and Tony didn't have much to say beyond "I'll be by in the morning." As this was definitely not the moment to discuss anything personal, Charlie nodded, and they left. As soon as they were gone, Charlie turned around to speak to Tam. Her friend was already halfway up the stairs.

"I'm going to bed," Tam said over her shoulder. "Good night."

Charlie let her go. She knew Tam knew that the conversation was coming, and knew also that Tam was deliberately avoiding it for as long as she could, but she was tired and wrung out and Tam was, too. Tomorrow would be soon enough for the talk they were going to have. For now, Charlie's head hurt, her stomach wasn't entirely over its encounter with Abell, and her joy over Bree was tempered by her knowledge that unless Tam could fix things, Michael would soon be losing the use of Hughes's body. What she really needed was a hot bath and a solid eight hours of sleep. Plus a handful of Tums.

And a couple of Advil.

Everything except the sleep she could do something about. But as long as Michael was in possession of Hughes's body, well, she had other uses for her time.

She went upstairs, ate the Tums, took the Advil, brushed her teeth, pinned her hair up, and turned on the bath. Her tub was of the big, old-fashioned claw-foot variety. She'd had it restored, and she loved it both because she simply liked looking at it and because it was big and deep and she could stretch out in it and soak.

That's what she was doing when she heard her bedroom door open and close again. Leaning her head back against the rolled lip of the tub, Charlie smiled and waited.

Michael walked into the bathroom. He took one look at her languidly lathering her arms with rose-scented soap and flames ignited in the depths of his eyes. Then he started to unbutton his shirt.

Charlie's heart began to pound.

"Did you have a nice walk?" she asked, spreading the lather across her shoulders.

"Yep." He took off his shirt, hung it on the hook inside the door, then took off his pants and did the same thing. Luxuriating in the hot water, Charlie looked at broad shoulders and honed abs and powerful legs, watched sinews flex and muscles ripple as he stripped off the rest of his clothes, and went all marshmallowy inside. When he stepped into the tub with her, she looked up the whole long length of him, saw how absolutely enormous he was with wanting her, and her body began to throb and burn.

"You're going to smell like roses," she warned, sliding over to make room.

"I can live with that," he said as he settled in beside her. Then he kissed her and pulled her on top of him, and the blazing sexual hunger that was always there between them raged to life, reducing her to a shivery supplicant in his hands and turning the air around them to steam.

Later, a long time later although exactly what time it was Charlie couldn't be sure, she opened heavy-lidded eyes on a room that wasn't quite pitch black but close enough, and discovered that she was alone in bed. She was still trying to focus enough to get a read on the numbers on the clock when she heard something over by the dresser, got a sense of movement near the bed.

Struggling up on one elbow, blinking groggily, she said, "Michael?"

A rush of movement, a jarring bounce as

something heavy hit the bed, and a fiery pain as a sharp object sliced through the top of her shoulder were her answer. Her heart leaped into her throat. Adrenaline spiked through her.

I've been stabbed.

Even as the horrified realization burst into her brain, a heavy hand clawed at her neck.

Screaming, Charlie flung herself out of bed.

CHAPTER TWENTY-SEVEN

"Help! Michael! Tam!" Charlie screamed as every tiny hair on her body shot upright. She landed on the floor, hard, and scrambled on hands and knees to get away from whoever was bouncing across the bed after her. She was sure it was a man; she couldn't see him, but he felt big. He blundered into the nightstand, knocking it over and sending it skidding. The ginger-jar lamp shattered. Tiny pieces of crockery flew everywhere. Horror turned her blood to ice. Her pulse pounded in her ears. A billion thoughts raced through her mind in a split second: What was happening? Who was he? What did he want? Abell — it felt like Abell, but it couldn't be. Abell was dead and this man was alive. She could hear the harsh pant of his breathing, see and feel the solid mass of his body as he came crashing after her in the dark.

Dear God, he wants to kill me.

Panic surged through her veins in a galvanizing tide. Even as she glanced back fearfully the intruder lunged toward her, a denser presence in a sea of black, and then from just a few feet away he launched himself at her. On her hands and knees near the far wall, she dived out of the way, rolling in the nick of time, shrieking like a steam whistle as he just missed her. He landed beside her with a heavy slithering thud, his knife — he had a knife with a long, thin blade — slamming into the dark wood just inches from her face. She could see the knife sticking into the floor, see it quivering with the force of the thrust, see him grab it by the handle and yank it out.

"Who are you? What do you want?" she cried, bolting for the door. He hurled himself after her and caught the tail end of the short loose nightgown she'd pulled on before falling asleep. With a shot of pure terror she felt the jerk of his hand as it fisted in her hem, and a terrified glance over her shoulder found the massive dark bulk of him looming up right behind her. Yanking her back toward him, he raised the hand holding the knife high. The blade slashed down again. She caught the glint of the blade, sensed the muscular force behind his falling arm, heard the rush of the movement. Throwing herself forward at the last second, heart jackhammering, she screamed like her life depended on it, which it did, and felt the blade slash through the thin silk at the back of her gown.

I can't get away. He's raising the knife again — this time it's going to slice through my skin . . .

Fear burning like acid in her mouth, she whipped around, grabbed a handful of the fragile silk, and jerked herself free.

Please God please God please God help . . .

Her bedroom door opened with a rattle of the knob and a soft rush of air. Charlie had about half a heartbeat to think *saved,* and then she recognized the shadowy figure in the doorway as Tam. Tam, who was no fighter. Tam, who couldn't help her. Tam, who if this madman got hold of her, would die, too.

"Run!" Charlie screeched as the man behind her roared and grabbed her by the shoulder and spun her around. Screaming "Charlie!" Tam hit the light switch instead.

Even as the near-blinding brightness from the overhead fixture flooded the room, the knife was already in motion. The blade flashed bright silver as it slashed toward Charlie's throat. Tam screamed "Charlie!" again as Charlie shrieked, dodged — and, amidst the debris of the tipped-over nightstand and the broken lamp and the various knickknacks scattered across the floor, spotted a gun.

Black and deadly-looking, it lay on its side near the closet. As she'd never owned a gun in her life, she knew where it had to have come from: it was the gun Michael had taken off Fleenor and left in the drawer of her nightstand.

Wrenching herself free of the tightening grip on her shoulder, shrieking with every bit of lung power she had left as she dodged the slashing knife one more time, Charlie threw herself on the floor, skidded across the slick wood, grabbed the gun, and rolled, coming up on her knees to point the thing at the intruder.

"Freeze!" she shrieked, in instant, instinctive imitation of every takedown she'd ever heard come out of the mouths of Tony and Lena and Buzz. Never mind that she was wearing a filmy, now torn and wildly askew pink silk-and-lace slip that barely reached to mid-thigh, or that her hair was tumbling in wild disarray around her face and there was a whole lot of bare skin on display. She sounded as deadly earnest in that moment as any cop ever had, and, miracle of miracles, the intruder froze. The gun was cold and heavy and her hands trembled as she gripped it, pointing it squarely at the midsection of the tall, burly, florid-faced man she was pretty sure she'd never seen before in her life, like she actually knew what she was doing. He stood there, breathing heavily, the knife gripped tightly in his hand, his eyes riveted on her face.

"Don't move," she warned, not daring to look away from him as her finger curled around the trigger. God, could she really shoot him? And didn't guns have some kind of safety feature where you had to deactivate something before you could actually pull the trigger? She didn't dare look at the thing to try to find out. "Tam, call the police!"

"I am." Voice shrill, Tam brandished her cell phone.

But even as Tam spoke into the phone Charlie could hear heavy footsteps bounding up the stairs. With a muttered "Thank God," Tam was already stepping into the room out of the way of whoever was coming. Afraid to take her eyes off the intruder, Charlie caught just a glimpse of a tall athletic form bursting through her bedroom doorway.

"What the —" Michael's words were bitten off as he took in the situation at a glance. Then he was beside her, breathless from his sprint up the stairs as he took the gun from her, holding it on the man with a deadly assurance no one could mistake.

Looking as if he was thinking about bolting for it, the intruder stared at Michael.

"Give me a reason," Michael said to the man in a tone that sent a chill down Charlie's spine, then glanced down at her in obvious concern.

"The police are on the way." High heels clicking, Tam flew across the room to Charlie's side. "I called Tony, too."

Charlie nodded in acknowledgment. As Tam hunkered down beside her Charlie registered peripherally that, instead of being dressed for bed, Tam was wearing plum-colored slacks with a purple wool jacket like she'd been out somewhere. The fresh scent of the outdoors clung to her. Charlie frowned, but tucked Tam's attire away as a matter to question later.

"Drop the knife." Michael's voice was still murderous. No surprise, the knife hit the floor. If the intruder had had any real intention to try to escape, he'd clearly given it up. "Kick it over here to me."

The man did. Without taking his eyes or the gun off the man, Michael bent and picked up the knife. Suddenly, the danger that had filled the room went away.

"Breathe wrong and you're dead," Michael said to the intruder, and then to Charlie, "You're bleeding. How badly are you hurt?"

"She's cut across the top of her shoulder. It doesn't look like it's very deep," said Tam. Charlie supposed the adrenaline spike she'd experienced had kept her from feeling anything before. Now she could feel the sting of the cut and the warm ooze of blood against her skin. She looked around at her shoulder. A long cut across the top of it was bleeding pretty freely, but as Tam had said the wound didn't look deep.

Didn't matter. She felt light-headed anyway, probably because as she'd looked at the wound she'd been hit with the realization that, if she hadn't awakened right when she did, she could easily have been killed.

Stabbed to death in her bed.

"I'm all right," she told them as Tam got to her feet and hurried toward the bathroom. Moving was beyond Charlie for the moment. The best she could do was try to regulate her breathing. Shaking her hair to one side to keep it away from the wound, she asked, "Who is he?"

"You mean he's not one of yours?" Michael's tone was only mildly edgy. Charlie shook her head, started to say *No.* Then she stopped. She'd thought she didn't know her attacker. But she had this sudden, niggling sense that she'd seen him before. Tam came back with a towel and Charlie's robe, distracting her. Draping the robe around Charlie while leaving her injured shoulder bare, Tam sank to the floor beside her, then folded the towel and pressed it to the wound, applying steady pressure. Charlie winced even as she murmured "Thanks."

"What's your name?" Michael asked the man. Charlie's attention refocused on the intruder, who was shifting his weight from foot to foot uneasily. His eyes were fixed on Michael and the gun. He was wetting his lips and breathing heavily. She could see his chest heaving beneath the long-sleeved black tee he wore with black sweatpants. A kind of wary confusion came into his eyes at Michael's question. He didn't answer.

Charlie stared at him. Michael was staring at him, too. Mid- to late thirties. Buzzed reddish blond hair. Broad face, meaty nose, thin lips. Light blue eyes. A big guy, at least six-two, husky. Not bad looking.

I was almost stabbed to death in my bed. That thought ran through Charlie's mind a second time, then stayed with her. She'd come across that scenario, that MO, before.

She looked at the knife in Michael's hand.

Long, thin blade, with a leather-wrapped handle. Wickedly sharp.

She had files in her office with an ME's sketch of a missing murder weapon that looked almost exactly like it: Michael's files.

Her heart started to speed up just as Michael said with a trace of surprise, "You're Detective Dan Foster with the Mariposa Police Department."

Even as Charlie had her own flash of recognition — she'd seen a video of this guy interviewing a handcuffed Michael inside the Mariposa police station right before Michael was charged with Candace Hartnell's murder — the truth hit her like a brick.

She knew, *knew,* who he had to be.

The Southern Slasher.

Her hands curled into fists. Her insides twisted.

"I'm with the Baltimore PD now," Foster said, frowning at Michael. "You know that. You're my damned lawyer."

Of course, Foster thought Michael was Hughes. And Hughes was Foster's *lawyer*? Hughes was a criminal defense lawyer; the case that had brought him to Big Stone Gap involved his client killing his girlfriend in the style of the Southern Slasher. Foster had to be the boyfriend suspected of murder. The true scope of his evil unfolded in Charlie's mind like a game of connect-the-dots.

Foster was a serial killer. The actions and motivations of serial killers almost always followed a pattern, and were actually highly predictable to someone who knew what to look for. To someone like her.

Fixing him with wintry eyes, Charlie said, "Your girlfriend was breaking up with you, wasn't she, Detective Foster? She rejected you, and you lost control and killed her because rejection is your trigger. Then you panicked, knowing you would immediately be the prime suspect because in any murder like that the boyfriend or husband always is."

Foster's eyes widened. Looking at her as if she'd suddenly morphed into a spitting cobra, he said in a hoarse, startled voice, "You don't know what you're talking about."

Charlie's eyes never left his. There was no longer any doubt in her mind that she was right. All the clues, all the little anomalies, added up to this man. This was her area of expertise, and she pulled on everything she knew to work out exactly what he'd done, and how, and why. Identifying psychopaths like Foster and figuring out what made them tick was what she did. She did it now, and all the pieces started falling into place.

She said, "I do know what I'm talking about. For one thing, I'm talking about this knife right here. The same knife you always use. You used it to slash your girlfriend to death, just like you used it to slash all your other victims to death. Monsters like you tend to be consistent in their methods of killing people, and you've used the same knife for every murder you've committed, haven't you? Do you think that knife can't be connected to all your previous murders? I'm betting it can."

"You're crazy." He looked at Michael and Tam as if seeking their support. "She's crazy."

Tam shook her head. Michael glanced down at Charlie, then looked back at Foster, his expression increasingly grim.

Charlie continued, "You killed your girlfriend because she rejected you, and then you panicked because you knew it was going to come back on you. You looked around for a scapegoat because the one you had already used, the one you had already framed, who had already been arrested and convicted of your previous crimes, was dead. Killed in prison." Charlie felt Michael stiffen beside her, as exactly who he was looking at dawned on him at last. Charlie went on, “Fortunately, he had a twin brother. Exactly when you ran across Mr. Hughes I’m not sure — probably when you joined the Baltimore PD — but run across him you did. You couldn’t have missed his resemblance to Michael Garland, so you did a little detecting — that’s what you do, after all, isn’t it, Detective? — and discovered that Michael Garland and Rick Hughes were indeed identical twins.”

Charlie could feel that she had Michael’s fascinated attention even though his eyes stayed fixed on Foster. She could feel the emotions seething through him: disbelief, hope, a rising anger. But it was Foster’s reaction that interested her most. His already florid face turned tomato red, and his eyes — his light blue eyes, which, along with his size and fair coloring would match Michael’s general description, Charlie realized — were bulging out of his head.

Chapter Twenty-Eight

"This is bullshit," Foster snarled. "Total bullshit."

Charlie shook her head. "I *know* what you did, Detective Foster. When you needed someone to pin your girlfriend's murder on, you decided that the easiest thing to do was make it another Southern Slasher murder. After all, it had worked beautifully for you before. Did Candace Hartnell reject you before Michael Garland picked her up in that bar? Yes, I'm sure she did. You were probably right there to see her leave with him."

Foster was starting to sweat. "You're pulling all of this out of your ass. *You weren't there.*"

Charlie smiled. It wasn't a pleasant smile. "Somehow you knew Michael Garland. You had it in for Michael Garland. You watched Michael Garland walk out of that bar with the woman who'd rejected you and you got angry. Then you came up with a way to make them both pay. Were you starting to feel the heat for the murders of the six women you'd killed previously? I think you were. I think you were worried that you'd left something behind, a hair, some saliva, something, although as a cop you knew how investigations were conducted and were very careful. But you were afraid you'd made a mistake and someone would figure it out, so you took what you must have seen as a golden opportunity to pin the blame on someone else and followed Michael Garland and Candace Hartnell back to her house. You waited outside until he'd left, and then you killed her. Did you call in a report of a possible drunk driver and have Michael Garland stopped after he'd left her house?" The look on Foster's face answered that. "Yes, you did. Very smart. And thorough. You're very thorough, aren't you, Detective Foster? So thorough that you took some of the DNA Michael Garland had left behind — it wouldn't have taken much — and salted those previous cases, your previous victims, which logged evidence you had access to because you were a detective. Then you made the supposed discovery that Michael Garland was the Southern Slasher and you got to play the hero." At the thought of what Michael had suffered because of this man, Charlie felt a ferocious anger flood her veins. It was all she could do to keep her voice even as she continued, "Did you enjoy testifying at his trial, Detective Foster? I bet you did."

"You can't prove any of this." Foster's voice was a croak. He was looking at her like he was afraid. Charlie was fiercely glad. He deserved to be afraid.

She said, "The police and the FBI can. Now that they have the road map, it'll be easy. Where you went wrong was killing your girlfriend, Detective Foster. You would have gotten away with the rest of it. But you're arrogant. You think you're smarter than everyone else. You should have just sat tight and hoped that the police investigating your girlfriend's death couldn't find enough evidence to tie it to you. But instead you came up with another brilliant plan, hired Rick Hughes as your defense attorney — probably the very next day. You salted the scene of your girlfriend's murder with something like a few hairs, anything containing DNA, that you either obtained from Hughes or you had saved from Michael Garland, and you waited for police to make the connection. Or, no, you didn't wait, did you? You're a doer, not a waiter. You told somebody, probably a cop buddy of yours, that your girlfriend's murder reminded you of the Southern Slasher killings you investigated back in Mariposa, and wondered out loud if maybe the real killer was still on the loose and out to get you, and the word got around. The only thing that was worrying you was that, having discovered how much he looked like Michael Garland, the convicted Southern Slasher, Hughes had decided to check him out." Charlie remembered the sense of evil she had felt the evening she had seen Hughes's Shelby parked across the street from her house, the evening she'd seen that brief, shimmery image of Michael in the neighbor's yard, realized that the evil must have been emanating from Foster who'd been nearby, too, and with that everything else, the rest of what Foster had done, fell into place. "You followed Hughes here to Big Stone Gap because you were afraid that he would realize he was being set up. When you saw him having dinner with me, coming home with me, you followed us and waited outside my house for him to leave." She shot a quick glance at Michael, noticed for the first time that he was wearing khakis and a blue shirt instead of the black pants and gray shirt he'd had on the previous night, and concluded that he had, indeed, left her asleep in bed to go back to the Pioneer Inn and change clothes. "When he left, and my house guest left, too —"

She slanted an inquiring look at Tam, who said in a squeaky voice, "I had an errand to run. I was gone for about an hour and a half. I just got back when you started to scream."

Charlie nodded and continued addressing Foster. "When I was alone, you broke into my house and tried to kill me, the woman you assumed Hughes had just slept with and had just left his DNA all over. That would have sealed the deal, wouldn't it? That would have made everyone think that Rick Hughes was the real Southern Slasher all along, and, while a regrettable mistake had been made in convicting Michael Garland, it was understandable because they were identical twins, and anyway the right twin would be captured and convicted now. You would have proved how much smarter than the authorities you are once again, and you would have gotten away with one more murder."

"You son of a bitch," Michael said slowly. She could feel the burning heat of his anger, and put a calming hand on the powerful leg beside her. He glanced down at her, and then she could feel him gaining control, reining his emotions in.

"That's crazy, all of it. You can't prove any of that," Foster said again. His voice was hoarse, his eyes were bright with fear and hatred as he looked at her, and if his face got any redder it would burst into flame. "Who the hell *are* you?"

Charlie knew that she was right in almost every detail. She would have known it even if he hadn't been looking at her like that because analyzing how serial killers thought and behaved was what she had dedicated her life to, but everything from his expression to his body language left her in no doubt that the scenario she had just described was close to the truth.

"I'm Dr. Charlotte Stone," she said, her eyes holding his. "Stopping serial killers is what I do."

"Wow," Tam said, nudging Charlie. "I thought I was the psychic here."

Charlie took a deep breath. Breaking eye contact with Foster, she glanced at Tam. "I study patterns of behavior. Everything he did fit a pattern. No psychic ability involved."

"Not one word of that fairy tale you spewed is going to be admissible in court." Foster seemed to be trying to get himself under control. His voice was stronger. Charlie knew how his mind worked: he still thought he was smarter than everyone else, and he would figure a way out. "It's all rampant speculation on your part. All of it."

Charlie shook her head. "The knife isn't speculation. Neither is the fact that you just tried to kill me. As for the rest, well, we'll see, won't we? It certainly gives investigators a good place to start."

Michael was frowning as he stared at Foster. "I'm as sure as it's possible to be that I never laid eyes on this guy before he pulled me out of that cell at the Mariposa police station. Why would he have it in for me? And where the hell did he get that watch?"

"I don't know, but it'll come out in the investigation," Charlie said. A commotion below announced a whole herd of new arrivals seconds before a man yelled, "Police!"

"I must've left the front door open," Michael muttered, while Tam yelled back, "We're upstairs."

As multiple sets of feet pounded up the stairs toward them, Tam jumped up, ran over, and grabbed Foster's arm.

Eyes widening, Tam stood stock still. Charlie, Michael, and, yes, Foster, too, were so surprised that all they could do was stare at her.

"I had to know for sure," Tam said, letting go and retreating to stand by Charlie, who with Michael's help was getting to her feet. Charlie understood — Tam had been reading Foster. She nodded and pulled her blue bathrobe closer around her as what seemed like half the Big Stone Gap police force burst into the room. While explanations were being given and Foster was Mirandized and handcuffed, Tam told Charlie quietly, "It's all true. He's the Southern Slasher. I felt so much evil in him, so much hate! He killed his girlfriend and all those other women" — she looked at Michael, who stood beside Charlie, and directed her next remarks to him — "and he hated you because you were the only one of — twenty-four, that's the number I got, twenty-four — the only one of twenty-four who undertook the mission in which his brother was killed who got back to this country alive. His brother never made it home from Afghanistan. The watch — Foster inherited the watch from him. Foster was wearing it the night he killed Candace, and he left it behind on purpose, in her bed, to incriminate you, because he knew you had an identical one. He hid your watch, which was intake material, when you were arrested. Only — I don't think the watches were totally identical. Something — something was different. The watch Foster left belonged to his younger brother, Dean Foster, who was killed during that twenty-four-man mission with you. Foster thought it was unfair that . . . He hated watching you go on with your life while his brother was dead."

Later, when Foster had been taken away and Charlie's wound had been treated and bandaged and she'd gotten dressed and told her story what felt like a hundred times, she was walking through the entry hall with Tony, Lena, and Buzz, who were on their way to the door. The three FBI agents were headed for the police station to conduct the first formal interview with Foster.

Charlie had just a moment of relative privacy with Tony, who bent his head toward her and asked quietly, "You doing okay with that guy?"

She had no trouble identifying "that guy" as Michael.

Nodding, she said, "We're fine. I'll let you know if anything changes."

"You do that," he said, and she knew that he meant for more than just information purposes.

Then Lena and Buzz caught up.

"That was a close call," Tony said to Charlie, totally professional now. "Too close. You need a home security system. Pronto."

"You attract serial killers like a dog does fleas." Lena sounded almost gleeful. "We can just cart you around the country with us and watch the arrest count pile up."

Charlie shook her head. "After this, I'm sticking to research. And I might write a book."

"Not that we don't appreciate the help, but that's probably a good idea," Tony said.

"If Foster had managed to kill you, his plan might very well have worked," Lena told Charlie. "At the very least, it would have taken the focus off him as a suspect in his girlfriend's murder."

"I hate thinking about that guy who got wrongly convicted as the Southern Slasher," Buzz said, grimacing. "Somebody dropped the ball on that one, and now there's no putting it right: the guy's dead."

Lena shrugged. "Nothing we can do about that."

Buzz frowned at her. "You know what, you've got more of a heart than you let on."

"Let's go, people." With a quelling look at the two of them, Tony opened the door.

Cold air swirled in. Outside, the world was the washed-out gray of a new dawn. To Charlie, Tony added, "I'll call you later," and walked out the door. Lena and Buzz followed. As they headed across the porch Charlie heard Buzz say to Lena, quietly so that Tony wouldn't overhear, "That heart you try so hard to hide is one of the things I love about you, you know."

Lena shot him a look that should have fried his eyeballs. "Stop it," she hissed. "I told you: We are not going there."

Buzz grinned at her, but Charlie missed the rest of the exchange as they went down the steps.

Charlie was still smiling at the idea that maybe Buzz was making headway after all when Tam called to her from the kitchen, where she and Michael were waiting.

"Cherie, come here." There was a sharpness to Tam's tone that made Charlie hurry back to them.

The first thing she saw as she stepped inside the room was that Michael was holding on to the back of one of the kitchen stools. He seemed unsteady on his feet. His face was absolutely white.

"What's wrong?" she gasped, rushing to his side, sliding a supporting arm around his back. Tam was beside him, too, looking at him with fear in her face.

It was Tam's expression that sent the first quiver of terror through Charlie's system.

"It's time." Michael sounded as if he was having trouble getting the words out. He was breathing hard, leaning on the kitchen stool like he needed its support to stay upright.

"Time for what?" Charlie asked as cold tendrils of foreboding started to wrap themselves around her heart.

The look Michael shot her was his answer. Then he said, "You know I'd give you forever, but I don't have it to give."

He's losing Hughes's body, Charlie thought, trying to get a handle on her rising panic. *That's all this is.*

"We'll figure something out," Charlie told him, doing her best to sound reassuring even though her heart was suddenly pounding. "Until we do, you'll hang out with me as a spirit just like you did before."

Charlie wasn't looking at Tam, but she heard Tam suck in a breath. She knew Tam: that indrawn breath couldn't mean anything good.

Michael gave a slight shake of his head. "I'm talking Spookville. I can feel myself getting pulled back in. You know I might not be able to get out. I may never be able to get out." He let go of the kitchen stool with one hand and hooked an arm around her, pulling her into an embrace.

"You can. You will. Oh, God, try to fight it." Charlie wrapped her arms around him, looking up into his hard, handsome face with alarm. The black seemed to be fading from his eyes. He was shaking, and he felt cold.

The slightest of smiles just touched his mouth. "Babe, here's a dirty little secret: Sometimes you fight and lose."

"Michael." Fear tightened Charlie's throat. She cast a desperate look at her friend. "Tam, isn't there something you can do?"

Tam made an inarticulate sound of distress.

"I love you," Michael said, and brushed her lips with his.

Then he collapsed.

Chapter Twenty-Nine

"Michael!" Charlie cried.

"Cherie, we have to lay him down."

Tam was right, Charlie knew. He was too big, too heavy. Between them, they were barely able to prevent him from crashing like a felled tree to the floor. They managed to lower him fairly gently, but that was all they could do. Pale and limp, he lay sprawled on his back, his eyes closed, his face slack. Still breathing, but clearly unconscious.

They knelt on either side of him.

Pain twisting through her, Charlie looked at Tam. "There's no way to stop this, is there?"

Tam shook her head. "No."

Before Charlie could do more than press an unsteady hand to his cold cheek, mist started to rise up out of Hughes's body. She watched it gather like a cloud of vapor inches above the supine form, hover for a moment, then whoosh up and to the side, where it took on form and substance.

A heartbeat later Michael stood beside the body of the unconscious Hughes. Still on her knees, Charlie looked up at him. He looked as solid and real in spirit form as Hughes did in life. His tawny hair was too long again, and shaggy. His perfectly sculpted face with its chiseled features had a healthy tan. His eyes — he was looking down at her — were once again their usual heart-stopping sky blue. He was wearing scuffed cowboy boots and faded jeans and a white tee that hugged more solid muscle than Hughes sported. He was her own outrageously handsome Michael, and Charlie's heart throbbed with love for him and pleasure at seeing him looking so completely himself again. That knee-jerk reaction was immediately supplanted by a spurt of fear: the prospect of him being once again swept off to Spookville made her stomach twist into knots.

He'd said that this time he might not be able to get out —

"Are you all right?" She sprang to her feet. She would have thrown herself into his arms, but the whole ectoplasm thing prevented that.

"Yeah." He smiled at her, a wry twist of

his lips. Something about it scared her all the way down to her toes. "No more serial killers, Doc. Promise me."

Charlie took a deep breath. The way he was looking at her was like he was saying good-bye. Her heart started to slam against her breastbone. "I promise," she said.

"Write that book. Be happy. Don't worry about me. I've got Spookville down."

"Michael." Her mouth was dry. "Please try. I want you to stay."

He glanced over his shoulder, out through the window at the shadowy backyard. To her nervous eyes as she followed his gaze, that familiar space suddenly looked almost sinister. She could feel the rising tension in him, the heightening emotion. The stress. The sense of dread. Like he was waiting for the other shoe to drop. Like he was waiting for something terrible to happen.

He looked around, met her eyes. His were a blazing blue. "Believe me, I want to stay. More than I've ever wanted anything. But Spookville is getting ready to take me no matter what I do, and I don't think I'm going to be coming back. You need to face up to that. You and me, we've had something great here, but we've both known from the beginning it couldn't last. Now you've got to go on with living, and I — I have to go on to what's next."

"There has to be something —" Charlie began desperately.

"There's not." He sounded, and looked, grim. "There's no help for it, babe. There's a path we've both got to take, and they don't go the same way. I want you to live your life, and have the best time, and marry and have kids, the whole nine yards. Then by and by, when you're like a hundred and twelve and you cross over, maybe we'll hook up." He looked over his shoulder again. His face tightened. "I got to go."

Terror stabbed her. "What? No. Not yet."

He looked past her at Tam. A silent message seemed to pass between them. Michael said, "You'll stay with her?"

Charlie felt rather than saw Tam's nod as Tam curled a hand around her elbow. As if to prevent her from —

"I love you," Michael said. His eyes burned into hers. His voice was low now, and husky. "You remember that." He turned and started walking away.

"Michael —" Her voice was sharp with panic. Tam's hand tightened on her arm as if to prevent her from following him. Charlie pulled away, running after him as he passed right through the kitchen door without opening it, gaining speed as he went. His gait was unnatural — it was as if he was being drawn by an invisible force. She saw that his booted feet weren't even touching the ground now. Reaching the door, she flung it open, burst out into the backyard. It was cold, barely light, smelling of earth, of damp. Dawn was just beginning to break. Shadows lay everywhere. Michael was already near the sunflowers. He was a couple of feet off the ground now, and getting higher. Darting after him, she cried, "I love you, too. Please don't —"

Go, she was going to say, but she stopped abruptly as he seemed to be jerked skyward. His back arched, he grimaced — she knew that look, he was in terrible pain, but he wasn't screaming *for her sake* — and then he was gone.

Vanished into thin air.

Charlie felt a scream crowding her lips, but she forced it back. There was no help to be had; screaming would do no good. She stared into the purpling sky where Michael had disappeared. He was gone. There was not so much as a ripple in the air.

Oh, God, who knew that you could actually feel your heart breaking? It was a burning, agonizing pain in the center of her chest.

"Charlie." Tam reached her, put a hand

on her back. Charlie sucked in a great, shuddering gulp of air and turned on her.

"You know something," Charlie said fiercely. "I saw him look at you. There's more going on here than just Spookville, isn't there? *Tell me.*"

Tam caught Charlie's hands, held them tightly. Her face was a study in distress. "I've wanted to tell you. He made me promise —"

"Tam."

Tam's shoulders sagged as she gave in. "Yesterday — I touched his arm. I read him. I didn't mean to: It was an accident. But when I did, I saw him in the *lieu de la mort* — the place of death. He was being tortured, horribly tortured. They — the *executeurs* — were waiting to destroy him, as they destroy all who go there. But he was holding them off, how I couldn't see. Then you were kidnapped, and he was allowed by them to see that you were in grave danger, and he made a bargain — if they would let him go to you, if they would let him save you, he would stop resisting. When they came for him again, once you were safe, he would allow himself to be destroyed. They did something to him to make sure that it would happen, that there would be no escape, and they let him return to you."

"Oh, no," Charlie whispered. She felt as if her knees would buckle. That explained so much — that explained everything. This whole time, he'd been trying to get her ready for life without him.

Tam said, "He wanted you to think that he was back in Spookville. He didn't want you to know that he'd been destroyed. He said you'd grieve."

"Grieve." The word didn't do how she felt justice. Great dark waves of desolation washed over her at the mere thought of Michael being destroyed. She had to force them back. She had to *think.* "That's what happened, isn't it? Just now. They've taken him away to be destroyed."

Tam looked at her like she would give anything not to have to answer.

"Yes," Tam agreed.

"No," Charlie said desperately. "No, no, no. He doesn't deserve it. He's *not* a killer. Anything he did, he had to do. Tam, please, there *has* to be a way to save him."

"There is something," Tam said, and Charlie grabbed on to her composure with both hands even as she felt it starting to come apart at the seams. "That's why I read the other man — Detective Foster. I could not lift a hand if your Michael was guilty of those heinous crimes, but since he's not, there's one chance, one thing we can try. My mother told me of it, told me the spell. But we must hurry. There's not much time before he is destroyed, and once that happens there is no undoing it. He'll be lost forever."

"What is it?" Charlie's hands tightened on Tam's so forcefully that the other woman winced and freed herself.

"Come with me to my car while I explain. Everything I need is in there, and like I said, we don't have much time." As she spoke, Tam broke away and ran toward her rented Kia, which was parked in front of Charlie's garage. Charlie ran beside her. Tam continued, "That's where I went this morning: to get the last component of the spell, just in case. I needed the blood of a chicken slaughtered just as the first hint of dawn appeared on the horizon. I went to a *sevite* — a spirit practitioner — that my mother knows near here to get it. It has to be used in the day it's received. I thought to go back every morning until — he was taken. I didn't know it would be so soon."

They had reached Tam's car by this time, and Tam popped the trunk. From it Tam took a Walmart bag and a Tupperware container of what could only be the chicken blood. Charlie was too agitated even to shudder at the sight of it.

"What are we doing?" Charlie asked as Tam closed the trunk.

"I'm going to send you back in time," Tam said, striding toward the garage. It was a single-car garage, not much more than a shed, actually. It was detached from the house, painted gray, with a solid white overhead door that was presently closed. "To the night that your Michael met that woman he was arrested for killing. I'm going to send you to him, and it's going to be up to you to stop what will happen. If he doesn't get arrested for killing that woman, then he will not go to prison, he will not be killed, and he will not wind up being snatched away by *executeurs* to be destroyed."

"You're going to send me back in time?" Charlie couldn't help it: her voice squeaked. She'd seen Tam do some amazing things, but she'd never imagined anything like this was even possible.

"We are going to try to reroute his path." Tam pulled a tube of colored chalk out of the Walmart bag, extracted a piece, and began drawing a large rectangle on the garage's smooth metal door. "You will only have a few minutes. You know where to find him on that night?"

Charlie thought of the bar where Michael had picked up Candace Hartnell. "Yes."

"You must picture that in your mind as you travel. Don't let your thoughts wander. You could wind up somewhere else."

"I can do that," Charlie said.

"That's his watch you're wearing, right?" Tam asked. She'd seen the watch before. She'd actually used it in a spell before.

Charlie touched the watch, which she'd put on when she'd gotten dressed. "Yes."

"That should help take you to him. Keep your hand on it while you go." Having finished with the rectangle, Tam sprinkled a rectangle of chicken blood on the gravel drive, the ends of which touched the chalk rectangle on the garage door.

"All right."

"There is one thing of which you should be aware — if you are successful, if this works, he might forget all about you. We will have rerouted his path. He won't wind up in your prison. On this new path of his, you two will never have met." Tam finished with the blood and set it aside, then pulled four stubby white candles out of the bag.

At the idea of Michael not remembering her, Charlie felt her stomach twist. But compared to him being destroyed — there was no choice.

"Tam." Charlie was still trying to get her mind around what was getting ready to happen. "Are you saying that if this works, Michael won't have gone to prison and will have spent the last five years simply going about his life?"

Tam nodded. She was setting the candles on the four points of the rectangle she'd drawn in blood in the gravel. "That's exactly what I'm saying."

"I'd do anything to give him his life back," Charlie said. Even if she wasn't in it. Even if he didn't remember her. More than she'd ever wanted anything else, she wanted him to have his life.

Tam put the last candle in place and straightened to look at Charlie. "He was willing to give up his soul for you; you're willing to give up your heart for him. I never thought I would be okay with the two of you, but I think perhaps you were meant to be. Soulmates."

Soulmates. She and Michael. There was a time when the thought would have boggled Charlie's mind. But now — it felt right.

Charlie felt her heart clutch as another thought hit her. "Will I forget him, too?"

Tam shook her head. "No. Everything that has happened, has happened. You will remember all of this, including being sent back in time and what you did to save him. His will be the path that is altered. But all of this has happened to him, too, and can't be erased. He has already experienced dying and being a spirit and meeting you. It's there in his soul, embedded forever, along with past lives and the in-between times and everything else that has ever happened to the entity that is now having a human experience as Michael Garland. If you are able to reroute his path, the body will be spared but the soul will not. The soul never loses anything that it has ever experienced. As a result of what we are doing, the soul will simply loop back and merge with the body at the point where the path is altered. The memories of what has happened during those years will still be there. They may be buried, in the same way we can't access past lives while we're on the earth plane. Or it's possible that they won't be, that he'll remember. I can't tell for sure." Tam pulled a long-handled lighter out of the bag and straightened again to shake her head at Charlie. "Now step inside that rectangle. What I'm going to do is light the candles and cast a spell, which will create a wormhole through time. If I've done everything right, the door that I've drawn on your garage door should open. Step through it, hold on to your Michael's watch, picture where you want to end up, and you should be taken there. When the spell wanes, you'll be bounced right back here. Do you understand?"

Charlie nodded, and stepped inside the rectangle. Her heart pounded, her stomach knotted, and the fear of what was about to happen coursed through her. But the alternative — to do nothing and let Michael be destroyed without even trying to stop it — was unthinkable.

"I'm ready," she said, and took a deep breath as Tam lit the candles. The scent of lavender wafted in the air. The sky was just beginning to lighten up, just beginning to swirl with streamers of orange and pink. Behind her, Tam set something on fire — Charlie didn't even want to know what — and started to chant.

"Porta aperio. Tempus vade retro. Ab aeterno transire. Revertere!"

Charlie felt a rush of air, a shifting of the ground beneath her feet, and then the metal inside the chalk outline drawn on the garage door seemed to dissolve into swirling darkness.

Taking a deep breath, she walked into it.

CHAPTER THIRTY

Trulio's Bar and Grille.

The bar's name hung in big red neon cursive letters that glowed against the white painted wall of the long, low building that Charlie found herself in front of. She was in a paved parking lot that was surprisingly full of cars. It was night, or, actually, from the feel of it, the early hours of a morning. The weather was hot and clear — summer. A nearly full moon glowed palely in a sky studded with tiny stars. Smells of barbecue and car exhaust and fresh-cut grass hit her nostrils. The building's windows spilled light over the asphalt. The muffled strains of some popular song filled the air.

Glancing around — yes, this was real, as real as the driveway at dawn she'd just left — Charlie went up the shallow steps to the door, pushed it open and walked inside.

Then she stopped for just a moment to get her bearings.

The place was a combination bar and restaurant. Blue-collar and rowdy, it was packed, with the booths lining the walls all taken and patrons crowded three deep around the bar. A waitress took an order at one table. Another, carrying a heavy tray, pushed into the dining room through a swinging door, obviously coming from the kitchen. It smelled of grilled meat and booze.

Charlie looked toward the bar. Dark, gleaming wood. A long mirror fronted by a jumble of bottles and glasses. The bartender, a heavyset man with dark hair, filling a mug with beer from a tap. So crowded that at first it was difficult to spot her quarry.

But he was tall, he was blond, and he was loud.

"Hey, Billy, bring us a couple more," he called to the bartender. The deep, drawling voice that cut through all the background noise was so familiar that Charlie's heart clutched. There he was, long body planted on a bar stool, knocking back a drink as he talked to a pretty, dark-haired woman who was perched on the stool next to his.

Candace Hartnell. Twenty-five years old. Dressed in a blue jean miniskirt that left most of her long, slim legs bare. Clingy red tee with a deep scoop neck that wasn't shy about how much cleavage it revealed. Strappy, sexy high heels. Leaning toward him, flirting for all she was worth. Laughing, drinking, clearly in major lust with the guy buying the booze.

With no idea how this night was supposed to end.

Charlie's eyes narrowed as she watched Michael's hand slide up Candace's tanned and slender thigh. She couldn't help it. It was a purely visceral reaction.

It occurred to her that right here, right now, Michael was thirty-one years old. A year younger than she was. Feeling no pain, and out to get laid. They weren't exactly each other's types at the best of times. And she had dressed that morning with her professional persona in mind and, thus, was wearing a tailored long-sleeved white blouse with black pants and low-heeled shoes. Her hair was secured in a ponytail at her nape, and her makeup was minimal.

In other words, Sex Kitten R Not Us.

Too bad. He was leaving that bar with her if she had to drag him out by his hair.

The waitress who'd been taking the order at the table walked by. Charlie touched her arm.

"Excuse me, could you call me a taxi, please?" she asked. "I'll be at the bar."

The waitress nodded. Charlie would have tipped her, but, wait, she didn't have any money.

"Ten dollars when it gets here," Charlie promised. Michael would have to pay. Whether he liked it or not. "Come and find me."

The waitress's eyes widened. "Shouldn't be more than five minutes."

"Thanks."

With that taken care of, Charlie girded her loins and marched up to the bar. Thrusting herself between Candace and Michael, she got right up in Michael's face. He blinked at her in surprise. The sky blue eyes, the outrageously handsome face, the shock of tawny hair, the big, muscular body in the white tee, jeans, and boots that he'd been wearing on this, the last free night of his life — it was all there. He looked younger, happier, less touched by darkness and pain, but otherwise exactly the same. He was even wearing his watch — the one that she'd been clutching when she'd stepped through her garage door into that swirling darkness. A surprised glance down at her arm told her that she no longer had it. Of course: he hadn't lost it yet. Her chest tightened at the knowledge. To have him alive in front of her like this, to feel her body brushing his and know what was going to happen to him if she couldn't stop it, was both heartbreaking and galvanizing.

Taking a breath, she met his surprised blue gaze again and let fly.

"You leave me home alone with our kids while you go out trying to pick up women in a bar?" she yelled, stabbing her finger into his chest for good measure.

He reared back, looking at her like she was nuts.

"I had to get my sister up to watch our three little angels while I came out and found you," Charlie raged.

Michael gaped at her. "What the *hell*?" he said.

All around them, people were turning to look.

Under less dire circumstances Charlie would have smiled at the expression on his face. But these circumstances were dire.

"Honey, he's taken," she said over her shoulder to Candace Hartnell, who was looking as horrified as Michael was looking dumbfounded.

"Sorry. I had no idea — he never said he was married." She slid off that bar stool and skittered away like her skirt was on fire.

Yes. Charlie gave herself a mental fist pump. Mission partly accomplished. Next order of business: get him out of there. Charlie stayed where she was, leaning against the bar, sliding her hand up Michael's thigh.

"Now you're mine, handsome," she purred.

Michael's hand clamped down over hers, holding her hand in place on his thigh.

"Sugar, this ain't going anywhere," he drawled. He had a good buzz going, she could tell from the brightness of his eyes. "Psycho librarian types aren't exactly my thing."

Leaning close, she murmured, "How do you know until you try?" She slid a hand behind his head and kissed him.

Deep and hot and slow.

And there it was: the chemistry. The blazing sexual attraction that had always been there between them, the blistering passion, the fierce pull of desire.

It wasn't a fluke, and it wasn't a result of them being flung together by circumstance.

It was, she decided as his arms came around her and he pulled her tight against him and took control of the kiss, fate.

A touch on her arm. "Your taxi's here, Miss."

Charlie broke the kiss and looked around at the waitress. Michael's arms were tight around her waist. Her arms were around his neck, and she was nestled between his spread legs. The evidence of his arousal was right there between them, hard and unmistakable as it pushed against the notch at the apex of her legs.

"I need ten dollars," she said to him. He looked at her. His eyes were glittering. His face was flushed. He let go of her to pull out his wallet.

She took it from him, extracted ten dollars, and handed the bill to the waitress.

When she turned back to him, he was watching her. Naked lust gleamed in his eyes.

She smiled and ran a thumb over his lips. He caught her wrist, kissed her thumb.

"Come home with me," she said.

He nodded and stood up. She gave him back his wallet, and as he put a twenty down on the bar she spotted a permanent marker and scooped it up. Then she took his hand and led him out of the bar.

When they stepped out into the fresh night air, he seemed to sober up a little bit. Having caught sight of the taxi, she was pulling him purposefully toward it. They were almost there when his hand tightened on hers and he dug in his heels. She stopped — she didn't have any choice — and turned to frown at him. He pulled her back against him, back into his arms. The feel of his big, muscular body against hers was so sexy and at the same time so achingly familiar that she could have cried.

"Hey, psycho librarian, I don't even know your name," he said.

"Charlie," she answered huskily, looking up at him. Then she went up on tiptoes and kissed him, a lush but brief kiss because she was afraid she was running out of time. Breaking off the kiss, she stepped back and took his hand. Flipping the lid off the permanent marker, she started writing on the smooth inner flesh of his forearm.

"Hey," he said, but he didn't pull away, merely watched curiously as she wrote on his arm.

"This is my name, and address, and a date," she told him. She'd written only her first name, because it occurred to her that if he tried to find her before five years had passed the outcome might be bad. The address was her house in Big Stone Gap, and the date was five years and one week in the future. "You come to this address on that date. I'll be there."

He was frowning at her.

"Sweet thing, in five years I could be on the other side of the world."

Having finished, she stuck the marker in her pants pocket and looked up at him.

"Let's get in the taxi," she said. In case she ran out of time, she wanted to make sure he didn't go back in the bar. She tugged him toward it.

He went, but said, "My car's here."

"You're drunk, and I can't drive."

"I'm not drunk."

Her patience frayed. They were at the taxi now, and, with a brief "Hi" for the driver, she opened the back door. "Michael. Just get in the damned taxi, would you please?"

With the urging of the smallest of shoves from her, he got in, and she slid in beside him. Closing the door, she breathed a sigh of relief.

"Where to?" the driver wanted to know.

"How close is the nearest hotel?" Charlie asked him.

"I thought we were going to your place," Michael said.

"Hotel?" Charlie prompted the driver, then, to Michael, she murmured throatily, "Hotels are so sexy."

"Right along this road," the driver said. Charlie could tell from his tone that he'd heard her comment to Michael. If she'd been able to see his face, she was sure she'd have just watched it turn red.

She said, "Take us there."

The taxi took off.

Michael was looking at her. His eyes gleamed at her through the darkness that shrouded the backseat. He was much bigger and stronger than she was, and she'd had ample evidence of his self-defense skills, so she was pretty sure he didn't feel threatened. But apart from the hot-and-heavy, let's-get-it-on vibe he was putting out, she thought she detected a degree of wariness.

"How'd you know my name?" he asked. He was holding her hand, but his grip was a little tighter than loverliness called for.

"I'm going to tell you something that is going to sound impossible," she said. "But it's true. I need you to listen, and I need you to do what I tell you." Lying, she improvised to add a little extra *oomph* to her words: "Cap and Hoop and Sean sent me to you with this message."

"What?" he practically yelped, and dropped her hand.

"I'm from the future," Charlie said, keeping her voice low in hopes that the driver would miss most of what she was saying. "I know it sounds crazy, but it's not. To prove it —"

She bent close, whispered her knowledge of how Sean had died in Michael's ear so that the driver couldn't overhear. When she finished and sat back, he stared at her, clearly stunned. Increasingly conscious of the clock ticking, Charlie couldn't give him time to process. Instead, she plunged on.

"Detective Foster of the Mariposa Police Department is a serial killer who was going to kill that girl you were talking to tonight and frame you for her murder and his previous murders," Charlie said. Michael was looking at her now like she was a bomb he feared might be going to explode at any moment, but she didn't care. "If you had stayed in that bar, if you had gone home with her — her name is Candace Hartnell, by the way" — she knew he didn't know it at that point — "she would have wound up dead, stabbed to death, and you would have found yourself on death row, convicted of her and six other women's murders. You would get killed in prison." No need to go into the whole he-then-came-back-as-a-ghost-and-she-was-there-now-trying-to-save-his-soul thing, she decided. That was unnecessary for her purpose, and would probably be too much information for one sitting. "You need to get out of this area. Move somewhere else and start over. Do not pick up any girl in any bar within a hundred miles of here. Do not pick up any girls, period, within a hundred miles of here. Just go. As soon as possible."

A tingly feeling was spreading over her skin, and Charlie was afraid she was almost out of time.

"I think I'm getting ready to disappear," she said. "Check yourself into the hotel and stay there tonight. Do not leave it for any reason. Then tomorrow, pack up your things and go. Start over somewhere else."

"Somebody put you up to this." Michael's face was hard now. He was looking at her like he didn't believe her at all.

The tingle was increasing. She was starting to hear a humming sound.

Time was up. She knew it. Grabbing his hand, Charlie said fiercely, "Every word I've told you is the truth. In the future you and I are in love, and I've come back here tonight to try to save your ass. You —"

Just as quick as that, a blackness darker than the darkest night enveloped her like a blanket. The humming noise turned into a roar, and Charlie felt the earth fall away around her. Her head spun; her stomach dropped.

Then she fetched up on her driveway.

Standing in the cool air of a brightening dawn staring at the solid white metal inside a chalk rectangle drawn on her garage door.

Weak-kneed and trembling. With no idea if what she'd done had succeeded in saving Michael or not.

"Dieu merci," Tam said devoutly. *Thank God.*

Charlie turned, saw Tam, and stumbled out of the charmed area into her friend's outstretched arms.

Nearby, one of Mrs. Norman's roosters began to crow.

Chapter Thirty-One

Michael didn't show up.

The date Charlie had written on his arm came and went, and there was no sign of him. No word. Tam sent out psychic feelers into the universe, but couldn't pick up a trace of him.

Charlie even tried Google. Google couldn't find him, either.

That was bad.

She started to feel this giant emptiness in her chest, like there was a hole where her heart had been.

The time travel had been real, not a hallucination brought on by Tam's spell or something like stress. She knew that because during that journey she'd lost his watch. She could only suppose that wherever he was he had it now.

She had succeeded in keeping him from being killed in prison. She knew that because his grave in the graveyard of the

First Baptist Church had disappeared.

When she checked the prison records, there was no mention of his name.

There was, however, a Dan Foster, formerly a detective with the Mariposa Police Department, on death row.

A new subject for her research, if she'd been going to continue working at the prison.

She wasn't. As she had promised Michael, she was going to take a break and write a book. She'd already found an agent and been offered a contract with a sizable advance.

It was because of the NARSAD, she knew. That was still a huge deal, and she was still thrilled to have won.

Tam was planning to accompany her to the award ceremony, and Tony and Lena and Buzz would be there as her guests. She was glad they would be with her on what would be one of the most important nights of her life: they were, all of them, family to her now. Tam and Lena had taken her shopping after double-teaming her to deplore what they described as her nonexistent fashion sense. She'd let them pick out what they liked: her only proviso was that the dress couldn't show too much skin, and it couldn't be bright.

They'd settled on a form-fitting black lace evening dress.

She packed up her office at the prison. She checked in on Paris and Bree and the rest of the kids, and was pleased to hear they were recovering and doing well. She meant to keep tabs on them for the foreseeable future because, well, somebody needed to, and she felt responsible for them after what they'd been through together. She even stayed in phone contact with Rick Hughes, who'd awakened in her house with the most distressing condition: he'd lost nearly three full days from his memory. Doctors told him he was most likely suffering from hysterical amnesia, and blamed the stress he had endured during the kidnapping.

He kept asking if he could come up and they could get together for a meal and a chat, but Charlie wouldn't agree. Tony had had FBI investigators confirm the fact that he and Michael were identical twins, that they had been adopted separately, and that Hughes's parents had kept the truth from him. They'd even altered the date on his birth certificate to coincide with the date they'd brought him home. At some point, that was information Hughes probably needed to know, but Charlie didn't feel like it was up to her to enlighten him. The truth was, she didn't think she was ever going to want to see Rick Hughes again for the rest of her life.

To be in the presence of someone who looked so much like Michael and yet wasn't Michael would cause her more pain than she could endure.

Which was what she was doing: enduring. She was going on, because she had her life with many good things in it and she was a survivor. Trading Michael's memory of her, of them, for his life was something that she would do all over again, every single time the situation came up.

Now she just had to learn to live without him.

The NARSAD banquet was held at the John F. Kennedy Center for the Performing Arts. Dinner was first on the schedule, followed by the awards presentation, and then dancing. It was a black-tie affair, crowded and glittering, with a live orchestra and so many luminaries that Charlie was dazzled way before her name was called to receive her award.

As she stood to go to the lectern and say a few words everybody in the room rose to applaud. They were smiling and clapping, and as she looked around she felt almost shy. At her table, her friends beamed at her. Tony was clapping like crazy, looking beyond handsome in his tux. Tam was her usual glamorous self in a gold sequined gown with a slit that rose halfway up her thigh. Lena was a curvy seductress in a dark red satin gown that made the most of her curves. Beside her, Buzz, who was also looking handsome in a tux, had the biggest grin Charlie had ever seen on his face.

Lena had accepted his proposal and was flashing a brand-new diamond ring on her hand.

"When you asked me what I wanted, I started thinking about it," Lena had confided to Charlie earlier. "And finally I figured it out: I want him. Everything else we can work out."

So there was good news all around.

Charlie's was the last award to be given out, and as she walked back to her table from the lectern the dancing started. The band struck up, and couples began twirling around the floor. Clutching her trophy — it was crystal, engraved with her name, and beautiful — Charlie watched Tony stand up as she approached and knew he meant to ask her to dance.

She was so, so fond of Tony.

She was putting her trophy down on the table and Tony was opening his mouth to ask her when suddenly Tony's gaze shot past her and he froze.

Frowning, Charlie turned to see what he was looking at.

Her heart lurched. Her breathing suspended.

Michael was walking toward her, threading his way along the edge of the tables, head-turningly gorgeous in a black tux.

"Is that — Rick Hughes?" Lena asked with surprise.

"No," Tam answered, and that's when Charlie knew for sure that he wasn't an illusion, wasn't a bad case of wish fulfillment or anything else. That Michael was real and solid and alive and *there.*

As much as he and Hughes looked alike, there was no mistaking Michael for anyone else.

Not for her.

He saw her looking at him, and lifted a hand in an acknowledging wave.

Charlie sucked in a deep, slightly shaky breath. Until that moment, she hadn't even realized that she'd been clutching the back of her chair for balance. Now, as he reached them, she let it go.

"Hey," he said to her, like they'd last met

maybe an hour before. His gaze swept the table. "I'm Michael Garland," he introduced himself, and shook hands all around.

Then he looked back at Charlie, and said, "Do you want to dance?"

Speechless, she nodded, letting him take her hand and pull her onto the dance floor and into his arms.

The band was playing "Moon River." She was nestled against Michael's chest, looking up into the most beautiful blue eyes she'd ever seen.

Her heart pounded. Her pulse raced. She felt dizzy, woozy, disoriented.

"You look surprised to see me," he said.

She nodded. Stunned was more like it, but she couldn't manage to say it. Couldn't manage to say anything. She was lucky she was upright, and doing the moving-breathing-thinking thing.

"Ain't no river wide enough, babe," he said, and smiled at her.

That's when she knew for sure it was real. That's when joy flooded her veins and her head cleared and she was able to catch her breath and actually say something.

"You remembered," she said.

"Not until two days ago. I'd almost forgotten about the crazy woman who wrote her address on my arm and told me she was from the future and yelled at me before she vanished right out of a taxi until I found myself in a shrink's office. See, the military reached out to some of us vets with an offer of counseling, and I took them up on it. So there I was, spilling my guts, and this chubby, bearded shrink asks me if I feel any remorse. Bells go off in my head: It's like I can hear this infuriating woman repeatedly asking me the same thing. Then, boom, it hit me, and I remembered the whole thing. Everything we went through together. Up until then, I'd been explaining away that night by telling myself I was drunk off my ass."

"Oh, my God," she said, eloquence being beyond her for the moment.

He nodded. "I remembered going to prison, and dying, and Spookville and the whole nine yards, just like that." His grip on her tightened. Charlie was so focused on Michael that she was scarcely aware until then that they were dancing, but there they were, circling the floor, just one of dozens of beautifully dressed couples moving as the music swelled around them. She was suddenly conscious of the solid muscularity of his chest against her breasts, of the hard strength of his arm around her, of how big and warm his hand felt clasping hers.

He's here with me. He's alive.

Her body was starting to adjust. She could feel the worst of her shock starting to fade. She was breathing almost normally.

He continued softly, "I remembered you. I remembered falling in love with you."

Her heart shook.

"I love you," she said.

He said, "I know."

Her eyes widened and she stiffened in his arms. All of a sudden she was fully functional and back to normal, except for the whole bubbling-over-with-happiness thing that was at one and the same time the most wonderful feeling she'd ever had and totally outside her experience.

The look on her face must have been something to see, because he grinned at her, a gloriously charming grin that made her toes curl in her ridiculously expensive high heels that had been selected for her, courtesy of Lena.

"I love you, too," he said.

She frowned at him and laughed at the same time and let him twirl her around until she was dizzy and a little bit worried that they might be making a spectacle of themselves on the dance floor with all her professional colleagues around, so she made him stop.

It was when her head quit spinning that it hit her. Clutching his hand more tightly, looking up into his hard, handsome face, she said, "Michael. Oh, my God. We've got forever."

He looked down at her. His eyes were tender on her face. "Babe, what we've got ourselves here is a lifetime. For now, with you, that's all the forever I need."

ACKNOWLEDGMENTS

So many people go into the creation of a book. I want to thank my wonderful editor, Linda Marrow, whose invaluable insights are always right on the money. I also want to thank her assistant, Elana Seplow-Jolley, who worked so hard on this, as well as the entire team at Ballantine Books. More thanks to my agent, Robert Gottlieb, who is always there when I need him. And last but not least, thanks to my husband, Doug, for hanging in as usual.

ABOUT THE AUTHOR

Karen Robards is the *New York Times* and *USA Today* bestselling author of forty-seven full-length books and one novella. The mother of three boys, she lives in her hometown of Louisville, Kentucky.

karenrobards.com
Facebook.com/AuthorKarenRobards
@TheKarenRobards

The employees of Thorndike Press hope you have enjoyed this Large Print book. All our Thorndike, Wheeler, and Kennebec Large Print titles are designed for easy reading, and all our books are made to last. Other Thorndike Press Large Print books are available at your library, through selected bookstores, or directly from us.

For information about titles, please call:
(800) 223-1244

or visit our Web site at:
http://gale.cengage.com/thorndike

To share your comments, please write:
Publisher
Thorndike Press
10 Water St., Suite 310
Waterville, ME 04901